SECOND
Act

ALSO BY NANCY HERKNESS

Second Glances series

Second to None: A Novella

Second Time Around

Wager of Hearts series

The CEO Buys In

The All-Star Antes Up

The VIP Doubles Down

The Irishman's Christmas Gamble: A Novella

Whisper Horse novels

Take Me Home

Country Roads

The Place I Belong

A Down-Home Country Christmas: A Novella

Stand-Alone Novels

A Bridge to Love

Shower of Stars

Music of the Night

SECOND
Act

A *Second Glances* NOVEL

NANCY
HERKNESS

Montlake
Romance

Text copyright © 2019 by Nancy Herkness
All rights reserved.

Published by Montlake Romance, Seattle

www.apub.com

Amazon, the Amazon logo, and Montlake Romance are trademarks of Amazon.com, Inc., or its affiliates.

ISBN-13: 9781503905337
ISBN-10: 1503905330

Cover design by Letitia Hasser

Cover photography by Wander Aguiar

Printed in the United States of America

To my sister, Damon, and my cousin Robert,
with profound gratitude for your unwavering support.

Chapter 1

He had just enough power left in his burning lungs and spent legs to sprint around the next street corner, trying not to skid on the wet, slushy sidewalk. The pounding footsteps behind him punched an extra shot of adrenaline into his system, giving him a burst of speed as he leaned into the turn. He spotted a break in the row of facades just ahead. Five strides, four, three . . . and he was there, cutting hard left between two multistory brick buildings into an alleyway where his pursuers couldn't shoot him for the next few moments, at least.

"Oof!" The last lungful of breath was forced out of him as he slammed into a body that wasn't supposed to be there.

"Ow!" said a female voice.

His arms went around her as he spun his back hard against a wall to keep from crashing onto the dirty, cracked pavement. Hugh exerted every muscle in his carefully trained body to maintain his balance and that of the woman in his arms. But she was struggling to get loose.

He held on to his temper as he sucked in gulps of oxygen. "Lady, you should not be here."

"But I almost had her," she said, her face turned away. "Now you've scared her back into hiding. Would you please let me—?" She finally looked up at him, her gray eyes opening wide. "Oh my God! Hugh!"

Hugh had the strangest sense of being pulled backward through time as he stood with his arms locked around the squirming woman.

"Cut! What the hell?" The director's furious voice echoed off the walls. "Where did *she* come from?"

"She came from my distant past." Hugh gazed down at the astonished face of his ex-fiancée, her long, silky brown hair twisted into the same lopsided bun he'd found so endearing the first day they'd met. Her eyes held surprise but also the soft light of compassion that had drawn him to her from the start. The generous curves of her mouth reminded him of the first time he'd kissed her, hoping he'd read the signals right and that she would kiss him back. When she had, his world had shifted under his feet.

"Hello, Jess," he said.

It had been eight years since he'd last seen her—the day she'd handed him back her engagement ring before she left him—and he had no idea what she'd been doing in the intervening time. Jabs of guilt and regret lanced through him because that was his fault. His pride had kept him away from the woman he'd once loved with all his young heart and soul.

Bryan stomped up to them, his bushy red hair sticking out in all directions, with the movie's crew, bundled up in their motley array of cold-weather gear, trailing behind him. "I don't care if she's known you since you were in diapers. This is an active movie shoot." He glared at Jess. "Did you not see all the barriers and signs? And where is our goddamn useless security?"

Hugh released her with an odd reluctance. "Jess, meet Bryan Ostroff, the director of *Christmas Best*," he said. "Bryan, this is Jessica Quillen, my ex-fiancée." He felt the group's attention sharpen and focus on the woman at his side. He wrapped his arm around her slight shoulders in a gesture of protectiveness.

Even Bryan stopped shouting long enough to give Jessica a once-over. "I didn't know you had an ex-fiancée," he said before his anger returned. "And I don't give a shit, since she ruined the fourth and about-to-be-perfect take of the chase scene."

Jessica shrugged off Hugh's arm and stepped toward Bryan with her hand held out. "Please accept my apologies, Mr. Ostroff." The director hesitated only a moment before he took her hand. Hugh had seen Jess handle even tougher customers the same way, so he wasn't surprised that she had disarmed Bryan's indignation with her sincere good manners.

"I've been trying to catch a pregnant stray dog for about a week now," she continued with an earnest smile. "I was so focused on following her that I guess I didn't notice all this." She gestured toward the array of cameras, barriers, and people. "I'm so sorry."

When there was an animal in need, Jess didn't let anything stop her from going to its aid. Her total commitment to caring was what had made her shine like a beacon to him all those years ago on another movie set. "You haven't changed," Hugh murmured.

"I told you I wouldn't," she said, her tone holding a glimmer of sadness.

Old pain and regret ripped through him. She'd been true to herself.

"Can you have this touching reunion on your own time?" Bryan said. "We need to finish this scene before we have to bring out the floodlights." He beckoned to one of the assistants, a clipboard-toting woman in a sweatshirt and cargo pants, before turning back to Jessica and moderating the exasperation in his tone. "Almost Mrs. Baker, could you please go with Margaret here? She'll take you to Hugh's trailer to wait."

"I wasn't planning to stay," Jessica said, thrusting her hands into the pockets of her quilted maroon jacket.

"Fine. Whatever." Bryan was already walking away as he shouted instructions at the cameramen.

"Please wait. I'd like a chance to talk," Hugh found himself saying.

Jessica glanced at the purple sports watch strapped around her wrist before starting to shake her head as she looked back up, her expression guarded. This was a new Jess. In the old days, she had never hidden her feelings from him.

Hugh gave her the seductive smile that made millions of women fall in love with the suave secret agent he played. "Doesn't your ex-fiancé rate as much time as a pregnant stray dog?"

Her sweetly curved lips flattened into a frown. "The dog needs help. You're well taken care of."

"I very much want to know what you've been doing. Find out how you came to be here in South Harlem. It's been a long time." Hugh injected a subtle note of pleading into his voice.

"It's been a *really* long time, so why do you suddenly care about what I'm doing?" Fury sparked in her eyes before she made a gesture of apology. "Sorry, that was uncalled-for. I'm just frustrated about losing the dog again."

He hadn't expected the anger. "No, you're right, it's been too long. I'd like to apologize, but I can't right now." He nodded toward the bustle of the film crew. "If you can spare the time . . ."

She hesitated, so he threw in a bribe. "There are sandwiches in my trailer, just in case you haven't eaten recently."

He knew the memory had caught her when the corners of her mouth twitched. Back when they were a couple, she had worked at a large emergency animal hospital in Los Angeles. When things got hectic, she would work through lunch, the hunger making her cranky by the time she got home. If she snarled at him when he said hello, he would make a beeline for the kitchen and assemble a peanut-butter-and-jelly sandwich at top speed, handing it to her without another word.

"That's not why I'm in a bad mood," she said with a raised eyebrow. "But you've convinced me to stay."

A surprisingly powerful wave of satisfaction rolled through him. "Thank you, Jess. We're almost done with this scene," he said. "Then they have to reset the cameras to shoot in the alley. That's when we'll get a rest period."

He waved the waiting Margaret forward. As the two women walked away, he watched his ex-fiancée's back, noting the slush-spattered jeans and thick-soled, black leather boots. Another wave of nostalgia rolled over him. Jess had never cared what she wore, and yet her very unconcern had made her more beautiful in his eyes.

"Hugh!" Bryan's voice yanked his thoughts away from the woman who had dumped him. "I want you on the main street again. You need to get back up to full speed before you take the turn."

He banished Jessica from his mind and returned to the role every moviegoer in the world knew him as: Julian Best, super spy.

Jessica sat with her hands cupped around a mug of hot tea, gazing around Hugh's trailer. With its four "slide-outs," it was almost the same size as the apartment they'd lived in together eight years ago in Los Angeles and far more luxurious than the South Harlem Victorian row house she owned now. The trailer's built-in tables and cabinets were all done in a burled blond wood that gleamed in slashes of late-afternoon sunlight. A crystal bowl of fresh fruit and a vase of purple-and-white flowers stood on the table in the fully equipped kitchen.

In the seating area, the chairs and sofas were upholstered in cognac leather, their plump cushions inviting her to relax in front of the giant television. Margaret had told her that Hugh watched the dailies on the huge screen. She'd even showed Jessica Hugh's bedroom, which included one entire slide-out devoted to a brilliantly lit, mirrored makeup area.

"Not that Mr. Baker needs much makeup," Margaret said. "He has one of those faces that the camera loves. And he gets better as he gets older." There was adoration in the woman's voice.

Jessica had been too shocked and then too distracted to examine her ex-fiancé's face closely, but she'd watched him mature through his movies. Margaret was right about his camera appeal, but it was more than his brilliant turquoise eyes, his sharply sculpted jawline, and that sinful mouth she remembered too vividly, all framed by thick, nearly black hair. Hugh had charisma and a seductive edge of darkness. When he was in a scene, all the other actors faded into insignificance. It was impossible to look away from him. She'd been engaged to all that, but once she'd accepted that she couldn't stay with him without losing herself, she'd known she needed to get out of his way.

However, because she'd loved him so deeply that it seemed embedded in the marrow of her bones, she'd been happy for Hugh as he rose to stardom after she'd given back the ring. It was good to know that she'd done the right thing, even though it had ripped her guts out.

She had watched every one of his movies on the day it was released. The first one had been agonizing because the pain of their failure as a couple was still so fresh. Seeing Hugh larger than life-size on the big screen had stirred up memories both joyful and miserable, and she'd spent the entire two hours with tears streaming down her face. Thank God she'd gone alone.

Over time, the anguish had lessened and she could appreciate the movies themselves, seeing Hugh more as Julian Best and less as the man she'd loved too much to hold him back. This was what he'd been born to do, and she applauded the drive and talent that had rocketed him to the top of his profession, despite the fact that it meant leaving her behind.

His palace on wheels illustrated the level of what he'd achieved in a concrete way. Pushing away the contrast between her situation and his, she picked up one of the double-decker sandwiches from the platter Margaret had insisted on setting in front of her. She lifted the top slice of artisanal bread to reveal a thick layer of perfectly cooked steak. Taking a bite, she closed her eyes to savor the way the tender meat melted on her palate. Then hunger got the better of her and she devoured the rest of it at high speed.

She eyed the abundance on the platter and considered stuffing a sandwich in her pocket to lure the stray dog out of hiding. She hadn't intended to spend her day off chasing down a terrified dog, but she was afraid the starving creature would give birth before dying as she tried to care for her puppies. And then all of them would perish. The thought sent a pang of guilt through her as she sat in luxury, waiting to chat with a world-famous movie star.

Which brought her to the question of why Hugh wanted to talk to her after eight years of silence. In the months after their breakup, she'd called him several times, getting his voice mail and leaving messages. He'd never returned them, so she'd given up.

His total withdrawal had been like a knife blade in her heart. She'd become an obstacle to his career, a weight that she didn't want him to have to carry as he climbed ever upward, but she'd thought she could still be some small part of his life. He'd called her his best friend as well as the only woman he'd loved wholeheartedly. But he had cut her out of his world as though she hadn't existed.

The misery came slashing back, and she jolted to her feet in search of a diversion.

She poked around the kitchen, grabbing a bottle of water from the well-stocked refrigerator. She stopped to inhale the potent fragrance of lilies from the flower arrangement before spotting a couple of photos on the wall. The one that caught her eye was of Hugh and Gavin Miller, the bestselling author who wrote the Julian Best books. She'd heard that they had become friends. The photo must have been taken at some sort of awards ceremony, because both men wore tuxedos and sexy smiles, which evoked a nearly breathtaking effect.

A wave of desire surged through her as she recalled what Hugh looked like under the tuxedo, all lean, hard muscle, the kind of body that made him believable as a highly trained secret agent . . . and made his love scenes steaming hot.

She gulped down some cold water just as the door flew open. Hugh bounded into the trailer to stand in front of a vent set in the polished wood paneling, shivering in a white dress shirt that clung to every curve and contour of his shoulders and torso. He held his hands up to the flow of warm air and threw her a wry look. "It's fu . . . rrricking freezing out there." He turned his hands to warm the palms, and she remembered the way those long, powerful fingers had once played over her bare skin, sometimes with gentle seduction, sometimes with rough craving.

She'd never thought of herself as wildly passionate until she met Hugh. It wasn't even his looks that had made her want to jump into bed with him every time they came within ten feet of each other—although they didn't hurt. It was that he held nothing back when they made love. All his formidable barriers dropped, which brought out an answering intensity in her.

A frisson of awareness ran through her. She really needed to get away from Hugh and the memories he kept dredging up.

He rubbed his hands together and turned to her with his slanting smile. "Sorry, but I didn't want my fingers to fall off due to frostbite. Let me grab a sweater and we'll catch up."

Jessica nodded because words had deserted her. She pivoted to watch him stride into his bedroom, the tailored wool of his trousers pulling tight over the muscled planes of his butt. He returned, tugging a silver-gray sweater over his head and down the expanse of his chest. Settling the hem at his narrow waist, he said, "Ahhh, that's better." Then he ran his fingers through the dark waves of his hair, smoothing out some of the rumple the sweater had given it.

Jessica curled her hands firmly around the water bottle because she wanted to finish the job of fixing his hair for him. Then she noticed something familiar about the sweater. "Is that the one I gave—?" She cut off her question, because it was absurd.

Hugh looked puzzled for a moment before he glanced down at his chest and back up again. "Yes. You sent it to me when the first Best movie came out." He winced. "I never thanked you for it, did I? Forgive me for being a total ass."

Pleasure and pain surged through her in equal waves. He'd loved beautiful clothes but couldn't afford them when they were together. Just before the premiere of the first Julian Best movie, she'd wanted him to know she was celebrating for him, despite his refusal to return her calls. So she'd gone to an Armani store with her credit card in hand. When she had touched the sweater in the store, the knitted silk had flowed over her fingertips like a soft Caribbean sea. The price tag had made her choke, but she'd closed her eyes as she signed the receipt.

"I can't believe you still have it." Or that he remembered he hadn't thanked her, a discourtesy that had sliced a fresh wound in her heart.

He ran his palm down the flat plane of his abdomen. "It's my lucky sweater."

"I thought you made your own luck." It had been one of his favorite sayings when he set off for yet another audition.

"I was young and arrogant when I believed that. Now I understand how often fate intervenes." He dropped onto the built-in sofa and stretched out his long legs, plucking at the fabric of his charcoal trousers. "They cut these things so tight I can barely move. And they expect me to run in them."

Jessica perched on the edge of the sofa three feet away from him, wondering if they were going to stick to superficial topics. "Have you ever split a seam while filming?"

"Many times, but wardrobe just sews it up again." He fixed his intense blue gaze on her. That focus had astonished her the first time she'd experienced it. She'd never before met a man who made her the entire center of his attention. He'd made her feel extraordinary for the first time in her life. He had truly *seen* her.

"How are you, Jess?" He scanned her face. "You look beautiful. But tired."

She squelched a desire to snort. Hugh was surrounded by gorgeous, perfectly dressed and made-up women all the time. Here she sat in often-washed jeans, a long-sleeve gray T-shirt, and soggy boots. She was pretty sure her bun was a sloppy mess, too. "Beautiful, no. Tired, yes."

Hugh shifted to lean closer to her, his face tight with displeasure. "You *are* beautiful." He locked eyes with her for a long moment before he sat back. "What's making you so tired?"

Irritation prickled through her. After years of ignoring her, he was suddenly concerned about her well-being? "Oh, I don't know, maybe running a single-practice veterinary clinic here in South Harlem." She grimaced. "It's a constant balancing act." Balancing the patients' needs against their owners' ability to pay; balancing her desire to help every animal brought through her door against the need to sleep; balancing the competence and compassion of her staff against the amount of money she could afford to compensate them. The one thing she had no balance between was her work life and her personal life. She had neither time nor energy for the latter.

Hugh's expression showed profound understanding. She reminded herself that he was a very talented actor. "And you won't turn away a single animal," he said.

"How can I?" She asked herself that question almost daily as she stayed past regular office hours.

"You're going to burn out," he said. "Can't you hire another vet to help you?"

"I had one for a year, but she wanted to pay off her school debt, so she went someplace that could offer her a higher salary." Jessica shrugged. "Not that I blamed her, but it's too frustrating and time-consuming to train someone, only to have them leave as soon as they have enough experience to get a better job."

"I can imagine." Hugh stared at something across the room for a few moments before speaking again. "I'm sorry we lost touch."

Annoyance flared into anger. "*We* lost touch? I left half a dozen voice mails for you. You didn't answer them."

"I—" He dragged his hand over his mouth. "It was too soon."

"And now it's too late." Jessica set the bottle on a side table and pushed off the couch. She didn't want to get ensnared by Hugh's dark magnetism again. "I should get going."

Hugh stood, too, towering over her in the space that suddenly seemed small. "I behaved like a jerk." Then he did the thing that used to disarm her every time. All the hard lines of his face went soft, and his voice dropped to a smooth rumble. "Let me start to make things right by treating you to a meal."

He's an actor. With an effort of pure will, she quashed the part of her that wanted to find out more about what had happened after she left or simply to bask in his still familiar, still tempting presence a little longer. "It's been good to see you, Hugh. I wish you luck with your movie. This is the one it took Gavin Miller so long to write, isn't it?"

"You've paid attention to Julian's progress, then?" He looked surprised.

"Of course. It's not hard when you're on the cover of a magazine at least once a month." She scanned the trailer to see where Margaret had put her coat. Spotting it draped over a kitchen stool, she edged around Hugh to grab it. "I really have to go."

He took the coat from her hands to hold it for her. "Give me your cell phone number. I'd really like to take you out to dinner while I'm in New York."

She gave him a tight smile. "Sure, I'll break out my designer scrubs." Their last big fight had been about what she wore on the red carpet.

"I deserved that," he said, his voice projecting genuine remorse. He gently tugged a stray strand of hair out from under her coat collar, the whisper of his fingers against the nape of her neck sending pleasure rippling through her. "Please. You can wear rags, as far as I'm concerned."

"We live in different worlds," Jessica reminded him . . . and herself. "It's better if we keep them from clashing."

And safer. After eight years, he could still make her feel things she thought she'd put behind her.

He huffed out a breath of frustration. "You and I never agreed about that."

The door of his trailer vibrated as someone rapped loudly on it. "Hugh, can I come in?" a melodious woman's voice called.

Muttering something under his breath, he ran both hands through his hair in an uncharacteristic gesture of hesitation. Then he walked over to open the door.

"Hello, sweetheart." The woman kissed him on the cheek. "It's frigid in my trailer, so I thought I'd review my lines in the warmth of yours. You don't mind, do you?"

She was stunning, of course, with auburn hair, green eyes, and a wide, generous mouth that undoubtedly incited all kinds of sexual fantasies in the male mind. And Jessica recognized her as the actress who'd been cast as Julian Best's new love interest.

The woman's gaze found Jessica, and she started. "Oh, I'm so sorry. I didn't realize you had company. I'll leave."

"No, *I'm* leaving," Jessica said. She zipped her coat with a flourish.

"Jess, this is Meryl Langdon, my costar," Hugh said, his tone dry. "Meryl, meet Jessica Quillen, my ex-fiancée."

Meryl held out her hand with alacrity, but her face held curiosity. "A pleasure," she said, her grip on Jessica's hand friendly. "I didn't know Hugh had an ex-fiancée."

"Ancient history," Jessica said.

"Neither you nor Hugh is old enough to call it ancient," Meryl said with a thread of laughter in her tone.

No wonder she'd gotten the part of Julian's love interest. Even the timbre of her voice made you want to lean in to hear it better.

"Sometimes I feel older than dirt," Jessica said, pulling on her gloves. "Nice to meet you. Bye, Hugh!" She gave a breezy wave and slipped out the door before he could react.

As she stepped down onto the gritty sidewalk, she hunched her shoulders against the slicing winter wind. Or was she trying to duck the image she had of Meryl and Hugh entwined on the big bed in the trailer? They would make a dazzling couple with clothes or without.

As she slogged off in the direction where she'd last seen the stray dog, she muttered, "I should have taken the damned sandwich."

Chapter 2

"Your last cat spay just face-planted!" Caleb, one of Jessica's vet techs, yelled through the operating room door. "She was up and aware one second, then collapsed. Gums are white. Breathing slow and shallow. Heart rate down to ninety beats. She's on oxygen, but she's not waking up." Then he was gone again.

"Oh, hell!" Jessica muttered into her mask as she dropped the scalpel back on the tray. She'd been about to make the first incision for a neuter. "Keep him sleeping," she said to Tiana, the vet tech handling the anesthesia. "I'll be back."

She raced down the hall to the recovery room, where Caleb was massaging the limp cat wrapped in a towel. The cat's small black-and-white face was covered with an oxygen mask, and she lay on top of a heating pad.

"How long has she been on oxygen?" Jessica asked, removing the little mask so she could press the cat's gums to check the capillary refill time. Not good.

"About three minutes. No response."

"Get a pulse ox on her." Jessica unwrapped the towel and pressed her stethoscope to the cat's chest while Caleb clipped the heart and oxygen monitor between the cat's toes. "Heart rate is still depressed." She felt the cat's ears and paws. "Cold extremities."

The monitor began its monotonous beeping, but far too slowly.

"Oxygen saturation is rising," Caleb said, reading the monitor. "But nothing else is."

"It might be a bad reaction to the anesthesia," Jessica said. "I'm going to administer atipamezole to try to reverse the effects. What's the cat's weight?"

Caleb checked the chart. "Two point seven kilograms."

Jessica did a fast mental calculation as she unlocked the medicine cabinet and grabbed the bottle of atipamezole. Ripping a syringe out of its sterile packet and shoving a needle on it, she drew in the liquid and ran back to the recovery table. Caleb had already positioned the cat's hind leg, so Jessica felt for the muscle and jabbed the needle into it.

Caleb covered the cat with the towel again and resumed his massage to stimulate the cat's system. Jessica replaced the oxygen mask over the little creature's face.

"What's her name again?" Jessica asked. She'd done so many surgeries that day that they'd all blurred together.

"Boots," Caleb said. "Mrs. Lopez just adopted her."

"Come on, Boots," Jessica said in an urgent voice as she checked the monitor. "Come back to us, baby."

Slowly but steadily, the beeping of the pulse ox sped up. A few minutes later, the cat blinked open her golden eyes.

Jessica and Caleb grinned at each other over the cat's swaddled body.

"You did it, Doc," the vet tech said. "You brought her back."

"*We* brought her back. You did a great job, Caleb," Jessica said. She methodically checked all of Boots's vital signs and breathed out a sigh of relief. The cat was stable.

"I have to get back to surgery," she said. "Keep a close watch on her until you're sure she's on solid ground."

"You got it, Doc."

Jessica scrubbed in again and bolted back to the OR, where the male cat still slept tranquilly on his back, his hind legs splayed out and anchored to the table.

"Okay, time to give up the family jewels, buddy," she said, picking up her scalpel. A few incisions and knots, and the job was finished. Her assistant gently wrapped the limp cat in a towel and carried him out of the operating room.

Carla Watkins, the clinic's receptionist and office manager, strolled into the surgery. "Honey, you got company in your office."

"And I've got six more surgeries to do. Who is it?" Jessica stripped off her surgical gloves and mask. Carla was usually a tigress about fending off drug reps without appointments, so it must be someone she felt Jessica would want to see. Which could only mean her brother.

Aidan had arrived at her house unannounced yesterday, dropping his duffel bag in her front hall and giving her his trademark "forgive me because I'm your brother and you love me" smile. But she hadn't felt forgiving, especially because he had a noticeable tan and his shoulder-length brown hair showed sun-bleached streaks of blond. Considering the gray, skin-numbing, postholiday dismalness outside her window, that meant Aidan had been traveling somewhere warm and tropical. She hadn't had a vacation in three years, so the thought didn't improve her reception of her brother.

She'd forced herself to hug him, but then she'd had to leave before she said something she'd regret. That's why she had been so focused on capturing the starving dog. The animal's plight kept her mind off her sibling's lack of responsibility.

Her brother had been gone—although his clothes were still strewn around her sparsely furnished guest room—when she got home from her encounter with Hugh. Aidan's absence had provoked a mixture of relief and annoyance, especially when his return had been heralded by the slam of the front door at one in the morning, waking her up. Admittedly, her sleep had been fitful. Seeing her ex-fiancé had set off a train of memories that had whipsawed her between nostalgic joy and soul-searing agony.

"Is it Aidan?" Jessica asked as she washed her hands.

Carla raised her eyebrows. "Is he back in town?" Her voice vibrated with disapproval.

Jessica nodded, but her heartbeat sped up. The only other visitor she could imagine Carla allowing in was Hugh.

Carla's expression went from judgmental to admiring. "No, it's someone a whole lot more interesting. Says you're friends from way back." She threw Jessica a quizzical glance before she bustled out the door.

As Jessica dried her hands, she tried to calm the nerves fluttering through her now that she was sure who it was. She hated reacting to Hugh this way. She should be able to ignore him the way he'd ignored her for eight years.

When she started down the cracked gray linoleum hallway, Geode, the office's resident cat, bolted past her to skid into the supply closet. Her visitor must have awakened the stranger-averse kitty and sent him running for cover.

She reached her office, a former storeroom into which she'd crammed a wooden desk she'd found on the curb and some assemble-it-yourself oak filing cabinets on top of which Geode usually slept. Her one indulgence was a high-end ergonomic chair on wheels, which was currently occupied by her ex-fiancé, his back turned to her so the width of his shoulders was evident above the chair's back.

"What on earth are you doing here?" She stopped on the threshold, her hands on her hips, and he swiveled to face her, his own hands lifted in a gesture of mock self-defense.

"You didn't give me your cell number, so I had to come find you." He rose, his presence filling the cramped space with that mesmeric energy unique to him.

"You could have just called the clinic." He wore a perfectly fitted navy-blue suit, and she realized he must be in costume as Julian Best. He looked out of place amid the battered furniture and the snapshots of patients in cheap plastic frames hung on the walls.

He smiled in a way that lit up his vivid eyes. "I find it's more effective to appear in person."

She thought of her no-nonsense office manager's reaction. "I'll bet you do."

He came around the desk to stand in front of her. She forced herself not to close her eyes as the exotic scent of sandalwood wafted into her nostrils. "You promised me dinner," he said.

"I'm pretty sure I turned you down," she said, veering past him to drop into her desk chair. That put one piece of furniture between them, but it was better than none. "Look, I appreciate the invitation, but I work until at least seven o'clock every night. I'm too exhausted to go out after that."

He scowled. "No wonder you look tired. You need a life outside work."

She just stared at him as he echoed the words she'd once said to him, when their engagement unraveled. Except it hadn't been his actual work that was the problem. It had been the extracurricular activities: the parties, the awards ceremonies, the promotional appearances. He'd claimed he had to do them all to succeed, and he'd wanted her by his side.

At first the chance to dress up and be glamorous had been fun. When she'd run through her limited wardrobe, she and Hugh had gone on a shopping spree, spending part of the advance his agent had given him. He'd bought a tuxedo that she made him put back on when they got home, just so she could peel it off him slowly and with great attention to each revealed inch of skin. She'd bought dresses and shoes and costume jewelry, most of which Hugh picked out. He could look at a piece of clothing and know it would look great on her. Because he paid attention.

However, the tension kicked in when the invitations began to conflict with her work schedule. Being low vet on the totem pole, she often got scheduled for evening hours. She had found someone to trade assigned slots with three weeks in a row to accommodate Hugh's work-fueled social schedule. The fourth week, she balked. He'd first tried to guilt her into it, saying he needed her presence to give him confidence. She'd pointed out that not only was it unfair to her colleagues to keep asking them to rearrange their week, but it made her look unprofessional.

"You don't have to worry about that," he had said. "Once my career takes off, you'll never have to work again."

She'd stood speechless for a long moment, wondering how this could be the same man who had chosen the perfect outfit for her because he seemed to know her almost better than she knew herself.

And they'd had a huge fight.

That's when she had begun to realize that their needs were veering in sharply different directions. He wanted someone who could smile with dazzling sincerity on the red carpet with a battery of cameras pointed at her, not someone who came home in blood-spattered scrubs with a hunger headache.

The ugly memory fortified her decision to avoid Hugh in the present time. She took a deep breath. "Aidan just arrived for a visit, so I don't want to leave him alone."

Carla happened to be passing by the doorway just then and made a loud, derisive noise.

"I sense a false note in that statement," Hugh said, an undercurrent of amusement in his voice as he nodded toward the now empty corridor. "How is your brother?"

She didn't want to talk about it. "He's fine. Enjoying New York City."

"He always took advantage of the nightlife when he came to LA."

Hugh had been very generous about taking her younger brother along to the fancy Hollywood parties he'd wangled invitations to. Back then, she and Aidan had been wide-eyed innocents, not understanding what went on in the bathrooms, bedrooms, and pool houses at those events. Hugh, of course, was well aware—he'd had the innocence kicked out of him in his teens—but he'd shielded them from the seamier side of the industry he'd chosen. She had to give him credit for that.

"He's doing the same thing here," Jessica said. Without a job to support it. But Aidan was good at getting other people to pay for his pleasures.

"So you can have dinner with me while Aidan is off clubbing." Hugh crossed his arms and leaned against the door frame. "You must at least have Sunday off."

"A lot of my clients work, so I'm open on weekends." She finally threw in the towel. She knew Hugh wouldn't give up until he'd gotten what he wanted. "Yesterday was my day off. That's why I chased the stray into your movie shoot. We can have dinner next Wednesday."

A frown drew down Hugh's slashing eyebrows for a split second. Then he nodded. "Wednesday it is. Tell me where to pick you up."

"Why don't I just meet you at the restaurant?" She didn't want him to see her fixer-upper row house, which was only about a third of the way toward fixed up. She'd bought the run-down building dirt cheap when she'd moved to New York, foolishly believing she could renovate it in the spare time she never had.

"You can't possibly think I'd agree to that," he said.

"I know. It's just . . ." She surrendered and held out her hand. "Give me your phone and I'll put my contact info in."

The phone he passed to her was a work of art, its ultraslim shape wrapped in brown leather with gold accents that had the unmistakable luster of fourteen karats. She tapped in her address and phone number, running her fingers over the exquisite case before handing it back. He'd finally gotten the beautiful things he'd craved.

He swiped a few times, and her phone pinged in her lab-coat pocket. "Now you have my number," he said. "I'll be in touch about the time."

"How about seven?" Jessica said.

"I need to check the shooting schedule." He glanced at the elegant gold watch on his wrist. "In fact, I have to get back to the set."

But there was one question she wanted an answer to. "Hugh, why do you want to have dinner with me after all these years?"

He gave an elegant shrug, the fabric of his jacket pulling tight across his broad shoulders. "You remind me of when I was a different man."

Hugh ducked into the limousine waiting for him outside Jessica's clinic. He hoped like hell that the scene between his archenemy and his love interest had taken longer to shoot than expected. Otherwise, everyone would be standing around waiting for him to show up.

Nobody would dare to complain, because Hugh was always on time and always knew his lines. Of course, he expected everyone else to do the same, which was why directors loved him. His less professional fellow cast members were not always as enthusiastic about his high standards. That meant he needed to stick to them himself.

However, he had felt an overwhelming need to find Jess. So much so that he had been less than fully focused on his performance this morning. He'd decided he should fix the problem by tracking her down.

Then he'd told her only part of the truth. She did remind him of another time and place, when he'd felt good about himself. Because Jess had loved him, he had felt worthy of that love. When she had handed back the ring he'd gone into debt to buy for her, the blow had felt physical. He could still remember groping for the back of their hideous plaid sofa so he didn't crumple to his knees. Of course he'd realized they were having some problems, but he knew how great her capacity for love was. He'd counted on that.

Then she'd rejected him.

He'd been so devastated that he couldn't bring himself to speak to her after that terrible night, although he'd saved her voice messages and played them over and over again. Finally, one of his friends had deleted them because his behavior was deemed unhealthy.

Then he had let too much time go by, and his pride threw up a senseless but unyielding blockade to keep him from reaching out to break the silence between them.

Now he knew that while he'd been pretending to be a fictional character, Jessica had been saving lives in a place that truly needed her. Not to mention that she was clearly struggling financially. He'd noted the cracked linoleum floor in the hallway of her veterinary clinic and the motley array of chairs in the waiting area. Except for the desk chair, the furniture in her office looked as though it had been scavenged from a dumpster.

However, when he'd glanced into the examining room he'd passed by en route to Jessica's office, the equipment gleamed with cleanliness and looked far more up to date than the computer on her receptionist's desk. Of course, Jess would spend her money on the best care for her patients.

Guilt shot needles into his chest, and he caught himself rubbing at it with his palm.

The Julian Best movies had made him a fortune once Gavin had helped him negotiate a cut of the profits instead of a flat fee. The overseas distribution of the films turned out to be a box-office platinum mine. After this movie released, he intended to apply for membership in Gavin's favorite hangout, the ultraexclusive Bellwether Club, which required that the applicant have amassed a fortune of a billion dollars, starting from scratch.

Yes, he'd put a large percentage of his earnings into the foundation he'd started to help foster kids like the child he'd once been. But he just wrote checks and made the occasional visit to the organizations his money funded. He wasn't down in the trenches getting his hands dirty like Jess.

The thought added to his nagging sense of dissatisfaction with his life.

Maybe this was just a side effect of the new, softer Julian Best. In the novel this movie was based on, Gavin Miller had killed off Julian's old lover, the Machiavellian double agent Samantha Dubois. Gavin claimed it wasn't because Irene Bartram, the actress who played Samantha, had interfered with Gavin's love life, but Hugh didn't believe it. Not that he had any sympathy for Irene. She was a first-class bitch.

Julian's new love was a normal woman, not involved in the spy game. Gavin's wife, Allie, had come up with the idea as a way to humanize the super spy. It also increased the stakes—Julian would have to work doubly hard to protect her since, unlike Samantha, she didn't have the skills to protect herself.

So maybe Hugh's sudden longing to be normal, to be more in touch with real life, was nothing more than too close an identification with Julian's character.

The limo eased to a stop by Hugh's trailer. He heaved a sigh of relief when no stressed-out production assistant paced the curb outside it.

But when he stepped inside, Meryl was artfully arranged on his sofa, her long legs crossed at the ankles to show off the graceful arch of her feet in their high-heeled pumps. Her skirt was slightly rucked up to reveal an expanse of smooth thigh. This time his internal sigh was not one of relief.

"Hugh, sweetie!" she said in her honeyed voice. "Bryan told us to take a break, so I thought I'd run lines with you. Since you weren't here, I raided your fruit bowl." She held up a half-eaten pear. "Hope you don't mind."

"How long a break?" he asked.

She glanced at the large clock that hung on the wall opposite the sofa. "Another fifteen minutes. They were having some technical difficulties with the sound. Too much ambient noise in New York City. Who'd have thought?" Her tone was heavy with the irony he generally appreciated.

In fact, he liked Meryl. She was prepared and professional. Unfortunately, she'd also hinted that she would like to extend their relationship to off the screen. Five years ago he might have felt the same way. Now he wanted to do his job and leave it behind him when he exited the set.

The problem was that Meryl was so subtle he'd had no opportunity to turn her down. And he didn't want to risk killing the chemistry she generated between them, because it showed up on the dailies. That's one reason Bryan had cast her.

Or maybe she was even cleverer than he thought and knew exactly what she was doing to steam up the camera lenses.

"Must be garbage pickup day," Hugh said. "I've had far too many scenes ruined by the crash of dumpsters being emptied."

Meryl gave a throaty chuckle. "I worked on a movie in Hawaii where they had to pay one helicopter sightseeing tour to shut down for three days because of the rotor noise. Cost them a fortune and the tourists were grumpy, but we got our shots. That's the movie business. You do whatever is necessary."

Something in her tone implied she meant more than just stopping helicopter noise. A faint disgust moved through him. "What lines did you want to run?" he asked, propping a hip against the kitchen counter.

Meryl swung her legs off the sofa so she could pick up a sheaf of papers from the coffee table, causing her skirt to slide even farther up her thighs. He had the odd thought that Jess looked sexier in her green scrubs than Meryl did with her calculated display of flesh.

She patted the sofa beside her and gave him the smile of a temptress. "Why don't you sit here, and we'll start right after we wake up and realize that we're locked in a pitch-dark shipping container."

Chapter 3

Jessica inserted her key into the lock only to discover her front door was already open. "You're not in Iowa anymore, Aidan," she snapped under her breath as she stepped in and shot home the dead bolt behind her. The thick oak door wouldn't offer much protection if it wasn't locked.

Between Boots the cat reacting so badly to the anesthesia and Hugh showing up in her office, it had been a strange day. Thank goodness Boots seemed to have made a full recovery. However, Jessica still hadn't regained her equilibrium after Hugh's visit.

"Jess! Come on in here. I have a surprise for you." Aidan's greeting came from the living room.

"In a minute." Jessica shrugged out of her puffy coat and hung it up in the hall closet. She stood for a moment, letting her gaze wander over the quarter-sawn oak paneling and the white and yellow roses depicted in the stained-glass window by the front door. The front hall was the last room she'd had a chance to renovate before she had gotten too busy with the clinic. It soothed her irritation with her brother a bit to admire the results of all her labor in stripping and revarnishing the wood.

She took a deep breath and walked into the living room. It was still a work in progress, with only one wall rescued from the garish 1960s wallpaper that was especially cringeworthy against the exquisite Victorian woodwork. The carved marble mantel was sooty with smoke stains while the wooden planks of the floor still bore the nail damage from the wall-to-wall green shag carpet she'd pulled up.

Seated on her blue crushed-velvet sofa were Aidan and a man with white-blond hair, drinking two of the craft beers she kept in reserve for a really bad day at the office.

The man rose and set his beer on one of the veterinary magazines strewn over the mahogany coffee table. "Jessica, you probably don't remember me, but I'm Pete Larson. From Wellsburg." He smiled, his teeth straight and white.

"Pete? The last time I saw you, you were . . ." She held her hand up level with her own head. Now he towered well over six feet with a breadth of shoulder that his blue button-down shirt outlined to good effect.

Pete laughed. "I had a growth spurt after you left for college." He was a year older than Aidan, which made Pete two years younger than Jessica.

"I'll say." Jessica held out her hand across the table. "It's good to see you again. Where did Aidan find you?"

"At a bar," her brother said. "You need to get out more, sis. Fellow Iowans are everywhere."

She'd made a concerted effort to leave Iowa behind, so Aidan's supposed enticement didn't convince her to increase her socializing. But no one in her family had ever understood her desire to get away.

"You look great," Pete said, genuine admiration in his gaze. "And you run your own veterinary practice in New York City. I always knew you'd make a success of yourself."

Jessica sat down on a carved walnut chair she'd found on the curb and refurbished. He was a nice man to say she looked good in her rumpled scrubs.

"Want one of these excellent beers?" Aidan asked, holding up his bottle. "You have good taste in beverages."

Jessica decided she'd better enjoy her own beer before it disappeared. "If there are any left."

Aidan headed for the kitchen while Pete leaned forward, his elbows resting on well-muscled thighs clad in khaki chinos. "I'm sorry to barge in on your evening like this. Honestly, I don't go to bars much myself. Some folks from work talked me into it, and there was Aidan. We started reminiscing, and he thought you'd want to join the fun."

A long-forgotten memory surfaced, making Jessica cringe inwardly. When she was a senior in high school, Aidan had persuaded her to accompany him to a party, mostly so she would drive him there. After pushing through the crush of bodies, she'd realized it was a younger crowd and had been headed for the front door when Pete had caught her wrist. "Let's dance," he'd shouted over the din of voices and music as he towed her toward a dark room where bodies gyrated.

Thinking one dance couldn't hurt, she'd joined the writhing crowd. After a few fast dances, the music had turned slow. Pete had pulled her into him, his chest and arms ropy with muscle from hauling hay bales on his family's farm. She'd hesitated because it was not cool to get involved with your younger brother's friend. Wellsburg was a tiny town, and word would get around. But it felt good to be pressed against his solid, male body and when he inexpertly sought her mouth with his, she'd let him kiss her.

Soon, they'd stopped dancing altogether.

When the music had picked up speed again, she had broken away, making it clear that the kiss had been a onetime deal. Pete probably didn't remember any of it, but she felt a flush heat her cheeks.

"Are you thinking about what I'm thinking about?" He gave her another smile, this one a little flirty. "There's one memory I've held on to for years. You kissed me at a party when I was about, oh, fifteen. It was the best kiss I'd ever had."

"I was hoping you'd forgotten that. Especially since I wasn't so nice about it afterward."

28

"No, you let me down easy. I knew I had no business kissing my friend's big sister." He chuckled. "But that didn't stop me from enjoying it."

Aidan reappeared with her drink, which kept her from having to respond. Pete sat back on the cushions while Jessica took a gulp of beer.

"Did you all start without me?" Aidan asked, looking back and forth between them.

"Just a short warm-up," Pete said with a wink for Jessica.

"Good, because I don't want to miss anything," Aidan said. "Jess, do you remember when the Schmidts' sow got loose and lay down in the middle of Route 23? She must have weighed about five hundred pounds. No one could get her to move, and traffic was backed up in both directions."

Jessica laughed. "All four members of the police force surrounded her, and she still wouldn't budge."

"I've never known a hog to be impressed by a badge," Pete said, deadpan.

"So they called in the vo-ag teacher and he said to get Jess," Aidan said, nodding to his sister. "I was jealous because you got out of class."

"I didn't understand why Mr. Hansen thought I could move a pig, but I wasn't going to argue with missing trigonometry."

"Everyone knew you were amazing with animals, even when you were a kid," Aidan said. "And you did manage to get her off the road."

"You used some kind of exotic food, didn't you?" Pete asked.

"Exotic only to a sow in Iowa," Jessica said. "Pigs like fresh fruit, and I figured oranges were something she wouldn't usually get fed. Also, oranges have a strong aroma, to get her salivating. I fed her one orange to hook her on the taste and then laid a trail of fruit from the sow to the side of the highway."

"And so was born the legend of Jessica the Sow Whisperer," Aidan intoned.

"Maybe we should talk about some of *your* escapades," Jessica said to her brother, as she remembered she was annoyed with him.

"Pete's already heard them all," Aidan said with an airy wave of dismissal.

"In that case, how did you end up in New York, Pete?" Jessica asked.

"Work," he said with a shrug.

"He's being too modest," Aidan said. "He got headhunted from a tech firm in Silicon Valley. Now he's the CFO of a hot start-up."

"What kind of tech?" Jessica asked.

"Capturing, packaging, and selling data exhaust," Pete said with a twinkle in his eye. "Aren't you glad you asked?"

She laughed. "It sounds like a cross between hard drives and automobile engines."

"You're not too far off," Pete said. "Why don't you have dinner with me Saturday, and I'll explain it more fully? Or not, depending on your preference." His tone was wry.

Jessica rocked back in her chair. She hadn't had—or wanted—a date in months, and all of a sudden two men had asked her out within the same day. The memory of Hugh's intense blue eyes flitted through her brain.

She caught sight of her brother's face and realized he looked like a cat that had dunked its head into the cream pitcher.

"Thanks, Pete, but I'm tied up at the clinic on Saturday. I appreciate the offer, though."

"What night would work better for you?" he asked without any hesitation.

Something about how unfazed he sounded in the face of her rejection made her look at him again. He wasn't the fifteen-year-old boy she had kissed and dumped. Pete Larson was a broad-shouldered, full-grown, very attractive man with his pale blue eyes, corn-silk hair, and big, square hands. He wore his khakis and his blue button-down shirt with the ease of someone who didn't need clothes to prove his worth.

He waited for her answer without rushing her, his patience showing a confidence that piqued her interest even more.

She decided she deserved some fun, even if she paid for it by being exhausted the next day. "How about Sunday? But I turn into a pumpkin at nine."

"I hear you," Pete said. "Monday mornings are rough. We'll start early, then. I'll pick you up at six." He pulled out a cell phone that was far more utilitarian than Hugh's. "What's your number?"

Jessica reeled it off and heard her phone ping with a text notification. It reminded her that she'd never read Hugh's text message.

"You've got my number now, too," Pete said, rising from the couch to his impressive height. He came around the table and took her hand, enveloping it in the warmth of his. "I'm looking forward to Sunday," he said with that perfect smile.

A little shiver of attraction ran through her. Pete was so different from Hugh—so down-to-earth, solid, and Iowan, without any of her ex's dark intensity—that her reaction surprised her. But maybe Pete would be exactly the right counterbalance to Hugh.

While Aidan walked his friend to the door, Jessica picked up the empty beer bottles and carried them into the kitchen. She had plunked them in the sink to rinse when she heard Aidan's footsteps heading up the stairs.

"Aidan," she called. He wasn't going to get away without explaining his sudden unemployment—and his plans to remedy it.

The speed of his steps accelerated.

"Aidan James Quillen, get back down here right now," she shouted as she marched into the living room.

The footsteps stopped and then sounded again, but in the reverse direction.

"Jeez, you sound just like Mom," her brother said as he reached the bottom step. "And that's not a compliment."

"We have to talk," Jessica said, pointing to the chair where she'd been sitting.

"Sure thing." Aidan perched on the chair with a nonchalance that she saw right through. She had to admit that he looked good. His rangy frame had filled out, so that he appeared more man than boy now, even in faded jeans and a T-shirt with a beer logo on it. His tan brought out the slight tint of blue in his gray eyes, and his sun-streaked hair waved down to his shoulders. That and his unshaven scruff gave him the look of a model in an advertisement for outdoorsy living. However, that just ratcheted up her irritation with him.

"You've been avoiding me," she said, sitting on the couch. "So I know the news is bad. What happened this time?"

He shrugged. "I asked for time off to see a lunar eclipse at Machu Picchu with some friends, but my boss wouldn't give it to me, even though I had the vacation days saved up." He spread his arms wide. "It was an opportunity of a lifetime. I couldn't turn it down."

"If you had the necessary vacation time, why wouldn't your boss let you go?"

"We had a big project that was behind schedule and he claimed that he needed me there to get it done. Which was total BS, because I wasn't even working on that project."

Sympathy for the boss she'd never met flooded Jessica. "Maybe he needed you to take up the slack on your project so other people could focus on the big one."

Aidan wouldn't meet her gaze. "He was just being a jerk. He didn't like me."

Jessica could imagine why. Aidan was a wizard at programming when he was interested enough to focus on the job. But keeping his attention on a project long enough to complete it was a challenge.

"Did you quit or just not show up?" Jessica asked.

"I resigned in an e-mail from the airport," Aidan said. "That's more than he deserved."

"You can't keep pulling this crap, Aidan. Pretty soon no one will want to hire you."

He gave her a complacent smile and tapped his temple with his index finger. "There's pure tech genius in this brain. People beg me to come work for them."

Jessica shook her head. "Word gets around. You don't want to become known for being unreliable."

Not to mention that Aidan had complained about the lower pay at the last two jobs he'd taken. She suspected that his reputation had preceded him at the higher-paying tech companies.

"Don't worry, sis, I won't become a permanent resident here." His tone was resentful.

She gave him a long, steady look. "You know that's not what I'm worried about."

"Yeah, yeah," he said. "You're concerned about my future, when I'm not so young anymore and need health insurance and a pension plan." He gave her his little-brother grin. "But I'm young now and I want to enjoy life while I can. I'm not a workaholic like you."

His last words felt like a smack in the face. She *wasn't* a workaholic. She put in long hours because her patients needed her, not because she preferred work over pleasure. In fact, her job gave her pleasure. Sucking in a deep breath, she counted to ten before she said in an even tone that she was proud of, "A job is called a job for a reason. You have to show up even when you don't want to in order to get paid. If it were all fun and games, people would do it for free."

"Don't talk to me like I'm twelve," Aidan said, but his sulky expression made him appear about that age.

"Then don't act like you are." She held up her hand in apology. She didn't want to fight with him any longer. "Sorry, I had a rough day."

"That's why I brought Pete over," Aidan said in a blatant redirection of the conversation. "I thought he would take your mind off things, cheer you up."

"You're such an altruist," Jessica said with heavy sarcasm, but she gave up on trying to drum a sense of responsibility into Aidan. He seemed to be impervious to the concept. He was good-looking, highly skilled, and charming. In the real, imperfect world, his combination of attributes meant he could always find a job, even if it wasn't always a good one. He had skated happily through life that way—so far.

"Hey, Pete's a great guy. I'm glad you're going out with him." His expression shifted to concern, making him look entirely adult. "I worry about you, Jess. You may think I have too much fun, but I don't think you have enough. Your clinic has kind of taken over your life." He shook his head as she opened her mouth. "I know you do important work. I think that's great. But you've got no balance."

Her irresponsible little brother was talking about balance? Yet she'd had the same thought yesterday and the sense that her life was becoming single focused had niggled at the back of her mind for the last couple of weeks. She'd ascribed it to the postholiday letdown when the once-pristine snow had frozen into gray, grit-filled heaps with no colorful decorations to distract the eye from them.

"Maybe Pete won't be the right guy," Aidan continued. "But you have to get out there again. I mean it's been eight years since you broke up with Hugh. How many guys have you dated between then and now?"

He might as well have body-slammed her into the couch. Hugh had just shown up in her life again, and now her brother was insinuating that she was still pining after him. Yes, it had taken her a while to get over the end of their engagement, but she didn't turn down other men because of that.

"I've dated plenty." Once, twice, three times at most. Maybe because it was impossible for them to measure up to a man who was now half the world's romantic fantasy. The thought made her look at Aidan with a mix of respect and dismay. When had he become so perceptive about her love life?

"But you haven't let anyone stick around, or I would have known. Maybe you're still hung up on Hugh."

She would have denied it if the memory of Hugh standing in her office doorway hadn't risen up in her mind. She'd fought it down at the time, but for a moment she'd wanted to press herself up against him from knee to shoulder, inhale his scent of sandalwood and clean, intense masculinity, and feel his arms come around her to hold her as though she were the most incredible person he'd ever met.

"It's sweet of you to worry about me, but I'm doing fine," she said. Aidan's concern made her heart glow with a soft warmth. He'd definitely matured.

"I think you'll really like Pete." Aidan's stomach rumbled loudly, and he grinned as he flattened his palm over it. "Did you eat dinner yet? I thought I'd get some Chinese takeout."

"I'll treat if you go pick it up." She had no idea how much money Aidan had left after his trip to Machu Picchu, if any.

When Aidan tramped off into the winter night to retrieve their dinner, Jessica stretched out on the sofa, felled by a combination of exhaustion and beer on an empty stomach. As she settled, her cell phone dug into her hip, so she fished it out of her pocket.

Two text messages showed up as unread. She swiped open Pete's, which read: Mexican, Brazilian, or Japanese? She liked his simple directness and being given a choice.

Then she swiped on Hugh's.

I should have done better.

She slapped her phone down on the sofa cushion with a growl of exasperation. Hugh had managed to phrase his message so it was almost, but not quite, an apology.

Chapter 4

Jessica admired the way the light from the pillar candle in the cut-crystal holder turned Pete's hair to spun gold. They'd texted back and forth about the fact that Wellsburg, Iowa, had none of the choices of cuisine he'd offered her before they settled on Brazilian. She'd expected a small, casual place in Soho, but he'd taken her to a sophisticated midtown restaurant with modern twists on classic South American dishes. The napkins were heavy white linen, the roomy chairs upholstered in taupe leather, and the room sleekly modern.

In a way, she was disappointed in his choice. She would have preferred him to act more like the solid, uncomplicated Iowan farmer she had assumed he would grow up to be. This was the kind of restaurant she could picture Hugh frequenting, and she wanted Pete to offer a counterweight to her ex-fiancé's unwelcome pull on her.

Of course, she might have been tipped off when Pete had come to pick her up in a dark-green Range Rover. Aside from the cost of the high-end vehicle itself, keeping a car in the city was expensive. Keeping a big car was even more so.

She also noticed how at ease Pete was in the urbane setting. Although his attire wasn't on the level of Hugh's custom-tailored suit, Pete looked downright elegant in a subtle blue windowpane plaid blazer, gray trousers, and a blue-and-white-striped shirt.

It was becoming harder and harder to think of him as her brother's high school friend. Which made Jessica glad she'd worn slim-fitting black pants, a lavender cashmere sweater, and kitten-heeled ankle boots. It was her go-to outfit for dress-up dinners out. As she had torn the dry cleaner's plastic off the trousers, she realized she hadn't worn them in at least four months. Maybe Aidan was right. Maybe she needed to get out more.

"I recommend the *moqueca capixaba*," Pete said, looking up from the menu to catch her watching him. The corners of his mouth kicked up in a slight smile. "The broth has a nice combination of curry and coconut milk."

"You eat here often?"

"It's near my office, so I sometimes bring business colleagues here." He scanned around the room. "I like the place, and the food is dynamite."

The waiter glided up to take their order. Jessica took Pete's recommendation about the fish stew, so he ordered white wine for both of them, his choice making the waiter nod in approval.

"How did you end up in Silicon Valley before this?" she asked when the waiter left.

He smiled full-on, sending a little slide of heat through her. "You inspired me."

"Me? How?" Other than that miscalculated kiss in high school, she and Pete had been mere acquaintances through Aidan.

He twirled an empty wineglass on the tablecloth. "You were so focused on getting into college so you could become a veterinarian. I'd never really thought of school as a means to an end. In fact, I wasn't even sure I wanted to go to college. But you changed my thinking."

"Wow, I had no idea I was ever a good influence on anyone," she joked, but with a glow of satisfaction. She'd certainly never been able to exert any sway over Aidan.

"In my opinion, you're a pretty damn good person."

"Um, thank you. That's really nice."

He must have sensed her discomfort and went back to his story. "You—and Aidan, if truth be told—also got me looking beyond Wellsburg, Iowa," he said. "So I went to Bucknell University in Pennsylvania."

"When you decide to look farther afield, you go for it," Jessica said. Underneath his easygoing facade, Pete must have a pretty powerful drive, since it had gotten him all the way to a top-shelf college in Pennsylvania. The realization both impressed and unsettled her. Hugh's overwhelming desire to succeed was what had driven them apart.

"I got a scholarship," he said with a shrug. "The place seemed like a foreign country, but their business school was famous for its accounting major. And that's what I wanted to study."

"Then you continued to broaden your horizons by moving to Silicon Valley?"

"I got recruited, and California sounded even more foreign than Pennsylvania." He shook his head. "Silicon Valley sure was, too."

"More exotic than Manhattan?" Jessica had followed a similar geographical path, now that she thought about it.

"Oh, yeah. At least it snows here." He winked just as the waiter arrived with the wine.

She was no longer surprised when Pete tasted it with the expertise of a connoisseur. Once the waiter had filled both their glasses, Pete raised his. "To Iowans with broad horizons."

They touched glasses with a muted clink. The wine was delicious, but she'd expected that. "How broad are yours?" Jessica asked. She held up the wine. "Have you been to Brazil?"

"A couple of times, although most of my days there were spent in conference rooms." Pete grimaced before he entertained her with a few stories of his journeys to various foreign locales. He'd traveled far more widely than a couple of trips to Rio.

"How about you?" he asked. "Where have you been?"

"Edinburgh, to the veterinary school for some postgrad work." She'd loved wandering around the historic city where almost everything was older than Iowa.

Pete smiled. "I spent a few days there once. Great city. Then I got the crazy idea that since I was in Scotland, I should play golf, so I drove over to St. Andrews. I thought I was a decent golfer until I landed in one of their pot bunkers. There's one called Hell, and that's exactly what it felt like."

Jessica liked his self-deprecation. The conversation flowed easily through the appetizers and the main course as they traded memories of their hometown and the people in it.

When the waiter offered them dessert menus, Pete checked his watch before he gave her a glinting smile. "I think we can have one more course before I have to take you home."

The pleasure of Pete's company had made Jessica forget all about her self-imposed curfew. "My fairy godmother will probably cut me a break just this once," she said, taking the heavy vellum menu. "After all, the whole point of eating dinner is to get to dessert."

"That wasn't *my* point in having dinner with you," Pete said, his smile changing to something less playful and more intent.

A flush crept up her cheeks. Torn between being flattered and being uncertain of where she wanted this to go, she dropped her gaze to the list of sweets. "What is a *brigadeiro*?" she asked.

"It's a classic Brazilian treat," Pete said. "Sort of like soft chocolate fudge, only here they serve it in a glass with a spoon."

"Well, it's chocolate, so I'm going with that." She put her menu down.

Pete ordered a cheese platter. "And a Sandeman forty-year-old tawny port for each of us," he added. "You appear to have a sweet tooth, so it seems like the right after-dinner drink."

After the waiter departed, Pete lounged back in his chair. "You can tell me that it's none of my business, but Aidan says that you were once engaged to Hugh Baker."

Jessica almost choked on her last swallow of wine. Why the hell would Aidan share that with Pete? "Did he also tell you that it was a long time ago?"

"He did, but I don't imagine you forget someone that famous. I'm surprised no one in Wellsburg ever mentioned it."

"Hugh wasn't Julian Best back then, so it wasn't big news." His casting as the super spy had brought the problems in their engagement to a crisis point, in fact. "It also didn't last long." Their entire relationship had been seventeen months of first heaven and then torment. She wished she didn't remember both so vividly.

The waiter presented them with two tulip-shaped glasses filled with a tawny liquid. Glad of the interruption, Jessica took a sip and savored the sweet burn on her tongue and the smooth slide down her throat. "Nice."

He acknowledged her compliment with a pleased nod. "Kind of hard to compete with Julian Best, though."

She decided to address the easy part rather than the implication that Pete considered himself in competition with her ex-fiancé. "Everyone gets that wrong. In real life, Hugh isn't a suave, dangerous, tuxedo-wearing secret agent. He's an actor who takes on a persona on the set. At home, he's just a regular guy with morning breath, poor taste in neckties, and an addiction to cheese puffs. The only thing not normal about Hugh is that he's never had a bad hair day in his life. I hated that about him."

Pete swirled his port in the glass. "Good to know that he's almost human."

Hugh had been quite human when they'd met on the set of a low-budget indie movie he was starring in. *Starring* was a loose term, because the focus of the movie was a pack of dogs, one of whom had died during filming. That was where Jessica had come in. She'd been fresh out of vet school, working at the big, cutting-edge veterinary hospital in Los Angeles where they treated everything from dogs with gunshot wounds to a king cobra with pneumonia. When the movie got some bad press for allegedly working the dog to death, the director contracted with the animal hospital for a vet to be on set all the time. Since Jessica was the newest and therefore least valuable member of the staff, she'd gotten the job.

Turned out the dog had died because it had a heart defect, not because the director was inhumane, so her job was easy. When the dogs weren't required for shooting, she kept them hydrated and in the shade of a canopy set up especially for the canine actors. When the dogs were in action, she helped the grateful dog trainer wrangle them for the cameras. She'd been so focused on the dogs for the first couple of days that she had paid no attention to the human actors.

Then Hugh had come over to visit the dog tent. His beauty was blinding. The black hair, the surreal turquoise eyes. She'd asked him if they were colored contact lenses, which had made him laugh. The bone structure of his face was striking, with its clean, slashing angles that made the camera linger. He was in costume, which meant jeans and a ripped T-shirt that displayed the symmetrical ridges of his abdominal muscles and the dusting of dark hair over his pecs.

He'd told her that he needed to interact more with the dogs to deepen his interpretation of his role. Jessica had seen no reason to doubt him, since he seemed like a celestial being who could have no possible interest in her. But Hugh later confessed that he'd used that as a ploy to talk with her, an admission she'd found both baffling and immensely flattering. As far as she was concerned, someone who looked like Hugh didn't need an excuse to chat her up, but part of his appeal was that he felt he had.

When Hugh asked her out for dinner a few days later, she thought she'd heard him wrong.

"Poor choice of topic, I guess," Pete said, pulling her mind back to the present.

"It's fine," Jessica said. "I'm long over Hugh." Or so she'd thought until the last couple of days.

Pete lifted an eyebrow in a way that indicated he wasn't convinced, so she decided not to mention that she'd just run into her ex. "Our lives have taken very different directions for a reason."

"I hear you," he said. "Opposite coasts and all."

"And different stratospheres."

Except Hugh was on her coast at the moment. But that wouldn't last. The Julian Best movies always shot in a multitude of exotic locations. Hugh would move on and forget her existence again. Annoying that the thought hurt.

She welcomed the arrival of dessert and cheese. The *brigadeiro* was rich and silky with the contrast of a crunchy cookie-crumb topping. "This is worth turning into a pumpkin for," she said.

Pete held out a small chunk of bread topped with cheese drizzled with honey. "Try this aged pecorino. Next time you might skip the chocolate."

As she took it from him, her fingertips brushed his. A ripple of awareness ran through her. Something shifted on Pete's face as well. When she bit into his offering, his gaze was on her lips. The sweetness of the honey brought out the sharp, smoky flavor of the cheese. "Mmm, you might have made a convert," she said, polishing it off.

"Have some more." He started to assemble another morsel.

"No, that's your dessert."

He smiled straight into her eyes. "Watching you eat it is my dessert."

She sucked in a breath as a shiver rolled up her spine. He was leaving her in no doubt of his interest. If only she could stop comparing him to Hugh.

He switched his focus back to the cheese, saying, "Any chance you're a hockey fan? I have luxury box seats at the Rangers game next Saturday."

Should she start down this road? She liked the comfortable rumble of his laughter, the admiration that glowed in his eyes, and the deft movements of his big hands as he put together another cheese sample. Pete appeared so straightforward and uncomplicated, without any of Hugh's sharp, dangerous edges.

"If it's like the cheese course, I could be persuaded," she said.

A slow smile lit his face. "I'll pick you up at five thirty, if you'll be done with work by then. No problem if you aren't. I don't need to hear 'The Star-Spangled Banner' being sung badly."

"I'll be ready." She tried to finish up by four on Saturdays. Otherwise she was just too exhausted the next day.

He looked at his watch again and signaled the waiter for the check. "Time to go, so I can get you home on time, as agreed."

She liked the fact that he was a man who remembered his promises and kept them.

Chapter 5

"It's Monday, so why are you smiling?" Carla asked as she placed a plastic takeout container and a bottle of water on Jessica's desk.

"Because I'm starving and you brought me food." Jessica unsnapped the cover and snatched up the sandwich. Taking a huge bite, she sighed with appreciation and mumbled, "I love curried chicken salad."

Geode hopped up on her desk in a bid to share her lunch, but she set him back on the floor, ignoring the annoyed twitch of his fluffy orange tail. "Curry wouldn't agree with you, buddy."

Carla sat down in the other chair and crossed her arms. "I ain't talking a chicken salad kind of smile, honey. That's a man kind of smile." The manager's eyes widened, and her voice took on a note of awe. "Did you go out with that movie star? He'd put a giant, happy grin on *my* face."

Jessica had decided not to mention her upcoming dinner with Hugh. Carla would make all kinds of erroneous assumptions. "Nope. I had dinner with a fellow Iowan. From my hometown, in fact, so we had a lot of memories to share."

"Is he a tall, strapping, good-looking Iowan?"

"You might describe him that way." Jessica took a swig of water to hide the smile that had started the interrogation. After stewing about it half the night, she'd decided to enjoy whatever this was with Pete. She could use it to take her mind off Hugh.

"I knew it was a man," Carla said, sitting back with a smug look. "He better be a good man or he'll be hearing from me."

"Haven't you learned that Iowans are all nice people?"

"Nice ain't what you want. You need some fun."

"He could probably make me a terrific corn maze," Jessica said, taking another bite. "It's considered an art form in Iowa."

"A corn maze." Carla snorted. "Yeah, that's what I meant by fun."

"You'd be surprised at what you can do in the far corners of a corn maze."

"If it involves dirt, cows, and insects, it's not my idea of a good time." Carla smoothed the red silk scarf she'd dressed up her sapphire-blue scrubs with. "I'm thinking a king-size bed with six-hundred-thread-count sheets and the big strapping Iowan stretched out across it, buck naked."

Jessica choked on her water as she pictured Pete in that scenario.

"My job here is done," Carla said with a smirk as she stood up and strolled out the door.

Jessica took another bite of her sandwich. Pete had texted her earlier to say how much he'd enjoyed the evening before.

In contrast, she hadn't heard a word from Hugh. She knew he worked long hours when he was filming, but she'd expected something about their upcoming dinner, especially after the cryptic message. She'd considered canceling but decided that she was curious to find out what he was like now that he was so successful and famous. Not surprisingly, he seemed different, more self-assured and less focused on something always beyond him, yet his intensity and magnetism were the same as the man she'd once been engaged to.

"Hey, Doc, can I talk to you about Khonsu over at the center? I'm worried about—" Diego stuck his head around her office door, his dark hair pulled back in a ponytail. "Oh, sorry, I didn't know you was . . . were eating."

Jessica beckoned him in. "I can eat and listen at the same time."

As Diego eased himself down onto the chair, it creaked under his weight. The boy was only thirteen, but he had the height and breadth of a large man. Ironically, he wanted to use his strength to protect helpless animals. He was so terrific with them that Jessica had taken him on as an intern. His ambition was to become a veterinarian, so she helped him with his science courses in school, too.

As if to prove Diego's animal-handling skills, the usually standoffish Geode leaped into his lap and butted his head against the boy's chin. Diego stroked the orange-and-white cat absently. "Shaq been having diarrhea bad for a couple of days. And now Khonsu got . . . has got the runs, too. I promised Felicia and Isaiah I'd talk to you about it, since they're the dogs' owners." The boy's hand paused on Geode's back. "Could you come take a look at them?"

"Of course," Jessica said.

Diego's face lit up with relief. "Sorry to make you come to the center, but since there's two of them . . ."

The George Washington Carver After-School Care Center was one of South Harlem's treasures. It offered a safe after-school environment to disadvantaged neighborhood kids ages eight to thirteen, along with computer access, homework help, and healthy food, all at no charge. But what made the center special to Jessica was their K-9 Angelz program, the brainchild of the center's director, Emily Wade Varela.

The K-9 Angelz allowed the kids to adopt rescue dogs who then lived at the center. Taking care of the dogs taught the children responsibility, gave them a sense that they were needed, and, of course, offered the best benefit of all, unconditional love. In turn, the dogs were given a wonderful home.

Jessica supported the program by providing veterinary care at cost—and sometimes even less than that. She also made house calls when necessary. Honestly, she enjoyed seeing the kids and the dogs interact, so her visits there were a pleasure, even though they required extra time.

However, the diarrhea was worrisome in an environment where multiple dogs lived together. "I'm glad you came to me right away," she said. "We don't want any more dogs to get sick if we can help it."

Fortunately, her patient load was relatively light that afternoon, and several could be taken care of by the vet techs. Jessica managed to get free by four thirty, when she indulged herself and Diego in the luxury of a ride share to the Carver Center.

Powell, the security guard, greeted them at the door. As they passed the kitchen and dining area, Jessica heard the clatter and scrape of dishes and the voices of the children eating their snack, as the staff diplomatically called the hearty dinner they served in the late afternoon. For some of the kids, it was the best meal they'd have all day.

Diego headed down the stairs to the ground floor, where a large room had been converted to a bare-bones but cheerful kennel. A couple of windows offered natural light that made the cream-colored walls glow. Ten crates of assorted sizes were lined up on the long side wall, while two big ones stood slightly apart with plastic tarps underneath them.

As soon as the dogs saw Diego and Jessica, a chorus of barked greetings rose, and a medium-sized black dog trotted over from where he'd been lying on a plaid dog bed. Diego put down Jessica's vet bag, which he'd insisted on carrying, and bent to give the dog a pet. "Hey, Mario, boy." Then he put his finger to his lips and said in a commanding voice, "Quiet."

Only a few more yaps sounded before all twelve dogs fell silent.

"The kids have been working hard on training, I see." Jessica was impressed.

"They listen to me better than to their owners sometimes," Diego admitted. He knelt and stroked Mario, the dog whose life he'd saved the year before after the little creature had been hit by a car. Now Mario and Diego were devoted to each other.

She opened her bag and pulled on a pair of sterile gloves before handing Diego a pair. "Okay, let's take a look at Shaq and Khonsu."

"They're in those crates over there," Diego said, pointing to the two separate ones she'd noticed earlier. "I figured I should try to isolate them as much as I could."

"Excellent thinking," Jessica said with a nod. "You're going to make one terrific vet."

Diego's brilliant smile warmed her heart. His early life had been rough, according to the center's director. His mother was missing in action, and his father was a loan shark who wanted Diego to use his size to intimidate deadbeat customers. The boy refused, so his father had told him to go sleep on the street. Luckily, Diego had found his way to the Carver Center and eventually been adopted by one of the board members, Violet Johnson. The boy had blossomed in his new environment, becoming the unofficial leader of the K-9 Angelz program.

When she swung open the door to the crate labeled "Shaq," the giant brindle pit bull stood up, much to Jessica's relief. "C'mon, boy," she said, inviting him to step out onto the tarp.

Shaq wagged his tail as she checked his gums and his skin elasticity. "His hydration is still good," she said, wrinkling her nose as the big dog passed very stinky gas. "How's his appetite?"

"Shaq never quit on a meal in his entire life," Diego said with a snort.

"Have either of the dogs vomited?"

The boy shook his head. "Just a lot of diarrhea."

"That's fun to clean up. Okay, Shaq, back in your crate for now." Jessica latched the door and pulled on a clean pair of gloves. "Now for the other invalid."

Khonsu sat up when she opened the crate door, his oversized ears pricked up and forward. "Here, boy, come see me," Jessica coaxed. The medium-sized black dog rose slowly and stepped out of the crate before sitting down once more. Again, she smelled the unmistakable odor of gastrointestinal issues. "Hmm, he seems less peppy than Shaq. How long has he been showing symptoms?"

"About twenty-four hours, I think," Diego said. "I was in church most of yesterday, so I wasn't around here."

"He's okay on the hydration," she said after checking his skin and gums. "How about his appetite?"

"Not as strong as Shaq's, but he's still eating."

"I'm guessing that it's giardia, but I'll need to take some fecal samples to confirm the diagnosis. In the meantime, I'm going to start them on metronidazole." She rummaged around in her bag for the plastic bottle of pills she'd tossed in when packing the duffel.

"I'll get you the Pill Pockets," Diego said, going to a shelf of neatly arranged dog supplies.

Jessica took the bag of treats that camouflaged the meds and stuffed a pill in one. Shaq swallowed it with enthusiasm. "Let's just cross our fingers he doesn't throw it up," Jessica said as she prepped a pill for Khonsu.

She knelt in front of the smaller dog and waved the morsel under his nose. He cooperated by gulping it down.

Jessica stood and put her hands on her hips as she surveyed the twelve crates enclosed in one area, a perfect breeding ground for the easily transmitted parasite. She didn't want to take the dogs back to her office for fear of spreading it even farther.

"Here's what we need to do," she said. "Keep the two dogs separate from the others, just the way you already have. In fact, if we can find a different room to move them to, that would be the best. Everything they touch—their bowls, bedding, toys, leashes—has to be kept separate as well. They can't go out in the dog playground with the others. Most important, they need to poop someplace completely isolated, and then the mess has to be removed right away."

If it was giardia, the whole kennel area would have to be cleaned and disinfected. She should shut down the center's popular dog yard, but until she confirmed the diagnosis, she didn't want to go to that extreme. It would put a huge burden on the already overworked staff of the Carver Center. Not that they would complain. Everyone who worked there was devoted to helping the kids.

"Right now, I'm going to take Shaq out for a walk to see if I can get a stool sample," Jessica said. "You can start isolating the two patients' equipment."

An hour later, she had her answer. Shaq had giardia. She plunked down at her desk in her quiet office and called Emily Varela's office to give her the bad news. The director sighed in resignation when Jessica explained the measures that needed to be taken. "Well, I knew when I started the K-9 Angelz program that it wouldn't be easy. I'll bring the staff up to speed and see if I can set up an isolation room."

"I'll send a vet tech over tomorrow to supervise the cleaning," Jessica said before disconnecting.

Tiana stuck her head in the door. "Hey, Doc, all the boarding patients are settled in and doing fine. You need anything before I go?"

Jessica glanced at the clock on the wall and winced when she saw that it was nearly seven. "Thanks, but I'll be heading home soon myself."

"See you tomorrow," Tiana said.

Jessica groaned as she leaned back in her chair. She'd expected to be done by five today. Tomorrow included evening appointments, so she'd be working for twelve hours.

The thought of walking home and stopping to pick up dinner somewhere along the way was suddenly more than she could handle. She pulled her phone out of her scrubs pocket to call a ride share and discovered several text messages piled up.

One was from Aidan, telling her that he was cooking dinner for them both tonight. She typed back, You are an angel! She added an emoticon of a smiley face with horns and a halo.

Then she scrolled to the next text. It was from Hugh: I've been thinking about you ever since we ran into each other.

His words sent a strange flutter through her chest. In the midst of filming a major motion picture, the movie's star was thinking about her.

He'd sent a second text right after that. I'll pick you up at six on Wednesday. I tried to make it earlier, but the shooting schedule is wall to wall. I look forward to learning who you are now.

That reminded her of what had made Hugh so fascinating. The intensity with which he had focused on her both flattered and made her nervous.

Who *was* she now?

Chapter 6

At seven forty-five the next evening, Carla walked into the examination room where Jessica and Tiana were wrestling with a German shepherd mix who didn't want to have his temperature taken. "Hon, you gotta stop and eat something," the receptionist said to Jessica. "I saw your dinner still in the bag on your desk."

"I'm a little busy right now," Jessica said, holding the dog's haunches so he didn't leap off the table. "In fact, could you get Matthew in here to help?"

"As soon as this one's done, you take a break," Carla ordered.

Jessica knew better than to argue when Carla was on the warpath, so she nodded.

"Mattie!" Carla yelled down the hallway. "Get your butt in here and help out the doc."

With the assistance of the extra tech, they got the dog's examination completed. As soon as the dog and his owner exited, Carla appeared at the door and gave Jessica her "don't mess with me" look.

"I'm going, I'm going," Jessica said, stripping off her gloves and tossing them in the trash before scrubbing her hands and arms.

"I nuked it for you, so it might be edible," Carla said. "You got two more patients and then we're closing up."

She'd lost track of the time and forgotten to eat . . . again. It wasn't as though she was losing weight, because she was often so ravenous after work that she would grab some fat- and carb-filled fast food and stuff it down at nine o'clock at night. She really had to choose healthier meals.

When she got to her desk, she found Geode sniffing a tuna melt and a walnut-and-pear salad from one of her favorite places, the Ceres Café. When she bit into the sandwich, she tasted tarragon, garlic, lemon, and a sharp, tangy cheddar. "I'll save you some tuna if you let me eat in peace," she said, shooing the cat off the desk.

Her cell phone pinged with an incoming text message, but she ignored it until she'd polished off half the sandwich and several forkfuls of salad.

She glanced down to see Pete's name and swiped it. Business trip got canceled. Would really like to see you before Saturday.

A shimmer of pleasure suffused her body. It felt nice to be wanted. She mentally reviewed her schedule. She was committed to Hugh on her evening off, and the rest of the week was filled with work.

Maybe a late drink on Thursday night? Nine-ish?

There was virtually no delay before he replied, As long as I don't get in trouble with your fairy godmother, I'll be at your door then.

A smile curled the corners of her lips. She may get huffy and leave some residual mice and pumpkins around. But if you don't mind me in rags, it's all good.

My first response about what I'd like to do with your rags could get me in trouble, he texted back, so I'll just say that I find you beautiful in whatever you wear.

He was upping the level of flirtation. Her stomach felt unsettled by the escalation, so she gave Geode his promised treat and packed up the rest of her dinner.

Her phone pinged again, and she debated whether to read it or not. She wasn't sure she could handle another exchange with Pete right now. But she looked anyway and found Diego's name on her screen.

Khonsu vomited. Not looking so good. Can you come?

"Oh, dear," she muttered as she texted him back: Two more appointments and then I'll be there.

When Jessica walked through the front door of the Carver Center, Emily was leaning against the reception desk, wearing her usual tailored skirt and blazer and talking with the night guard. A look of relief crossed the director's face when she saw the vet.

"Diego is downstairs with Khonsu," Emily said as she pushed off the desk. "We cleaned out a storage room and moved both dogs in there. I'll show you where it is." She led the way to the stairs, her low-heeled pumps clicking on the gray linoleum. "It would be devastating for Isaiah if something happened to his dog. But you already understand that."

Jessica nodded. "Khonsu isn't a puppy or elderly, so giardiasis shouldn't be fatal for him."

"You've saved more than one of our dogs," Emily said. "I trust you to pull Khonsu through."

But Jessica had lost plenty of patients over the years. Every single one of them broke her heart a little, but the dogs at the center were especially precious because the kids loved them without reservation.

At the foot of the stairs, Emily bypassed the kennel area, turning into a narrow hallway with several doors leading off it and pushing open the second one. "There's not a lot of room in there, so I'll leave you to it." She wrinkled her nose as the stench wafted out into the corridor. "Not to mention that you need a gas mask to survive in there."

Jessica laughed as she walked into what was really a large closet.

"Doc, it's so good to see you." Diego knelt by Khonsu's crate, his brown eyes clouded with worry. "He wouldn't take his metro, and then he vomited. He seems really weak."

Jessica put on sterile gloves before opening the door of the crate to find the dog curled in the corner on a towel. His oversized ears were folded back against his head, and he did nothing more than lift and drop his tail twice when Jessica reached in to pet him. "Hey, boy, I can tell you're not feeling so great."

She pulled the towel forward to bring the dog closer to her and pinched up his skin at his shoulders, frowning when it didn't settle back in place immediately. "He's very dehydrated. Let's give him an IV of sodium chloride fluid. You want to prep the cephalic vein the way I showed you at the clinic?"

Diego's face lit up. "Sure thing, Doc."

Jessica pulled a tray out of her duffel bag and supervised while Diego laid out the equipment necessary to shave and sterilize Khonsu's leg. The boy worked with careful but sure movements before shifting around to hold the dog and occlude the vein for Jessica to do her part. Once she had the catheter in the vein and firmly taped in place, she let Diego hook up the IV of electrolytes. Khonsu lay listlessly through it all.

"I wish he was being cooperative because he trusts us," Jessica said, "but I'm afraid it's because he's weak."

"Yeah, he took a turn for the worse all of a sudden." Diego stroked the dog's head with a look of concern.

"I'm going to give him an injection of Cerenia to prevent any more vomiting," Jessica said. "Will you keep him still for me?"

Diego immediately moved into the proper position for immobilizing the dog. "Tiana's been giving me lessons about how to hold an animal," he said. "Sometimes it's not so easy."

"Tell me about it," Jessica said, remembering their struggle with the big shepherd mix.

Khonsu didn't react at all when Jessica gave him the injection. She muttered a mild curse under her breath before she could stop herself, but Diego just nodded. "He's in rough shape. How come it's hitting him so hard?"

"He must have some sort of immunodeficiency." She glanced at her watch. "You should go home. You have school tomorrow."

"I don't want to leave him alone," the boy said.

"He won't be, because I'm staying here." Diego still looked torn, so Jessica gave his shoulder a little push. "Go! Tomorrow is my day off, which means I can sleep late."

The boy got to his feet with slow, reluctant movements.

"One more question," Jessica said. "Are any of the other dogs showing symptoms?"

His expression lightened. "Not a one, Doc."

"That's because you caught it right away and isolated these two." Although some of the dogs might actually have the giardia parasite without any outward indications. But Diego didn't need to know that right now. "You should be very proud."

The boy ducked his head, but she saw the pleasure on his face. "Thanks, Doc. I'll tell Ms. Emily you're staying."

"Don't forget to wash your hands!" Jessica dumped her own gloves before she pulled out her phone to call Aidan. "Damn it," she said, when the phone showed no signal and no Wi-Fi. The thick cement walls of the basement closet must be blocking reception.

She walked out to the staircase and got a weak signal, so she texted her brother about her plan to spend the night at the Carver Center. His response was: You're such a sucker, sis. I mean, such a good person.

She snorted, but his brotherly snark cheered her up.

Footsteps sounded on the stairs, and Emily rounded the corner. "Khonsu must be bad if you're staying the night," she said, her kind face tight with worry.

"He's severely dehydrated. For some reason, the giardiasis has hit him harder than normal. But he's on an IV now, so he should perk up." She hoped.

"I assume you don't have to be with him every minute, so I've made up the cot in the nurse's office for you to sleep on." Emily gestured an apology. "It's on the third floor, which means you'll have a lot of steps to climb."

The mention of a bed sent a wave of fatigue through Jessica. "I'd climb Mount Everest for clean sheets right now."

"I know the feeling," Emily said. "I'm heading home, but you have my number if you need anything. James, the night guard, is here. He loves the dogs, so he'll be happy to help."

"Does he clean up diarrhea?" Jessica asked with a grimace.

Emily laughed and waved good night as she started back up the stairs.

Visions of resting on a soft pillow danced in Jessica's brain while she checked on Khonsu again. He still wouldn't lift his head, but when she pinched up the skin on his neck, it settled back into place a little more quickly. "You're getting hydrated, buddy," she said, stroking his head. "Now you need to find some energy. Guess you don't want to go out, huh?"

Shaq stood up and wagged his tail at the word "out," so she swapped gloves and gave him some love. Then she trudged up three long flights of stairs.

The flights seemed to get longer each of the five times she traveled up and down them during the night to check on the dogs and clean up both poop and vomit. However, at six the next morning, Jessica was rewarded when she found Khonsu sitting up on his towel.

Sure enough, his gums were pink and moist, and his skin snapped right back on his neck. She blew out a sigh of relief and removed the catheter. She wouldn't have to tell Isaiah that his K-9 Angel hadn't made it through the night.

She sat back on her heels and considered climbing the stairs to sleep until the staff came in. But the third floor seemed so far away, and in the corner, there was a big, soft dog bed that Diego must have been using to sit on. God knew she'd slept on dog beds before. She zipped up the hooded sweatshirt she'd commandeered from the nurse's office and curled up on the bed, falling asleep as soon as her eyelids closed.

"Dr. Quillen is sound asleep downstairs in the quarantine room," Emily Varela said after welcoming Hugh to the Carver Center. He liked the fact that she treated him with warm courtesy but no awe.

"The quarantine room?"

She smiled. "It's a large storage closet that we put a couple of dog crates in to keep the sick ones from infecting the rest of the K-9 Angelz. Those are our rescue dogs."

"She's sleeping in a closet?" Painful flashbacks from his childhood rose up and clawed at his throat.

"It's not as bad as it sounds." Emily turned toward the stairs. "I'll be happy to show you."

"I don't want to take up any more of your time. Please just point me in the right direction, and I'll find her." He wanted to talk with Jess privately, because he wasn't sure how the conversation would go.

Emily hesitated a moment before she said, "At the bottom of the stairs, turn left and go into the hallway. The closet is the second door down."

Playing a character who fought for the good guys had its perks. People tended to trust him without knowing why.

He jogged down the stairs. When the shooting schedule had changed unexpectedly, it had left him with the whole day free. All he could think about doing with that time was seeing Jessica again, so he'd taken a chance and arranged for a helicopter to New York from Boston.

Of course, he hadn't told Jess that the shoot had moved to Boston or that he was flying down early to see her. If he was already here, she couldn't tell him not to come.

However, it had taken him most of the helicopter flight to track down her whereabouts. Fortunately, Aidan had proved helpful, but her brother had warned Hugh that Jess might refuse to leave the sick dogs.

Which was why Hugh preferred not to have Emily as a witness to their discussion.

A chorus of barking greeted him when he reached the foot of the staircase. Various-sized crates stood in a neat line down one side of a spare but immaculate room. These must be the K-9 Angelz Emily had referred to. He understood why an infectious dog would need to be separated from the pack.

The narrow hallway led into the bowels of the building, although it also was clean and well maintained. When he came to the second door down, he put his hand on the knob and lowered his head to listen. No sound emanated through the metal, so he cracked the door open.

The odor that wafted out made him jerk back a step and blow out a huff of disgust. If Jessica was in there, he couldn't imagine how she was breathing. Bracing himself, he pushed the door farther ajar.

First he saw two crates with the sick dogs lying in them. Neither barked, he assumed because they didn't feel well. Leaning farther in, he found Jessica, curled up in the corner on a faded brown dog bed, an overlarge gray hoodie zipped up over her hot-pink scrubs, her hair in a crazy tangle, and her hands tucked under her cheek.

The small, close space, her tightly curled body, the ill-fitting hoodie, all yanked him back to when he was eight years old. His new foster mother had taken him upstairs to show him his bedroom and opened the door to what had once been a walk-in closet but now held a cot and a plastic set of drawers. The hanging bars had been left in place, but they were too high for Hugh to reach back then. He had nothing that required hanging up, anyway.

His foster mother had told him he would be sleeping in there because he was small and didn't need any more room than that. His meager clothing and few possessions, including his mother's photo, had gone in and on the chest of drawers. Of course, when the social worker visited, his things got moved into the youngest son's room, but the kid didn't want Hugh sharing his space, so he went back to the closet as soon as the social worker left.

It wasn't the worst place he'd ever slept, but his child's soul had been shredded by this clear indication of how unimportant he was to his new family.

All those wounds gaped wide, pouring out the agony of being unwanted. He strode into the storage room with one goal—to get Jess out of there.

He shook her shoulder gently. "Jess, wake up. We need to go."

Her eyelids fluttered open halfway, an expression of bewilderment on her face. "Hugh? No, it can't be." She closed her eyes and snuggled her cheek back against her palm.

Without further thought, he went down on his knee, snaking one arm under her shoulders and the other under her legs, and brought her up against his chest before he rose again. Thank God for all the muscle-building workouts his personal trainer put him through in order to be convincing as a secret agent.

Jessica woke up enough to grab his shoulder as he exited the stinking storage room and kicked the door shut behind him. "Hugh? What on earth? It can't be six o'clock already!"

"I got the day off, so I came early," he said, walking down the hallway. The fist that had clenched around his heart eased more and more the farther away he got from the closet. He filled his lungs with clean air.

"You can't just scoop me up and whisk me away to wherever you think you're going. I have sick dogs to tend." She began to squirm, so he had to tighten his grip to keep her from falling.

"Emily said you texted someone named Diego that the dogs had pulled through fine." He kept walking. "I promise to find another vet to come check on them."

"Do you think some busy vet will just drop everything to make a house call to the Carver Center?" She sounded both annoyed and incredulous.

"Yes, I do. My assistant can find someone to do virtually anything. You can speak with the vet yourself when he locates one."

"Your assistant. Of course." She subsided for a moment, and he thought she actually nuzzled her nose against his neck and inhaled. Not that he blamed her after she'd spent the night in that horrific stench.

He reached the bottom of the staircase and put his foot on the first step.

"No," she said, struggling in earnest. "I'm a full-grown woman. You cannot carry me up a flight of stairs."

"If you knew how many weight machines I have been tortured by, you would be reassured that I can, in fact, carry you up the stairs." Now that he had her warm, curvy body against him, he was reluctant to release it, even though she smelled a bit like the closet. Her silky rat's nest of hair brushed against his cheek, and he enjoyed the feel of her arms wrapped around his neck.

"There might be people up there," she said. "Please don't embarrass me in front of my clients."

That was a plea he could not ignore. As he set her down on the floor, she staggered slightly, so he had an excuse to pull her into him again, the press of her breasts on his chest sending a streak of desire down his center. "Jess, you're exhausted."

"I just need a shower and a couple of hours of sleep," she said, her palms flat against his shoulders as she pushed away.

"I have an entire hotel suite waiting for you," he said. He'd planned to fly her to Gavin's mansion on the beach in Southampton but had scrapped the idea when he found out how she'd spent the night. So he'd reserved the penthouse at his favorite Manhattan hotel. Although he was staying at Gavin's house in the city while filming, he wanted total privacy for Jess to rest in. "Without any ulterior motives except to wrap you in the luxury of rest and give you the pampering you deserve." That was true at the time. Now that he'd touched her, his motives had become murkier.

She shook her head. "I have plans for today."

A shock of disappointment ran through him. "Plans that can't be postponed?"

She rubbed her hands over her face in a gesture of fatigue. "I don't know."

"Jess, let me take care of you for one day." He cupped his hands over her shoulders in an effort to communicate his earnest wish. "I'd like to do this. For old times' sake."

An odd expression crossed her face, one he couldn't read. "Why?"

"For starters, you were sleeping on a dog bed in a room that reeked of shit. Clearly, you need rescuing." And he needed to save himself from his memories.

"It's not the first time I've slept on a dog bed, and it won't be the last." She shrugged out of his grasp. "If you could just take me home, that would be great."

"I've ordered chocolate croissants from room service. There's a bathtub the size of a lap pool. You can watch the boats go by on the Hudson River while you bathe." He decided not to mention the enormous bed, even though he genuinely had no intention of joining her in it. He shifted forward so that she would look at him as he softened his voice. "Jess, you take care of all those animals but not of yourself."

She always had. The generosity of her caring was one of the things he had loved about her. However, it also took its toll on her.

"Chocolate croissants?" she repeated, and he knew he had her. "It's not fair to play on my vulnerabilities."

"You know better than to expect me to play fair." He smiled. "So you're going to let me treat you?"

"No strings attached." She gave him a direct look with her clear, gray eyes.

He spread his arms wide in a gesture of innocence. "Just one old friend helping out another."

"We've gone past being friends," she said.

She was right, in a way. The attraction between them had been too strong to stop at mere friendship. They'd gone from working together to being lovers. Friendship had blossomed later. "No reason we can't be now."

"Huh" was her cryptic response. She stood at the bottom of the steps for a moment. "I guess I'll leave my medical bag here, in case I have to come back, but I need to get my purse from Emily's office."

"I'll get it for you so you don't have to climb any more stairs." He wanted to put his arm around her waist to help her up these steps, but they were too narrow for two people to walk abreast, so he contented himself with walking close behind her.

"No staring at my butt," she said.

He grinned at her show of spirit. "It's covered by a giant sweatshirt, so there's not much to see."

She harrumphed.

When they reached the top of the stairs, Emily was waiting with a large purse in her hand, which he guessed was Jess's.

"Khonsu is out of the woods," Jessica said to the director. "Shaq's doing fine, too."

"Diego told me. That's wonderful news," Emily said. "Thank you so much for caring for them through the night. We're so lucky to have you."

"It's just my job," Jess said. She swayed a little, so Hugh stepped closer and slipped his arm around her.

"I appreciate your telling me where to find our dedicated doctor," he said. "Now it's time to make our exit."

Emily held out the bag with a wide smile. "I had a feeling you might want this."

Jess reached for the bag, but Hugh snagged it first, slinging it over his shoulder. Emily's smile turned approving. "I like a man who can handle a purse," she said.

Hugh winked and steered Jess out the front door. Anticipation flickered through him as they walked down the steps to the limo. Being with Jess reminded him of a time when everything seemed possible, even love.

Jessica slid onto the leather seat of the limo, making a quick scan of the opulent wood paneling, the thick gray carpeting, and the heavily tinted windows. She knew she was loopy from sleep deprivation, so she went back to debating whether she should really go to a hotel with Hugh. The thought of eating food someone else fixed for her and taking a long, luxurious bath had tempted her beyond resisting. But there was more to it than that. There was Hugh himself.

When she'd awakened to find herself cradled against the hard, warm wall of his chest, held by the tensile strength of his arms, it had felt . . . wonderful. He had smelled good, too, something she appreciated after a night with sick dogs. She had turned her head into the place where the soft cashmere of his black sweater stopped at his throat to inhale the combination of sandalwood and clean man.

She groaned as she wondered what odors *she* was exuding.

Just then the car door opened, and Hugh settled onto the seat beside her. As the limousine glided away from the curb, he smiled. "I promise you won't regret coming with me."

The slightly crooked slant of his lips was so familiar and so tempting. She shook her head. "I'm confused. It's only ten o'clock in the morning. Aren't you supposed to be shooting blanks at bad guys?"

"We had some permit problems, so my scenes got canceled for today." There was a funny note in his voice that she couldn't quite pin down. "I decided it was the perfect opportunity to spend more time with you."

She ignored the flutter of gratification that gave her. "How did you even find me?"

He barked out a short laugh. "It wasn't easy until I got hold of Aidan."

She sucked in a breath when he took her hand and twined his fingers with hers, his touch on the sensitive Vs between her fingers setting off a tingling awareness. He looked down at their hands. "Thank you for spending your day off with me."

His words pinged against her heart. How could this man at the pinnacle of his world feel gratitude toward her for agreeing to spend a few extra hours with him? Yet she could tell he meant it. "I may spend most of it sleeping, so don't be too grateful yet," she said.

"Well, I *would* recommend a bath first," he said, his turquoise eyes lit with amusement.

That stung, even though she knew it was true. "I was taking care of two sick dogs. What do you expect me to smell like?"

The amusement left his face. "I know all about it. Emily is a staunch admirer of yours. She says you've saved more than one of their rescue dogs."

"That's what veterinarians do." But she couldn't help the flicker of pleasure it gave her that Hugh had repeated Emily's compliment.

"Not all of them. You've always been extraordinary in your commitment to your patients." She wasn't sure if he considered that a good thing or a bad thing, since it had caused much of the friction in their past, but then he continued. "That passion is what makes you a great vet."

His grip tightened, and the press of his palm against her skin sent licks of heat up her arm. She slipped her hand out of his grasp and spread it open on her thigh. She didn't want Hugh to affect her that way.

"I appreciate the endorsement." When she glanced up at him, his smile was gone and he had folded his arms across his chest. Did it bother him that she had withdrawn her hand? "Do you have any pets now?"

The tension eased in his body language as he stretched out his long, black-denim–wrapped legs and crossed them at the ankles. "My lifestyle isn't conducive to keeping animals, except maybe goldfish. Too many lengthy absences in foreign countries."

"You were never much of a dog person, anyway."

"Ironic, given how we met, isn't it?" The shadow of hurt had left his eyes. "I didn't encounter any dogs at your house when I stopped by to persuade Aidan to tell me where you were. I assumed you'd have several, probably three-legged, blind, and missing an ear."

Jessica laughed at his jibe about veterinarians' propensity for adopting animals whom no one else would. "Same problem as yours. Too many hours away from home. Although we have an office cat who tolerates very few people other than me."

"Because you're an animal whisperer. That hasn't changed," he said.

"I'm the same as always. You're the one who's become so different. A superstar. Famous the world over. Meeting kings and queens. You even have my office manager, Carla, awestruck, and she's almost impossible to impress."

"You of all people should know that's just the outward trappings. You told me often enough." Something twisted in her chest at the melancholy in his voice.

"Aren't you happy? You've succeeded beyond anything we dreamed of."

She saw the old, familiar darkness in his eyes as he said, "I never thought success would make me happy."

No, he'd thought it would prove that he wasn't worthless, the way he'd so often felt as a child. "But you should be. The entire world has acknowledged that you're brilliant and talented."

The angles of his face took on a stark edge. "I'm no longer much interested in the world's opinion."

"Because you've won, so you don't need it anymore." But she wasn't sure that was true. Hugh had been abandoned by his parents when he was too young to remember them. It sometimes seemed like nothing could ever fill the void left by that ultimate rejection. Not even her love.

"You should go to sleep until we get to the hotel." He shifted to the seat facing backward, signaling an end to that topic. "Stretch out and make yourself comfortable."

Opening one of the limo's compartments, he pulled out a pillow and a blanket. She couldn't help admiring the way his muscles flexed under the fabric of his sweater or how his inky hair curved against his temples. He pinned her with his striking eyes. "Lie down. I'll make sure someone takes good care of your patients while you're sleeping."

His words somehow sent exhaustion spiraling through her, so she slid down on her elbow and curled her legs onto the seat. He leaned forward to position the pillow under her head. His face was close enough so she could see lines at the corners of his eyes and mouth that hadn't been there when they were engaged. But those marks of maturity only made him more magnetic. When he brushed a strand of her hair off her cheek, just that tiny contact made her shiver with delicious sensation. She slammed her eyes shut to ward off any further reactions.

But he wasn't finished. She felt the blanket drift down over her before he pulled it up around her shoulders to tuck it in with little strokes of his hands. Heat rolled through her body.

Hugh had had that effect on her from the first time he'd touched her under the dog tent. All he'd done was lift her ponytail off the back of her sticky, sweaty neck and blow a breath against her skin, but the graze of his fingers had vibrated all the way down between her legs. She had been glad he was behind her and couldn't see her eyes close or hear her stifled gasp. In fact, the one thing all their problems had never lessened was Hugh's sexual pull on her.

But then, millions of women felt the same way about him.

Chapter 7

Jessica had been sure she wouldn't be able to fall asleep with the fraught tension of Hugh's presence in the enclosed space of the limo, but once again she awoke to the sound of his voice. "We're here."

She bolted upright, knocking the pillow to the floor. "You're not carrying me into a hotel."

He raised both hands in surrender. "I wouldn't dream of it," he said as the passenger door swung open.

She scrambled out of the car to find they were parked in a narrow alley, the car drawn up in front of an undistinguished metal utility door. The driver trotted over to knock, and it opened to reveal a woman in a dark suit. "Welcome, Mr. Baker, madam." The woman smiled as she nodded to Jessica.

"This is the antipaparazzi entrance," Hugh said, putting his hand on the small of her back and moving her toward the door. The warm imprint of his palm in that particular spot brought back their times on the red carpet when his career had begun to take off . . . and she had begun to think she was the wrong woman for him.

She shook her head to banish the memories.

"Please follow me," the woman said, leading them along a corridor illuminated by sleek, modern crystal sconces. She stopped in front of an elevator door, where she pressed a card against a square black pad before pushing the call button. "Your key, Mr. Baker," she said, turning to offer the card to Hugh. "If you need anything, touch the concierge button on any of the phones in your suite. I'll make sure you're taken care of."

The elevator door slid open, and Hugh ushered Jessica into the steel-and-wood-paneled car. "Where are we?" she asked, once again feeling the unsettling quiver of attraction caused by Hugh's presence in a small space. It was counterbalanced by the equally unsettling sense of his wealth and prominence, as evidenced by the private entrance, the personal concierge, and the understated elegance of the hotel that reeked of money.

"The Wooster 44 in Soho."

"I've never heard of it."

"That's why I like it. Most people haven't."

Because it was so exclusive only movie stars and their ilk frequented it.

The elevator stopped, and the door slid open to reveal a huge room with windows for two of its walls, allowing the late-morning light to wash through the space. The steel canyons of Manhattan stretched away in one direction while the other side displayed the parade of boats and ships plying the Hudson River. "Wow!" she said, stepping out onto the patterned stone floor.

A faint aroma of bacon wafted through the air, making her stomach grumble, so she pushed aside her sense of not belonging in this place. "I smell more than chocolate croissants."

"You need some protein, too," he said. "Would you rather eat or bathe first?"

"Bathe! Where's the bathroom?" She was desperate to wash off the stink and dirt of her night's labors.

He pointed to a curving staircase off to the side. "Next floor." He scanned her face with a frown. "You should leave the door unlocked. I'm afraid you'll fall asleep and drown."

"I caught up on my sleep in the limo." She didn't want to even think about having him near a tub. She'd seen the famous bath scene in *Best Laid Plans*. It had made cinematic history for being the hottest love scene that didn't involve sex.

His frown remained. "At least answer if I call out to you. For my peace of mind."

His worry seemed genuine, and she felt a guilty delight. "The tabloids would have a field day with that story, wouldn't they? 'Actor's Ex-Fiancée Drowns in Penthouse Suite Tub: Did she ignore the warning and take the hair dryer in with her'?"

Amusement chased away Hugh's frown, but he shook his head. "It would be a lot more lurid than that."

"Then I'll make sure not to die there." She headed up the stairs, gliding her palm along the gleaming polish of the banister's highly grained wood. Starbursts of crystal and chrome lit the stairwell.

Oddly enough, even in this opulent setting, Hugh seemed more like the man she'd loved eight years before. His desire to feed her a proper meal, his concern that she would fall asleep and drown all brought back the early days of their time together. He'd massage her feet when she got home from work. He'd go grocery shopping and pick up her favorite brand of cookies without her asking for them. He'd inquire after the progress of the patients she was particularly concerned with, even remembering their names.

Hugh had noticed everything about her in a way no one else had. She'd been alone and independent for so long—working like a dog to get into and then graduate from vet school, moving far away from Iowa to work—that it felt delicious to be cared for so tenderly. Her heart had melted and opened to him, absorbing his attention like a thirsty sponge. He had made her feel worthy of being loved by someone like him.

But all that had faded away when he'd become Julian Best. So which person was Hugh now?

She had no answer, so she kept walking up the stairs.

On the next level, the floor was carpeted in a velvety taupe that her sneakers sank into. She padded down the hallway to find a huge, double-height bedroom bathed in winter sunlight. Sliding doors opened onto a terrace dotted with large pots and chaise longues that would have been inviting if the temperature had been higher. But it was the king-size bed that made her stop . . . because Hugh's smoky voice and slanting smile and honed body made her think thoughts she shouldn't. She told herself that the bed looked seductive only because she wanted to fall onto it and sleep, not because she could picture Hugh laying her back on it and coming down on top of her.

As liquid fire ran through her veins, she averted her eyes from the expanse of inviting cream linens. Giving the bed a wide berth, she discovered a bathroom that made her gasp.

An enormous oval tub was set in front of floor-to-ceiling windows that faced the river. She wasn't sure how she felt about being naked in front of all that glass. Then she saw an elegantly lettered sign set on the edge of the tub that explained the glass was mirrored on the outside so no one could see in. She was not the only person with exposure issues.

Turning on the faucets full force, she inspected the toiletries in their elongated bottles lined up on the tub's ledge. She picked the bath salts marked "relaxation" and tipped them into the steaming water, releasing a cloud of geranium-and-bergamot fragrance. Stripping out of her smelly scrubs, she eased down into the embrace of the swirling water with a happy "ahh."

When was the last time she'd taken a long soak in a tub instead of a quick, practical shower? It had to have been several years.

She lathered up her hair with a rosemary-and-mint-scented shampoo, which reminded her of the times Hugh would join her in the bathtub at their apartment, sliding down behind her in the soapy water, his long, muscular legs framing hers on either side. He'd start out with his clever fingers working suds into her hair, but she'd feel his erection against her backside and things would progress from there, leaving the bathroom floor puddled and Jessica nearly boneless with pleasure.

As though she'd conjured him up with the power of her thoughts, a knock sounded on the door. "Are you still breathing?" Hugh's perfectly modulated voice carried through the heavy wood. "I have a glass of champagne for you."

She jumped, creating a small wave that sloshed against the bathtub's sides. "You can't come in. I'm in the tub."

His velvet chuckle seemed to ripple through the water and over her skin. "How about if I swear not to look? I'll just hand you the glass and exit."

It seemed stupid to be modest with her ex-fiancé, but she found herself feeling shy. She'd put on a few pounds over the last eight years, and Hugh rolled around half-naked with gorgeous, rail-thin actresses in front of the camera—and undoubtedly in private, too.

On the other hand, sipping champagne in the giant bathtub while she watched the river traffic sail by seemed like a decadent experience not to be missed. "Just a minute." She snatched a towel from the pile by the tub, wetting it so she could wrap it around her underwater. "All right."

The door opened so fast he must have had his hand on the knob. He walked in with his head turned away in an exaggerated posture of averting his eyes while he carried the slender champagne flute to her.

Despite the soggy towel, she felt exposed in ways that made her body prickle with a heavy sensuality. She reached up and snagged the glass, her fingers brushing Hugh's so that a tingle shot up her arm. "Thanks. You can go now."

He laughed but strode back through the door. She took a sip of the light, fizzing champagne and wished he'd brought the whole bottle.

The door opened a crack. "Let me know when you need a refill. There's a call button by the tub." The latch clicked into place again.

She tossed back the champagne in an attempt to douse her unwanted reaction to his presence but only succeeded in making herself light-headed as the alcohol hit her hungry, sleep-deprived system hard.

She finished her bath in a haze of fuzzy-headed longing, her nipples tightening just from running the soapy washcloth over them.

"Damn you, Hugh," she huffed as she climbed out of what should have been a soothing spa experience. Winding a thick towel around her like a sarong, she opened the mirrored cabinet over one of the double sinks to discover an array of toiletries that made her sigh. She wove her hair into a neat braid before she lavished a lily-of-the-valley cream all over her body and rubbed chai-spice foot balm into her tired arches.

Turning, she eyed the pile of dirty, crumpled scrubs on the floor with revulsion. Putting those on over the expensive cosmetics she'd just used seemed blasphemous. She opened a random cupboard door and found several silk robes. The smallest one covered her from shoulder to midcalf, its softness making her practically purr as she drew it on over her now-glowing skin.

She would ask the hotel to wash her grubby clothes before she had to don them again.

As she started toward the bathroom door, it struck her that the counter was bare of anything except the hotel-supplied toiletries. She flicked open a couple of cabinets. Nothing except some discreetly packaged condoms, also provided by the hotel, which made her chuckle.

Where was Hugh's stuff?

Tightening the bow of her belt, she went through the bathroom door and padded into the bedroom, reveling in the luxurious feel of the carpeting against her clean, bare feet.

She stopped when she saw Hugh standing in front of the windows, his hands thrust into the pockets of his jeans, his shoulders hunched with what looked like tension. But her attention wandered over the length of his legs and the curve of his butt. He had a great butt.

She must have made a sound, because he pivoted toward her. His expression went from somber to intense as his gaze raked over her. "You look . . . clean." He gave the last word an inflection that brought the flames of her desire roaring to life.

"I probably smell a lot better, too." She tried to shrug away her unwelcome reaction to him.

He walked to a table that appeared to be sculpted from a single block of wood and picked up the champagne bottle. "Would you like another glass?"

"I should eat something first," she said, still feeling muzzy headed. "Alcohol on an empty stomach is a dangerous thing."

"Of course." He seemed off balance, a rarity for Hugh. "Downstairs." He gestured for her to precede him.

She looked around the bedroom instead. No suitcase. No shirt draped over a chair. No phone charger coiled on the dresser. "Where are your things?"

"My things?" He looked around the room as though they'd disappeared without his noticing.

"Clothes. Toothbrush. What normal mortals travel with."

"Ah, those things." He gave her a guilty half smile. "They're at Gavin's. I usually stay there when I'm in New York."

"Then what are we doing at this hotel?"

"Giving you some much-needed rest and food. And a bath. In private with no obligation for social niceties."

"You shouldn't have rented a whole suite just for me to take a bath. I have a perfectly functional bathroom at home. It's ridiculous." Yet it was also grand and oddly sweet. A pinwheel of pleasure spun in her chest.

Hugh chose that moment to close the distance between them. He raised his hands to cup her shoulders, his touch radiating through the silk of the robe. His eyes held shadows, and his expression was somber. "When I saw you in that stinking closet, curled up on a damn dog bed, I needed to do something for you. All I could think of was getting you out of there and to a place of comfort and ease. Please accept this as a small gift for being who you are."

"I don't need anything for being me." But she remembered that he had often brought her little presents when they were together, things he would see on his way home from an audition or a carpentry job. A silver necklace with a tiny cat hanging from it by its paws. She still had that, tucked into its little blue velvet pouch. A moose-tracks ice cream sundae because the flavor was hard to find. A hand-thrown bud vase glazed in shades of purple, her favorite color.

It had touched her because he chose them with care, an endearing trait in a man who might easily have been self-centered. She huffed in frustration with herself and him. "I thought you were staying here."

"Why does that matter?" He smiled as he squeezed her shoulders gently. "You've already dirtied the towels, so we can't give it back now. Relax. Enjoy." He released her. "Now let's get some food in you before you get any crankier."

"I'm not—" He lifted an eyebrow. "I'm a little irritated, is all." But he was right, of course. He hadn't forgotten that she got grouchy and headachy when she went hungry for too long.

She shoved her hands in the pockets of the robe and started toward the door. When she moved, the fabric brushed against her bare skin, reminding her that she was naked beneath it. She should have put on her panties at the very least, because somehow she felt as though Hugh could see right through the silk. And that sent a zing of heat down into her belly.

"Do you think the hotel could wash my clothes real fast?" she asked as Hugh came up beside her in the hallway.

"Of course. I'll give them a call."

"'Just touch the concierge button,'" Jessica mimicked. "I think I need a concierge at my place."

Hugh was silent.

Comprehension hit her. "You have one, don't you?"

"Just my assistant, Trevor."

"Only one?" She exaggerated her skeptical tone.

He gave a short laugh. "I'm not that high maintenance."

"I wonder if Trevor would agree."

"He has often told me what a pleasure I am to work for." He sent her a sideways glance heavy with irony.

"Thank goodness you know how unreliable that compliment is."

When they reached the foot of the stairs, Hugh gestured toward the spacious, glass-enclosed living area. A table covered in taupe linen had been set up in a spot that commanded views on both sides. Hugh pulled out one of the chairs for her. When he pushed it back in, she could swear she felt something brush the top of her head. Had he just kissed her hair? She must be imagining things.

He opened the doors of a warming cabinet that stood next to the table, reaching inside to pull out a linen-lined silver basket. The muscles of his back bunched and stretched like waves under the close-fitting fabric of his sweater. "Chocolate croissants."

Now memory welled up inside her like tears. He used to have a chocolate croissant waiting for her on the kitchen counter when she got home from a night shift at the animal hospital. He would lay a single blossom alongside it with a little note explaining what his choice meant in the language of flowers. She examined the roses in the center of the table, perfect half-opened blossoms in pale pink with touches of yellow, and wondered if they had some significance.

Flipping back a corner of the napkin covering them, she picked up the warm, flaky pastry and put it on her plate. "And one for you?"

He shook his head. "My trainer would blow a gasket."

She let her gaze skim down his lean, ripped body. "Seriously?"

"Julian Best eats nothing but filet mignon and caviar, so Hugh Baker does, too, when the movie is being shot." He grimaced. "Along with beets, spinach, soybeans, and far too much kale. No sugar, no carbs." His expression turned wry. "I have to *look* like I'm capable of hanging on to the skid of a hovering helicopter with one hand while saving the damsel in distress with the other."

She had no problem believing in his physical capabilities. She'd felt the steely strength of his arms as he lifted and carried her without so much as breathing hard. The memory sizzled through her body.

"I'm glad I'm a vet and can eat whatever I please." Jessica took a bite of the croissant and moaned with pleasure at the combination of light, buttery roll with semibitter dark chocolate. When she glanced at Hugh, he was watching her with an odd, nostalgic smile playing around his lips.

"You still like chocolate croissants." He gave a nod of satisfaction before turning back to the warming cabinet and pulling out more food. "We have eggs scrambled with caviar and cream cheese. Pumpkin-spice pancakes with caramel syrup. Filet mignon topped with a poached egg. Sides of chipotle-spiced bacon, pheasant sausage, or venison hash."

"You could feed a small army with all this," she said as he laid out plate after plate, the long fingers and fluid grace of his hands holding her gaze. "Stop!"

"Some of it's for me. Just the protein, of course," he said, settling into the chair across from her and digging into a plate of steak and eggs.

"So what's it like to be a superstar . . . besides the torture of dieting?" Jessica asked, cutting a bite of pumpkin pancake. "I need details so I can wow all my friends." She wanted to keep it light so she wasn't as conscious of wearing nothing but a robe while she faced a man who could light her up with just his voice.

He gave her that tantalizing half smile that pinged around her nerve endings. "Not as glamorous as it looks, but it pays well. I have a house you'd love. Right on the beach on the Monterey peninsula. You can hear the sea lions barking and the male elephant seals coughing while the otters float on their backs smashing shells with rocks."

"Sounds noisy." But she'd love to be surrounded by that kind of racket.

"We get whales, too, grays and humpbacks."

"That's spectacular, but you got off topic." She debated between more pancakes or the caviar and eggs, deciding to sample the latter.

He chewed a bite of filet and swallowed, the muscles in his throat working under the smooth skin. "You remember what it's like on a movie shoot. A lot of standing around waiting. Then makeup has to touch you up. Then you do the same damn scene for the tenth time but have to make it look fresh." His voice was flat and indifferent.

She waved her fork. "But what about the parties and the red carpets?"

"As the phrase implies, the carpets are all the same color. Not much difference from one to the other." He raised an eyebrow. "You weren't a big fan of those occasions."

Their worst fight had been after the Academy Awards. Hugh's agent had gotten him invited when he had been cast in the first Julian Best movie. The movie's PR people had whipped up a storm of curiosity about the unknown but up-and-coming actor. Hugh got his Armani tux for free, but Jessica had to deal with her own dress—and their budget didn't run to couture.

She'd gone to a Goodwill store in LA that was famous for getting designer castoffs from the stars and found a spectacular red Givenchy gown. When the television commentator had asked her who had dressed her, she said, "Goodwill." She'd gotten a laugh, but Hugh had been furious. She understood now that he'd had a severe case of nerves, but when he'd hissed in her ear, "Don't embarrass me again. Tell them it's vintage Givenchy," she'd been horrified and hurt. Especially since they'd been joking about the dress's provenance on the way to the ceremony in the limo Hugh's agent had sent for them.

That was the beginning of the end for Jessica. Hugh had plunged deeper and deeper into a world she felt out of place in. She didn't have it in her to spin her life in a way the PR people found acceptable, so she began to avoid the publicity events that Hugh thrived on, the distance between them growing with each missed occasion.

"I'm just more comfortable in scrubs than Armani," Jessica said as Hugh waited for her to respond to his comment about the red carpet events. "Speaking of which, aren't you going to call the hotel about getting mine washed?"

"It's not really necessary. While you were in the tub, a messenger delivered the bag of clothes I asked Aidan to pack for you." He gave her a rueful smile. "I shouldn't confess this, but I like having you in something that has only a sash holding it closed."

She had a vision of him tugging the knot of her sash loose, pushing the sides of the robe open, and cupping her breasts in his long, elegant hands. She grabbed a glass of water and took a gulp. "Oh, please, you do love scenes with Irene Bartram."

Distaste tightened Hugh's lips. "Irene is about as sexy as a boa constrictor."

"But she's stunning!"

"It requires every ounce of my professionalism as an actor to get into bed with Irene."

Jessica couldn't help the little smirk that curled her lips. It had about killed her to watch Hugh running his hands over Irene Bartram's exquisite body in that first Julian Best movie. Because he'd touched the actress the same way he used to touch Jessica, and she couldn't imagine that it wasn't sexy to feel Irene's flawless, creamy skin under his palms. He certainly projected extreme arousal. After the first movie, time and distance had made the love scenes easier to watch, but she'd always felt like she couldn't measure up to Irene.

"So you're happy that her character got killed off in the latest book?"

Hugh's smile held a dark edge. "In so many ways."

"Wait, wasn't she engaged to the author but they didn't get married?" She leaned forward. "Did he do in her character because they broke up?"

"Gavin broke the engagement well before he decided to eliminate Irene's character."

"Are you and he really friends, or is that just a PR thing?" Keeping to neutral topics seemed the safest course of conversation. She took another bite of the eggs, the caviar adding an intense blast of saltiness.

Hugh shot her a sardonic look, as though he knew what she was up to. "Gavin and I are genuine friends. While the first movie was being filmed, we discovered that we have certain similar elements in our pasts. It gave us a common ground, and the friendship grew from there."

"Was he in the foster care system, too?"

"No, he had a father, a mother, and a stepmother. But that didn't make his childhood a happy one. His stepmother was of the evil variety."

She'd sensed a dark side to the author of the Julian Best series, especially when it came to the dynamic between Julian and Samantha Dubois, Irene's character. Julian knew Samantha was a double agent who was capable of betraying him at any time, but he had a continuing relationship with her anyway. It struck Jessica as twisted. "Did Gavin's mother die?"

"She abandoned him when his father became physically abusive. Gavin just recently reconnected with her. It turned out his father had forced her to stay away and refused to allow her to communicate with Gavin."

"That's so sad and awful." Although not quite as awful as Hugh's experience during and after foster care. He'd bounced from foster home to foster home and then been shoved out of the system at age eighteen with nothing but a garbage bag of hand-me-down clothes.

"You don't have to feel sorry for him anymore. He's blissfully married. In fact, his new wife is the one who convinced him to give Julian a normal, wholesome love interest." Hugh's expression held a trace of longing as he spoke of Gavin's life.

"So she helps him write?" A pang of guilt hit Jessica. Did Hugh envy Gavin having a wife who participated willingly in his working life?

"He calls Allie his muse, so I suppose she does in some way." He surveyed the array of half-eaten food in front of Jessica and gave her one of his disarming smiles. "I bathed and fed you, so you must repay me with the story of your life."

"Is that a line from a movie?" she asked with suspicion. He sometimes borrowed from film scripts.

"C'mon, Jess, tell me how you ended up in New York City. It's not where I imagined you."

She began to cut the remainder of her pancakes into tiny pieces and wished she'd insisted on changing into her clothes. They would provide some psychological armor. "After we split up, I didn't want to be in LA anymore. Too many memories." She gave him a quick upward glance to find him looking unhappy. "So I e-mailed my favorite professor at Iowa State about a difficult case I was treating at the animal hospital and mentioned I was looking to relocate. Another of her students had started a practice in South Harlem, but the vet's father had gotten very sick, so she needed to go home to Iowa to help him. My prof asked if I'd be interested in taking over."

She looked at Hugh again. His turquoise eyes were laser focused on her while his dark brows were drawn down in a furrow. "It was about as far away from LA as I could get, so I jumped at it. I also wanted to practice normal veterinary medicine, rather than getting nothing but high-pressure emergencies all the time."

"It appears that you get your fair share of emergencies here," he said with a dry note in his voice.

"Life would be boring if I didn't face the occasional challenge," she said, arranging the pieces of pancake into a pattern on the plate. She didn't want to see any of the emotions crossing Hugh's face.

"Do you enjoy the work?"

"Very much. My patients' owners are so appreciative of what I do. My staff is awesome. And the community supports the clinic." She smiled, feeling on safe ground now. "The Carver Center's K-9 Angelz program is an incredible benefit to the kids there."

"Actually, I'd like to tour the center." He hesitated a moment before saying, "I have a foundation that funds programs for disadvantaged kids. Maybe it could help the K-9 Angelz, too."

"That would be terrific. I'll let Emily know." She smiled. "I should have guessed you'd be involved with helping kids. Why have I never heard about it? Your PR people should be all over that."

"My foundation is not about photo ops. It's about saving as many kids as I can from what I went through." His face was tight with annoyance.

"Hey, don't bite my head off! I just thought other people might donate money if Hugh Baker's name was associated with it."

"Sorry." He raked his fingers through his hair, making her remember the satin feel of it against her own hands. "I've had to battle hard to keep that part of my life private. The kids shouldn't be scrubbed and decked out in their best thirdhand clothes before being paraded in front of a bank of cameras so that I look virtuous to my adoring fans."

"I get it. You don't want a cause you care about on a personal level turned into a media circus."

He fixed his gaze on his empty plate and spoke in a strained voice. "When I was in the group home and prospective foster parents were scheduled to visit, they made us shower, brush our teeth and hair, and put on our least ratty clothes before they lined us up in the living room. We knew we were on display, and we hated it. The reek of desperation in that room . . ." His voice trailed off and she knew he was lost in the terrible memory.

Reaching out, she laid her hand over his where it rested on the tablecloth, the sharp bumps of his knuckles pressing into her palm. "Look where you are now. You've left all that behind you."

He lifted his head, his features hard with the bleakness of his past. "You never leave it behind."

Her heart wrenched in her chest. He might have a face that sold millions of movie tickets, but behind it was still Hugh, the man she'd wanted to love for the rest of her life. Feelings she'd thought long gone rioted through her.

She pulled her hand away from his and pushed back her chair. "May I have my clean clothes so I can go home?"

He was out of his chair and around the table before she had finished standing up. He gripped her shoulders as he had upstairs and looked down at her. "Stay. Please. It's so good to see you. I've missed you."

His voice rumbled, low and persuasive, playing her nerves and emotions like a violin. The strength of his hands on her shoulders sent a thrill of sexual awareness curling through her. The scent of sandalwood and Hugh enveloped her in a sensual cloud.

She felt her body soften and melt, yearning toward the man she'd given her heart and soul to without reservation eight years before. And madness seized her. It had been so long since she'd felt this way, so cared about, so focused on, so worthy of attention. She wanted to feel it again, just once more.

She thrust her fingers into the silky darkness of his hair and rose on her tiptoes, finding his lips with hers, feeling the electricity crackle between them as their bodies pressed together. Her breasts ached with pleasure when the hard wall of his chest crushed them.

"Jess," he breathed into her mouth before he grasped the back of her head in one hand and wound his other arm around her waist to yank her against him. The kiss exploded into demand and answer, setting her alight with delicious sensation.

No matter what he had become in the last eight years, her body still knew him on the most primitive level as her mate. And it responded with abandon, desire sliding downward to turn hot and liquid within her.

She released his hair and shoved her hands up under his sweater to feel the texture of his skin and the springy hair running down the center of his torso. The muscles of his abdomen tightened, and he moaned into her mouth.

She felt a jerk on her sash and then her robe was pulled open. A brief draft of cooler air drifted across her skin before his hands cupped her buttocks under the sumptuous fabric, his fingers kneading close to her yearning as he held her belly tight against his erection.

Yanking the hem of his sweater upward to bare his chest, she tore her mouth away from his to tongue his nipples, a touch he'd enjoyed in the past. "Oh dear God, Jess," he rasped out, his grip on her bottom turning convulsive. She reveled in her power to drive him over the edge.

For the second time, she found herself swung up in his arms as he carried her to one of the huge velvet sofas that curved through the living room. "I want to feast on you," he said, lowering her onto the cushions before he ripped his sweater off over his head and stared down at her. "I want to touch every inch of you."

His words made her writhe with frustration. "That will take too long. I want you inside me now." She opened her legs in invitation and knew she would get her wish when his face went incandescent with lust.

"I wasn't expecting . . . ," he said, an expression of near pain twisting his lips. "I don't have a condom."

"The bathroom," she said. "They stock everything in there."

"Of course." A look of such relief crossed his face that she nearly laughed. Except she was suffering from frustrated arousal as well. He strode toward a door she hadn't noticed, hauling it open and disappearing while she heard the bang of drawers being opened and closed.

The noise sent a splinter of sanity through her brain, making her sit up and pull the edges of the bathrobe back together. She should leave now, get away from this man who could fascinate and destroy her at the same time.

"Found them!" he shouted, holding the box of condoms aloft in triumph as he stalked toward her with long, impatient strides and a look on his face that turned her insides into pure, molten desire.

She tore off the bathrobe and lay back against the caress of the plump sofa cushions.

He knelt over her with one knee between her thighs and a foil envelope between his teeth as he jerked his belt buckle open and unzipped his trousers. She reached up to take the condom from him and pull it out of the packet while he stripped off the rest of his clothes.

"You're so beautiful," she said, stroking the condom down over his cock before she traced her fingers over a bulging muscle in his thigh. His body was more defined now, all youthful roundness honed away.

He came down on top of her, braced on his forearms, his hips between her thighs. "You have the beauty," he said. "Inside and out." He lowered his lips to hers and slid into her at the same time.

Her mouth opened on a cry of delight and his tongue drove into it as his hips flexed in the same rhythm. His weight held her in place while he moved inside her at a relentless pace, the exquisite ache within impelling her body into an upward arch, her nipples brushing the soft hair on his chest.

"Hugh," she said on a moan when he lifted his head to look down at her, his jaw tight with restraint. "Please!"

"You liked this," he said, shifting so he could slide his hand down between them. He found her clit with his fingertip.

Her focus drew in so that all she felt for a long moment was his touch on that one tiny, intensely sensitive spot. Then the sensation exploded outward, shooting fireworks into every nook and cranny of her body while her muscles slammed into orgasm around him.

"Ahh, Jess!" he shouted as his climax pumped in counterpoint to hers, amplifying every twinge of pleasure.

And then they collapsed into the sofa, gasping and panting and quivering with release. Hugh lay partly over her, so she could feel his heart pounding against her while his breath whistled past her ear. Shudders of after-pleasure trembled through her as she sucked oxygen into her depleted lungs.

"I was not expecting that." His voice came out in a rasp from somewhere near her shoulder.

"You said that already."

"I did? I can't remember anything before the cataclysm that just hit me."

"It was a good one," she said on a breathy laugh.

He rolled so that he lay on his side with his back against the sofa's cushions, his head propped on one hand. "Watching you come always set me off." He smoothed some damp, clinging hairs off her forehead.

The present broke over her. Despite his earlier vulnerability, this was not the Hugh Baker she had once fallen asleep with every night. This man was rich beyond belief, had a face recognized by hundreds of millions, and was a lover of glamorous women. His burning ambition for all those things had destroyed their relationship. What the hell was she thinking?

Goose bumps rose on her arms as she felt the chill of reality. Yet when she lifted her gaze to his, he smiled like a cat who'd found a whole pond of fat goldfish. If it was an act, it was a darned convincing one.

"Whatever you're thinking, stop it," he said, tracing a line along her collarbone and down over the swell of her breast.

Her skin seemed to shimmer wherever his finger roamed. "What if I'm thinking that you're the greatest lover of all time?"

He snorted. "Then you wouldn't look like someone just threw a bucket of cold water over your head."

It was that actor's eye, always watching other people in case he could use something from them in his work. It made him far too perceptive when it came to reading her.

"What's bothering you, Jess?" His finger gently circled her nipple.

An arrow of arousal shot from her breast to the V of her thighs. "I can't think when you do that," she said with a gasp.

His smile was pure wickedness. "Then my plan worked." He bent to suck where his finger had been playing, his hand moving down to rest on her belly.

"Hugh!" Her hips lifted without any conscious thought on her part.

"An invitation," he purred against her breast, skimming his hand lower to curve between her legs.

"I can't . . ." But her body belied the protest, her muscles loosening and opening to him.

He stroked her with a featherlight touch, dipping one finger just barely inside her when she began to pulse her hips. Then he shifted down the couch in a display of flexing muscles that made her breath catch even before he touched her clit with his tongue.

And then she lost the ability to care about anything but the feel of his mouth on her. Until she came again, crying out his name while heat and satisfaction rolled through her in waves.

When he lifted his head, his eyes were glazed with desire as he licked his lips. "Your taste hasn't changed," he said. "And it still goes straight to my cock."

"Finish inside me," she said. "I just can't promise to help."

He shook his head. "You're still coming down from your orgasm. And every good actor knows that building anticipation makes the final climax all the more intense." He moved up beside her again, wrapping an arm around her waist to pull her satiated body against his. His erection nestled between her buttocks, making her nerve endings quiver despite their overload.

He'd succeeded in scattering her worries, and she decided to leave them that way. Feeling like this was so much nicer than being virtuous. For today, she would pretend that she was having a brief, meaningless sexual fling with her ex-fiancé, not with a world-famous movie star.

It wouldn't change anything about her life.

Hugh savored the feel of Jess's luscious bottom cradling his half-erect cock. The fragrance of expensive cosmetics rose from her hair and skin to waft past his nostrils, but under it he could still detect the familiar, distinctive scent of Jess herself. When he'd been inside her, when he'd tasted between her legs, it had felt like a homecoming.

He hadn't been lying when he said he hadn't expected this, hadn't even hoped for it, although she'd been in his thoughts whenever he wasn't involved in shooting a scene. His dinner invitation to her had been a nostalgic whim mixed with curiosity and guilt. He wanted to know what had happened to her in the years that he'd refused to be a part of. However, seeing her curled up on the dog bed had triggered such a powerful reaction that he hadn't cared about anything except taking her as far away from there as he could get her.

Self-reproach gnawed at him even as he tightened his embrace on her waist. Had he somehow pressured her into making love without realizing it? No, she had initiated this. Of course, that didn't mean he had been forced to go along, but as soon as she tunneled her fingers into his hair and touched her soft lips and body to his, he had lost the ability to stop.

But he didn't want just her body. He wanted to know everything about the past eight years, even though he had no right to pry into her life anymore. He was the one who'd let their lines of communication lapse, even knowing that as his fame increased, Jessica would feel less and less comfortable trying to get in touch. He had been damned if he was going to reach out when he had been hurt. She had given up on him, so he would show her just how far he could go without her.

Back then he had been young and blind to everything but his drive to reach the top—and so very stupid. When he'd thought he needed a sophisticated pretender on his arm on the red carpet, he had really needed Jess. She'd loved him with everything in her, no reservations. He'd loved her in return with all the intensity of someone who had never been loved fully before. Yet he'd somehow found a way to damage her feelings for him without understanding what he'd done.

Now he was consumed by the need to know why she had broken the engagement. Because Jess didn't quit easily.

He shifted restlessly as he faced the truth. His refusal to reach out to her through the years had nothing to do with Jess or her actions and everything to do with his childhood.

He had felt abandoned . . . again.

Hours later, Jessica lay beside Hugh in the rumpled bed, their arms and legs intertwined, watching the lights of Manhattan blaze through the windows. The weight of reality settled on her shoulders while she admired the bird's-eye view of her adopted city with its soaring, glass-skinned towers and gridded streets winking with red taillights. This was what New York looked like from Hugh's perspective. She belonged down where you could see the grimy, cracked sidewalks and the weariness on people's faces as they stomped through the gray haze of winter. He stroked her bare shoulder with his thumb, almost as though he didn't realize he was doing it.

"I don't think I can move," she said.

"There's no need to." He hooked his knee around hers to angle her closer to him.

"Ever again."

"You can stay in this room as long as you like."

"What time do you have to go back to work?" She splayed her hand on his chest to feel his slow, steady heartbeat.

"I have to leave here at four in the morning."

"Are you riding into the rising sun or something?"

"No, I have to get back to Boston."

She levered herself up so she could see his face. "Wait, you aren't filming in New York anymore?"

"We moved to Boston two days ago."

"I—but—that's a long way to go for dinner." He'd traveled to New York because she was here. That probably wasn't a big deal for him. His assistant had undoubtedly chartered a helicopter or jet or something.

"I wanted to see you." His simple statement burrowed into her heart, a place she no longer wanted him. "We're filming virtually non-stop for the next few weeks. They aim to get the movie out for next year's Christmas season, given the theme. So I foresee quite a bit of air travel in my future."

Did he mean air travel in order to see her again or to get to the different locations? "Where else are you shooting?"

"DC. Miami. Prague. Dubai. Singapore. Palau." He ticked each one off on his fingers. "I've missed one somewhere, but it doesn't matter. I'll find a way to get back here as often as I can."

"I . . . Hugh . . ." She didn't know how to explain. "I thought this was a one-night-stand kind of thing."

They were so close together that she felt his body go rigid. "I know you," he said, "and you're not that kind of woman."

"I just . . . I mean . . . you're you and I'm me. If anything, the differences between us have only increased."

"So what was this?" His voice was a growl.

"A day out of time and reality."

He untangled himself from her in swift, efficient movements before he swung his legs off the bed and stalked away, his bare skin all light and shadow in the glow from the buildings outside. He rubbed his hand over the back of his neck, making the powerful muscles of his shoulders ripple, before he pivoted toward her. "Isn't it possible that we've both changed?"

She sat up, clutching the covers tightly to her chest with one hand, and swept her other hand around the huge room with its glittering view. "It would take a seismic shift to accommodate this."

"I don't care about this," he snapped. "It's just a way to buy the privacy that other people take for granted."

"Exactly."

He let his head fall back and blew out a long breath. "I'd forgotten how stubborn you can be."

"Not stubborn, practical." She rolled to the side of the bed and stood up, dragging the coverlet with her. "We've had this conversation before, and we both know how it ended. I think it's time for me to leave."

"No. Please. I'm sorry. Let's not part this way." He held out one hand, palm up. "Come back to bed. Just to sleep."

Regret and sorrow showed in the stark angles of his face. A sting of guilt pierced the flood of old emotions that swamped her better judgment. She hesitated. She didn't want to leave on an unpleasant note, either.

He seized the sheets in one hand and flipped them back in an invitation. "A few more hours."

"All right, but I'll leave when you do." She unwound her makeshift sarong and dropped it on the bed before slipping between the covers. Hugh slid in beside her, his weight rolling her toward him, even as he snaked an arm around her waist and snugged her back against his chest.

"Thank you," he said, his voice rumbling by her ear. "I . . . thank you."

She settled back against him, laying her arm over his and tucking her hand there.

Just a few more hours.

Chapter 8

Jessica plodded down the stairs from her bedroom the next morning, a headache wrapped around her temples like a vise. She had dragged herself out of the giant, warm hotel bed when Hugh got up to shower well before dawn. He'd insisted on coming with her in his limo, where they'd nearly made love again. Then she'd stumbled into her own bed for a couple of more hours of sleep. Now she could feel the twinges of soreness in private places that had gotten an unaccustomed workout the day before.

The smell of coffee drew her like a magnet. She followed the delicious scent into the living room, coming to an abrupt halt when she saw the furniture shoved to the center of the floor and covered with drop cloths. "Aidan?"

"In the kitchen, big sis. I have scrambled eggs."

Jessica groaned at his cheerful voice and trudged into the kitchen. "What's going on in the living room?"

"Good morning," her brother said, standing in front of the stove, dressed in ripped jeans and a bleach-spotted green T-shirt. "Pour yourself a cup of coffee. I'll tell you after you've drunk at least half of it."

He knew her well. She followed his instructions without argument, stirring two spoonfuls of sugar into the fragrant brew before she took a large swallow and sat down.

"You look wiped. Late night?" her brother asked with a teasing glint in his eye. He plunked a plate of eggs in front of her before he sat across from her at the small oak table with his own breakfast.

"Yeah." He knew who she'd been with, and she didn't want to talk about it—or even think about it. "What's with breakfast? And the living room?" she asked again, tasting the eggs. They were surprisingly good.

"I got to thinking," Aidan said. "I'm unemployed and living here rent-free. I should contribute, so I'm going to finish stripping the wallpaper and redo the floor."

Jessica raised her eyebrows in surprise and disbelief. "Do you know how?"

"YouTube," he said without batting an eye.

Since she'd used the internet for her home improvement projects as well, she had no grounds on which to object. "I'd appreciate that." She also wondered where this uncharacteristically constructive urge had come from.

"Just want to be useful." His tone was breezy, which made her look at him with suspicion. "Okay, so Hugh might have said something to me yesterday when he was here looking for you."

She closed her eyes on a wince at the sound of Hugh's name. It had been darned hard to say good-bye in the wee hours of the morning. She knew it was just familiarity, but she'd felt so comfortable and safe cradled in his arms.

"Didn't go well?" Aidan asked. "I figured since you hadn't come home, maybe . . ." He shrugged. "Sorry, Jess."

"It was . . . fine. But he's off to film in faraway places, and I'm back to being a hardworking vet. That's the end of it."

Curiosity was written all over Aidan's face. To his credit, he didn't pursue it. "Do you have any supplies for the wallpaper stripping?" he asked. "I want to see what I already have to work with."

But Jessica couldn't stop herself. "What did Hugh say to you?"

Her brother shifted on his chair. "He pointed out that I had some free time and that it was clear you could use a hand. I'd forgotten that he did carpentry to make money before he got famous. He gave me some tips on repairing the floor and the wood trim."

And she'd forgotten that Hugh was one of the few people Aidan would listen to. Her brother had always been dazzled by her ex-fiancé's glamour. The effect was probably even greater now that Hugh was a superstar. She was both grateful to Hugh and embarrassed that he'd seen her shambles of a living room. She hoped Aidan didn't feel free to ask Hugh for more advice on home renovation just because he now had her ex's current phone number.

In truth, she didn't have much faith that Aidan would finish his do-it-yourself project, but any progress was better than the way the room looked now. "The stripping supplies are in the basement under the steps. You're great to do this, bro. By the way, the eggs were delicious." She stood and picked up her empty plate.

"I'll do the dishes," Aidan said. "I know you need to get to work."

She gave an exaggerated start. "I don't know what alien stole my brother and left you in his place, but I'm going to send her a thank-you gift."

"Ha-ha." But he grinned. "What kind of gift would an alien want, anyway?"

"Depends on where in the universe she's from." She set her plate in the sink before coming back to ruffle her brother's hair. "Don't let the chemical fumes damage your brain."

"So I hear some fancy Manhattan vet checked up on Khonsu and Shaq yesterday," Carla said, standing in the surgery room doorway while Jessica prepped for her first case. "And I hear some hot movie star swept you away from the Carver Center in a limo."

Heat flushed Jessica's neck and face. "Yeah, Hugh's an actor, so he believes in making a dramatic exit."

Carla walked into the room and peered at Jessica. "Girl, you got a dreamy little smile on your face that tells me he didn't just give you a lift home." She held up her hand. "It's none of my business, though, so you don't have to tell me any details about where you went or what you did with the hot movie star."

Jessica pulled out a fistful of paper towels and focused on drying her hands. "He's my ex-fiancé. We were engaged for about six months and haven't seen each other for eight years. So yesterday was just nostalgia."

Very physical nostalgia. Her body still hummed with a bone-deep satisfaction. When Hugh's image drifted into her thoughts, satisfaction changed to anticipation, which would remain a profound, unfulfilled ache. Their farewell at four in the morning had been pretty final, although Hugh had promised to send her tickets for the movie's premiere next winter. She gave a mental snort. Or he would ask his assistant, Trevor, to send the tickets.

"You were engaged to Hugh Baker?" Carla's eyes went wide. "And you never mentioned that?"

"We haven't been in contact since I gave back the ring, so it didn't seem relevant to my current life." Nor to her future life.

"What about your friends who want to live vicariously?" Carla said, but her tone was softer. "You can tell me later when you're not worn out from whatever wore you out." She winked and sashayed out of the room.

Jessica couldn't help smiling. Carla's sass always lifted her spirits.

"Here's your first victim," Caleb said, carrying in a huge tomcat. "Ready to get denutted."

Her surgery schedule was light, mostly spays and neuters, which she could do in her sleep, so she finished up in time to take a full hour for lunch. She was reading a newly arrived veterinary journal with her feet propped on her desk and Geode on her lap when Carla leaned in.

"This is your week for good-looking male visitors," she said. "This one's blond." And she was gone.

Jessica lifted Geode off her thighs and dropped her feet to the floor with a thump, guilt spearing through her as she assumed it was Pete. She hadn't spared a thought for him since Hugh had awakened her in the storage closet at the Carver Center. She tried to straighten her bun as she heard heavy footsteps coming down the hall.

But the man who came through the door was a stranger, albeit a striking one. He wore a well-cut tweed jacket and charcoal trousers and held a large vase of vividly hued flowers that could barely compete with his brilliant green eyes. "Dr. Quillen?" he said in a cultured voice. "I'm Will Chase. I'm on the board at the Carver Center and wanted to thank you for your care of Khonsu and Shaq."

Jessica stood up to accept the vase he held out. "You didn't need to bring me flowers for doing my job, but I appreciate their beauty." She sniffed at a rose and smiled. "They smell a lot better than the sick dogs, too."

He smiled back. "Spending the night with them in the basement storage room went above and beyond. Those dogs happen to be important to some kids I am especially fond of, so I wanted to express my gratitude in person."

"That's very kind of you." She set the flowers on top of one of her filing cabinets, where their extravagance looked out of place among the cheap furniture. She'd put them out in the reception area after he left so they would cheer her clients. Jessica plunked back down on her ergonomic chair. "Have a seat," she said to her still-standing guest. His manners went with his voice.

Will eased himself into the rickety chair in front of her desk, crossing his legs in an elegant motion. "I'd like to make a donation to the clinic," Will said.

"Seriously, the flowers are enough." Her clinic wasn't a nonprofit, so she couldn't accept donations, anyway.

He shook his head with a smile. "Would you like me to give it to the Harlem Animal Shelter? I know that's where most of the K-9 Angelz come from."

His relentless refusal to accept no for an answer reminded her of Hugh, although Will Chase covered his obduracy with a veneer of smooth charm.

"The shelter does great work and they could use the money," Jessica said. "They would be a worthy recipient."

He rose and held out his hand. "Carla says you're on your lunch hour, so I won't take up any more of your time, but I had to meet the miracle worker of the K-9 Angelz in person."

His grip was firm and warm, exactly what she would expect, given his refined exterior. "No miracles involved, just some metronidazole and IV fluids. Nice to meet you, though."

He released her hand with another beguiling smile. "To a layman, that seems miraculous enough. The Carver Center is fortunate to have you."

Jessica didn't have long to wait before Carla strolled into her office. "You know who that is, right?" she asked.

"A Carver Center board member," Jessica said.

"He's Kyra Dixon's fiancé. And a billionaire."

"No wonder the flowers are so nice," Jessica said. "Wait, is he the person who started Ceres for Canines, all because Shaq has a sensitive stomach?"

"Nailed it. You know, if I didn't like you so much, I'd go work at the Carver Center," Carla said. "A lot of hot, rich men hang around there. Of course, now they're starting to hang around here, so I guess I'll stay."

Jessica chuckled and stood to pick up the flowers. "You can put these on the reception counter so everyone can enjoy their beauty."

"You know, you're allowed to keep something for yourself every now and then," Carla said as she took the vase.

"I don't spend enough time in here to hog the flowers." Jessica glanced at the time on her computer screen. "And we both have to get back to work."

However, when she returned to her office after she'd finished her afternoon appointments, a water glass filled with a handful of blossoms sat on her desk. Carla had shared the wealth.

Jessica dropped into her chair with a smile and pulled out her cell phone to check her text messages. She'd felt a couple of vibrations while she was examining her last patient.

When she read the names of the senders, she tilted back in her chair and closed her eyes with a groan. One message was from Pete. The other was from Hugh. Seeing their names side by side on her phone made how she'd spent yesterday seem so much worse somehow.

Leaning forward again, she debated which one to read first, opting for Pete's. It was bound to be fairly innocuous. Does nine still work for you? it said.

"Oh my God!" She'd completely forgotten about having drinks with him that evening. She checked the time and flopped back in her chair with relief. She still had three hours before he would be at her door. It had been an easy day, thank goodness.

Although she was a little worried that her lack of sleep would catch up to her, especially if she had a drink. Light day at the office, she typed. Could you make it at eight? That will get my fairy godmother off my back.

His response was nearly instantaneous. The sooner, the better. See you at eight.

Now she had to hurry. She swiped open Hugh's text and felt her heart lurch in her chest.

Yesterday was a good day.

Jessica sat beside Pete on the leather-upholstered banquette in the high-sided booth. His body wasn't quite touching hers, but she could feel the heat of it. Every now and then, his arm or shoulder brushed against her when he moved. It should have been pleasant, since he smelled clean and healthy and male. But her body still felt imprinted with Hugh's, so she had to stop herself from shifting away.

"You're quiet tonight," he said. "Tough week?"

"A couple of the Carver Center's dogs got a severe case of giardiasis, and trust me, you don't want the details about that. I was afraid we might lose one of them, so I put him on an IV and spent the night at the center."

"I'm guessing you pulled him through."

Jessica nodded. "He's well on the road to recovery now."

"Would you rather go home and get some sleep?"

"No, I need to do something . . . normal." Instead of spending an entire day in a penthouse suite having sex with a movie star.

Pete looked a little taken aback. "I'd hoped for 'fun' or maybe even 'pleasurable.'"

"Sorry, 'fun' is a much better description." She took a sip of the excellent Manhattan she'd ordered. "I'm tired of my work. Tell me about yours."

"I suspect the details of my job are right up there with those of giardiasis. It's just a lot of numbers."

She shook her head. "You don't have to scrub down numbers with rubber gloves and bleach."

"That bad?" he said. "Although I was accused of laundering money on one occasion."

His sly sense of humor surprised a real laugh out of her. "You made that up."

"I was innocent as the driven snow, of course—well, guilty only of some clever, creative accounting—but the accusation was real."

"Ouch. Who accused you?"

"Just a jealous competitor. The SEC never got involved, thank God." His expression turned serious. "Did you know Aidan has applied for a job at ExDat?"

"No! I thought he was enjoying a little vacation before he started job hunting." Actually, it looked like an extended vacation. She frowned into her drink. Pete wasn't going to ask her if he should hire her brother, was he?

"The job he's aiming for is way out of my area," Pete said, easing her mind. "Aidan would be in the data handling and analysis part of the business, while I'm just a number cruncher. But I don't want whatever happens with Aidan to affect us."

Us. The word made Jessica take a bigger swallow of the Manhattan than she should have. It seemed a little soon to be talking about "us." Or was she still under Hugh's influence? Then she thought of Aidan's propensity for quitting jobs when he got bored. "I'd hate for Aidan to affect our friendship, either," she said, trying not to emphasize "friend-ship" too much.

Relief showed in Pete's pale blue eyes, so he must not have noticed her use of the word. He covered Jessica's hand where it lay on the wooden table, his big, square palm heavy on top of her fingers. "I put in a good word for him, but HR knows that I have no idea what the tech guys actually do, so it might not carry much weight."

"You didn't have to do that," Jessica said, slipping her hand out from under Pete's. "He needs to get the job on his own merits."

A flash of disappointment crossed Pete's face. "Oh, he will, but having a connection gets his résumé looked at faster and with closer attention."

"They'll check his references, too, I assume?" She didn't want Aidan to make Pete look bad when he quit abruptly. She wasn't going to rat out her brother, but one of Aidan's past employers might. That would make her feel less guilty somehow.

Pete shot her a sharp glance. "They're pretty thorough, but is there something I should know?"

"No, they'll all tell your HR people how brilliant my little brother is." That much was true.

Pete looked as though he wanted to ask more, but he moved on to another topic. He was a pleasant companion: attentive, nice-looking, and easy to be with. Forty-eight hours ago, she might have been glowing in his company. But Hugh's turquoise eyes and clever hands and lust-inducing body kept rising up between her and her current date.

She put down her empty glass. "This drink is hitting me hard after last night's—I mean, *Tuesday's*—all-nighter. You see, I can't even remember what day of the week it is." She gave him a rueful smile. "I don't want to be rude and fall asleep on your shoulder, so maybe I should go home."

"Nothing would make me happier than to have you dreaming on my shoulder," he said, giving her a slow, intimate smile before he signaled the waitress.

"Er, thank you." She wanted to respond to that smile, but instead it made her uncomfortable. Because she'd had sex with Hugh yesterday and couldn't forget the heady sensations.

She just hoped the effects would fade with time.

Hugh poured himself a mug of coffee in the kitchen of his trailer. He needed the heat to ward off the chill of an outdoor night shoot in frigid Boston. Settling on the sofa, he cursed and shifted as the gun in the shoulder holster dug into his ribs. He'd worn enough of them that he should be more accustomed to their presence. Of course, his harness wasn't meant for comfort. It was designed to fit tightly over the black turtleneck and emphasize his chest and shoulders for the cameras. As he plucked at the straps irritably, his gaze fell on his cell phone, lying on the coffee table.

Picking it up, he swiped to Jessica's response to his text message: Yes. That's all she'd said. One short word. That should tell him all he needed to know regarding her lack of interest about remaining in contact with him. She'd made it pretty clear the morning they'd parted, but he'd hoped she might have changed her mind.

Because when he wasn't working, he couldn't stop thinking about the hours they'd spent together.

He scoffed at himself over all the elaborate plans he'd made for yesterday, borrowing Gavin's helicopter and mansion on the beach. Yes, he'd wanted to show her what resources he had at his fingertips now, even if they belonged to someone else. In some ways, not having to own what he needed was even more impressive. Why he thought Jess would care about any of that, he wasn't sure. He'd just needed to prove something—to himself, not her, it seemed.

But then he'd seen her on that dog bed, and his past had risen up to shake him by the throat.

He couldn't complain about the outcome. They had always been good in bed together, and he'd felt the old spark of attraction flare to life again almost from the moment he'd slammed into her in the alley. She must have felt the same magnetic pull between their bodies, but it shocked him a little that she'd given in to it. She wasn't the sort to engage in sex for its own sake. With her it had meant there was something more going on. Which was why he hadn't expected her to banish him from her life again when they said good-bye.

At the time, though, his attention had been only on the way every curve and texture of her body, every sound and scent of her, had fanned his desire higher. He knew where to touch her and she knew where to touch him . . . and when. It had been not comfortable—because that was far too bland a word for the explosion between them—but maybe effortless, with no friction but the kind they required to climax. Their bodies melded together without thought.

His cock stirred at the memory. Not a good thing when he could be called back on set at any time. He rubbed a hand over his face to clear away the images of Jess under him and over him and cradled between his legs in the bathtub.

He took another sip of coffee to find it had cooled to an unpleasant lukewarm temperature. Walking to the kitchen, he dumped it down the drain and poured another steaming mug. He remained standing with his hip against the counter while he stared out the trailer window at the empty city sidewalk that could be anywhere in the world.

Maybe that's why he couldn't banish Jess from his mind. Shooting on multiple locations always left him feeling disoriented. The lines between Hugh Baker and Julian Best blurred as he spent more and more time in character. Jess offered an anchor to reality. Always had, even back in the old days.

Of course, then he'd gotten sucked into the world of Hollywood make-believe and wanted her to join him there, because it had cast its bedazzling spell over him. The truth was that he'd known on some level that he was selling out, and he took out his guilt over that on Jess.

Yeah, he'd been a real asshole, but he thought he needed a woman who would be an accessory to his glorious rise to stardom, someone who would charm the directors and the studio executives. Of course, Jessica could do that in her own inimitable way, but he wanted her to be like everyone else in Hollywood—glitzy, worldly, and, truth be told, always playing an angle.

He was relieved when someone banged on his door. All this introspection was depressing and something he'd learned to avoid. "It's open," he called.

Bryan's long-suffering assistant, Timoney, came up the steps. "We're done for the night, so you can go back to the hotel."

"What about the duck boat scene in the harbor? Are we shooting it tomorrow night?" The weather was forecast to be even colder then, so he wasn't enthusiastic about the postponement.

"The scene's been scratched. Bryan doesn't like shooting in Boston. Bad angles, bad weather, bad permits." She shrugged at the artistic whims of her boss. "He's decided to rewrite those scenes for New York. We're headed back there tomorrow. I assume your assistant will arrange your transportation. And you'll have at least the morning off, because the writers need time to rework the script."

"Poor bastards. Bryan will have them up all night." And then he'd have to learn the new script as quickly as possible. He just hoped they kept most of the same lines. Despite all that, his pulse quickened at the prospect of being back in the same city as Jessica.

"He's already ordered in four urns of coffee for them," Timoney said.

"Do I need to try to talk him out of this?" Hugh had sometimes used the leverage of his stardom to persuade Bryan out of hasty decisions that would cause major problems for the film.

"Nah, I think it's for the best," Timoney said. "No one liked that duck boat scene, anyway. It was just there because we couldn't get permits to film on the bridge like in the book. We can probably get a bridge in New York."

Hugh winced inwardly. That meant a whole new set of stunts, many of which he would do himself as a point of pride and authenticity. Despite his daily workouts with his trainer, at this point in the schedule, his body was beginning to feel the strain of being a super spy who had no fear of death or injury. "Then I will leave the writers to mainline coffee."

The door swung open again, and Meryl glided up the steps, wearing a ski jacket over the ruined blue evening gown that was her costume for the night. "Oh, I guess you heard. Back to the Big Apple."

"Good. I don't have to notify you," Timoney said, checking off something on her clipboard before she plodded back down the steps and closed the door.

"Since we have tomorrow morning off," Meryl said, her voice a low purr, "I thought we might do some sightseeing. I've never been to Boston before. Will you show me the sights?"

If he'd been uninterested in Meryl's advances before, he found them downright distasteful now. Not her fault, though. "My apologies, but I need to get some extra sleep. Makeup complained about the circles under my eyes this morning."

"Ah, that just adds to the dangerous edge of Julian Best," Meryl said, tracing his cheekbone lightly with her fingertip. "All those ghosts haunting him."

He forced himself not to jerk away from her touch. "Chris O'Toole grew up in Boston. He'd be happy to tour the city with you." Chris played the villain's evil but conflicted sidekick in the movie.

"Really?" Meryl was too subtle to pout, but he caught the fleeting look of frustration that crossed her face. "I didn't know that about Chris. He'll make a downright fascinating tour guide." She flicked a lock of auburn hair over her shoulder. "I hear he's gotten the lead in that psychological thriller Bryan's making next."

"You sound surprised," Hugh said.

She made a wry face. "He's not exactly leading man material, is he?"

"Chris is very talented, and that's what matters to Bryan."

"You can't really believe that," she said. "It takes a lot more than talent to succeed in this business."

"He's got discipline and drive, too," Hugh said.

"But he's not tough," she said. "Not like the two of us."

He wasn't sure he wanted to be part of Meryl's club.

"I'll see you in New York," Hugh said, giving her a little bow of dismissal.

"I meant that as a compliment, baby," she said, standing on tiptoe to brush her lips against his cheek before she made her exit, the door clicking shut behind her.

Without conscious thought, he swiped at his cheek with the back of his hand, as though Jessica would be able to see some residue from Meryl's kiss.

What made his gesture even more ridiculous was that Jessica might not want to see him at all.

Chapter 9

Jessica had spent the whole workday waffling back and forth about whether she should cancel her date with Pete on Saturday. If she did, his expensive hockey tickets would be wasted. If she went to the game, he would believe that she was interested in him as more than a fellow sports fan.

Now she strode along the slushy sidewalk toward her house with the debate still raging. She'd hoped the exercise and the cold would clear her mind, but so far, the circle continued. She decided that she would make a decision before she arrived at her house . . . and then stick to it.

As she walked up the steps to her front door, she decided to go to the hockey game. Maybe more contact with Pete would start to banish her memories of Hugh.

In truth, she hadn't thought that Hugh would have such an impact on her, even given their recent intimacies. After all the misery and trauma of the end of their relationship, she should have been wiser about letting him get anywhere near her. Maybe if she conjured up some of the hurtful things he'd said and done, she would remember the real Hugh.

She'd spent so much time trying to forget those awful incidents that it took some effort to open her personal Pandora's box. When she did, the flood of emotion made her press her hand to her midsection as the pain hit her. A collage of limousine interiors whirled through her brain with Hugh sitting beside her in his tux or some other carefully chosen outfit as he told her what she'd said wrong at the ceremony or the party or whatever they'd just been to. He'd called it coaching and smiled about it. She, who had once thought of herself as an outgoing, friendly person, had become increasingly mute.

His criticism had hit her hard, because the old Hugh had been her greatest cheerleader. When she agonized over a mistake she'd made at the animal hospital, he would point out all the reasons she couldn't have known what to do or how someone else had put her in a difficult position. He had shown her how to forgive herself, a gift she treasured.

She shook her head as a fresh wave of longing hit her. That part hadn't been what she needed to remember.

Pulling herself out of the past, she tried the door. One of the three locks was actually secured, which was progress, she supposed. "Hello, Aidan," she called as she peeled off her gloves and shrugged out of her coat.

"Oh, hell!" said a voice that was not Aidan's. "What time is it?"

"It can't be . . ." She dropped her coat on the floor and practically ran into the living room.

There Hugh was, standing on a ladder beside her brother, his left wrist raised to check his watch while he held a trowel in the other hand. Plaster dust whitened his hair, red T-shirt, and jeans. "I'm sorry. I lost track of time," he said, giving her an apologetic look. "Let me just finish repairing this crack and I'll get out."

"What on earth are you doing here in the first place?" Dismay— and an uncontrollable thrill of excitement—made her voice sharper than she wanted. How could she shove him out of her mind if he kept showing up in living, breathing full color?

"I texted him for advice," Aidan explained. "He said he had the day off from shooting so he'd show me how to properly repair the plaster." He looked from one to the other of them. "Is that a problem?"

"But I thought you were in Boston," Jessica said, wishing her ex-fiancé didn't look just as good in dirty jeans as he did in a tailored suit. That was one of the things that made Hugh so in demand as an actor: he could make any role seem intense and sexy, even a handyman.

"Our esteemed director took a dislike to Boston and moved us back here. The writers stayed up all night tearing the script apart to set the scenes in New York." Hugh shrugged, sending up a little puff of white dust. "They're still hard at work, so I had some free time. Doing something constructive with my hands was an appealing alternative to sitting around waiting. I meant to be gone before you got home."

"Why does it matter if you're here?" Aidan asked.

"Because we're not engaged anymore," Jessica said. "So he shouldn't be working on my house." But she remembered that Hugh would often tackle a home improvement project to unwind from a difficult day at work on a movie set. He said it allowed him to use a different part of his brain. Maybe he really had planned to leave before she saw him there.

"I don't see what difference it makes," Aidan said. "He's good at this. Besides, it will increase the resale value of your house if you can say that the famous Hugh Baker plastered the walls." He grinned, but neither of his listeners laughed.

"Let me finish this up and then I'll clear out." Hugh turned back to smooth wet plaster over a crack that the wallpaper had covered up.

"Chill, sis," Aidan said, climbing down his ladder. "Your wall is going to look a lot better because he came over. This kind of repair takes skill and experience."

Jessica tried to quell the riot of her emotions, but it was impossible not to watch the ripple and flex of Hugh's back muscles as he swept the trowel across the wall. She forced herself to return to the hall to hang up her fallen jacket. She closed the closet door and stood facing it as she took several deep, controlled breaths.

"I'm done." Hugh's resonant voice came from close behind her, and she spun around. He ran his fingers through his hair, creating dark lines through the dust that clung to it. "I shouldn't have come, but I needed to do something real. It won't happen again, I promise."

"I overreacted," she said, noticing the shadows clouding his turquoise eyes. "You were just being helpful. I ought to be grateful, as Aidan pointed out."

"No, you told me good-bye, and I should have respected that." He gave her a rueful grimace. "I'm a slow learner when it comes to you, Jess." He half turned away before shaking his head and facing her again. He squared his shoulders and fixed her with a direct gaze. "I've been thinking about our past a lot in the last couple of days. I owe you an apology for how I treated you eight years ago."

She held up her hand to stop him, but he continued. "I'm the one who destroyed our relationship." He shoved his hands into his front pockets and looked down for a moment while Jessica tried to think of some way to halt the deluge of unwelcome apology.

Hugh lifted his head again before she could speak. "I was so focused on succeeding in Hollywood that the minute I got a toehold, I hurled myself up the cliff face like a desperate man."

She had known that, even then, had sensed the desperation that had him in its grip. She had tried every way she knew to reach past that, searched for the right words to break through to the person she loved, but he was a man possessed, his gaze turned away from her and locked on the brass ring.

"But I left behind the person who was most important to me. You," Hugh continued. "Even worse, I hurt you. I can't forgive myself for that."

"No more, please," she said, her heart twisting in her chest. She didn't want a contrite Hugh. She'd tried to tear him out of her heart eight years ago because she couldn't bear the pain he'd inflicted on her. This remorseful Hugh would find his way back in all too easily. Then he'd revert to being a movie star and leave her bleeding on the floor again.

"Jess, I wish I could go back and unsay all the terrible words I threw at you. All I can do is assure you that they weren't true and I didn't believe them even then. I should have apologized when it would have meant something."

"It means something now," Jessica said. "More than you can imagine." She still carried the scars from some of the ways he'd made her feel wrong. It helped to know that maybe she wasn't.

"I wish . . ." He pulled his hands out of his pockets and made a tiny gesture of futility. "I know too much time has gone by." His mouth twisted into a travesty of a smile. "The one thing I could repair was your wall."

"You've repaired some other things, too," Jessica said, her voice wavering slightly.

He pressed a kiss on her forehead, his lips warm and gentle. "You were always a better person than I am." Then he was out the front door in three strides.

Jessica touched her forehead, still feeling the brush of his mouth on her skin.

Hugh accepted the bottle of imported beer from Gavin Miller and went back to staring out the window into his friend's Manhattan garden. "I shouldn't have gone there without her permission," he said.

"Probably not," Gavin said agreeably from somewhere behind him.

Hugh took a swig of the beer and watched a pigeon pecking at the flagstone terrace two floors below him. "I fully intended to be gone before Jess got home."

"Yet you stayed. I wonder what that could mean." Gavin's tone was sardonic.

"It meant that I wanted to finish the job." Hugh pivoted to see his friend sprawled on the leather sectional sofa, his long legs crossed at the ankles as he drank his own beer. "I wanted to give her something that I couldn't just buy." He lifted the bottle and his other hand. "To get my hands dirty."

"Well, according to our housekeeper, you also did a fine job of getting your clothes dirty," Gavin said.

Hugh chuckled. "Ludmilla practically ripped my filthy clothes off my body so she could wash them right away."

"Gavin—Hugh! I didn't know you were here," Gavin's wife, Allie, smiled as she walked into the room, her bright red ponytail swinging with every step. "I hope you've come back to stay with us."

"Hugh's just like a college kid." Gavin tilted his head back to look up at his wife. "He only comes to our house to drink our liquor and do his laundry before he departs again."

People often commented that Hugh and Gavin could be brothers, and they indeed shared the same dark hair, height, and build. But Hugh knew it wasn't their features that struck people as similar; it was the stark, almost harsh angles that cast shadows on their faces. They'd both grown up without love in their younger lives, and it showed in the depths of their eyes and the set of their jaws. Yet when Gavin's gaze rested on his wife, all the lines and edges of his countenance seemed to blur with tenderness.

Allie sent a smile across the room toward Hugh. "Your laundry will just add to the value of our house if we ever decide to sell it."

"It doesn't have quite the cachet of 'George Washington slept here,' I'm afraid," Hugh said.

"Well, I'd rather have you than boring old George," Allie said. "I wish I could hang around and talk, but I have a patient to see."

Hugh raised his eyebrows. "I didn't know physical therapists worked such late hours."

"My patient is a very prominent person with a very demanding schedule," Allie said. "I try to be accommodating."

He noticed she wouldn't even offer a pronoun to indicate the patient's gender, such was her concern for confidentiality. He wished he had more people with Allie's discretion in his own life. "Your patient is very fortunate."

"Damn straight," Gavin said. "Will you call me when you're headed home, sprite?"

Hugh found Gavin's nickname for Allie odd. She seemed a woman with her feet firmly on the ground, not some wispy, airy imp. In fact, she reminded him of Jessica. Both were healers to their core with a warmth and vitality that somehow got transmitted to their patients.

"Always," she said, her voice sounding like a caress. When she leaned down to give her husband a kiss on the cheek, Gavin turned his head so her lips met his. Hugh knew it surprised Allie, because he saw her eyes widen and then flutter closed when her husband put his hand on the back of her head to hold her there longer.

When Allie straightened, her redhead's complexion betrayed her feelings with a flush of pink.

Hugh cleared his throat in an overly dramatic way just to bother Gavin.

The writer grinned at him. "And that is how to kiss your wife properly."

Allie's cheeks burned an even brighter rose, but she put one hand on her hip and struck a sassy pose. "He thinks that will keep me from falling in love with one of my patients the way I did with him. It's kind of like that old saying about when a man marries his mistress, he creates a job opening."

Hugh barked out a laugh. "I'm so glad you agreed to marry Gavin."

Pleasure sparkled in Allie's eyes as she turned them back to her husband. "So am I."

"Oh dear God," Hugh said. "Now he looks unbearably smug." But he was envious of the palpable connection between the two of them.

He'd felt that once . . . and never again. But he put that down to his well-earned cynicism.

Allie waved good-bye, and Gavin's gaze didn't leave her until she was out of sight.

"I can't believe I almost screwed up your relationship," Hugh said, referring to the time he'd accused Allie of using Gavin for her own ends. Of course, he'd been fed false information by the scheming Irene Bartram.

"You didn't screw it up. I did." Gavin turned somber. "Nothing should have shaken my belief in Allie's integrity, because I knew her—and I loved her."

"Trust has never been our strong suit, you and I." Hugh leaned his hip against the windowsill. "Doesn't it bother you to have her working so late?"

"It used to, but I've learned to handle it."

"She's very careful about confidentiality, which I admire," Hugh said. "Do you know where she is or who the patient is?"

Gavin examined the label on his beer bottle. "We have an understanding. She only takes patients our doctor and friend, Ben Cavill, refers to her, and she must use our driver, Jaros, to go to them." He lifted his gaze to Hugh. "So, technically, I do not know where she is or who the patient is. However, if need be, I could find out quite swiftly." He bared his teeth in a shark's smile. "And I would not hesitate to do so."

"But why take the chance that you'd need to?"

"You've met Allie, so I'm surprised you think I could stop her." Gavin gave Hugh a sardonic look but then grew serious. "Let's face it, I'm just an entertainer. I spin stories about a spy who can't possibly exist. Allie heals people. That's a lot more important than anything I do. Not only that, but she's brilliant at her job, so I would be doing humanity a disservice if I tried to convince her to stay home with me." He gave a short laugh. "God knows what would have happened to me if she hadn't taken me on as a patient. The real reason, though, is that she would come to hate me if I interfered with her calling. Her work is part of who she is and why I fell in love with her. I'd be a fool to attempt to change that."

Hugh put down his beer on a side table and clapped his hands together a couple of times in mock applause. "That was quite a speech."

Gavin bent at the waist in an ironic, seated bow.

But the speech had made Hugh squirm inwardly at the memory of how he'd treated Jessica's work in their past. He winced as he thought of the many times he'd demanded that she change her schedule to accommodate his, as though his meaningless parties were more important than her healing sick animals of all kinds. He'd needed her beside him to shore up his belief in himself, to remind him that an extraordinary person thought he was worthy of her respect and even more, her love. So he had trampled on the qualities that he loved most in her: her compassionate spirit, her boundless love for other creatures, and her skill at healing.

"If your profession is unimportant, what does that make mine?" Hugh said to Gavin with a lift of his eyebrow. "At least you conjure characters into being out of thin air. All I do is mouth the lines you've written for me. I'm essentially a puppet."

"Did I hurt your feelings? I'm so sorry."

"Ha! You take joy in irritating me."

Gavin shook his head. "I didn't say what we do is worthless. The world needs to escape, even to believe that someone like Julian Best is working behind the scenes to battle evil for all of us. I dreamed him up, but you've brought him to life as the living, breathing embodiment of my words. Remember, storytellers were revered in ancient times. Too bad those days are over."

"At least a few of us still get paid well." Hugh waved his beer bottle around to indicate their elegant surroundings. Gavin owned not one but two town houses side by side in Manhattan, one to live in and one to run his writing empire from.

"But we've gotten off topic," the author said. "We were discussing the woman from your past. I never got the chance to meet her back then. You'd broken up by the time we became friends. You should bring her to dinner."

"Who do you think you are, my mother?" Hugh repeated the question that had become a dark joke between them, since both had lacked a loving mother figure in their early lives.

"I'd like to meet the woman who you commandeered my helicopter for."

Hugh knew Gavin didn't really care about the helicopter. "You'd have done the same thing for Allie."

"Allie is my wife, not my ex-fiancée," Gavin said.

"Would you care about her well-being any less if you split up?"

"That would depend on why we parted," Gavin drawled.

Hugh let his gaze rest on his friend and was rewarded when Gavin shifted on the sofa and said, "Yes, I would still care. I cared even when I thought Allie had used me. Of course, we've already established that I was an idiot."

"Neither one of us is very good at relationships. We didn't have any sterling examples to learn from."

"Speak for yourself," Gavin said. "I am happily married and intend to remain so for the rest of my life."

A sharp pang sliced through Hugh. He could have had that, but he'd thrown it away. "I apologized to Jessica," he said. "For being an asshole."

"It's taken you this long to realize that's what you are?" Gavin asked. "I could have told you much sooner."

"It seems to me you live in a glass house in this case."

"I've mellowed since I fell in love with Allie." Gavin dropped the taunting. "How did Jessica respond to your apology?"

"She said it helped repair some of the damage."

"Is that what you hoped she would say?"

No, he'd wanted her to throw herself into his arms and say all was forgiven. "It was a start."

"What is it you're looking for, Hugh?" Gavin sat forward. "You haven't mentioned her in years."

Hugh straightened to stare out the window again. He hadn't mentioned Jess because thinking about her was like probing an unhealed wound, so he didn't. "I see how happy you are, and I want the same thing."

"Well." Surprise sounded in Gavin's voice, which gave Hugh a moment of satisfaction. "I wasn't expecting that. I thought this was a simple exercise in atonement and self-flagellation."

"It is, but I can't help wondering . . ." Hugh gulped down a mouthful of beer. Seeing Jess again had made him feel like he was missing a piece of himself, a piece he hadn't realized he'd lost.

"You've told me that she didn't want the kind of life you offered her. Now she's built a life she does want, so maybe you should leave well enough alone."

Hugh pivoted to look at his friend. "Maybe the life I have to offer is different now."

Gavin snorted. "She runs a low-cost vet clinic in South Harlem. How exactly does that tie in with what you do?"

His words were an eerie echo of what Jess had said to him all those years ago about how different the things they wanted from life were. On the surface, she was right, but they shared a drive to succeed at whatever they did and a strong commitment to hard work. He'd just been too self-absorbed to give her room to do what she needed.

Hugh shook his head. "You're right. My presence can be disruptive, thanks to Julian Best's fame. I should stay the hell away from her."

At least until he was sure of what he really wanted.

Chapter 10

"Goal!" Pete leaped to his feet, and Jessica jumped up to cheer, too. Her companion's enthusiasm for the game and his colorful running commentary had proven contagious. She was rooting for the New York Rangers as loudly as he was.

"That's evened things up," Pete said, giving her a high five. "Now we'll take the lead."

She was glad to have something to focus on other than just conversation. Sitting across a table from Pete would have been hard with Hugh's face and words still roiling through her brain from their encounter the day before. The hard-fought hockey game provided an excellent diversion.

The luxury box hosted twelve guests, all of whom Pete had introduced her to. They were either employees of ExDat or their significant others. It had become obvious to her that Pete was a big wheel in the company by the way their fellow spectators treated him. There was liking, certainly, but also respect and some deference, all of which Pete was clearly comfortable with.

When the end-of-game horn sounded, the arena erupted in celebration of a Rangers come-from-behind win. Jessica stood and joined the victory cheers. Pete's face was lit with fierce pleasure. He took his hockey seriously.

"Yes! I knew they'd do it," he shouted into the din. He wrapped his arm around Jessica's shoulders and pulled her against his side in an exuberant hug.

She let herself relax into him because it was nothing more than his way of sharing his excitement at the win. But when she smiled up at him, he leaned down and kissed her, a real kiss, not just a "hey, my team won and I'm happy" kind of kiss. His lips felt strange and unfamiliar on hers. Because he wasn't Hugh, of course. Anger flared, and she reached up to thread her fingers in his pale hair so she could kiss him in return.

She was damned if Hugh was going to ruin this.

Pete wrapped his other arm around her to bring her closer as the kiss deepened. She tried to sink into it. She wanted to feel heat sear through her. Pete knew what he was doing, but her body refused to acknowledge his skill, remaining quiescent and indifferent.

When the cheering subsided and the spectators began to file out of their seats, Pete released her mouth, but his gaze stayed on her face, his eyes blazing with desire. "Now *that* was the right way to celebrate a win," he said with a scorching smile.

Jessica laughed, even as she realized she'd made a mistake. "I had no idea hockey was so exciting," she said. "It went to my head."

"There's another game tomorrow night," he said, his arms still around her. "I'll get tickets."

She smiled and leaned away from him so he let her go. "I can only handle one work night out a week," she said, sidling sideways to exit the row of seats. As soon as they were back in the luxury suite, he wound his arm around her waist while the group collected their coats and said good-bye.

And it remained there, a heavy, uncomfortable weight, as they walked the two blocks to the parking lot where his big Range Rover waited, gleaming darkly in the city lights. He made a wry face as he held the passenger door open for her. "I wish you didn't have to work weekends."

"Me, too," Jessica said, although it was providing a useful excuse to hide behind right now. She really wanted to give Pete a chance—he was such a solid, trustworthy guy—but Hugh's allure was too vivid and fresh.

When they arrived at her house, Pete double-parked in front and escorted her up the stairs. His kiss was meant to persuade, to seduce, and to promise, but she felt none of the hot, melting response Hugh's kisses evoked, so she ended it as soon as she could and slipped inside her door.

She walked into the kitchen to find a note from Aidan, saying he'd gone out. She pulled a bottle of wine out of the fridge and poured herself a glass before wandering into the living room. Pushing Pete out of her mind, she examined Aidan's progress on the walls and had to admit that her brother was doing a good job.

It cheered her up to have one part of her life moving forward in a satisfyingly concrete way. Until her gaze fell on the perfectly smooth plaster where once there had been a long, jagged crack. She closed her eyes and groaned.

Would she ever be able to look at that wall again without thinking of Hugh?

The next morning, Aidan sat across the kitchen table from Jessica, sporting sweatpants, a flannel shirt, and a hangover as he nursed a mug of coffee between his hands. "I'm glad I don't have to go to work today," he mumbled.

She cut another bite of the pancakes she'd made for herself. Aidan had taken one look at the fluffy golden disks and turned green. "That's why I don't party hearty on Saturday night," she said.

"You don't party hearty any night," he said. "You work all the time."

"Hey, I went to a hockey game last night."

Aidan brightened. "With Pete, right? Did you have a good time?"

"The luxury suite was great. It had its own bathroom. A really nice one with snazzy glass tiles."

Her brother rolled his eyes. "Figures you'd be more interested in that than the actual game."

"In fact, I enjoyed the game. The Rangers had a come-from-behind win, which was pretty exciting. Pete knows hockey, so he explained the more esoteric rules."

"Are you and Pete, um, getting along all right?" Aidan asked.

Touchy question, but she kept her tone casual. "We get along fine. Why?"

"Um, I need to tell you something." Aidan looked anywhere but at her.

"Sounds like something I won't like." She put her fork down.

"I might have applied for a job at ExDat, but it's not in Pete's division or anything, so it's not a big deal." Now her brother met her eyes. "But I'm glad you're doing okay with Pete."

"Are you seriously implying that I should keep dating Pete so you can get a job with his company?" Of course, she had considered the same dilemma when Pete had told her.

"Not really, no. It's just good that you like him." Aidan had the grace to look sheepish.

"Did you keep in touch with him between high school and now?"

"I saw him every now and then at parties when we both came home during college vacations, but not after that. It was a surprise to run into him here in New York. He's a good guy," Aidan continued. "Not as rich or famous as Hugh, but solid."

It seemed unfair that everyone compared Pete with Hugh, including Pete. Even worse, *she* compared them. "Fame doesn't mean a whole lot to me—"

"That's obvious."

"Hey, I was about to say that I wouldn't mind being a little richer, though."

"You and me both," Aidan said with a grimace. "Getting this job would be a step in the right direction."

"The truth is that Pete already told me you'd applied for the position. He wanted to make sure it wouldn't affect anything between him and me."

"Did he think I might get it?"

She decided not to tell him that Pete had supported his application, so as not to raise her brother's hopes. Although after seeing Pete with his colleagues at the game, she was no longer convinced that his recommendation was as negligible as he claimed. "He said it was an entirely different area than his and he didn't know much about it."

Aidan's face fell. "I thought he might have some pull, since he's pretty high up in the company."

"I'm sure he has some influence, but he's not going to share that with me in a social setting."

"Good point." He cheered up enough to grin at her. "Well, since you don't hate him, maybe you could just keep dating him a little longer, for my sake."

She threw her wadded-up paper napkin at him and got up to go to the clinic.

Chapter 11

Jessica stopped chewing her bite of ham-and-cheese sandwich as she read the e-mail Carla had forwarded to her in the batch of Monday-morning messages. She hadn't had time to check them until her very late lunch. The e-mail was from a veterinarian who'd heard about the clinic and liked what Jessica was doing for the community. The vet wondered if there might be a part-time opening for her.

Aidan's comments about the fact that she worked constantly echoed in Jessica's brain. Even Hugh had warned her that she was going to burn out. And for all Pete's patience with getting her home early, he would grow tired of that . . . if she let him stay around long enough.

Jessica scanned the e-mail again. She'd tried hiring another vet a couple of years ago, and it hadn't worked out, as she'd explained to Hugh. However, that had been a full-time position and she hadn't been able to offer a competitive salary. She might have adequate funds to keep a part-timer committed. But why would a fully qualified vet want to work part-time? There had to be a catch.

Carla came in with a green zippered pouch tucked under her arm. "I've got too much cash in the drawer, so I'm going to the bank now. And don't worry, Caleb's coming with me."

Jessica made sure never to keep much cash in her office. She didn't want to take the risk of exposing her staff to the dangers of robbery.

She nodded and then pointed to her computer screen. "Do you think this e-mail is legit?" She could hear the excitement in her own voice.

"You mean the vet who wants to come work here because we do good things?"

Jessica nodded.

Carla put her free hand on her hip. "Honey, I try not to look a gift horse in the mouth, but you better dig into her references real thoroughly, is all I'm saying."

"I will." Her receptionist's reality check doused some of her enthusiasm. "But I might be able to take an occasional Saturday off."

Carla's skeptical expression softened. "You sure deserve it, so let's hope she's what she claims to be."

Jessica's fingers flew over the keyboard as she asked the vet for her résumé and references, as well as when she could come in for an interview. As she hit send, a text message pinged on her phone. When she saw the sender was Hugh, she eyed her phone like it was a rabid raccoon. Should she touch it or run far away?

She'd spent Sunday trying not to think of Hugh. She'd focused on Pete and how much fun she'd had at the hockey game . . . and drinks . . . and dinner. She'd reminded herself that Pete understood where she came from, that they had a whole background in common, that he'd made a success of himself, too.

But when Pete had texted her a couple of times, she'd pleaded a busy day at work and given him short, noncommittal responses. She felt like a low-down, two-timing cheater, even though no promises had been asked for or made. There was just something about how Pete treated her that made her believe he expected more of their relationship than she was prepared to give yet—or maybe ever.

Because Hugh rose up at every unguarded moment, his turquoise eyes blazing with arousal as she remembered him braced over her, moving inside her, touching her in the places that pleased her most. But it wasn't just the sex. It was the defined muscles of his shoulders rippling as he smoothed plaster over the crack in her wall with focused care. And the sadness etched in the lines around his mouth when he apologized for hurting her at the end of their doomed engagement.

She squeezed her eyes closed and rubbed them as though that could stop the parade of images.

"You got a headache, Doc?" Diego's voice held concern.

She pulled her hands away from her face and beckoned him into the office. "No headache. Just thinking about something I shouldn't be."

"I hear you." Diego sat on the ramshackle chair in front of her desk. "I think we got another case of giardiasis at the center."

"Damn—darn it!" Jessica said, watching Diego politely suppress a smile. She knew he'd heard a lot worse, but she agreed with Emily about providing good role models for the kids, even though she didn't work at the center. "I'll stop in on my way home. Which dog is it?"

"It's Pari, the newest K-9 Angel. Maybe she's the one who brought it in."

"That's a strong possibility," Jessica said, impressed with Diego's analysis. "She might have shed the infectious cysts without showing symptoms herself. She's the small, brown, curly-haired one, right?"

Diego nodded. "Naveen's dog. I'll go with you to the center." He stood up.

"Don't you have homework to do?"

"One of our teachers was sick, so we had study period. I got a lot done then."

"I guess Violet will make sure you do the rest."

Diego grinned. "She sure will."

Three hours later, Jessica and Diego walked up the front steps of the Carver Center. Jessica was proud of herself for still not having read Hugh's text message. Fortunately, she'd been crazy busy right up until the moment Carla declared the office closed for the day. Now her phone felt like it was scorching through the pocket of her scrubs.

"Evening, Doc, Diego," Powell said from behind his desk as she and the boy shucked off their coats. "Got another sick dog, I hear."

"Naveen's new one," Diego said, starting down the hallway.

"There's big excitement upstairs." Powell tilted his head toward the staircase. "We got us a real, live movie star visiting." He gave Jessica a quizzical smile. "Your friend."

Diego stopped. "You mean Hugh Baker? For real?" Then he looked at Jessica with a hint of embarrassment. "Carla told us you know him."

Jessica was still dealing with how just hearing that Hugh was in the same building as she was sent an electric shock of nerves through her. She fumbled her phone out of her pocket. Maybe that's why Hugh had texted her.

Are you free this Wednesday? I'd like to talk. Just talk.

Sexual heat prickled over her skin and soaked deep down into her belly as his words evoked memories of the last Wednesday they'd spent together. She hadn't intended to do more than talk the last time, and look where she'd ended up.

"Doc? Doc?" Diego's voice finally penetrated the Hugh-induced cloud of lust wrapped around her. "You okay?"

"I'm fine. Just got an unexpected text." She held up her phone. "You go on upstairs to meet Mr. Baker. I'll take a look at Pari."

Diego hesitated for a split second before he shook his head. "I'll go with you."

Jessica saw the longing on his face as he glanced up the stairs. "Let's go up first, then. We'll check out Pari after you meet the movie star."

The boy's dazzling smile was a gift in itself. "That'd be dope."

"Leave the doc's bag here," Powell said. "I'll look after it."

Preceding Diego up the stairs, Jessica lifted one hand to push at her bun, wondering how mussed it was after she had yanked off her knitted cap. Then she dropped it to her side. She refused to pander to her annoying obsession with her former fiancé. However, she did give a tug to the hem of her scrub top, feeling an unwelcome spurt of relief that she'd worn her favorite purple one with the flattering pin tucks.

With each step, she felt her heart beat faster. Was it because she wanted to see Hugh or because she was afraid to?

As she neared the top of the steps, she could hear his beautifully modulated voice rising and falling. He was telling a story about a movie stunt that had gone wrong, and she found herself caught up in the tale before she could even see him.

When she reached the first floor, she dodged sideways to join the row of staff members leaning against the wall, their rapt attention on the man sitting in one of the mismatched armchairs in the lounge. He was wearing a black T-shirt and jeans, which should have made him blend right in, but his ineffable charisma made him practically glow, drawing every eye to the flash of his turquoise eyes, the glossy ebony of his hair, and the starkly beautiful planes of his face.

One of the dogs sat beside him, its expression blissful as Hugh absently stroked its head with his long, elegant fingers. He gestured with his other hand, demonstrating how he'd leaped from a third-story window, only to discover that his safety harness hadn't been properly fastened.

She thought she'd escaped his notice, but he swept his gaze around his audience like the pro he was and it snagged on her. The fingers stroking the dog went still for a long moment, and there was the tiniest break in the flow of his words. But only she noticed before the show went on.

Diego joined a group of older kids who were propped against the back of a sofa, and Jessica could see him fall under Hugh's spell. She should slip downstairs to take care of Pari now, but she found herself ensnared as well. The movements of Hugh's hands, the stretch of his T-shirt over the muscles of his chest and shoulders, and the long, denim-clad legs wound their fascination around her like a silken net.

She caught her breath as he described how when he fell, he could feel the safety harness slipping off his chest and away from his shoulders while he tried to grasp one of the straps as he heard the screams and shouts of the film crew. Just when he thought he had lost the harness and was going to crash into the ground at full speed, his watch snagged on a buckle, giving him enough time to grab the strap and break his fall, although he nearly wrenched his shoulder out of its socket. He lifted his wrist as he described the bruise that wrapped around where the watchband had been mashed against his skin. "But I've worn that watch for every stunt since then. It saved my life."

He looked around. "Know what I learned from that experience?"

"Use a stunt double," one kid called out.

"Don't jump outta third-floor windows," another one said.

"Wear *two* safety harnesses" was the final suggestion.

Hugh laughed, a deep, rich rumble of amusement. "All excellent advice. But I can't always take it." He leaned forward to make sure he had their attention. "I learned to check the safety harness myself and to do it twice. Because no one cares about your fate as much as you do. Your future is always in your own hands."

Jessica felt her heart twist. No one had cared about Hugh as a child. Not to mention that there had been no safety harness for his younger self.

A chorus of "yeahs" and "amens" rose in agreement with his words.

"They care here." It was Diego, his voice booming out. "They got our backs here."

Jessica saw Emily stand up straighter and smile at the boy's words.

This time the sound of agreement was louder and longer. All the staff members were grinning by the end of it, and some wiped at their eyes.

Hugh nodded as the room quieted. "You're right, and you're lucky to have this place. But your life is still your responsibility. You have value, every one of you, and you should always act that way."

Jessica knew he'd never felt valued. Never believed that he mattered in any way. Which was why he'd been so focused on succeeding as an actor. In his roles, he'd found a way to pretend to be someone who was worthy of attention. She'd understood that from the first time he'd told her about his past as a foster child.

But she'd assumed he had left that behind when he rose to the pinnacle of his profession. Now millions of people wanted to know what he ate for breakfast, where he bought his socks, and whom he was sleeping with. He had all the attention he'd craved. Yet she could still see the foster child looking out of his eyes as he spoke to the kids.

She didn't want to feel any more sympathy for Hugh, so she slipped away and down the stairs. She stopped to grab her duffel from Powell and tromped down to the basement. The dogs greeted her with surprising enthusiasm, given that she usually arrived bearing needles. But dogs were very forgiving that way. Far more than people.

She made the quiet signal, and most of them stopped barking. "Where's Pari?" she asked, walking along the row of crates with their neatly lettered name tags. There was an empty space toward one end and no sign of Pari, so she checked the storage closet where she'd spent the night. The one Hugh had carried her out of.

The little brown-and-white mutt stood up when Jessica opened the crate's door. "You look better than Khonsu did," Jessica said with relief. When she called the dog's name, Pari ambled out of the crate.

After a thorough examination, Jessica had to agree with Diego's diagnosis. She got out the metronidazole and dosed Pari with half a tablet. After giving the ailing little creature some gentle petting, she put her back in the crate.

Pulling out a script pad and pen, she sat cross-legged on the floor and started a note to Diego. She wanted to dodge out of the center before she ran into Hugh. She didn't have an answer for him about Wednesday.

"You just can't stay out of this closet, can you?"

The black velvet of Hugh's voice shimmered through her, even as she inwardly berated herself for not just texting Diego about the meds so she could escape sooner. "I go where my patients are," she said, continuing to write without looking up. "You did a nice thing, talking with the kids."

Out of the corner of her eye, she saw Hugh's legs fold down until he was squatting beside her, his forearms resting on his knees. "I like kids," he said.

She finished her note and stuck it to the bottle of metro with a strip of surgical tape. "They'll be telling everyone about meeting a famous movie star. It will make them feel important in front of their friends." She turned to look at him, getting the full wallop of his extraordinary face about two feet from hers. Good thing she was already sitting down.

He nodded. "It's the least I can give them." Because he understood that any little thing that gave a disadvantaged kid a positive moment in the spotlight could help.

Damn it! She didn't want to see this side of him right now.

"Need a lift?" He held out his hand, only the tiny twitch of one corner of his lips betraying his deliberate pun.

She couldn't ignore his offer, so she braced herself and laid her palm on his. The strength of his fingers and his arm as he rose and pulled her up with him sent heat corkscrewing deep inside her.

"I have tickets to *A Question of Desire* Wednesday night. I was hoping you'd come with me," he said, her hand still enveloped in his.

Those were the most in-demand tickets on Broadway, impossible to get because the cast was filled with marquee names who were contracted for a limited run. But Hugh could get anything he wanted now, of course. "You sure know how to tempt a girl," she said, stalling even though she knew she'd say yes. It was impossible for her to resist going to a fabulous play with Hugh as her date. No woman possessed that kind of willpower, even if she wondered about the motive behind the invitation.

His blue eyes went smoky, but he didn't take advantage of her opening for a flirtatious comment. "And dinner first, I hope," he added.

His thumb traced over her knuckles, a touch that sent a tingle flickering across her skin. But she looked him straight in the eye. "Just dinner and the play."

He nodded. "No other expectations."

"Sounds good," she said. But Hugh hadn't been responsible for her previous insanity.

It was her own weakness she had to fight.

Chapter 12

Jessica had come close to wearing scrubs for her dinner with Hugh. After all, he'd claimed he would be fine with that, and she wanted to test him to see if that was true.

Instead, she'd fallen back on the New Yorker's uniform of black trousers, black boots, and a silky black top with a draped V neck. She'd broken out her long-disused curling iron to add some soft, sexy waves to her hair and left it loose and shining around her shoulders. A gold chain dotted with chunks of polished carnelian circled her neck a couple of times and lay against the bare skin of her décolletage. She might not be a movie star, but she could still play up her assets.

Of course, that would appear to conflict with her avowed intention of not sleeping with Hugh. If she'd wanted to help herself keep her vow, she should have worn a bulky, shapeless turtleneck.

But the flicker of heat in Hugh's eyes when she opened her front door gave her a little blip of satisfaction.

He transferred the heat to her by brushing the warm, chiseled curve of his lips against her cheek. "You look beautiful. And don't make some comment about that being an empty compliment just because I hang around with movie stars." He focused that intense gaze on her and repeated, "You. Look. Beautiful."

She reminded herself that he was an actor, so he could project sincerity at will, but something made her believe him this time. "Thank you. So do you. As always."

He wore black trousers, a black shirt open at the neck, and a pale gray woven blazer. The monochromatic color scheme made his turquoise eyes blaze like lasers. But she caught a flash of discomfort cross his face. He made a dismissive gesture, and she nearly pointed out that he didn't take compliments any more graciously than she did. "Come in out of the cold while I grab my coat."

"You won't need it. The limo driver will let us out right at the door."

"Right. I forgot about that handy feature of riding in a limousine." She picked up her purse and a red wool wrap from the front hall table. "Okay, then."

Hugh leaned forward to glance through the hallway door into the living room. "Aidan's making good progress on the wallpaper stripping."

"He is." Much to her surprise. Her brother was sticking with a project despite it being boring, dirty, and without compensation. She chose to interpret his actions as showing both maturity and appreciation for his sister, which warmed her heart. "He's going to strip and refinish the woodwork next."

Hugh nodded his approval. "Is he job hunting, too?"

"Sort of." Aidan had been invited to come in for an interview at ExDat.

"Meaning?" he asked.

"He has one job interview scheduled for next week."

"I wish him luck." Hugh put his hand on the small of her back to steer her toward the front door. She was sure she could feel the exact outline of every point of contact through the thin silk of her top, the heat of his palm a counterbalance to the piercing cold of the night air.

To steady herself, she said, "Speaking of interviews, I have one scheduled with a vet who wants to work part-time at the clinic."

His fingers pressed more firmly against her back for a second. "You sound excited about it."

"I could use the help, so I'm hoping she's as qualified as her résumé says she is. And that her references check out."

"Do you think they won't?" He opened the limo door for her.

She looked up at him. "Not a lot of vets want to work in South Harlem part-time, so I'm a little concerned that something in her background makes it hard for her to find another position."

"Maybe she just wants to go where her help will be most valuable." Something about his tone made her try to read his expression, but his face was in shadow.

"I hope so." She bent and slid onto the leather seat of the limo. Hugh closed the door, leaving her alone in the luxurious car for a few seconds. She skimmed her fingers over the polished wood paneling and admired the subtle lighting. A privacy screen shut the passenger compartment away from the driver, turning the space into a cocoon of intimacy.

Hugh entered the limo on a waft of chilly winter air that made her shiver. The cold didn't usually affect her that much, but being around Hugh seemed to heighten her senses. Now the rich scent of his soap drifted past her nostrils, and she couldn't resist a deep inhale.

"When's the interview with the vet?" he asked.

"The interview? Oh, it's Saturday." She'd been sidetracked by the memories his soap evoked.

He nodded. "Maybe you can get an extra day off after you hire her."

"*If* I hire her."

"I'm being optimistic."

Hugh was never optimistic about people. "Do you know something about this vet that I don't?" she asked, turning to find him staring straight ahead. "Hugh?"

He shifted to give her a look of astonishment. "How would I know anything about her?"

"Good question," Jessica muttered. Would Hugh be able to conjure up the perfect veterinarian to work for her? Something about his responses made her suspicious. However, Carla had said not to look a gift horse in the mouth, so she would keep the rest of her questions to herself.

"How did you spend your day off?" he asked.

"Sleeping late. Running errands." She gave a little laugh. "I even picked up some paint samples for when Aidan finishes stripping the walls. I can't believe my living room might get renovated in this decade."

"You know, I'd really like to give him a hand when I have a break from shooting. I get genuine satisfaction out of doing that kind of work." He gave her a wry look. "Every now and then."

She remembered the time she'd visited him on a job site, where he'd been doing the kitchen cabinetry. He'd shown her how he'd dovetailed the drawers and made her run her fingers over the sanded edges of the cabinet doors to savor their smoothness. Then they'd made very illicit use of the expensive granite that topped the kitchen island. "Thanks, but it's not a good idea."

Instead of arguing with her, he leaned back in the corner of his seat while an odd smile played over his lips.

"What?" she asked.

He shook his head. "It was an interesting answer."

"It was honest." She tried to figure out why it had made him smile but couldn't. "What did you do today?"

"Froze my balls off climbing around on a bridge. Of course, Meryl did the same thing in a ripped-up evening gown, so she was even colder."

"Hey, you're the one who wanted to be an actor."

"I'll like it better when we get to Palau."

A pang of loss rattled her. "When do you leave New York?"

"In about ten days. We're doing the bridge scene, another chase scene, and some interior shooting here before we depart for DC."

She let her gaze skim over the length of him, taking in the legs stretched out across the limo's carpet, the shoulders wedged against the door, the powerfully elegant hands, one resting on his thigh and the other on the leather between them. She lingered on the lines of his jaw and cheekbones and knew it was impossible for her to forget this man, no matter how many miles or years separated them.

The thought sent a slash of depression through her. She needed to remember the Hugh who had made her feel like a failure, not the man who had made her peanut-butter-and-jelly sandwiches and massaged her aching feet at the end of a long day. To remind herself of why she had given back his ring, even though she loved him. Because otherwise her heart would break all over again when he got on the plane to DC and never looked back.

"I'd like to stay in touch this time," he said, as though he had read her thoughts. He reached across the space between them to take her hand from her lap and curl his fingers around it.

"Why?" The simmer of his skin radiated deep into the bones of her fingers.

"You're part of who I am." He stroked his thumb over the back of her hand.

The friction of his movement sent tendrils of sensation winding up her arm and through her body. She couldn't pull free without making a fuss, so she tried to ignore his touch. "Just old friends, then." Maybe she could manage that if he was halfway around the world.

His thumb went still, and he said in a flat tone, "Just old friends."

At the theater-district restaurant, they were seated in a private corner, screened from the rest of the room by half-height walls. Hugh had explained that the owner was a former actor who understood the need for recognizable faces to be hidden so they could dine uninterrupted. As a result, many celebrities patronized her establishment, which brought in the general public hoping to catch glimpses as the famous folk entered and exited.

Now Hugh sat across the linen-covered table from her, the angles and planes of his face thrown into relief by the shadows of the candlelight. "Has anyone ever done a bust of you?" she asked as she slathered butter on a warm apple-raisin roll.

His eyebrows arched in perplexity. "Not that I'm aware of."

"They should. It would be a shame not to capture that incredible bone structure in three dimensions."

He dropped his gaze to the spoon he was fidgeting with.

"You still don't like it when people compliment your looks," she said, remembering his reaction at her front door. "I thought you'd be used to it by now."

He put down the spoon and met her eyes. "It's not what I want people to think about . . . the ones I respect, anyway."

"I don't understand why it bothers you." She bit into the crusty roll and sighed with pleasure.

He shrugged and took a sip of red wine. Then he surprised her. "When I was a young kid, potential foster parents were scared away by my looks. I heard one man say my eyes were unnatural. The bone structure everyone admires so much made me look older than I was, harder, less innocent. I would have preferred to be a blond cherub with round cheeks and brown eyes. Those were the kinds of kids who got chosen."

Jessica put down her roll. "You never told me that." She was stunned by the anger she felt that he had concealed such an important piece of the puzzle that was him.

"There were a lot of things I didn't tell you," he said, his voice tight. "I recreated myself when I became an actor. I didn't want anyone to know who I'd been."

"I wouldn't have loved you any less. And I might have understood you better." Although they'd both been so young then.

138

He locked his blue eyes on her. "I couldn't take that risk. You were so smart, so accomplished, so *normal*. I needed you to be dazzled by me so you didn't realize who you were really in love with."

Jessica rocked back in her chair. "But you told me about being a foster child, so why not tell me the rest?"

He gave her a crooked smile that held no amusement. "I was playing on your sympathy. I didn't want you to know the whole truth."

"You didn't have to play on anything. I loved you." And then it struck her like a flash of lightning. He hadn't felt lovable. How could he, when no parent had ever been there to tell him he was? Her heart seemed to contract into a fist of sorrow. She stretched her arm across the table to lay her hand over his. "I'm so sorry," she whispered through a constricted throat. "I didn't realize . . ."

His brows drew down into a near scowl. "Sorry for what?"

"For—" She'd been about to say "for you," but that sounded ridiculous when she remembered whom she sat across from. "For not understanding better."

Hugh didn't like the pity he saw clouding the clear gray of Jessica's eyes. However, he did like the fact that she was touching his hand. He was also glad she hadn't been offended when he'd called her normal.

In his world, normal was rare, but other people didn't always comprehend that. Normal meant two parents, a home where they had to take you in, a significant other who didn't care what part you could get for her or him, and being able to eat cheese puffs whenever you wanted to.

Dear God, he was turning into a whiner.

He rotated his hand under Jessica's so he could feel her palm against his. She had the hands he'd expect of a working vet: short, unpolished nails, slightly chapped skin from the constant washing, and a strength developed from continual use. He remembered how they'd felt moving over his body during their night of lovemaking and felt the stirring of desire again. His gaze slipped down to the swell of her breasts exposed by her top's curving neckline.

She wanted to be just "old friends."

"Hugh? I didn't mean to upset you."

"Upset?" He shook his head. "Just thinking about the past."

The little worry line formed between her eyebrows. He used to smooth it with his thumb when they were lying in bed together, usually naked.

"We were young and ambitious. Both of us, not just you," she said. "Maybe our attention wasn't on each other as much as it should have been."

"Don't feel guilty," he said, putting his other hand over hers to hold it there. "I was the one who tried to make you into someone different. I fell head over heels in love with a hardworking veterinarian. Why would I want you to be anyone else?"

"It goes both ways. I loved an up-and-coming actor. I should have expected the publicity that went along with that." Honestly, she'd been fine with it—even enjoyed their forays into an alien world of sparkling glamour—until Hugh started to dissect her public appearances under the microscope of his disapproval.

"Let's stop worrying about our youthful mistakes," he said.

"And try not to compound them with more recent ones," Jessica said.

He knew exactly what she was referring to. "I don't consider our night together a mistake."

She pulled her hand away from his. "It wasn't a good idea."

"That's the second time you've used that phrase in reference to me. I believe I'm offended." Unless he could interpret it to mean that he affected her more than she wanted.

She folded her hands on the table and looked down at them.

So he could interpret it his way.

She lifted her head to look him in the eye as though she wanted to strip away all his masks. "What do you want from me?" she asked with quiet intensity.

"Nothing. And you don't want anything from me. That's the point." He moved his hand to the center of the table, palm up, and held his breath while she stared down at his invitation. For a long moment, he thought she would refuse it. But then almost in slow motion, she pulled her left hand from the security of her right and laid it on his. Relief washed through him like a heady taste of champagne as he closed his fingers around hers ever so gently, because he didn't want to scare her away.

He nearly cursed out loud when the waiter arrived with their appetizers and he was forced to relinquish the delicious contact with her gentle vitality.

Watching her savor the onion tart with parmesan and pancetta almost made up for it. Unlike so many actors he knew—including himself at times—Jess ate with gusto, her face an open canvas of bliss. He barely took his eyes off her as he picked at his pear-and–goat cheese salad, his concession to the Julian Best diet.

"This crust is heaven," she said, a dreamy smile curving her lips as she cut another bite. "Like butter made flaky."

A tiny crumb lodged in the corner of her mouth, and he imagined himself licking it off, sending a jolt of arousal straight to his cock.

"My salad is equally delicious . . . if one is a rabbit," he said.

She waved her fork in his direction. "Ha! It's only fair to have a guy worry about his weight every now and then."

"Stick with me and you'll hear many, many guys moaning about their weight. It's an occupational hazard."

"Thank God my clients don't judge me by my appearance." She grinned. "Because there's no way I'd wear Spanx to work."

"It was a lot easier when I was twenty," he said. "I could eat anything and not show it."

"Like three bags of cheese puffs in twenty minutes," she teased, referring to a night when he'd gotten drunk at a cast party, accepted a dare, and then puked up bright orange for the next few hours. "Of course, you purged those before they could turn into love handles."

"Ah, but it got the attention of Lorenzo d'Albo, so it was worth the repulsiveness." Stupid to be cast in a movie because you ralphed up cheese puffs, but the director had remembered Hugh's stunt when he'd auditioned for d'Albo a week later, just by coincidence. Being memorable often paid off in Hollywood.

"I couldn't believe you ate cheese puffs again the next day. I would have been off them for life."

"Iron stomach." He patted his hard, flat abdomen. But the ability to eat virtually anything had been a necessity in foster care.

The waiter whisked away their empty plates, and Jessica reminded him of another embarrassing story from their time together. He retaliated with an equally disconcerting moment in her life. Soon they were one-upping each other and disagreeing about what had really happened eight years before. And laughing. Just like old friends.

He loved it and he hated it. Maybe he didn't know exactly what he wanted *from* Jess, but he knew that he wanted *her*.

For the first time in her life, Jessica regretted the appearance of dessert, because it signaled the end of dinner. Not that she didn't find the rich-but-light-as-a-feather chocolate mousse layered between thin sheets of chocolate sponge cake nearly orgasmic, but she and Hugh were having so much fun. Trading stories took her back to those sunshine-filled days in California when her life opened out before her with what seemed an endless array of pure possibility. So many paths had spread out in front of her; she felt like she had all the time in the world to explore them. Part of the thrill was the prospect of having Hugh by her side for the journey.

When he was laughing with her over their meal, he seemed like the Hugh she'd known eight years ago. But when the last mouthful of mousse cake had been savored, while Hugh paid the bill and accepted the waiter's discreet but heartfelt speech of admiration with practiced ease, she watched the younger Hugh disappear within the star.

Strange to realize how much she missed that old Hugh.

Chapter 13

The limousine pulled up to a plain metal door well away from the regular entrance to the theater.

"Is that the stage door?" Jessica asked.

He shook his head as he pulled out his phone and tapped at the screen. "Too obvious. This play is prime paparazzi territory, and they'll be watching the stage door. So we're going in through the delivery entrance." His phone beeped with an incoming text. He glanced at it and stowed the phone in his pocket before he put his hand on the door handle. "Get ready to dash."

A bubble of delighted laughter escaped her throat as Hugh took her hand and pulled her across the sidewalk, his strides so long that she had to trot to keep up. It felt ridiculous until she saw a man with a camera running in their direction, shouting, "Hugh! Hugh Baker!"

Hugh angled his body between her and the photographer for the last two steps before the door swung open and they hustled into the utilitarian, behind-the-scenes area of the theater. A flash of bright light made her blink.

"Damn it!" Hugh muttered. "Now they'll be watching for the limo. I'll get a regular sedan to pick us up." He squeezed her hand. "I don't think they got you in the photo."

"Would you care if they did?" Jessica asked as they followed the stagehand who'd opened the door for them down a narrow hallway.

Surprise flickered across Hugh's face. "I thought *you* would. You weren't big on being photographed in the past."

"I was always worried that I would hurt your image." Because Hugh had been so concerned about it. She liked to match her sneakers to the color of her scrubs, but that was the extent of her attention to fashion. "Now I imagine your image is virtually bulletproof, and we're not an item, anyway."

He laced his fingers between hers. "I would be proud to be photographed with such an impressive woman by my side."

Their escort stopped in front of an elevator and pressed the call button. "The box is on level four. Someone will meet you at the elevator up there."

Hugh nodded his thanks while Jessica stared at him, fighting the unsettling pleasure evoked by his words and his touch. There was a potent, almost sexual intimacy in having his fingers thrust between hers. A shudder ran through her when he lifted her hand to brush his lips over her knuckles while they waited for the elevator door to slide open. The flood of sensation almost obliterated the fact that he'd called her impressive, but she hung on to the memory.

The backstage elevator was barely large enough to allow the two of them to squeeze in, which magnified her awareness of Hugh a thousandfold. His scent enveloped her, his clothing rubbed against hers—even his breathing was audible in the charged silence that fell between them while the creaky contraption crawled slowly upward.

"I want to kiss you." Hugh's voice was a rasp. "Badly."

She knew it would be a mistake, but she couldn't stop herself from looking up at him. His eyes blazed down at her, sending a flash of heat searing through her belly. "Yes," she whispered.

Somehow he pivoted in the small space and sandwiched her between the back wall and his muscled body, the living, breathing solidity of him making her feel fragile and feminine. Threading his fingers into her hair, he tilted her face up and brought his mouth down on hers in a kiss that merged promise and demand. She locked her fingers around the swell of his biceps and hung on as lips and tongues met in a dance of seduction that melted her insides into pure desire.

An electronic ping sounded from what seemed like a great distance, and Hugh lifted his mouth from hers. "I don't care if I see this damned play, but you deserve to." Before she could tell him she didn't care about the play, either, he had shifted his delectable body away from her and turned to face the door.

An older woman dressed in a black usher's uniform, with a pile of programs resting in the crook of her arm, stood just outside the elevator, her expression a mixture of awe and shock.

"Good evening," Hugh said without any sign of embarrassment. "We're going to Box C."

"I know . . . of course," she stuttered before composing herself and gesturing toward the luxuriously carpeted and wallpapered corridor. "This way, Mr. Baker. We're honored to have you with us this evening."

Hugh put his hand on the small of Jessica's back to allow her to go first. When it slid lower to rest on the upper curve of her buttock, she had to swallow a gasp of arousal. Hugh had always been clever at touching her in ways that seemed acceptable to the public eye but that sent her nervous system into a paroxysm of lust.

The woman led them to a paneled door, pulling out a key on a long chain attached to her belt to unlock it. Inside was a tiny antechamber with two spindly gilded chairs, hooks for coats, and another door set in the red velvet-covered wall. "Enjoy the show," she said, handing them each a program. "If you need to leave, you can open the door from the inside. When you want to return to your box, I'll be outside with the key." She stood silent for a moment, as though she were debating something.

"Would you like an autograph for someone?" Hugh asked with a smile.

"Oh, yes! My nephew is crazy about your Julian Best movies. He would be so thrilled."

Hugh took a program from her stack and pulled a silver pen from his pocket. "What's his name?"

"Eric with a *C*," she breathed, watching Hugh scrawl over the cover. When he handed her the signed program, she nodded approvingly. "Thank you for your graciousness. May I say that I know several actors who should take lessons from you on how to behave toward their admirers?"

"I appreciate that," Hugh said before he closed the door.

"How did you know that's what she wanted?" Jessica asked.

He sighed. "I've seen that look on a thousand faces. They have someone to whom they want to give the gift of my autograph, but they don't want to impose or seem unsophisticated. Since I appreciate their generally good intentions, I like to give them what they're hoping for."

For a moment, she cupped his cheek with her palm. "You're a surprisingly nice movie star."

He snorted. "That was more insult than compliment."

"Take it any way you want." Jessica gave him a quick slant of a smile.

His look went hot. "I'd rather take you."

His words were like a torch tossed onto a pile of dry kindling. Her body was immediately engulfed in flames of wanting.

She glanced around the closet-sized, windowless room with its two closed doors, one locked by the usher, the other leading to the private box for watching the play. "Is anyone else sitting in the box?" Her voice sounded almost muffled as it was absorbed by the thick, luxurious fabric on the walls and the plush carpeting on the floor.

A look of puzzlement narrowed his eyes for a split second, and then comprehension dawned. He had her against the velvet-covered wall before she even registered that he was moving. But before he did anything more than hold her there with a light pressure, he said, "Tell me this is what you meant for me to do."

"Yes," she said, bringing her hands up to undo the buttons of his shirt. "I've lost my mind, but this is what I want."

"Jess," he breathed, his gaze on her fingers as they traveled down the front of his chest, yanking the buttons out so she could flatten her palms against the lightly furred surface of him. She spread the silk open and kissed his pecs, his nipples, and the triangular indent at the base of his neck, inhaling his scent as she drank in the feel of his skin against her lips.

"Jess," he said again, his voice like sandpaper. When he flexed his hips into her, she felt the rock-hard length of his erection.

The ache between her legs intensified. "I want to keep touching like this but with you inside me," she said, working her hands down between them to his belt buckle.

He pushed her hands aside and practically tore open his belt and fly, releasing his cock with a shove of the waistband of his boxer briefs. She started to reach for him, but he was already yanking up her top and freeing the button at her waistband. He jerked down her zipper before kneeling to slide her trousers down to her ankles, holding them while she lifted first one foot and then the other. He parted her thighs and curled his fingers around them while he kissed his way up to her crotch, pressing his mouth to the thin lace covering her clit and flicking at it with his tongue.

Lightning seemed to streak through her body, sizzling across her nerve endings and hardening her nipples to points of pure sensation. She dug her fingers into his shoulders to anchor herself.

"More?" he asked, his breath a caress through her panties. "Or inside you?"

"I don't know."

His laugh was partly a groan as he ripped her panties down to her ankles so she could kick them away. He stood and slipped a finger inside her, his eyes on her face as he stroked in and out. Tension tightened in her belly, and she grabbed his wrist. "No, your cock inside me."

He produced a condom from his back pocket. "Thank God!" she said on a wave of relief.

"I'm a quick study," he said, rolling it on.

He bent and hooked one hand behind her knee to pull it up to his hip, opening her. She guided his cock into position and nearly came when he thrust up into her. The hollowness was filled and stretched but still aching for more. But he didn't move, just impaled her and stayed seated deep inside.

Her bare behind was pressed hard against the soft wall covering, her clit was pressed against the base of his cock, and she was filled with his hard length. "Oh, yes," she gasped. "Yes, like this."

"Raise your arms," he commanded as he tugged up the hem of her top and peeled it off over her head. Her bra followed, and his hands were on her breasts. First he cupped them against his palms, so sparks seemed to shower through her chest. Then his fingers were on her nipples, rolling and tweaking until her hips moved with his touch.

"My turn," Jessica said, leaning forward and tonguing his flat nipples while she traced the striations of his abs with her fingertips. His muscles rippled under her touch, and his breath rasped in gusts over her head, stirring her hair.

"I can't wait any longer," he said, seizing her other knee and lifting her off the floor completely, her back braced against the wall, his hands holding her legs against his waist. He began to move inside her, building fast to a hard, plunging rhythm. Her orgasm seemed to hit every muscle in her body, and she clenched around him, both inside and out, squeezing her thighs around his waist, digging her ankles into his butt, and clutching his shoulders with her hands while her body bowed hard into him.

He drove into her again, and she felt his climax pumping within her while he uttered her name on a cry of completion.

Then his weight was against her, using the wall to hold them locked together. His heart thundered against her chest, and the scents of aftershave and sex enveloped her. "Jess," he said. "Oh God, Jess."

His cock softened, and he shifted his hips to slip out of her, the small movement sending a gentle ripple of pleasure through her belly. "Ahh," she sighed.

He lowered her still-booted feet slowly to the carpet before he stepped back to rake his gaze down her body. "You are so incredibly sexy in nothing but boots and a necklace."

She realized she was naked and he was fully clothed but for an open shirt and fly. "Why are you so much better at undressing me than I am at undressing you?" she asked, looking around for her panties.

"Practice." He gave her a wicked grin and scooped up a wisp of lace from the corner before handing it to her.

Suddenly she remembered that he was the legendary Hugh Baker, fantasy lover of women everywhere. Which meant that she had forgotten it while they were having sex against the wall. He'd been just Hugh, pleasuring her with his mouth and hands and cock. Nothing more than a man she wanted to touch and be touched by.

That was dangerous thinking. He was not just Hugh. He would never be just Hugh again.

By the time she had pulled on her trousers and shrugged into her shirt, Hugh was put back together without any sign that he'd just had explosive standing sex. Grabbing her purse, she rummaged around to find her brush.

"Let me," he said, holding out his hand.

"You're going to fix my hair?" But she handed him the brush.

"I've spent a lot of time with stylists," he said, taking her shoulders and turning her around so her back was to him. Delicious tingles danced over her scalp as he stroked the brush down through her tangled tresses, stopping to unravel the occasional knot with deft fingers.

"I think I might have another orgasm right now," she said, her eyelids fluttering closed so she could savor the pampering. There was a moment's stillness before she felt his fingertips on her scalp, massaging ever so gently. "That, yes," she said on a happy exhalation.

"You see, I remember how much you loved to have your hair brushed." His voice was a low rumble close to her ear. "Although you weren't quite as vocal about it then."

A confusion of emotions and memories tumbled through her. The times she would come home from work and Hugh would sit her down on a kitchen chair, put a glass of wine in her hand, and go fetch her brush from the bedroom. Not only did he brush it until she sagged into boneless relaxation, but then he would braid it, the gentle tugging on her scalp an extended pleasure.

But he'd stopped doing it after his career began to take off. Instead, he would comment on her lack of makeup or suggest that they shop for a new outfit for her to wear to an upcoming Hollywood party.

She shoved the corrosive thoughts back into the dark corner where she tried to corral the guilt and pain from the end of their relationship.

The first lilting notes of a waltz drifted into their velvet antechamber, making it seem as though they were enclosed in a small, exquisite music box. "The play's starting." She could hear anticipation in his voice.

"Then let's go see it." She stood and took the brush from him.

"Intermission can't come soon enough," he said with a hot smile, but he opened the inner door for her.

She stepped through to find herself in a small box looking down on the stage. Four velvet-and-gilt armchairs were set in a precise arrangement, with two at the front of the box and two behind. Hugh leaned past her to shift the two front chairs to the side. "Sit here next to me," he said, indicating one of the back row chairs. "I don't want to be seen. It might distract the audience from the play."

She sank onto the cushioned seat while his fame pressed down on her shoulders like a fifty-pound bag of kibble. She eyed him surreptitiously in the dim glow cast by the spotlights trained on the still-closed curtain. It struck her as awful to be that famous.

He seemed to sense her gaze, because he reached out and took her hand, resting it on her chair's arm, his fingers tucked around hers.

The curtain went up, and his grip tightened slightly as he leaned forward, his attention on the stage.

She tried to keep her focus on the drama playing out before them, but after about ten minutes, she caught a flash of movement out of the corner of her eye. Turning slightly, she watched as Hugh mimicked a gesture one of the actors had just made. He must have been trying it out to add to his own repertoire. He'd said at dinner that the young actor cast as the lead was brilliant. It seemed that Hugh was willing to learn from him. Her respect for his dedication to his craft surged, and she squeezed his hand.

Hugh swung around to catch her watching him and lifted her hand to his lips for a brief but potent kiss. However, his attention went back to the play almost immediately. Jessica angled herself in her chair so she could watch him and the action on the stage at the same time. Several more times he imitated movements, but on a couple of occasions he shook his head and frowned.

When the curtain came down for intermission, Hugh rose and pulled her up with him. "Let's go someplace more private," he said with a wicked smile as he led her through the door to the antechamber.

But reality had laid a cold blanket on her reactions to him. When he wound his arms around her, she braced her forearms against his chest to hold him away. "I want to know what you didn't like about the play."

His eyebrows drew down. "What I didn't like?"

"You shook your head a couple of times. Why?"

"Good God, I don't remember or care right now." His gaze drifted to her lips. "I have better things to do."

She shook her head. "You were copying gestures, which was fascinating. But I'm curious about what earned your disapproval."

His grip on her eased slightly as he thought. "The moment when Finn sees Catriona for the first time. I thought he reacted wrong. He doesn't give a damn about anything other than possessing her body, but he played it as a mooning, love-struck boy. It was too soft and emotional for the ruthless man Finn is." He focused on her again. "Now can I get back to possessing *your* body?"

Before she could stop him, he brought his mouth down against her neck, sipping at her skin. Her body forgot all about the burden of Hugh's celebrity and ignited with the same pure lust Finn had felt for Catriona. But she kept her arms between them. "Isn't it hard to be so famous?" she gasped out as electric desire ricocheted down into her gut.

Hugh grunted and drew her earlobe in between his lips.

"Oh, Hugh, there!" She tilted her head so he could have better access, and he responded by tracing the whorls of her ear with his tongue.

All the words she'd planned to use as a barrier between them evaporated, and she found herself straddling his lap while he sat on one of the little chairs and drove up inside her. His hands massaged her breasts, winding the tension tighter and tighter until her orgasm crashed through her. He kept still as her muscles clenched around him but then burst into a whirlwind of motion, driving hard and deep until he climaxed with his mouth open over her nipple, his groans vibrating against her.

She dropped her head to his shoulder while the aftershocks spun through her in exquisite succession. As she sat splayed over his thighs, she wondered idly how Hugh managed to short-circuit her good judgment, her modesty, and her sense of self-preservation. Yet she couldn't regret the indulgence. It had been too long since she'd felt this kind of soul-searing abandon. Since she'd given him back his ring, in fact.

That thought made her sit up.

"What's the rush?" Hugh asked, putting his palm behind her head and pressing her back toward his shoulder.

"I need to visit the ladies' room."

"Of course," he said, his hands going to her waist to lift her off his lap and set her on her feet. He traced down her cheek with one finger. "The line should be gone by now."

She stood a moment to take in the length of him sprawled in the spindly chair, the black silk shirt hanging open from his shoulders to expose his sculpted chest, his fly unzipped with his still partially erect cock resting in the nest of dark hair, his eyes glinting with almost bemused satisfaction. Any photographer would sell his soul to capture Hugh Baker in this pose.

Grabbing her panties, she dressed quickly. "How long until the play starts again?" she asked as she scooped up her purse.

Hugh glanced at his watch. "Maybe another five minutes. It depends on what's happening backstage." He smiled. "That's the fun of live theater. Disaster is always imminent." He began to button his shirt. "You don't have to worry. When you're in a box, you can come and go at any time."

"I don't want to miss a minute of the play, though." She opened the door as little as possible to slip out, just in case anyone was lurking in the corridor, hoping to spy a famous audience member. When she dashed into the bathroom, what she saw in the mirror made her swear. Her whole face and neck were rosy with the flush of sexual satisfaction, her lips were swollen and her lipstick smeared, and her hair was a crazed mass of waves. Anyone who saw her would know exactly what she'd just done.

After a glance around to make sure no one in the restroom was paying any attention to her, she repaired the damage to her hair and makeup. There was nothing she could do about the glow that colored her skin or shone in her eyes, so she stayed in the shadows as she darted back to the box and knocked on the door.

"I missed you," Hugh said, capturing her in his arms as soon as he let her in. He was bending to kiss her when she put her hand across his mouth.

"I put all my face paint back on so I don't look like I just had sex in a theater box. Don't mess it up," she said.

He chuckled against her palm and then flicked it with his tongue, the warm, moist touch sending a tingle down her arm.

"Stop it," she said, pulling her hand away.

"Tempted?" he asked with a wicked look while he slid one hand down to squeeze her behind before he turned to open the inner door.

The curtain music ended just as they sat down.

Jessica felt guilty, because Hugh didn't respond to the play as he had in the first act. Instead he was attentive to her reactions, which led her to focus on the show more closely.

By the time the curtain came down again, she had tears streaming down her cheeks. "That was amazing," she said, accepting the little package of tissues Hugh pulled from his breast pocket so she could mop her face. When the audience surged to their feet for a standing ovation, Jessica joined them. Hugh stood as well but faded back into the shadows of the box so his face was hidden.

The actors were still bowing when Hugh seized her wrist midclap. "I've arranged for us to go backstage, so we need to leave now."

Sure enough, the usher was hovering near the box door when Hugh opened it. She led them to the same secret elevator and sent them back down into the bowels of the building, where another escort took over. By the time their companion said, "In here," and pulled open yet another door, Jessica had no idea where she was in relationship to the stage. "It's Ms. Jocanda's dressing room," the stagehand said, standing aside to let them pass. "She said to treat it like your own." He closed the door behind him.

"Wow! Rose Jocanda offered you her dressing room." The British actress was the top marquee name in the play. Famous for her versatility and ability to convert quirky roles into star turns, she had won a couple of Oscars and earned several Tony nominations. "I guess it would be uncool to ask for a selfie with her."

"Ask away," Hugh said. "She's used to it."

Jessica looked around the small, tidy room. The most prominent feature was a large mirror framed by lightbulbs hung over a Formica countertop loaded with cosmetics and a couple of wig stands. A rolling rack filled with colorful costumes stood against one wall, while a small sofa spanned the other. On the table in front of it, a vase of yellow roses added an extra pop of color.

"It looks just like I imagined a theatrical dressing room would," Jessica said. "Only neater."

Hugh sat down on the sofa. "Rosie's famous for her tidiness. She says it's too unsettling to have things jumbled up in her private space."

Jessica was fascinated by this glimpse into the actress's psyche. "What else does she say?"

"About what?" Hugh patted the cushion beside him.

"Anything." Jessica sank down beside him. "Acting."

"Acting? I'm not sure I've ever talked with her about it. I can tell you about the time we finished shooting a scene and decided to go swimming in—"

The door flew open, and Rose Jocanda strode in, yanking her blonde wig off as she walked. She perched it on one of the empty stands and turned, her dark hair still pinned flat to her scalp. "I had to get that dreadful, itchy thing off my head." She held out her arms as Hugh and Jessica rose. "Hugh, love! So good to see you!"

Jessica watched in awed bemusement as the actress threw her arms around Hugh and kissed him soundly on the lips, leaving a smear of her vivid red lipstick on his skin. As soon as she released him, Rose reached up to scrub it off with her thumb. "Don't want to make your lovely companion jealous," she said before offering her hand to Jessica. "And you are a talented veterinarian, Hugh tells me."

The actress had the same crackling, larger-than-life aura Hugh did, only hers was quintessentially feminine. Even the weirdly exaggerated stage makeup couldn't overwhelm the woman's delicate bone structure or the intelligence shining in her green eyes.

"Yes, I'm Jessica Quillen, and I'm a vet," Jessica said, shaking hands. "You were amazing in the play. But you're incredible in every role. I'm a great admirer of yours."

"You know, people think we get tired of hearing that, but we never do. Thank you so much," Rose said with such utter sincerity that Jessica almost believed her. "Let me fluff my hair and then we'll snap a photo with you and Hugh. I can't resist a selfie."

Hugh threw Jessica an "I told you so" look.

"She's only including me because we're a package deal tonight," Jessica muttered while Rose returned her hair to a cascade of glossy waves.

"There." The actress put down her brush, checked her makeup, and picked up a cell phone from the countertop. "Hugh in the middle so we're the bookends." Rose arranged them and held the phone high. "Always shoot down to hide the chin sag."

After taking several photos, she tapped away at her phone.

"You're posting it on social media, aren't you?" Hugh's tone was indulgent, though.

"Hell, yes," Rose said. "Me with the fabulous Hugh Baker's arm around me? That's an event to be shared. And I sent you a copy, too, so you can share it with Jessica, who can digitally cut me right out of the picture." She winked.

"You were brilliant in the scene with Frederick," Hugh said. "You gave us that tiny, first glimpse of the anguish beneath the steel, just enough to make your ultimate unraveling entirely believable. Well done."

Rose lit up at Hugh's words. "I kept overplaying that scene at first, but I pulled back a little bit more every performance until I felt it was tightly coiled enough to explode at the end." She cupped Hugh's cheek. "You can always put your finger on the key moment. It's a great gift to hear I did it right."

This time Jessica believed Rose meant her gratitude. That an actress who played Shakespeare and Ibsen valued Hugh's compliment on her performance opened her eyes to another side of him. She'd been focused on his celebrity, not on his talent. Rose reminded her that Hugh had worked hard to hone his acting skills when they'd been together, studying great performances in movies, attending plays to absorb live theater, taking lessons from acting coaches he admired. Tonight, during the first act, he'd demonstrated that he was still upping his game.

"I mustn't monopolize you," Rose said, checking her hair in the mirror again. "The whole cast is dying to see you. And of course to meet your charming friend."

She led them out the door and down a narrow hallway to a lounge packed with people talking and taking photos with their cell phones.

"Darlings, I've brought Hugh Baker," Rose said in a voice that silenced the buzz of conversation. "And his friend Jessica."

Jessica had to give Rose credit for introducing her when she was clearly an afterthought. Although she would have been just as happy to fade into the background in order to observe Hugh in his element.

"Oh my God, Hugh Baker!" Dorian Greer, the young actor who had been given the lead over more prominent candidates, raced up and pumped Hugh's hand. He bestowed a sweet smile on Jessica before turning to the room. "This man is the reason I am standing in this place with all of you. He championed me for the role and supported me through all the auditions. I owe him my career."

Jessica sensed Hugh's discomfort in the tightening of his grip on her hand and his subtle shift to move her slightly in front of him.

"Let's not get ahead of ourselves," Hugh said with a smile. "Your career is up to you and your talent, which you have in abundance."

It was interesting that Hugh had told her how terrific the young man was in his role without mentioning that he had been involved in getting Dorian the part.

"All right, I will take the hint." Dorian flung up one hand. "No more public gratitude, but it will always be here." He touched his chest over his heart with a graceful gesture.

After that, a parade of people came up to greet Hugh. Some were clearly old friends, some were awestruck, some were fawning, but everyone treated him as though he were a visiting monarch. And he played the role well, responding with graciousness, encouragement, and courtesy, yet he was always cloaked in that impenetrable detachment that Jessica knew all too well. Only with Rose and Dorian did he let down his guard.

Jessica was introduced to all the actors and included in several selfies with Hugh. She finally excused herself from further photos since she knew that no one, except possibly Hugh, wanted her there. Besides, it was entertaining to watch her sometimes irascible ex-fiancé pose with a smile on his face that she suspected was entirely false.

When they began passing around glasses of wine, Hugh leaned down to murmur in Jessica's ear, "Theater wine is god-awful. Let's go find some good stuff to drink."

"I don't want to take you away from your friends," she said.

"I'm having dinner with Rose and her husband next week, so we can catch up then." He started down the hallway.

"She's far from your only friend in the room," Jessica said, letting him pull her along with him. "In fact, I'd say you have at least fifty."

Hugh threw her an irritated look and kept walking.

"Okay, so they were mostly people who wanted to say they'd met Hugh Baker, but you must like some of them. By the way, why didn't you tell me you'd helped Dorian get the part?"

Hugh halted at a spot where two corridors intersected, glancing right and left. "It's a damned rabbit warren down here."

"Go right. I remember that weird pipe hanging down."

Hugh made the turn down the hallway. "He exaggerated. I was impressed with his performance in a play in LA and hooked him up with a hungry junior agent. When this part came up, I put in a good word for him with the director. Nothing heroic."

"Maybe not heroic, but generous."

"If I can't use my influence to help talent find its audience, what's the point?"

"Some people might consider Dorian competition."

Hugh kept walking. "If he's better than I am, he deserves the part." His tone turned cynical. "I don't worry much about talented actors. It's the famous ones who could take the plum roles away from me."

"No one's more famous than you are."

"The public is fickle." By some miracle, they had arrived at the elevator, and Hugh pushed the call button. "I'm not getting younger, whereas Julian Best never ages."

"They wouldn't dare replace you as Julian!"

"They can and they will, as soon as I cross whatever invisible line the producers decide is too old to appeal to the broadest demographic."

The elevator door glided open, and they squeezed into the small space together. Hugh slid his arm around her waist and pulled her against his side.

"Does that bother you?" Jessica asked, trying not to be sidetracked by the feel of his body pressed to hers.

"Sometimes. And other times I almost wish they would find another Julian. Thank God Gavin allows Julian to grow and change in his books or I might die of boredom."

"Is that why you've never done Broadway? Because you would play the same role night after night?"

The elevator doors opened, and he moved them forward just enough to step out into the hallway. "My agent tells me I can't afford to do Broadway."

"You would have been terrific as Finn in this play," she said as they walked toward the door.

"Julian always takes precedence." His voice held the tiniest edge of regret. Pulling out his fancy phone, he tapped at the screen and waited for a returning ping. "The sedan is right out front." He took her hand. "Ready to make a run for it?"

Jessica felt like the heroine in one of Hugh's movies as he threw open the door and pulled her along with him at a jog. Despite the unassuming dark sedan, two photographers lay in wait, shouting as they ran beside Jessica and Hugh, cameras flashing. Hugh ignored them, heading straight for the car without breaking stride.

The chauffeur had the back door open, so Hugh helped Jessica scoot onto the back seat before joining her. The door slammed shut, but the photographers kept shooting through the window until the driver pulled away from the curb.

"Wow! That was weird." Jessica blinked several times to clear the flash from her eyes.

"I'm sorry you had to deal with that." Hugh's voice was tight with fury. "Those were bottom feeders. The real pros don't bother me without my permission, because they know they'll get more access that way."

"You can't control what other people do," she said.

"You'd be surprised what you can control." He sounded hard and jaded, but then his voice shifted to a purring rumble. "Can I tempt you back to the hotel room?"

"Twice wasn't enough?" she said, even as flickers of heat licked along her nerves.

He lifted her hair to kiss the side of her neck so his breath grazed her ear when he spoke. "Never enough when it comes to you."

Arousal shuddered through her. Shaking her head was the hardest thing she'd ever done. "I've got to work tomorrow."

To her surprise, he kissed her again but leaned back against the seat. "As do I." He gave the driver Jessica's address.

"And you have to worry about how you look for the cameras." No one cared if she had bags under her eyes, but for Hugh it was a different story.

"Meryl assures me that exhaustion makes Julian look all the more authentic." He gave her a whimsical smile.

A spear of jealousy sank itself into her chest. "Did she really notice that you looked tired? I'm sorry."

"Don't be. I used it as an excuse to avoid her plan to sightsee around Boston."

"You didn't want to see the Old North Church, where Paul Revere hung his lanterns? It's very historic."

"If you'd be my tour guide, I would happily view it."

Jessica couldn't stop a satisfied smile from curling her lips. "We could visit Plimoth Plantation, too, and see how the Pilgrims lived."

"I draw the line at bad actors pretending to be—" Jessica's cell phone emitted an electronic claxon that made Hugh flinch. "What the hell is that?"

She was already yanking it out of her bag. "A medical emergency. I have to call my service. Can you ask the driver to head for the clinic?"

She hit the speed dial for her answering service to find out that a cat she'd spayed the day before had ripped out her stitches and was bleeding from the wound. She told the owners to meet her at the clinic so she could resuture the incision.

"What's the problem?" Hugh asked.

"The main one? Cats are jerks," she said with a laugh before she explained the issue. "Now I've got to decide which one of my vet techs to roust out of bed to assist."

"Does it require a trained professional or just an extra set of hands?" He held up his hands like a surgeon who'd just scrubbed in.

"You want to help with cat surgery? This isn't like playing a doctor in a movie. It involves real blood and guts. Well, hopefully not guts, unless the problem is worse than I think it is." She scrolled down to Caleb's number.

"You know I'm not afraid to get my hands dirty." He sounded pissed off and something else. Insulted? Hurt?

She lowered her phone. A willing helper was all she needed. "Since I know you can take direction, I will accept your generous offer. Caleb will be grateful, since you've saved him a midnight trip to the clinic."

He nodded, and she caught the look of satisfaction on his face in the glow of the streetlights. "How do you know I can take direction?"

"Because your appearance at the clinic made an impression on Carla. She's been reading up on you—and sharing it with me." Jessica had listened, fascinated by the information her office manager had tracked down on the internet.

"My apologies."

"No, it makes for very entertaining lunch conversation, especially when it's contradictory. One question I could lay to rest for her was whether you are gay or not. Of course, I couldn't rule out bi."

Hugh snorted out a laugh. "That was from years ago. I can't remember how that rumor got started."

"Well, it seemed at direct odds with the orgy of supermodels you supposedly participated in at some Las Vegas hotel. Although I suppose some of the supermodels could have been guys." She chuckled. "As far as I can tell, the only thing you haven't done is been kidnapped by aliens."

He didn't laugh this time. "That doesn't happen anymore, Jess, I swear. The PR people at my agency are very savvy. They make sure none of the gossip rags steps over the line with any really libelous stories."

"I didn't believe any of it," Jessica said, surprised at his intensity. "I know it's just made up to sell papers."

"It's foul and unsavory. I don't blame you for not wanting to be dragged through the mud like that."

She realized that he was thinking about their past together. "That wasn't why I—"

The car came to a stop and the driver interrupted her. "We're here."

Chapter 14

Shareena and Cornell Adams stood in front of the clinic, peering hopefully at the sedan. Jessica swung her door open before the driver could get to it. "How's Zora doing?"

Cornell lifted the cat carrier he held, from which loud meows issued. "She's not bleeding so bad now, but she isn't happy."

"Her complaining's got nothing to do with the stitches," Shareena said. "She just hates being in that case. We probably should have kept her in there tonight, but you can hear how she feels about being shut up. I thought she'd just settle down and sleep with us on the bed, but she woke up and got to jumping around. I heard her and saw the blood and bruises on her little belly. I feel so bad about that."

Cornell put his arm around his wife's shoulders and gave them a squeeze. "You can't stop Zora from being who she is, a high-energy little kitty."

Hugh had come around the car to join the group. "This is Hugh Baker," Jessica said. "Hugh, Shareena and Cornell Adams, the parents of our patient, Zora."

"Pleased to meet you." Hugh held out his hand, but it took a drawn-out moment for Shareena to stop staring long enough to shake it.

"You're famous. From the spy movies," she said before turning to her husband. "Cornell, you love those."

"Sure do," he said, releasing his wife to give Hugh's hand a hearty shake. "I can't wait for the next one. It's been a while."

"I'm pleased to hear that," Hugh said. "I'm in New York because we're shooting it right now."

"I like them, too," Shareena said, "but Cornell's a real fanatic. He knows the dates they were released and everything."

Jessica had been listening with half an ear as she unlocked the metal screen that stretched across the whole storefront of the clinic and stooped to lift it.

"Let me do that." Hugh's voice came from right behind her as he reached down to grip the handle. She stood back and admired the way his lean body straightened in one smooth motion, taking the heavy screen upward with him.

"Thanks," she said, fitting the key into the front-door lock. "Okay, let's get Zora stitched up again." She flicked on the lights. "Hugh, can you grab the cat case and come with me? Shareena, Cornell, make yourselves comfortable." That was a bit of a stretch, since her waiting area held a mishmash of donated chairs, some of them pretty flimsy. "You can make tea or coffee in the kitchen down the hall, if you'd like."

"We're good, Doc," Cornell said. "We're grateful you'd come in to take care of Zora in the middle of the night."

"Of course," Jessica said. "She's my patient."

She headed down the hall, hearing Hugh's footsteps behind her, along with the cat's continued vocalizations. She pointed to the door into the surgery room. "If you'd put Zora on the floor in there, I'll grab us both some scrubs. Meet me in my office."

Rummaging around in the supply closet, she pulled out her own scrubs and then a set of Diego's, laughing when Geode shot in through the closet's open door to blink at her indignantly from a dark corner. Although most of her staff wore their scrubs to work, she kept spares for emergencies like this. She carried them to her office to find Hugh inspecting the photos displayed on the wall.

"You have a lot of grateful patients," he said as he accepted the folded green scrubs and placed them on her desk. He began to unbutton his shirt. "Tell me what we'll be doing with Zora," he said, yanking the shirttails out of his trousers and shrugging out of it.

The sight of all that bare skin flowing over the curves of his muscles made her suck in a breath as the low simmer from their earlier lovemaking flared into full-on flames again. Thank God he pulled the baggy top on before he went to work on his trousers. But how on earth could a man look so good wearing shapeless green cotton?

"Um, what?" she said, remembering he'd asked her a question.

A devilish glint danced in his eyes. "I asked you what I'll be helping you do with the cat. But you seem distracted."

"That's because I wasn't expecting you to do a striptease in my office."

He looked taken aback. "Sorry. I'm used to changing costumes in front of a waiting camera crew, so I didn't even think about it." The turquoise of his eyes went hot. "However, I'd be delighted if *you'd* do a striptease."

She gave him a saucy smile as she headed for the door. "Nope. I'll change in the scrub-in room and meet you in surgery."

"Don't I need to scrub in, too?"

"The scrub-in room is just a sink in a closet. It barely holds one person. You can wash your hands when I'm done."

All the way down the hallway, she got lost in a vision of Hugh pressed up against her back at the sink in the tiny washroom, his arms around her, the soapy water sliding over their skin as they scrubbed each other's hands.

Oh dear God, she just kept slipping further and further under his spell.

Hugh came back from washing his hands to find Jessica placing a cloth-wrapped package on a table beside some tubes and a syringe, her movements practiced and efficient. Her hair was tucked under a surgical cap, a face mask dangled from her neck, and she wore bright purple scrubs. She looked every inch the brilliant, compassionate doctor, and he felt an odd surge of pride, as though he had some claim on her success.

"You never told me what we'll be doing with Zora," he said when the cat yowled in protest at her continued confinement.

"First, I'll sedate her. Then you'll help me intubate her for the anesthesia." She pointed to the package on the table. "You'll open the surgical pack *exactly* the way I tell you, so it remains sterile. Then I'll do whatever is necessary to close up her incision again. You'll turn off the anesthesia and she'll wake up good as new." Her smile turned crooked. "At least, that's what happens in a perfect world."

"You mean something could go wrong with this?" Such was his faith in his ex-fiancée's skill that he hadn't even considered the possibility of a problem.

"Zora's a young, healthy cat, and she was fine with the anesthesia yesterday, but there's always a risk with any kind of surgery." Jessica shrugged. "The risk is just far greater if you don't do it."

"A balancing act," Hugh said, knowing her shrug covered up a profound concern for the cat's well-being. "You said that about your clinic before."

"That was more about managing it. When it comes to my patients' lives, there's a whole different level of balance."

He took a deep breath. "What now?"

"Let me show you how to work the anesthesia machine." She pulled over a rolling contraption with many dangling tubes and a large green tank attached to it. Lifting one of the tubes, she said, "This is what you'll attach to Zora's tube." She pointed to a large silver dial. "This controls the percentage of isoflurane mixed with the oxygen. I want you to set it on two once we hook up Zora's tube and adjust it if I ask you to. At the end I'll ask you to turn it to zero to stop the flow of anesthesia but not oxygen."

Now Hugh was feeling a punch of adrenaline. "Got it."

"I need you to get Zora out of her case. You can put it up on the counter there. It shouldn't be hard, since she seems quite eager to exit."

Zora was now banging her paws against the metal gate at the front of the case. Hugh picked it up and found himself being stared at by a small, black cat with huge green eyes. "She makes a lot of noise for such a little creature," he said as he set the case down and unlatched the gate. He knew enough to hold the gate closed until he was ready to grab the cat.

However, once she was released from her prison, she calmed down and snuggled into Hugh's arms. He stroked her glossy fur before turning to bring her to the operating table. "You shouldn't be so trusting, Zora," he said before looking at Jessica. "Now I feel guilty about delivering her to you."

Jessica chuckled. "You have to remember that I'm helping her. Not to mention that she has no idea what's about to happen to her. That's the beauty of not having the capacity to anticipate the future. Sometimes I think animals are luckier than humans that way." Jessica gave Zora a quick scratch under the chin.

Hugh's guilt about capturing Zora ratcheted up a notch when she began to purr. Then Jessica went into full vet mode, issuing instructions swiftly but allowing him enough time to follow one before she went on to the next.

"Put her down on her stomach. Put one hand on the back of her neck to hold her." Jessica felt around the top of the cat's hind leg for a brief moment before she inserted the syringe halfway between her thumb and index finger. Zora barely flinched. "This will relax her enough so she won't mind the tube."

Sure enough, he could feel the cat's muscles soften and go limp under his hands.

"Okay, now is when you earn your pay," she said with a glinting smile. "Hold her head with your left hand and stick the thumb and forefinger of your right hand behind her canines so you can open her mouth. Stretch her neck a little forward to open up her throat for me."

Jessica pulled out the cat's tongue and stuck a long swab down her throat. "This is just lidocaine to suppress her gag reflex." She picked up a plastic tube, held it against the side of the cat's head, and adjusted a piece of gauze tied around the tube. Pulling out the cat's tongue again, she slipped the tube down Zora's open throat. Hugh felt the urge to gag on Zora's behalf, but the cat barely twitched.

"Okay, attach the machine and turn on the isoflurane." She was already tying the gauze around the back of Zora's head as Hugh fitted the tubes together. He set the dial precisely on the two and turned back to find Jessica doing something with another syringe inserted into a thin tube attached to the larger one. Now that his nerves had settled, his interest was caught, so he asked, "What does that do?"

She removed the syringe. "It inflates the little balloon at the end of the tube, which holds the whole apparatus in place. That way the tube can't be dislodged before we want it to be. All right, let's roll her onto her back so I can see what's going on."

If the little cat had been relaxed before, now she seemed almost boneless as he moved her. Her stillness gave him a shiver of unease because it mimicked death so closely. Jessica deftly secured the cat's legs to the table so she was splayed out, the wound on her belly clearly visible. She gave it a quick scan, nodded, and said, "Okay, you monitor her while I go scrub in and get sterile."

His fragile confidence evaporated. "Wait, you're leaving me alone with a wounded cat on anesthesia when I have no idea what I'm doing?"

She chuckled. "I'll be just down the hall. Yell if anything changes."

His nerves tightened and buzzed in a way they hadn't in years. He might have a perfectly functional pair of hands, as he'd pointed out, but he didn't know how to make sure the cat was all right. He spent what seemed like an hour flicking his eyes between the gauge on the anesthesia machine and the splayed-out cat. Neither one moved.

Jessica came back into the room with her hands gloved and her surgical mask over the bottom of her face. "See, I was only gone five minutes. And Zora survived."

"Longest five minutes of my life," Hugh muttered.

Jessica's gray eyes held a dancing light of amusement above the mask. "Now you're going to open the surgical pack. We don't want to break the sterile field, so I need you to follow my directions to the letter."

It was like choreographing an action scene. He had to fold back each layer of the cloth in a precise order, never allowing his hands to cross the top of the pack, and move to a new position at the side of the table for the next corner. When he was done, Jessica carefully lifted the sterile inner pack onto a steel tray beside the surgical table and opened it, revealing a gleaming array of scalpels, scissors, and needles.

What blood there was from the wound had dried, so Jessica gently wiped it away. Now he could see the torn and bruised edges of the skin with the ripped-out stitches on one side. "What's that other set of stitches underneath? They seem fine."

Jessica had begun cutting away the frayed skin at the edge of the wound, which made Hugh a little queasy. "Those are in the subcutaneous fat. There's another set below them in the internal body wall." She glanced up to flash him a dry look. "I have to do a lot of sewing in this job. My mother thinks it's hilarious, since she offered to teach me when I was a kid and I refused. Now I'm going to flush it with some saline solution to clean it." She picked up a syringe and squirted out the blood and gunk from the wound. "Now turn the iso down to one, please."

Her running commentary as she worked made Hugh forget about his earlier squeamishness. She handled the cat with a fascinating combination of confidence and gentleness. He couldn't take his eyes off her gloved hands, even as she began pushing the needle through the cat's skin. "Could you blot up that blood for me?" she asked as fresh bleeding began to obscure the skin. "There's gauze on the surgical tray. Just don't touch anything else."

He pinched up the gauze and carefully pressed it against the wound, soaking up the blood so Jessica could see where to place the needle next. An emotion he couldn't name welled up inside him. Maybe they weren't exactly saving the cat's life, but they were giving her a chance to heal and be healthy and happy. It seemed so much more real and important than anything he did.

"Since Cornell says Zora's a high-energy kitty, this time I'm going to set six simple interrupted sutures and tie off each one separately. That way if she pulls one out, the other five should still hold." She did something to the thread and snipped it off. He could see the neat purple stitch with a small knot on one side.

The next time the blood accumulated, Hugh blotted it up without Jessica having to ask. He fell into the rhythm of the stitching and knotting, anticipating how to help her. When she finished up the last suture, regret rolled through him. He wanted to keep working side by side with her, their bodies touching in a way that had nothing to do with sex but made him feel necessary to her. It reminded him of how a scene could flow when all the actors were in the zone, drawing energy from one another to feed the emotions they were portraying. When was the last time he'd felt that way?

"Roll her over on her side now." Jessica interrupted his thoughts. "Hit the two-minute button on the microwave."

"Are we feeding Zora a meal right after her surgery?" he asked, following her instructions.

Jessica chuckled as she spread out a towel beside the cat. "No, we're warming up a rice bag to make her cozy as she comes out of the anesthesia."

Hugh helped her shift the limp little body onto the towel. Jessica stood stroking the cat while they waited for the microwave to ding.

"Lay it along her back," she said when Hugh retrieved the toasty fabric cushion. He held the rice bag in place while Jessica wrapped the towel snugly around Zora.

"Okay, take the iso to zero," Jessica said. "But we'll keep the oxygen flowing to help her recover."

Hugh did his job while Jessica untied the gauze bow behind the cat's head. "As soon as she starts to stir, I'll deflate the balloon and take the tube out."

"How long does it take for her to wake up?"

"Somewhere between two and five minutes."

"I feel like she'll be mad at me for getting her into this," Hugh said, watching the still, white bundle with just a small furry head protruding.

"She may be, but she'll forget quickly, especially if you pet her. Animals tend to be quite forgiving. It's both a strength and a weakness."

The cat's throat moved, and Jessica became a blur of motion as she deflated and removed the tube before Zora became aware enough to be uncomfortable. "Now we just wait for her to wake up fully," Jessica said, stripping off her gloves and untying her surgical mask to let it hang down around her neck.

Hugh removed his gloves and leaned his hip against the counter, watching Jess while she watched the cat. "Thank you for trusting me to help you," he said. "That was one of the more fascinating experiences of my life."

Jessica gave him a startled glance. "It wasn't rocket science."

"It was . . . important."

Her gray eyes went luminous. "That's a nice thing to say. Not enough people feel that way about spaying a rescue cat."

"We helped another living being."

Zora let out a hoarse mew and began to struggle within the towel. Jessica loosened the fabric so the cat could move. She met Hugh's gaze again. "Now you know why I work long hours."

"Now I *understand* why you work long hours." Guilt raked through him. "I'm sorry I didn't get it eight years ago."

"Neither one of us understood what the other wanted," she said, her voice soft.

It was the wrong place and time, but the need to know overwhelmed him. "Jess, why did you leave me?"

"What?" She jerked her head up to give him an angry glare. "I told you when I gave back the ring, and it was hard enough then."

He rubbed at the back of his neck, hating to admit the truth. "I didn't hear a word you said after you handed the ring back to me. I was too . . . upset." Devastated. Angry. Hurt.

Abandoned.

The cat rolled onto her stomach and looked around woozily. Jessica petted Zora's head. "I need to care for Zora right now," she said.

"Of course. I shouldn't have asked." He straightened. "What can I do to help?"

She continued to stroke the cat. "Nothing. I'll take it from here."

He wanted to kick himself for destroying the fragile trust that had been built between them. His attention caught on the detritus on the surgical table and tray. "Let me clean up. Just tell me where to put things."

Her shoulders rose and fell as she drew in a deep breath. "Thanks," she said with forced courtesy. "Put the scalpel handles, forceps, and scissors in the sink. The techs will take care of them in the morning."

He carried her tools to the sink, setting them down carefully. As he followed her instructions and disposed of the other items in the proper receptacles, Jessica seemed to relax in his presence again. She scooped up the cat in the towel. "I'm going to let the Adamses see that Zora is okay but I'll keep her here in a cage overnight."

"I'll join you and give Cornell an autograph." He was using every weapon at his disposal to overcome his mistake.

This time her gratitude seemed genuine. "He'll love that."

The Adamses were relieved and appreciative that Zora's surgery was successful. Cornell grinned with delight over the autograph Hugh scrawled on a sheet of paper he found on the front desk.

Hugh locked the door behind them while Jessica carried the cat into the back to settle her in an empty cage. He followed the sound of running water and found Jessica washing up in the tiny scrub-in room. "Go change your clothes," she said, her gaze on her hands. "Leave the scrubs on the floor in my office." She gave him a quick upward glance and strained smile. "You did great."

He'd screwed up royally.

Jessica took her time dressing, partly because she was dog tired but mostly because she wanted to make sure Hugh was fully clothed before she faced him again. He'd reopened all the old emotional wounds, and she didn't need the physical issue to make the situation more fraught.

Why did he care eight years later what had led her to break the engagement? She had rehearsed her farewell speech over and over again, stomach clenching and tears streaming down her cheeks. Now he admitted that he hadn't even paid attention to her painfully chosen words? Or did he just not remember?

She yanked the brush through her hair, wincing as it snagged on a knot.

She didn't owe him any more explanation, and she should just tell him so, rather than excavating all that agony. Yet she couldn't ignore her new perspective on Hugh—his kindness with his fans, his generosity toward a young actor, his stalwart assistance tonight, even though he'd looked like he might throw up a couple of times. She smiled at that. Not to mention how he made her feel when he touched her. Like he found her the most extraordinary, fascinating lover he'd ever had.

She sighed, knowing she would put herself through the wringer again because the memory of their love still wielded power over her heart. Or maybe she was just a sucker, as Aidan claimed.

She adjusted her carnelian necklace in the mirror before she marched out the door.

Hugh sat in her ergonomic chair with his head tilted back and his eyes closed. A shadow of whiskers darkened his jawline, adding a slight roughness that enhanced his dark charisma.

Remorse nipped at her. She hoped it was true that the camera would love the fatigued look. "You should get some sleep," she said softly.

He lifted his head and opened his eyes slowly, making the revelation of the brilliant turquoise all the more dramatic. "Honestly, I'm too hyped up to sleep. I was just reliving the surgery. Who knows when I'll need to play a brilliant veterinarian?"

Jessica snorted at his use of "brilliant" before she sat down in the bilious-green vinyl chair that stood in front of the desk. "You asked why I broke the engagement."

He sat up. "I had no right to—"

She lifted her hand, palm out. "Maybe I can say it better now because I have more distance to give me perspective." She laced her fingers together on her knees and stared down at them, traveling back in time to her younger self to find the emotions she needed words for. "You were like a meteor blazing across the sky, growing brighter and brighter with each step you took toward your goal. I could see that you were going to succeed, because you had the talent and the drive and the discipline. But you needed a different partner to support you."

A strange, guttural sound made her glance up. Hugh had braced his elbows on her desk and dropped his head into his hands.

"It wasn't right or wrong. It was just a fact," she said. "Your career required a wife who enjoyed the social aspect of being a star, someone who could schmooze the producers and directors, someone who cared about designer gowns. I would never be that person." She had left out the part about his constant criticism making her feel like a failure. Tears pricked at the back of her eyes, and she had to swallow before she could speak the next words. "I loved you . . . too much to hold you back. So I made the hardest decision of my life."

"Dear God," Hugh said into his hands.

"Look at how right I was," Jessica said. "You've become the most recognized actor on the planet. You couldn't have done that with me dragging you down."

When Hugh lifted his head, anguish twisted his features. "All I knew is that you were leaving me. I couldn't comprehend anything else about what was happening. I was so stupid."

His pain squeezed her heart. "I didn't understand how much your childhood had affected you. I get it now. You thought I didn't love you enough to stay."

"I was an adult." He slapped the top of her desk with his open palm. "I should have acted like one."

"Don't say that, my love." She covered her mouth with one hand as soon as she realized what she'd called him.

His gaze locked on her before he shook his head. "That was pity."

Jessica wasn't sure that was true, but she didn't want to examine the possibility right now. "Not pity, just regret for what we once had."

Hugh pushed up to his feet, his movements stiff and slow. "Time to take you home."

"Hugh . . ." What could she say to him? "I didn't want to leave you."

"No one ever does."

Chapter 15

Jessica had turned that sentence over and over in her mind ever since. As they rode the short distance to her house in the town car, Hugh had shifted the conversation back to her veterinary work. He'd walked her to the door, kissed her on the forehead, and trudged wearily down her front steps while she watched through the stained glass window.

She'd thought her words might bring him some comfort. After all, she'd left him because she loved him, not because she didn't. Instead her explanation seemed to have dropped a greater weight on his shoulders.

Self-reproach had made her sleep fitful, so it had been tough to drag herself into the clinic. Which was why she winced when Carla waltzed into her office and slapped a tabloid down on her desk, saying, "You've been holding out on me, girlfriend."

Jessica looked at the page Carla pointed to. One of the bottom-feeding photographers had caught her and Hugh dashing out of the theater door hand in hand at the moment Jessica had looked up at him, laughing at how she felt like a spy movie heroine. In the picture, her expression translated to happy adoration. "Seriously?" Jessica said, picking up the offending paper to read the caption: "Hugh Baker's mystery date head over heels in love. Who's the new woman in the movie star's famously footloose dating life?"

Carla sat down in the other chair. "Looks like you and Mr. Hugh Baker aren't exactly history anymore."

Jessica dropped the tabloid on her desk. "You know better than to believe the crap they print in these things. Hugh and I just went to a play together." As long as she said nothing more, that was the truth.

"Then why are you looking at him like he hung the moon and the stars?" Carla grabbed the newspaper and scanned the photo. "Not to mention you've got that certain glow about you. Besides, even if you just went to a show together, that's more than you shared with me."

Now Jessica was going to have to lie. "He got some tickets at the last minute and invited me for old times' sake."

"He got tickets to *A Question of Desire* at the last minute? Honey, the scalpers can't even get tickets to that show."

Jessica shrugged. "Maybe he had another date who couldn't come? I don't really know."

Carla gave her a long, hard look. "I'll back off—for now. But other folks are going to see this—there are a couple on the internet, too, by the way—and start asking questions. What do you want me to tell them?"

"Most of the truth. That Hugh and I knew each other before he got famous. He's in town shooting the Julian Best movie and we got together again—just as friends. You can leave out the engagement part," Jessica added. "Too complicated."

"Oh, honey, in this day and age, someone's going to find that out anyway," Carla said, shaking her head. She stood and put the paper back on Jessica's desk. "You should keep that. It's your fifteen minutes of fame."

"Not exactly how I want to be remembered," Jessica said as she shoved the paper in a desk drawer.

"Hey, you could do worse than to be caught holding hands with that sexy hunk of manhood." Carla exited with a sly glance over her shoulder.

Jessica got up and closed the door before she pulled the paper out again. There she was, hair flying, necklace bouncing, face turned up to her companion in a galling expression of hero worship.

At least Hugh wasn't staring back into her eyes. His gaze was focused forward, and his jaw was set with determination as he towed her along. The camera had caught him midstride, so his long legs and muscled thighs drew the eye—or at least *her* eye.

She groaned and stuffed the paper back in the drawer.

She was coming out the door of her office when Diego walked by, carrying a large bag of dog food. As he passed her, the bottom of the bag broke and spilled kibble all over the floor, causing him to curse with words he never ordinarily used at the clinic.

"Hey, Diego, Tiana will take care of that," Jessica said, deciding he must be upset about something more than the dog food. "Come in my office for a minute."

"I spilled it. I gotta clean it up," Diego said. "Sorry about the cursing."

"Hey, Doc wants to talk to you, buddy," Tiana said. "I've got this."

Diego shrugged and trudged after Jessica into her office, flopping onto the green chair so hard that Jessica worried it might collapse under his weight.

"What's on your mind?" she asked.

He stared down at his hands where they rested on his thighs, his shoulders rounded. "I really messed up."

"What are you talking about? It's just some dry dog food. It'll take Tiana five minutes to sweep it up."

"Not that." He lifted a face of pure misery to meet her gaze. "You know when I put the sick dogs in the storage closet so they wouldn't infect the healthy ones?"

"It was a great idea."

He shook his head. "The health inspector came—a new one—and saw Pari in the closet. He say that go . . . goes against some code about

179

the treatment of animals 'cause there ain't no ventilation, and he going to report it to Animal Control and Welfare. Ms. Emily say he just in a bad mood and it wasn't my fault, but I should have took Pari out of there." His whole body slumped in the chair. "They might shut down the K-9 Angelz 'cause of me."

"What you did was perfectly correct," Jessica said. "I'll talk to the animal welfare folks and explain the situation."

The boy's face brightened. "I guess they might listen to a veterinarian."

"Of course they will." She couldn't bear for Diego to blame himself for some petty bureaucrat's hissy fit. "It's just a misunderstanding."

When he stood, his shoulders were square again. "Thanks, Doc. Tell me what they say."

After he left, she blew out a breath. She'd had some dealings with Animal Control and Welfare and knew a couple of people there, but she had no idea which department would handle the health inspector's complaint. Time to call Emily at the Carver Center.

"I hear you had an unfortunate encounter with the health inspector," she said when Emily answered.

The other woman sighed. "He's new, so he feels the need to throw his weight around. We just had bad timing with Pari still being quarantined in the storage closet."

"Does he really want to shut down the K-9 Angelz?"

"Who knows? He was probably just trying to intimidate me."

"I'll weigh in with my expert opinion if it will help." Jessica didn't want to barge in if it would only make things worse. Emily was a pro at handling bureaucratic red tape. "Tell me what division the complaint was filed with. I might even know someone there."

"They won't tell me much of anything other than that they're sending someone for a special inspection of the dogs on Friday sometime between noon and two. Your presence would probably impress the inspector, but I can't ask you to waste two hours of your valuable time just waiting around."

"The K-9 Angelz program is too terrific to lose because the health inspector had a bad day," Jessica said. "I'll find a way to be there."

She flipped through the contacts on her cell until she found the number of someone she could talk to at Animal Control. After she explained the situation, he said, "Doesn't sound so good, Doc. If Health is involved, we're gonna go over everything with a fine-tooth comb, just looking for violations. It's kind of an interagency courtesy thing."

"Is there anything I can do to make it go better?"

He huffed out a laugh. "Don't offer them a bribe, if that's what you mean."

Jessica chuckled, too. "It might have crossed my mind."

"Look, I know you and I know you'd never allow animals to live in unhealthy conditions. I'll drop in a good word for you, but that won't carry much weight. Mostly you're going to have to cross your fingers and hope whoever they assign to the inspection isn't one of the crazies or the nasties."

"Any chance you could find out?"

"Wish I could help you, but it's kept kind of secret, for obvious reasons."

Jessica sighed. "You've been great."

She stared at the wall with her patients' photos on it, only she wasn't seeing them. Scenes kept flitting across her mind's eye: Hugh with Shareena and Cornell; Hugh with the usher at the play; Hugh with the boys at the center. Hugh could dazzle anyone with his star power and charm. An animal welfare inspector shouldn't be immune.

Could she really ask him for such a favor after last night's drama? She had no idea what his feelings toward her were now. Her gut twisted, because her feelings about Hugh had become . . . complicated.

But the Carver Center was more important than her personal issues. Hugh cared about it, too. She'd seen that when he'd spent time with the kids.

If he didn't want to help her, he could always say his shooting schedule wouldn't allow it.

Tiana stuck her head in through the doorway. "Hey, Doc, Boots and her mom are in Room 1."

Guilt and relief made her jump up from her chair. She could put off the awkward phone call a little longer.

At six thirty, Jessica flopped down on her ergonomic chair with a sigh of relief. Carla had worked a miracle and cleared tomorrow afternoon's appointments so she could be at the Carver Center for the inspection. Of course, Jessica would have to work an extra two hours on Saturday to accommodate the rescheduled patients. Now she needed to see if Hugh could deliver the same miracle.

She picked up the cell phone she'd left on her desk because her patients had been wall to wall today. When she saw there was both a text and a voice mail from Pete, she winced. There was also a voice mail from Hugh.

Pete's text and voice mail were virtually identical. He wanted to talk as soon as possible, preferably in person, and his evening was open.

Hugh's message was less problematic. "Jess, I heard about the photos of us. I hope they don't cause you any embarrassment or trouble. If they do, call me immediately and my PR team will deal with it."

As she debated which difficult conversation to grapple with first, a wave of exhaustion washed over her. She slumped back in her chair, just like Hugh had the night before, and stared at the water stain on the ceiling. It would help if she could untangle her own feelings about the two men. Hugh tantalized her with his heat and brilliance but threatened to singe her heart again. Pete seemed to offer a steady flame that would warm her without leaving scorch marks.

Sitting up, she marshaled her thoughts before tapping Hugh's number.

"Five minutes to rest while we set up for the next scene," Bryan shouted. "Get makeup in."

Hugh grabbed the towel that his assistant, Trevor, held out and blotted the sweat off his face, careful not to smear whatever makeup remained after his exertions.

Trevor fumbled in his pocket and pulled out Hugh's cell phone, checking the screen. "You're gonna want this call," he said, handing the phone to his boss.

When Hugh saw it was Jessica, he walked away from the bustle of the set. For the first time he could remember, he was reluctant to talk to her. Last night had set things shifting inside him, and he wasn't sure where they would settle. So he addressed the least complex of the issues between them. "Jess, is the photo creating problems? I'm sorry."

There was a moment of hesitation. "Are you in the middle of shooting?"

"Just finished a fight scene." He tried to control his breathing, but he was still sucking wind from vanquishing a trio of armed enemies.

"I didn't call about the photo," she said in a rush. "Do you have a minute to talk or do you need to get back to work?"

A strange panic gripped him. What could she say to him in a minute except good-bye? He strode toward his trailer. "They're giving us a break to recover. Let me just go somewhere more private."

"I don't think privacy is necessary. I want to ask you a favor."

That stopped him midstride. "A favor?"

"A rather large one." She took a breath. "To make a long story short, a grumpy health inspector didn't approve of quarantining the dogs in the storage closet."

Hugh recalled the stench from when he'd found Jessica sleeping there and wasn't surprised, but he kept his opinion to himself.

"Now he's gotten Animal Control and Welfare involved, and they're coming to make their own inspection tomorrow between noon and two. If it doesn't go well, the inspector could shut down the K-9 Angelz program." Her voice turned pleading. "You saw how much the dogs mean to the kids. They'd be heartbroken."

He remembered the pride with which the kids had shown him their dogs, but even more the love that had shone in their eyes as they petted their charges. He started to agree with her, but Jess was on a roll.

"I'll be present to throw in my expert opinion, but I'm just a common, run-of-the-mill veterinarian. You, however, are a movie star, and I've seen how people respond to you." She paused, and he wondered what was coming. "Is there any chance you could get time off to come to the center tomorrow afternoon and bestow your magic charm on the inspector? If your schedule doesn't allow it, I totally understand. You have a gazillion-dollar movie riding on your shoulders. But if you could take a break . . ."

He muttered a curse. "We're in the middle of filming, Jess, and you're giving me virtually no time to rearrange things."

"It was a long shot, but I had to ask. Don't worry about it." He could hear the disappointment in her voice, and it twisted painfully in his chest.

"I didn't say no." But he would probably have to. He couldn't screw up the whole damn timetable, even for such a worthy cause. "Let me check the schedule and talk to Bryan. No promises, though."

"I wouldn't ask for myself, but—"

Trevor walked up and gave him an urgent hand signal that meant he was wanted back on set. "I have to go. I'll be in touch."

He disconnected before she could thank him and handed his phone back to his assistant. He didn't want to feel any more guilt when he failed her. "Trevor, what's my schedule for tomorrow?" he asked as he walked toward the organized chaos of the set.

Trevor tapped at his own cell phone and reeled off a list of times and scenes for the next day. Hugh frowned as he listened. It was a full day, but there were no giant action scenes, so some resequencing might be possible. He needed to nail this next take, to put Bryan in a receptive mood.

He would tell Bryan he wanted the time off because it was a cause he cared about, but to himself he admitted the truth: he couldn't stand the thought of letting Jessica down.

As much as she'd wished to thank him, Jessica had been relieved that Hugh was in a hurry. There'd been no time to discuss where things stood between them.

Pete was going to be a much tougher proposition. She'd texted to set up a meeting with him at nine at Philomena's, the bar they'd enjoyed last Thursday, and then dashed home to shower and change. She'd taken some care with her clothes, needing the armor of black jeans, a tailored white silk blouse, and her favorite plum suede boots. Even her hair had been carefully tamed into a neat bun. Leaving it down would send the wrong message.

Now she sat in the back of a ride share on her way to face him, wondering how to explain what had happened to make her life so tangled.

Pete was already sitting in a booth when she walked in, his pale blond hair glowing against the brown leather of the banquette. He stood and greeted her with a kiss on the cheek, but there was no smile in answer to hers. As soon as they were both seated, he waved a hand at the stemmed glass in front of her. "I ordered you a Manhattan since that was your choice the last time we were here."

"That was thoughtful of you."

He pinned her with his gaze. "I'm not going to beat around the bush because that's not my style. I saw the photo of you and Hugh Baker in the *Star*." He grimaced. "Not that I read that garbage, but a work associate does and remembered meeting you at the hockey game, so she shared it with me."

Jessica winced. That had probably injured Pete's pride on top of everything else. "The photo was a surprise to me, too." She wanted to say it was misleading, but she couldn't quite force the words out.

He locked his gaze on her face. "When I asked you about Hugh Baker, you told me your engagement ended a long time ago. You said you were over him. In that picture"—his voice turned hard—"you sure as hell don't look over him. And you might have mentioned the fact that you are still seeing him."

She didn't blame him for being upset. "When we talked about Hugh, I wasn't seeing him. Until the week before our conversation, I hadn't had any contact with him in eight years. Not a word. So when I ran into him—literally—while he was filming the new Julian Best movie, I didn't expect anything about our relationship to change."

"Whose relationship? Yours with Hugh or with me?"

"Both . . . either. What I told you was true—Hugh and I live in different worlds. Nothing made me think he and I would connect again."

Pete sat back, his expression grim. "But you did. So where does that leave us?"

She folded the corners of the paper cocktail napkin up over the base of her glass. "I don't know." She lifted her head to meet his eyes. "I hate to screw things up with you when I have no idea what's going on with Hugh."

He huffed out a frustrated breath. "Look, I don't shy away from some healthy competition. You're an amazing woman, so it doesn't surprise me that I'm not the only man in your life. I'm not even afraid to go toe to toe with a world-famous actor. But I can't compete with the past. Your relationship with Hugh Baker goes back a long way. I need to know if those old feelings are truly dead."

His words took Jessica on a roller-coaster ride of dismay, gratification, and finally, the stunning realization that she needed to admit the truth to Pete—and to herself.

She swallowed hard, glanced up at Pete, and then stared down into the golden liquid in her glass. "I thought those feelings were dead. I had buried my life with Hugh in a deep, dark corner of my heart, never to be resurrected." She forced herself to meet Pete's gaze. "Even when we talked again on the movie set, I didn't feel anything other than a sort of regretful nostalgia."

Pete's face seemed carved in stone.

"But we spent some more time together." She thought of how she and Hugh had made love the day he'd scooped her up off the dog bed. She should have known that it wasn't only her body that responded to Hugh. "I wouldn't say the old feelings resurfaced. Eight years is a long time, and we've both changed. But whatever brought us together back then is still there in some form. I just don't know whether there's any future in it. Only time will tell."

All she knew with utter certainty was that she'd fallen right back in love with Hugh, despite their past failure, despite the glaring differences between their two worlds, despite having no idea how he felt about her. As she watched Pete swallow the rest of his drink in one gulp, she wondered what the hell was wrong with her. Across from her sat a successful, attractive, decent man who wanted her. Why did she long for the man who'd hurt her enough to drive her away from him?

Pete set down his glass as though it was made of the most fragile crystal. "I appreciate your honesty." He signaled the waiter for the check and took his credit card out of his wallet to lay it on the table. She hated to have him pay for the drinks, but it seemed like the wrong time to argue about it.

"You're a nicer guy than I deserve," she said as a pang of regret rolled through her.

He shook his head, handing the waiter his credit card without even looking at the check. "I'm not nice. I just know when I'm beaten."

"I wish things had worked out differently." She meant that.

"Just don't say you really like me," he said, his mouth twisting in a grimace. "That would be the kiss of death."

"Deal," she said.

Pete signed the credit card slip and stood up. Jessica started to do the same, but he waved her back into her seat. "You should drink that cocktail. You might need it."

He walked out with a confident stride, and Jessica saw several female heads turn to watch him.

She picked up her Manhattan and downed half of it all at once, hoping the alcohol would wash away the guilt and remorse she felt over hurting Pete. The other half she swallowed in an attempt to drown her newly acknowledged feelings for Hugh.

But Hugh had fought his way out of the deep, dark corner she'd shoved him in, and now she couldn't banish him back into it. The glow of the Manhattan was starting to seep through her bloodstream, but all it brought was a desire to lay her head down on the table and cry until she fell into an exhausted sleep.

And wasn't that exactly why she hadn't wanted to love Hugh ever again?

"You did *what*?" Gavin jerked upright in his chair, nearly spilling the glass of scotch he held.

"I got Bryan to rearrange a few scenes so I could take tomorrow afternoon off. The K-9 Angelz is a program I believe in." Hugh didn't mention the string of creative curses the director had let loose when Hugh had made his request. But Hugh never asked for special treatment, so Bryan—or rather Bryan's assistant, Timoney—found a way to accommodate him.

"At least be honest with me," Gavin said. "You didn't disrupt a major motion picture for the kids and the dogs."

Hugh put his feet up on the coffee table in Gavin's den. "No, I suppose I didn't." He took a sip of his drink.

"What's going on with your ex-fiancée?" the other man prodded.

"Hell if I know."

"Well, I know it's more than you're letting on. Talk to me. I'm your best friend." Gavin paused a moment. "Possibly your only friend."

Hugh barked out a laugh. "Don't flatter yourself." But he found he wanted to talk about Jess. "She told me why she broke our engagement. Well, actually, I pressured her into it." He wasn't going to cut himself any slack.

"Something about how she hated being in the public eye all the time."

"That was my spin on it. She didn't enjoy the spotlight, but I was the one who made her feel uncomfortable about how well she handled it." He shook his head. "She decided that she was holding me back from my lofty goal of being a movie star. The woman who's saved countless animals' lives believed she would be an impediment to my career. God, I was such an idiot."

"No argument here," Gavin said. "However, it sounds to me like there's a fine line between what you believe and the explanation she gave you."

"Ah, it's subtle but significant. My theory assumed that she was thinking only of herself, but that's not Jess. She would have sucked it up and done what was necessary because she was always there to support me. I was such an ass about it that I convinced her she wasn't good enough at the publicity appearances. She didn't want to be the reason I didn't make it as an actor, so she took herself out of the equation."

Gavin stood up to refill his glass from the cut-crystal decanter. He tilted it toward Hugh. "Want another?"

"Why not? You serve damned good scotch." Hugh held out his glass for Gavin to pour more of the golden liquor into.

"So how does this revelation change things?" Gavin eased back into his chair.

Hugh had been trying to figure that out ever since Jess told him. "There's a lot of damage. In my mind, she abandoned me, so I abandoned her. She called me. I didn't return her messages. She even sent me a very handsome and expensive gift when *Level Best* premiered. I still have it, but I never thanked her."

"In short, you behaved like a real bastard."

"I behaved like I was still a teenage foster child, not a grown man. I understand that now. But then . . . she hit every hot button in my brain." He swirled his glass so the liquid formed a whirlpool. "It was like watching my mother walk away from the foster home all over again."

Gavin was silent, a rare occurrence. Hugh looked up to find the usually harsh angles of his friend's face gone soft with compassion.

"Don't you do it, too," Hugh said, an edge in his voice. "I don't want pity."

"It's empathy. I was also deserted by my mother." Gavin's tone was even. "It leaves scars that never quite heal."

Hugh nodded in acknowledgment of their shared experience.

"Jessica told you you'd already repaired some of the damage, so the case is not hopeless," Gavin said. "Which brings me back to the question I asked you the last time we discussed this: What do you want from Jessica?"

Hugh put his feet on the floor and stood up to walk to his favorite window. "I don't think I ever stopped loving her." He faced Gavin squarely. "I want her to love me again. I want to build a better relationship this time. I want it to last."

"That's definitive. How are you going to make it happen?"

"She's not indifferent to me," Hugh said, remembering their evening at the theater.

Gavin chuckled. "I won't ask how you know that. I can see it on your face. But that's not enough."

"It's a start. With Jess, there have to be emotions involved," he said. "I need to charm a grumpy animal welfare inspector tomorrow. That will earn me brownie points."

"All that indirect trust building is great as far as it goes, but you have to put your heart right out there for her to stomp on if she chooses to. You have to tell her exactly how you feel. I learned that lesson the hard way."

Hugh shook his head. "There's still too much about our past we need to resolve. She's not ready to hear how I feel yet."

"Or maybe you're just too afraid to tell her."

Chapter 16

Jessica poured herself a mug of fragrant coffee, plopped half a bagel in the toaster, and sat down across from Aidan. He was wearing plaid flannel pajama pants, a gray T-shirt, and a serious case of bedhead, his sun-streaked hair a rat's nest of spiky knots. She took a gulp of the life-giving beverage, carefully put the mug down on the oak table, and braced herself to make another confession.

Last night while she'd wrestled with the guilt she carried for hurting Pete, she realized that she might have also killed her brother's chances of getting the job at ExDat.

"You know the picture of Hugh and me in the tabloid?" Her brother hadn't been there when she'd gotten home last night, but he'd left the paper on the kitchen counter, open to the photo, making Jessica cringe all over again when she saw it.

Aidan nodded, his eyes half-closed, as he took a large swallow of his own coffee.

"Pete saw it, too, and he wasn't thrilled about it. Not that I blame him. Anyway, we won't be seeing each other anymore."

"Shit!" Aidan's eyes went wide with dismay. It took a moment, but he got past his first reaction and managed to give her a brotherly pat on the hand. "That's a bummer. Probably not a fun discussion to have with him."

She was touched by his sympathy. "I hope it doesn't screw up the job interview."

"Nah. Pete's not that kind of guy. Don't worry about it." Aidan's confidence seemed a little forced. "It's none of my business, but what's going on with you and Hugh, anyway? The picture made things look kind of, um, intense."

She made a face. "Pictures can be misleading."

"Yeah, but you wanted to marry Hugh once. Are you headed in that direction again?" He raised both hands, palm out. "Just to be clear, I think he's a cool guy, so I'm on your side either way."

His unconditional support sent a little tendril of warmth curling into her chest. "You're a pretty decent brother, you know."

Aidan grinned, which, combined with his bedhead, made him look about ten years old. "I keep telling you that. Are you going to answer my question or not?"

"Not?"

"I said it was none of my business." But he looked hurt.

"I don't know the answer," she said. "With Hugh, nothing's ever simple."

"You're always revved up by a challenge."

She sighed. "Do you think that's why I keep falling in love with him?"

Her brother's eyebrows rose. "Oh-kay, so that was an answer."

"It doesn't mean anything because I have no idea how he feels about me." She braced her chin on her hands. "We live such different lives. I just don't see how to reconcile them, even if he wanted to. We couldn't manage it eight years ago."

"I can't believe I'm saying this, but eight years is a long time. You've both changed. Maybe you could work it out now."

A spark of optimism flared. If her irresponsible brother thought it was possible . . . "I've considered that, but I figured it was just wishful thinking on my part."

"You're already in love with him again. If it doesn't work out, it's still going to hurt. But if you don't try, you'll pile regret on top of the pain."

"Wow! That's incredibly . . . smart."

"It's just logic. I'm good at that." He grinned again, his gray eyes bright now. "But you're welcome for the brotherly wisdom."

She laughed just as her phone pinged with a text. She pulled it out of the pocket of her forest-green scrubs and swiped into the message.

Schedule rearranged. Will be at the Carver Center at noon. Shall I wear Julian's tuxedo?

"Oh my God! I can't believe he did it!" Jessica shouted.

Aidan winced, his free hand over one ear. "Hey, keep the volume down. I haven't had my second cup of coffee yet."

"Sorry." She typed back, feeling the uncontrollable smile that stretched her lips wide: You are truly the Best! If you could carry a really cute puppy while wearing the tuxedo, that would be perfect. Thank you a thousand times over!

His response came back immediately. I'll let you know how you can repay me later. Now I have to go make up for this afternoon's lost time.

"Hugh got the afternoon off to charm the Animal Control inspector." As a warm glow spread through her, she couldn't help but wonder whether he was doing it for her or for the kids.

"To do *what*?"

"Oh, right, you don't know about the impending catastrophe at the Carver Center." She filled him in on the situation while she buttered her bagel, her appetite suddenly back in full force. She savored her first bite of the warm bread with its chewy crust and lightly crisped top. Bagels were one of the things she loved about New York.

"I don't know a ton about the movie biz," Aidan said as she ate with gusto, "but changing the shooting schedule in less than twenty-four hours seems pretty . . . significant. Are you sure you don't know how Hugh feels about you?"

Jessica sailed through her morning appointments on a wave of pure joy. Hugh was going to rescue the K-9 Angelz program. Yes, she had that much confidence in his ability to win friends and influence the inspector. But the joy came from Aidan's conviction that Hugh wouldn't have done something as difficult as changing the filming schedule unless he was trying to impress Jessica.

She took a car service to the Carver Center, not wanting to arrive with slush stains on her scrub pants. Emily greeted her at the front door with a hug. "Mr. Baker called to say he's running a little late due to work, but I'm not worried. I've never known an inspector to come at the beginning of the time window." She shook her head. "I can't believe you enlisted a movie star to help us, but I'm so grateful. The health inspector was quite prickly, so I'm concerned about what he might have reported us for."

The Carver Center's director was usually unflappable, so the inspector must have been downright awful. "We've got this," Jessica said. "But I'm going to take a look at the kennel area to see if I need to make any extra tweaks."

"Diego was here until ten o'clock last night scrubbing and polishing. He got all the kids to groom their dogs until they practically sparkle." Emily's eyes took on a militant light. "I can't believe a rational person could find anything wrong with our facilities."

Jessica remembered what her contact had said about nasties and crazies but decided to keep it to herself. "Diego is one amazing kid."

"I can't wait to see what he does with his life," Emily said. "It's going to be extraordinary."

Jessica agreed as she slipped off her quilted winter jacket and shrugged into the pristine white lab coat she'd brought with her. She kept it for occasions when she needed to look especially authoritative and competent. It even had her name and the clinic's logo embroidered on it in the same serious forest green as her scrubs.

"The lab coat is a nice touch," Emily said as she took Jessica's jacket to hang on a hook in the hallway.

"Let's hope it helps," Jessica said before she headed down the stairs to the dogs' quarters. Once she'd quieted the enthusiastic greeting, she scanned the basement space. Sure enough, it was immaculate, the floor so clean she wouldn't hesitate to eat off it, and the dogs' coats shone with brushing and good health. Even the windows had been washed, so the pale winter sunlight came through with maximum brightness.

She walked down the hallway to check on the storage closet where Pari was quarantined. The door was open to allow for ventilation, and she noticed that someone—her money was on Diego—had set up a fan in one corner to circulate the air. She nodded in approval as she spoke softly to the little dog. She felt badly about not petting Pari, but she didn't have gloves with her.

Her gaze fell on the brown dog bed where she'd slept, and memories of the power of Hugh's arms cradling her ignited flares of heat deep in her body. He'd gotten into all the corners of her life, a realization that made her uneasy.

She forced herself to focus on the room, giving it a thorough scan and finding nothing objectionable, before she strode out.

Upstairs, she joined Emily in the kitchen, where the director was chatting with Kyra Dixon, the center's chef.

When they heard the front door open, both Jessica and Emily jumped off the stools on which they had settled to wait.

"Good to see you, Mr. Baker," Jessica heard the security guard say, and her nerves fizzed.

Hugh appeared in the door to the kitchen, his brilliant blue gaze scanning the room until it locked on her. When he smiled, she read all the feelings in it that she had hoped for, and her heart unfurled like a flower in the spring sunlight.

"Jess," he said, coming toward her with his hands stretched out, palms up. She met him and laid her hands in his, loving the feel of his fingers closing around hers. He bent and kissed her in an unguarded way that took her back to the early days of their affair, when she'd been intoxicated by his every touch.

The kiss was not long, but it left her wrapped in a haze of desire. He released her hands to greet Emily and Kyra, who glanced between Jessica and Hugh with somewhat dreamy expressions. She had time to notice he wore a perfectly tailored charcoal-gray suit, which she guessed belonged to Hugh himself since it seemed less tight fitting than Julian's attire.

"No tuxedo?" she teased once she'd recovered enough to speak.

"It seemed implausible that I'd stopped in for a visit to the Carver Center while en route to Monte Carlo, so I came as myself." He turned to Emily. "On the way here, I had a few thoughts about how to explain my presence."

Jessica stood back and listened with openmouthed admiration as he outlined his plan to sway the inspector into giving a favorable report and discussed the timing of all of their entrances and exits, so as not to overwhelm the inspector and make him or her feel pressured.

"Brilliant!" Emily agreed with enthusiasm. "Now I guess we should all take our positions."

"Or as we say in the movie business, 'Places, everyone!'" Hugh said. He gave Jessica a private smile before he disappeared up the stairs to the lounge.

Kyra let out a long, exaggerated sigh and said, "You are one lucky woman."

"Hey, I've met your fiancé," Jessica said, remembering the tall, patrician blond who'd brought her the giant flower arrangement. "You're not exactly suffering on that front."

Kyra smiled. "I have no complaints, but I'm not immune to Julian Best's sexy edge of danger."

"You should hear him complain about his gun holster being too tight," Jessica said with a snort as she headed for the door. Hugh had suggested that she join the inspector in the kennel area, so she trotted back downstairs and worked her way along the row of crates, petting their tail-wagging inhabitants.

After about twenty minutes, her phone vibrated with a text message from Powell, using their silly code for the arrival of the inspector: The eagle has landed.

Jessica pulled her stethoscope out of her coat pocket and hung it around her neck, an extra costume prop Hugh had suggested. Soon voices and footsteps came from the stairs, so she swung open Shaq's crate and pretended to listen to the big dog's heart.

"This is Dr. Quillen, the vet who sees to the medical needs of all our dogs," Emily said smoothly. "Doctor, I'd like to introduce Arlene Washington from Animal Control and Welfare. She's here to ensure that we're doing everything we can to make our canine residents comfortable."

Jessica latched Shaq's cage and stood to shake hands. Ms. Washington was tall and thin, with wiry gray hair pulled back in a ponytail. She wore navy trousers and a matching windbreaker with the New York City government insignia printed on it in white. Tucked under her arm was an electronic tablet.

"As a vet, I appreciate the work you do to protect animals in the city." Jessica smiled with total sincerity.

Ms. Washington gave her a limp handshake without an answering smile, and Jessica's heart sank. Thank goodness she'd called in the cavalry.

"If I can answer any questions about the dogs' health, please let me know," Jessica said, trying again. "We have one dog quarantined because she has giardiasis. Because of the quick response of the dogs' caretakers, only three out of twelve canines have shown symptoms of the parasite. That's pretty impressive."

Ms. Washington nodded and looked around the kennel, her brow furrowed. She paced down the row of crates, peering into each one. The dogs all stood and wagged their tails, a couple barking a friendly greeting. "At least the dogs are doing their part to prove they're happy here," Jessica whispered to Emily under cover of Shaq's deep woof.

The inspector walked over to one of the windows, peering out into the snow-covered backyard. She flipped open the cover of her tablet and tapped at it for several seconds. "Let me see the quarantine room," she said, her tone flat.

Jessica's throat tightened at the mention of the trouble spot. They needed the big guns now, but there was no sign of Hugh.

"This way," Emily said, gesturing toward the hallway and falling into step beside Ms. Washington. Jessica walked behind them, wondering what Hugh was waiting for.

When they entered, Pari sat up and yipped. Ms. Washington showed her first sign of humanity when she knelt and put her fingers through the crate's wires to let the dog lick her fingers. "Are you feeling okay?" she asked. She straightened to her full height. "Looks like she's doing all right."

The dogs raised a chorus of greeting from the kennel area, and Jessica blew out a breath of relief.

"Dr. Quillen?" Hugh's voice projected clearly through the barking.

"Excuse me," Jessica said, stepping to the door before she raised her voice. "Mr. Baker, I'm in the quarantine room." She turned back to Ms. Washington. "I'm sorry for the interruption, but Mr. Baker has very limited time."

The inspector's lips tightened into a thin line. "So do I."

Jessica just smiled as Hugh's footsteps sounded on the concrete hall-way's floor. He came to the door, his broad shoulders filling the width of the frame. "Doctor, I have a—" He feigned surprise. "My apologies, I didn't realize you were busy."

"Ms. Washington, may I introduce Hugh Baker. You might recognize him from the Julian Best movies," Jessica said, somehow keeping a straight face. "Mr. Baker, this is Arlene Washington. She does the good work of making sure kennel facilities are keeping their boarders happy and healthy."

"A pleasure, Ms. Washington," Hugh said, taking the woman's hand in both of his and giving her the full focus of his intense blue gaze. "Thank you for your work on behalf of our fur friends."

For a moment, the inspector just stared at Hugh, and Jessica's heart turned to stone in her chest. Did Ms. Washington live under a rock and not know who Hugh Baker was? Maybe she hated spy movies. Maybe she hated all movies.

"You're welcome," the inspector said, her eyes never leaving Hugh's face. Everyone waited a beat, but that seemed to be her entire response.

Hugh appeared to think for a moment before speaking again. "You know, I'm here because I have a foundation that supports other kids' centers like this one. We heard about the Carver Center's K-9 Angelz program and believe it is something our kids would benefit from as well. So we're using this"—he swept his hand around the tiny room—"as our model. Dr. Quillen is acting as the veterinary adviser on the project."

Jessica hid her amused surprise. Hugh was improvising beyond the simple script he'd outlined for them.

"Perhaps you could assist me with the regulatory side of things." He smiled into Ms. Washington's eyes, his charm turned up to full wattage.

Jessica's knees had turned to rubber, so she wasn't surprised when the inspector broke at last and nodded so hard her ponytail bounced. "That could be worked out," she said.

"Excellent!" Hugh sounded as though he'd been granted his fondest wish. He pulled a business card and a slim silver pen from his pocket, scrawling something on the back of the card before he proffered it to her. "Here's my personal cell phone number. Do you have a business card I might take?"

Ms. Washington took the card by one corner and gaped down at it. "Your personal cell phone number," she repeated.

"And your card?" Hugh prompted after a moment.

The inspector looked flustered. "I don't have one." She slipped his card into an inner pocket and patted the others. "Maybe a piece of . . ."

Hugh produced another of his cards and held out the pen as well. "Just write your name and number on the back of mine."

She used her tablet as a writing surface and penned her information with great care. When Hugh's fingers brushed hers as he accepted the card, the inspector jerked slightly and gave him a nervous look.

"Do you know that I found Dr. Quillen sleeping on the dog bed in that corner last week?" Hugh said to Ms. Washington, pointing to the spot. "She was so concerned about one of the dogs that she didn't want to leave until she was sure the little creature would make it. That's an impressive commitment to the animals here, don't you think?"

Jessica's mind went straight to what she and Hugh had done afterward, making the blood heat up in her veins, but she managed to say, "Any vet would have done the same thing."

The inspector tore her attention away from Hugh long enough to acknowledge Jessica. "I've heard good things about you."

"This program has instilled a love of animals in the young people here that they'll take with them all of their lives," Hugh said, making another grand sweep with his arm. "They will go out as ambassadors of kindness to our fur friends. Maybe one of them might even become an inspector like yourself."

Ms. Washington swallowed before she said, "That would . . . well, maybe."

Hugh stepped out of the doorway and bent just slightly at the waist in an almost bow. "Why don't we go to the kennel area and you can use it as an illustration of how I should set up my own program?"

"I could do that," the inspector said, walking out the door. Hugh gave Emily and Jessica a wink before he followed the woman into the hallway.

They waited until the footsteps had receded. Emily quietly closed the storage room door and then made a show of fanning herself. "Oh my God, he had me nearly melting onto the floor, and he wasn't even looking at me!"

"Me, too," Jessica said, sagging against the wall as the adrenaline drained out of her system.

"Well, that's because when he looks at *you* like that, he means it." Emily glanced at her watch. "We're supposed to give him a little more time alone with her before we rejoin them. By then he'll have her eating out of his hand."

"And the K-9 Angelz will be safe." Jessica blew out a breath. "I don't think we could have done it without him."

"Yes, meeting Hugh Baker probably made her week. You know, I always feel a little sorry for the various inspectors," Emily said. "Everyone dislikes them so much, but it's a job that needs to be done."

"It's only the occasional bad apple who abuses the power they have. But you just never know which kind is going to walk into your place."

Emily twisted the door handle open. "Time to find out the verdict."

Once he got her talking, Hugh discovered that Arlene Washington knew her stuff and was genuinely concerned about the dogs' health and well-being, so his interest was no longer feigned. In fact, he was glad to have her contact information for future use.

But he knew the power of leaving them wanting more, so Jessica and Emily's reappearance played right into his plan. He looked at his watch—or rather, Julian's, since he hadn't had time to do more than strip off the black turtleneck and jeans and throw on his own suit—and smiled an apology at Arlene, as she'd asked him to call her. "If you're finished with your inspection, I'll walk you to the door. Otherwise, I'm going to have to say good-bye here. I have a scuba scene to shoot, and it takes a while to suit up." He made a wry face.

"I'm satisfied with what I've seen," Arlene said, tapping on her tablet again. She spared a quick nod for the other two women. "You've passed."

He could see the quick flicker of relief on both their faces.

"Thank you," Emily said sincerely but without any sign that she expected otherwise. "I appreciate your taking the time to come here. We always want to be sure we're doing things correctly."

He gestured for the women to precede him up the stairs, but as soon as they reached the top, he made sure to walk beside Arlene so he could focus his attention on her one last time. It wouldn't do for her to think that once the center's kennel had been approved, he had lost interest. He made a point of taking Arlene's winter coat from Emily and helping the inspector into it.

"It's been a pleasure and an education," he said, pulling the heavy metal front door open. He stepped out behind Arlene to find half a dozen photographers loitering on the sidewalk. As they scrambled into action, their cameras clicking and whirring, irritation burned through him. He supposed they had followed his limo from the movie set. That had been a tactical error on his part, but he'd been in a hurry.

Arlene stood frozen at the top of the steps, her mouth half-open. He forced a rueful half smile and offered his arm to her. "I'm sorry for the aggravation. Allow me to escort you past these nuisances."

She swallowed. "Sure," she said, putting her hand through the crook of his elbow. They walked down the steps side by side with Arlene looking like a deer in headlights. The photographers parted barely enough to let them through. He controlled his desire to give them a look that would make them move farther away. He could imagine the caption: "Hugh Baker angered when he runs afoul of the Big Apple's health department. Inspector hauls him off to jail."

His limo was parked by a fire hydrant a few steps away. The photographers followed them, so he bent to murmur in Arlene's ear, "May I offer you a ride anywhere?"

She shook her head. "My car's just down the block." With a flash of unexpected humor, she added, "I don't want to start any crazy rumors by getting into a limo with you."

He laughed. "You're a wise woman."

As he ducked into the car, he glanced back at the Carver Center to see Jessica standing at the top of the steps, an expression of stunned horror on her face while the photographers swarmed his ride. He closed the door and hit the driver's intercom. "Drive around until you lose these vultures and then circle back here."

"With pleasure, sir," his driver said. All his chauffeurs considered it a point of honor to be able to shake off the paparazzi.

He yanked out his phone to send Jessica a text saying, Don't leave. I'll be back once I lose the bottom feeders.

I'll be here.

Fifteen minutes later, the limo glided back into position at the fire hydrant. Hugh waited for a few moments, but no lurking photographers leaped out of hiding places.

As he walked up the steps, the door swung open. "Did you get rid of them?" Jessica asked, peering around him.

He stepped inside. "All clear."

"How do you stand that?" she asked.

Unease prickled through him, but he shrugged it off. "It comes with the territory. Let's get out of the hallway." He needed to kiss her until her distress melted away, so he started toward the stairs down to the kennel.

"Emily wants to thank you," Jessica said, veering toward the upward staircase.

"Later." He seized her hand and pulled her into him so he could murmur, "I think you should thank me first."

Her eyes lit with amusement that went hot when she met his gaze. But it wasn't just desire he saw in her face. There was something more, something that she hadn't allowed him to see before. Suddenly, his need went beyond distracting her from the underbelly of fame. Now he wanted to feel this new thing between them, to wrap himself in it as he moved inside her.

"Oh, in that case." She grinned before tugging him along at a brisk pace.

When they reached the bottom of the steps, the dogs set up their usual high-volume welcome, but he didn't care. He spun her back to the wall and leaned against her, reveling in the soft push of her breasts against his chest and the sigh of her breath on his mouth when he brought his lips down on hers. Her fingers were in his hair, then gripping his shoulders, then digging into his buttocks to bring him closer as she rocked into his erection.

"We can't do this here," she said as he slipped his hands up under her scrubs to fill his palms with the round weight of her breasts. Her nipples hardened when he rubbed his thumbs over the delicate lace of her bra, making him want to suck on her. His cock stiffened further at nothing more than the thought.

"The storage closet is private," he said. "All we need is something to brace under the handle. There has to be a broom here somewhere."

"Hugh! We can't!" But her voice was a breathless rasp.

"Are you sure you don't want me to suck on your breasts while I drive into you over and over again until your orgasm explodes through you?" He put every ounce of seduction he could command into his voice.

She went still in his arms for a long moment while he waited. "I know where the cleaning supplies are," she said at last.

"I adore you," he said, giving her a fast, hard kiss before he slid his hands out from under the green fabric of her scrubs. "Lead the way."

They retrieved a broom, and Hugh shoved it under the doorknob of the storage room before he ripped his jacket off and tossed it on the dog bed. Jessica shrugged out of her lab coat and added it to the pile. Then Hugh lost track of who unbuttoned, untied, unbuckled, and unzipped what until they were naked and Jessica had stroked a condom onto his cock.

"I'm not using that dog bed," he growled.

"It's more comfortable than you think," she said, reaching down to cup his balls.

"The corner," he hissed, walking her backward while her fingers danced over his sensitive skin and made him almost unable to think. He slid his hands under her naked buttocks and lifted her so she could wrap her legs around his waist, the hot, slippery center of her hitting his erection with the power of a stun gun, but one that gave pleasure, not pain. She levered herself up with her hands on his shoulders and let him slide into her in one swift movement.

"Jess," he hissed through clenched teeth as he felt her heat envelop him. "I want you so much."

"Yes!" she said, her inner muscles doing something wonderful to his cock. He took handfuls of her firm, round bottom to lift her so he could move, pushing up and half withdrawing, feeling the drag of her taut nipples against his chest, the bite of her fingers on his straining shoulder muscles, and the moist huff of her breath as she said his name every time he came into her.

Then all he could do was feel, as his world narrowed and focused on the place where the two of them joined, the tension building with each shift and thrust. She arched back, her body completely still for one suspended moment, and then she clenched around him, her orgasm stroking and kneading his cock so hard he had to fight not to come with her. He wanted to absorb every ounce of her pleasure before he took his.

As soon as she dropped her head onto his shoulder in completion, he let himself go, driving deep into her before his release tore through him, blanking his mind to everything except the detonation between his thighs.

As he held them both upright against the wall while they recovered, he realized he had been right. Things had changed. This time, there had been nothing held back, no barriers between them. "Jess, will you come to the hotel with me tonight? I want to have you in my bed, to sleep with you in my arms." He'd kept the penthouse suite in the hope that she might spend another night with him.

"Yes," she breathed against his bare shoulder without a moment's hesitation. "I want that, too."

His heart felt as though someone had made a fist around it and squeezed. Strangely, it felt as much like fear as joy.

He eased her feet down to the floor, relishing the slide of her skin along his. She leaned against him, her arms around his neck. "I have to get back to the set," he said, his hands on her waist. "I promised Bryan I'd return as soon as I could."

"You didn't, though." He could hear pleasure in her voice. "You *came* here instead." She chortled at her joke, and his fear evaporated.

"You always complained about *my* puns," he said, brushing his fingers over her ribs to tickle her.

She giggled and jerked away. "It's evil to tickle the woman you just made come until her muscles turned to mush."

"It was the only way I could get you to let go of me," he teased, scooping her panties off the messy pile of their clothing and handing them to her before he hurried into his own clothes.

"Well, that was way too fast," she said, still wearing only her lingerie.

Perplexed, he looked up from buckling his belt. "What was? The sex?" She had seemed just as eager as he was.

"No, you covering up that gorgeous body of yours."

He grinned with relief. "Practice born of many costume changes." He pulled her to him and ran his hands over her still-bare shoulders and back. "I'm glad you haven't covered yours up yet." He lowered his mouth to where one breast swelled above the lace of her bra and licked along the edge of the fabric.

"Hu-u-ugh," she breathed out, her hands clutching his upper arms.

"Hold that thought until tonight." He shifted upward to kiss her soft, pliant lips. "And bring your lab coat, so you can wear it and nothing else."

Desire heated her eyes as he set her away from him. "Shall I bring the stethoscope, too, and we can play doctor?"

He laughed and shrugged into his suit jacket.

"You were amazing with Ms. Washington." Her lips curved into a smile as she straightened his tie. "Tonight you have to tell me how much of what you said about your foundation is true. I kind of like the idea of being a veterinary adviser to the stars. Well, one star."

"Yes, one star only. I'm not big on sharing."

Jessica combed her fingers through his hair and sighed. "You still never have a bad hair day. So unfair."

"You can do your level best to mess it up tonight."

"I accept the challenge."

Her laughter followed him as he strode down the hallway. Never had he wanted to return to work less than at this moment.

Chapter 17

Jessica lay beside Hugh in the rumpled hotel bed, Manhattan's neon lights painting a kaleidoscope of colors across the sheets and their naked bodies. She shifted slightly to pull her stethoscope out from under her shoulder.

"If we damaged it, I'll buy you a new one," Hugh said as he took it from her to place it on the bedside table.

"Stethoscopes are pretty sturdy. They have to be." She snuggled in as he pulled her against his slightly sweaty side.

"Except I'm fairly certain the manufacturer wasn't expecting it to be used quite the way we did."

Jessica chuckled and spread her fingers over Hugh's chest, the rise and fall of his breath still noticeable after his exertions. "At least we know your heart is pumping just fine."

"A few other things pumped just fine, too." She nipped at his shoulder, making him growl, "It's your patients who are supposed to bite, not you."

She closed her eyes to bask in the press of his ribs against her breasts, the hard muscle of his thigh under the crook of her knee, the warm steel of his arm around her shoulders. If she'd thought her body was humming before, now it was singing an aria of sexual satisfaction, the music welling up from deep inside her. "I feel so good," she said on a sigh.

He traced a finger along her shoulder and down her arm. "You certainly do."

But that wasn't enough. No matter how hard she tried to convince herself it shouldn't be necessary, she couldn't let go of her need to have Hugh put whatever he felt into words. As Aidan said, it was going to hurt if he told her this was just an interlude because they happened to be in the same city at the same time. However, she wanted to know that right up front.

She levered herself up on one elbow so she could see his face. Its angles seemed less stark and hard edged somehow, and she brushed a fingertip along his cheekbone where it was lit by a slash of scarlet neon.

"You look like you have something to say." For a moment she didn't recognize the emotion that flickered in his eyes. Then she identified it as fear.

"Something good." She hoped, swallowing against the nerves that made her throat constrict. "It's different between us tonight, isn't it? We're more . . . open with each other, less cautious."

He tucked a strand of hair behind her ear, hesitating before he spoke. "Jess, I know it won't be easy, but I want to try again with you, with us. Would you be willing to do that?"

Disbelief waltzed with joy, so she was spun in the grip of first one and then the other, leaving her uncertain of what she wanted to say except "Yes!"

"Did you say yes without stopping to think about it?" He pushed up to a sitting position, taking her with him. Now he sounded jubilant.

"No, I've been thinking about us quite a bit, but I did say yes."

He shook his head, but he was smiling. "You're confusing me. Just say yes again."

She took his face between her hands and held it while she locked her eyes on his. "Yes!"

He wrapped his arms around her and kissed her with a tenderness that made her want to cry. When he released her lips, he drew back only a couple of inches. "We'll make it work this time. *I'll* make it work, I swear."

His vehemence was almost daunting, as though he would overwhelm any problem they might have through sheer force of will.

"That's something else I've been thinking about," she said. "It wasn't just you back then. I could have been more understanding."

"Don't say that. I've kept important things about my past from you." He slid his hands down her arms to intertwine their fingers. "I should have been honest with you . . . and with myself."

"Let's forget about that tonight and just enjoy the present." She wanted to hold on to the sweetness of the moment a little longer.

"Do you know how much I want to do that? But we can't move forward until I've repaired the damage from the past." He shook his head. "I owe you a full explanation for my unforgivable behavior over the past eight years, because there's more you don't know."

All the softness in his face was gone now. "Tomorrow," she said, still trying to spare him the pain.

He looked down at where their hands were joined and said in a raw voice, "I don't know if I'll have the courage tomorrow. Right now, I believe in your love."

"You should always believe in it."

His grip tightened. "I'm trying." He released her hands and shifted on the bed so he was silhouetted against the city lights, his face in shadow.

His deliberate obscuring of his expression made her feel strangely vulnerable, so she pulled the sheet up over her breasts.

"I told you that my parents dropped me at a foster-care center and never came back. That's not accurate." He looked away so she could see the sharp lines of his profile outlined by the lights of the skyscrapers behind him. "My father wasn't in the picture from the start. He was a brief relationship that ended when Ma discovered she was pregnant.

I never met him and never want to, although she often told me how much I look like him."

Jessica said nothing about it but she noted his use of the word *often*, which seemed out of place in the story. "I don't know if that's better or worse than him abandoning you *after* you were born. Maybe better?"

"It doesn't matter. It's just a fact in a sordid story."

"Not sordid," she said, hating his belittling of his history. "A tragic and terrible story."

He shrugged. "My mother took me to the foster-care center but made it clear that the situation was only temporary. She told them—and me—she was going to come back for me."

"Oh no." Jessica's heart contracted painfully. Despite his withdrawal, she needed to offer comfort and reached forward to lay her hand on the back of his where it rested on the bed. "That was cruel, even if her intentions were good."

He looked down at her touch but didn't acknowledge it in any other way. "Ah, but she did come back. More than once. I would get settled with a set of foster parents, and then she would show up on the doorstep, demanding my return."

"What? She could do that?" She tried to imagine how Hugh would have felt as a small boy when that happened.

"She wouldn't relinquish her parental rights because she was sure she could be a good mother to me . . . if she could just stop drinking."

He'd never told her why he had been put in foster care. Jessica had assumed his irresponsible parents just didn't want to be saddled with a child. "Did you want to go with her?"

"I couldn't pack my garbage bag fast enough every time. It didn't matter if I liked the foster family or not—she was my mother and she had come back for me."

"But she didn't keep you." So he had been whipsawed between joy at his mother's return and what? Crushing hurt and disappointment when she threw him back? Jessica forced herself to do nothing more than squeeze Hugh's hand when she wanted to throw her arms around him and rock him like the child she was picturing.

"Ma would go to AA meetings for a while. Then something would happen to upset her at work—she mostly waitressed—and she'd quit. Or I'd get sick and she'd have to use part of the rent money for the doctor and meds, so the latest landlord would get nasty. It always started with just one little drink to take the edge off her problems." He shrugged again. "But an alcoholic never stops at one."

"How old were you the first time it happened?"

"I'm not sure. Young enough not to remember much about it, except that she gave me back." His last words were raw with a pain that scraped over Jessica's nerves like a knife blade.

"You thought she didn't want you." She could barely speak through the heartbreak she felt for that little boy.

"The next time I was old enough to understand what would happen if she started drinking. I did everything I could think of to prevent it. I made the beds every day. I washed the dishes. I helped her clean the apartment. I took out the trash. I kept 'quiet as a mouse,' as she always admonished me when she left for work, because there was no babysitter, of course. She couldn't afford one."

Jessica winced. "How old were you?"

"About eight or nine, I think."

"Oh dear God!" She pictured the boy doing chores beyond his years because he thought it would help his mother stay sober. Tears burned in her throat.

"I didn't need a babysitter. The apartment was perfectly safe." His voice was harsh as he defended his mother.

"That wasn't what I was thinking of. It was you"—her voice broke on a sob—"working so hard to be perfect, believing you could change her behavior when her problems had nothing to do with you. I want to take that little boy in my arms and tell him none of it was his fault."

"But I was never good enough." Now his voice was harsh for a different reason. "Never good enough to make her want to stop drinking, so she could keep me."

Tears ran down Jessica's cheeks. "You know that's not true. She had a disease. That's what alcoholism is. She *did* want to keep you—look at how often she tried!—but the disease prevented it."

He let out a long breath. "It didn't feel that way at the time." Suddenly, he turned his hand under hers and clasped her fingers. "She screwed up my chances of being adopted by a stable family. I screwed up my chances, too, because I refused to cooperate in case she wanted me back again. At the same time, I still hoped someone would want to adopt me, just because it would prove that there wasn't something wrong with me."

"Who could blame you?" Jessica fought down another sob. "When was the last time you saw your mother?"

His grip on her hand became convulsive. "Six years ago. At the morgue in West Covina to confirm her identity. She'd been hit by a car. Her blood alcohol level was .21."

"I'm so sorry," Jessica whispered, the words inadequate to acknowledge his terrible loss. Her death meant that there was no chance for Hugh to ever have a real relationship with his mother.

He reached for her other hand and faced her, angled so she could see half of his face while the other half was still in shadow. "I didn't tell you this to make you pity me. I told you because that's why I reacted the way I did when you broke our engagement. Because I felt like that child who'd been abandoned all over again."

She nodded. "I understand."

"It wasn't your fault any more than my mother's alcoholism was mine. You had every right to feel the way you did. But when you left, I reverted back to that nine-year-old. Even worse, I refused to admit it to myself. I rationalized not contacting you with all kinds of lame reasons. Then too much time passed, and I couldn't break through my own stupid pride. I told myself you'd moved on." He ran his thumbs over the back of her hands. "But I never did. I couldn't, because I didn't have the guts to face what I had done."

His words sent a little shiver of disquiet through her. Was this just atonement for their past or did he want her now?

"Neither of us felt that we were good enough for the other," she said. "Kind of ironic. Except I was used to excelling at whatever I did, so I couldn't accept being less than the perfect partner. I felt like a failure all the time, and that made me miserable."

"That's on me. You were brilliant, but in your own wonderful way. I was too scared and blinded by the attention to see that." He dropped her hands and shifted close enough to hold her bare shoulders. "I meant it when I said you could wear scrubs on the red carpet as far as I'm concerned."

"Will Tiffany loan me a diamond necklace to go with them?" she teased.

"I'll *buy* you a necklace. You are the woman I want exactly as you are. Don't change. Ever."

"Change is part of life."

"Your compassion and integrity and capacity for love will never change. That's what I treasure."

His words burrowed deep inside her, soothing the old wounds and swelling the love for him she was beginning to be a little afraid of. It was so overwhelming and without restraint. She still knew so little of this older Hugh and how he lived and what he thought. To fall so completely in love with him again seemed dangerous.

"Will you forgive me so we can start over?" he asked, his voice low with regret.

"There's nothing to forgive. We had problems we couldn't overcome back then."

"I don't deserve it, but thank you, Jess." He used his grip on her shoulders to pull her in for a kiss that started out as a gentle exploration but flared into pure passion. When they tumbled sideways so they could entwine their bodies, Hugh smiled at her. "We're supposed to be older and wiser, but right now I feel young and horny."

Jessica laughed and ran her fingers over his stiff cock. "You certainly do."

Chapter 18

Jessica had to convince Hugh to let her depart without him in the wee hours of the morning. She pointed out that if the paparazzi had somehow trailed him to the hotel, they wouldn't pay any attention to her exit as long as she was alone. He'd admitted the practicality of that, but it had been hard to leave when he walked her to the suite's elevator stark naked. His powerful, masculine beauty still had the power to stun her.

She sat in her kitchen, smiling into her coffee like a woman madly in love, when Aidan trudged in. "How can anyone look so happy before noon on Saturday?" he groused as he poured himself a mug of caffeine. "Wait, last night, you were with . . . now I remember." He gave her a sly look and flopped down into the chair across from her. "But I don't want to know any details."

"Nor would I share them." In recognition of Aidan's new maturity and brotherly advice, she added, "Hugh and I have decided to give it another try."

"You mean, like a 'serious actually get married this time' try?" Her brother's sleepiness evaporated as he sat up straight in the ladder-back chair.

"We're not quite to that point yet. We just started dating again." But she was hoping that's where it would lead.

"Well, you almost married him before, so I figured you might not need a lot of time to make up your mind." He shrugged. "It's cool.

Everyone deserves a second chance. Although since Hugh's an actor, maybe it's a second act."

"Don't the hero and heroine always split up at the end of Act Two? That's not a good analogy." Jessica swallowed the rest of her coffee and stood. "Today's the day I interview the part-time vet candidate."

"You're doing an interview on a Saturday? That's weird."

"Not when your prospective employee prefers to work weekends." Jessica practically sang that sentence. The possibility of having a week-end day off was a golden dream. "She's got a kid, so she wants to be at the office when her husband is home to do childcare."

"Sounds like a win-win for both of you."

Jessica rinsed out her mug and put it on the dish drainer. "If she's as good in person as she is on paper."

The sun was surprisingly strong for an early morning in January, the rays managing to raise gleams of reflected light from the piles of frozen, gray snow that dotted the sidewalk and streets. Jessica found herself almost skipping as she headed toward the clinic, her gloved hands shoved into the pockets of her jacket for extra warmth against the frigid air.

She liked the city in winter. The cold kept the less savory smells down, while the food carts still emitted their mouthwatering aromas on clouds of steam. The dark, bare branches of the trees looked sculptural against the silver-blue sky, and the architectural details of the buildings wore puffy caps of snow that softened their hard surfaces.

Today, though, her buoyant mood was due to Hugh. It could have been raining cats and dogs but she would have danced through the deluge. Although whenever she thought of his mother's cruelty, she wanted to strangle the woman, even though she knew that his mom had at least tried to be a mother to Hugh. Of course, his mother was beyond her reach.

Jessica understood so much more about him now, especially his relentless drive to be a superstar. He couldn't risk being abandoned again, so he needed to have millions of people love him, even if that love was a fickle illusion. That's why he had tried to mold her into the perfect arm candy.

It also explained why he'd cut her off after she broke the engagement. He wasn't going to allow Jessica to tempt him with hope and then annihilate it.

A deep sadness for that little boy ran through the joy of her love for the grown man. But the joy was what made her hum as she strolled along the sidewalk.

Her humming stopped abruptly when she rounded the corner of the block where the clinic stood. Her first patient, Racha—a high-strung greyhound who'd been adopted after he'd retired from racing—alternated between barking hysterically and cowering behind his owner, Mateo Vega. The dog was upset because a horde of photographers stood in a semicircle outside the clinic's front door. Mateo tried to calm him, but the dog wouldn't keep quiet or stand still long enough to be soothed by words or touches.

"Holy crap!" Jessica stomped up the street to confront the paparazzi. "Get the hell away from here. Don't you see you're upsetting the dog? He comes in early to avoid crowds because they make him crazy." Carla always scheduled the skittish creature's appointments before the clinic officially opened.

Instead of leaving, the photographers whipped up their cameras and swarmed around her, clicking away. "Look over here!" "Think about your lover boy in bed." "Why'd you dump him back then?"

That drove Racha into a frenzy of barking and running in circles, so the leash tangled around the dog's slender legs. His owner did his best to keep it from bringing Racha down on the hard pavement. Thank goodness Mateo was a dancer with great balance and agility.

"If that dog gets hurt, I'm suing every one of you," Jessica said, digging out her keys from her purse as fast as she could.

The photographers backed off slightly, probably because she wasn't doing anything more interesting than unlocking the metal gate. She yanked it up, barely feeling the weight with the anger surging through her veins.

"Mateo, come on in." She beckoned as soon as she'd unlocked the door. "Get out of his way," she barked at the paps.

Mateo managed to get the frantic dog through the forest of cameras without anyone getting hurt.

"I'm so sorry," she said, as she locked the door behind them before she knelt to settle Racha down with some gentle stroking. "Who's a good dog? Who tried to scare away the evil paparazzi?" she crooned.

"I know you can't control those people, Doc. But why are they taking pictures of you?" Mateo's expression was baffled and concerned. "Is everything all right?"

Jessica sighed in relief as Racha sank to the floor and rolled onto his back, inviting a tummy rub. She hesitated and then decided everyone would find out soon enough anyway. "I'm dating Hugh Baker, which wouldn't be such a big deal except we were once engaged and it didn't work out back then."

Mateo's eyes went wide. "You mean *the* Hugh Baker, the one who plays Julian Best?" He fanned himself. "He is *so* hot. I'd date him, too, except he doesn't roll that way."

Jessica laughed and rose from her crouch by the dog. "Evidently."

"I'm happy for you, Doc," Mateo said, leaning in to give her a hug and an air-kiss.

Surprised but touched, she hugged him back. "That's nice of you. Now let's see what's going on with Racha's ears."

She led the way down the corridor to an examining room and pushed the disturbing encounter with the press out of her mind. It wasn't until Racha was ready to leave that she remembered the front entrance would be a problem.

"Luckily, we have a back alleyway," she told Mateo as she walked toward the rear of the building. "It's not scenic, but it should keep poor Racha away from the circling vultures. Unless they're staking out the back, too." She stopped for a moment. "I know, I'll go out front to attract their attention. Give me a minute and then zip out the back."

She walked to the front door, drew back the dead bolt, took a breath, and pulled it open. The paps sprang to attention, tossing cigarettes away as they once again started shooting. This time, though, she smiled and held out the hem of her bright red top. "Hey, guys, do these scrubs make me look fat?"

One of them laughed and lowered his camera. "You really are a veterinarian. I didn't believe it. I mean, Hugh Baker with a real person? It's strange."

"I couldn't agree with you more," Jessica said, turning to smile toward the other group of photographers. She even put one hand on her hip, remembering that little tip from the red carpet eight years ago.

Figuring that she had given Mateo enough time to escape, she backed toward the door again. "If I were you, I'd clear out before my office manager gets here. She's pretty scary when she's angry." With that, she dodged back in the door and locked it again.

Sitting down at her desk, she started to reread Riya Agarwal's résumé for her upcoming interview, but her anger at the photographers spoiled her concentration. Even Geode seemed to sense the waves of fury radiating off her, because he didn't attempt to sit in Jessica's lap, retreating to the top of the filing cabinet instead.

"How does Hugh stand it?" Jessica asked the cat, then answered her own question. "He lives in a bubble with back entrances and limousines and assistants named Trevor. But I live in the real world." She scanned her cramped office with its water-stained ceiling, hideous green chair, and brown vinyl tiles. This was where she belonged.

She heard the front door open and then Carla's footsteps pounding down the linoleum of the hallway. Geode leaped off the filing cabinet and fled. "What on God's green earth are those creeps doing out in front of our respectable clinic, bothering the hell out of anyone who tries to come in?" Carla demanded.

Jessica's stomach clenched. Even Carla was upset by the paps. "I know. They freaked out Racha, too."

Carla looked insulted. "I'm not freaked out. I'm pissed off." She sat down and pinned Jessica with a sharp look. "What gives?"

Carla angry was better than Carla distressed, so Jessica relaxed a bit. "It's my fault. Well, technically, it's Hugh's fault. When you date a superstar, the tabloids want pictures. Especially once they find out about the broken engagement."

"So now you're dating him?" Carla raised her eyebrows.

"We're giving it another try." Jessica realized she was going to be saying that a lot. No one cared if she dated Pete Larson, but everyone wanted to know about Hugh Baker.

"You're going to tell me all about it at lunchtime, but right now I got to get rid of some nasty paparazzi before they scare all our patients away." She jerked out of the chair and marched back down the hallway.

Jessica was tempted to watch the confrontation, but she had to get ready for work. As the vet techs arrived, not one commented on the photographers, but she was too busy to ask them about it. She hoped they hadn't felt harassed.

When her lunch break rolled around, she grabbed a bottle of water and one of the deli sandwiches Carla had ordered in before she shut herself in her office. She wanted privacy to check the texts that she'd heard come in on her phone.

Hugh's first text said: Right now I want Julian Best to die a horrible death so we can go back to the hotel room.

His second text was: Although I may not be able to make love to you until I've thawed out, because the East River is so cold that my balls have frostbite.

His third text read: I need to speak to Gavin about the next book taking place during the summer months or entirely in locations near the equator.

Jessica started to giggle.

There was a gap in the time stamps before he sent his final text: What I'm trying to say is that I'm counting the seconds until I can touch you again.

Her giggles stopped on a drawn-in breath. She felt as though he *had* touched her—in all her most sensitive places.

An impatient knock vibrated through the door before the knob turned and Carla walked in with her own sandwich.

"Give me a second," Jessica said as Carla sat down. She typed in: I've never had text foreplay before. I like it.

"You done?" Carla asked.

Jessica put down the phone with a little smirk.

"Now we're gonna talk, girlfriend," Carla said.

"I haven't heard any complaints about the paparazzi," Jessica said. "Did they get bored and leave?"

Carla gave her a triumphant smile. "They left, all right. I called a buddy at the precinct and told him our business was being disrupted. A couple of guys from the K-9 unit came over with their dogs and suggested that the photographers move along. The cops still remember what you did for that German shepherd—what was his name?"

"Brodie," Jessica supplied. One of the police dogs had been grazed by a bullet in a gunfight between the police and a drug dealer. It had happened nearby, so they'd brought the dog to her. "It was just a flesh wound, not a big deal."

"You know how they feel about their dogs. They're just like a human partner, and the cops don't take hurting their partners lightly." Carla pointed an accusing finger at her. "Don't change the subject."

"There was no subject. You just sat down and said we were going to talk." Jessica took a bite of her turkey sandwich.

"Hugh Baker is the subject, and you know it."

"What about him?" Jessica gulped a swig of water.

"Why are you back together?" Carla left her sandwich sitting on the paper plate on Jessica's desk while she conducted her interrogation.

"Wow, you really cut to the chase." Jessica started to peel the label off the water bottle. "He's shared some things with me that kind of explain what happened eight years ago." She looked at Carla. "But the real reason is that I never stopped caring about him. I just shoved it in a box and stuffed it down in a dark corner of my mind. When I saw him again, the old feelings came back to life."

Carla did something Jessica had never seen before. She hesitated, drumming her royal-blue fingernails on the matching scrubs that stretched over her knee. When she spoke, concern filled her voice. "I want to believe in the power of true love as much as anyone, but he's not the same Hugh Baker you fell in love with eight years ago. The man is in the stratosphere of money and fame. And it's not that I think you don't belong there, too, but that kind of success changes a person. He doesn't know what real life is like anymore, riding in limos, staying in penthouse suites, getting tickets to the hottest play on Broadway with a snap of his fingers."

"I think I can handle a penthouse suite without too much trouble." Jessica tried to lighten Carla's mood, but her words were an eerie echo of what she'd been thinking earlier.

"That's the good stuff." Carla waved her hand toward the front of the clinic. "There's the bad stuff, like everyone wanting to know your business, women throwing themselves at him, traveling all over creation for his job." She leaned forward, her brown eyes soft with concern. "I'm just saying that maybe you should go slow and find out how you fit into all that."

Since the same disquieting thoughts had crossed Jessica's mind, she shifted in her seat. She'd been so happy this morning. Why couldn't she go back to that blissful state? "So you think I should give up on him because he's rich and famous?"

"Just be careful, hon. Don't jump in with both feet right away," Carla said. "Although I can see in your face that it's probably too late."

"I tried to be practical and fall for someone less complicated," Jessica said, thinking of solid, stable, blond Pete, "but you can't control who you love."

"Yeah, that's why we have music and poetry," Carla said. "Because love screws with us all and we have to vent."

Four hours later, Jessica sank onto her desk chair again, wishing she could forget Carla's warning. But it had gnawed at her every time she had a break between patients. The paparazzi outside the clinic proved that she had been living in a dream world for the past two weeks. Being with Hugh was going to change her life in ways she couldn't yet comprehend.

Tiana stuck her head in the door. "Riya Agarwal is here. Carla said 'two thumbs up' and asked if you want Dr. Agarwal to come to your office."

"Sure, she might as well see the worst," Jessica said with a grimace at the dreadful green chair the vet candidate would have to sit in. She unearthed the doctor's résumé from under a pile of patient files and scanned the questions she'd jotted down. It felt good to have something normal and straightforward to focus on amid all the turmoil of the day.

A small woman dressed in black trousers, a white blouse, and a red blazer stopped in the doorway. "Dr. Quillen?" She had huge brown eyes, shiny black hair pulled into a fat bun at the back of her neck, and a shy smile.

Jessica stood and walked around her desk, holding out her hand. "A pleasure to meet you. Have a seat in the ugliest chair ever made."

Dr. Agarwal laughed as she settled onto the seat. "At least it is comfortable," she said in a musical voice.

Jessica went back to her desk chair and began to ask her questions. The doctor replied to every query with ease and expertise. The only odd note was struck when Jessica asked, just out of curiosity, how Riya had found the clinic. The other woman had an answer—she had looked up all the veterinary practices close to her and chose Jessica's clinic as the one she was most interested in—but it sounded pat and rehearsed, unlike her other responses. However, Jessica didn't care.

The clincher came when Geode strolled in and stopped to sniff at Riya's ankles. Without pausing in her answer, the doctor reached down to give the cat a gentle head scratch. Jessica doubted the vet even realized she was doing it. The famously shy Geode not only allowed Riya to touch him, he crouched and leaped onto her lap.

That was when Jessica offered Dr. Agarwal the job.

"I look forward to getting to know the ropes tomorrow," Jessica's new part-time colleague said as they finished up ironing out the details. Jessica had been thrilled that Riya wanted to start as soon as possible. Then she remembered this morning's unpleasant surprise. "I should probably warn you about a little issue we're having here at the moment. When you come in tomorrow, you may find some photographers hanging around in front. Just ignore them."

"Photographers? Why would photographers be here?"

Jessica sighed. "Do you know who Hugh Baker is?"

Riya's large brown eyes widened like a startled doe's before she nodded.

"He and I are dating, which wouldn't be big news, except that we were engaged eight years ago and broke it off."

Relief spread over Riya's face. "Oh, so you know. That makes me feel better."

"I know what?"

"About how I . . . about Mr. Baker being the reason . . ." The other vet trailed off as she sensed Jessica's incomprehension.

But her words triggered hazy memories of a conversation in Hugh's limousine. "Did Hugh send you here?" Jessica asked, making an effort to keep her voice even.

"I had my résumé posted on a job website, saying I was looking for part-time work in the New York area. He got in touch with me and suggested I apply here, even though there was no job opening posted." A worried crease appeared between Riya's eyebrows as she tried to repair whatever damage she had done. "He said many very positive things about you and your clinic, so I became convinced this was the right place for me."

Jessica didn't want to upset her godsend. "And I am thrilled that he did. You are going to be a great addition to the clinic."

A relieved smile lit Riya's face. "I am thrilled, too."

"Hugh! Come in for a minute!" Bryan shouted from the door of the production trailer as Hugh walked by, headed for his limo.

Hugh considered claiming that he was late for an appointment of some kind, but he owed Bryan for yesterday's rescheduling. Of course, the director was taking full advantage of that. He'd worked Hugh like a dog today, shoehorning in extra scenes to speed up the filming. All Hugh wanted to do right now was fall into bed with Jess and go to sleep . . . after making love to her, of course. That thought sent a shot of adrenaline right down to his cock.

However, he veered toward the trailer and plodded up the steps. "Good or bad?" he asked as Bryan waved him onto a chair in front of the large screen where the day's footage was reviewed.

"You tell me," the director said. "Run that last scene with Meryl again," he ordered the assistant.

It was the foreplay scene between Julian and Sara, which started with some clever banter, moved into emotional confessions, and culminated in a hard, passionate kiss. Hugh had been surprised and relieved when Bryan had declared the second take a wrap.

As he watched, he understood why.

"I can't believe the camera lens didn't fog up," Bryan said. "You two practically generated nuclear fusion. Every guy in the audience is going to thank you for what happens when he and his date get home."

Of course, he'd been channeling his feelings for Jess into his character's reactions to Sara. Meryl, being the talented actress she was, had used his energy to feed her own responses.

"If you do this for the actual love scene, it's going to scorch right through the film," Bryan chortled.

"Meryl did half the work," Hugh pointed out.

Bryan shook his head. "That heat is radiating off you, ace, but I'll make sure Meryl sees this, too. She needs to know what's possible when a pro is acting at the top of his game."

Hugh wasn't immune to compliments from a director whom he respected. His fatigue lifted somewhat. "I appreciate that, but it takes a talented director to make it happen."

Bryan grinned and slapped Hugh on the shoulder. "We are one helluva team. Now go get some sleep so we can make more magic tomorrow."

Hugh groaned inwardly about the Sunday shoot, but he'd agreed to it knowing that Jess had to work anyway.

On the way to the hotel, he fell asleep in the limo, starting awake when the driver opened the door. Jess had texted him that she was already there, so he practically bolted down the hallway to the elevator, his haste prompted by the thought of how soft and warm she would feel in his arms.

He strode out of the elevator into the suite, calling her name. She rose from the plush sectional couch, tossing aside the magazine she was reading, her face alight with welcome. He let his gaze wander over the swell of her breasts under her cream-colored sweater and the swing of her deliciously rounded hips as she walked toward him. He wanted to feel every inch of her sweet, lush body against him right now.

They met halfway for a kiss that both shattered and healed him. She'd left her satiny brown hair loose around her shoulders, the scent of a citrusy shampoo drifting up from it. He buried his fingers in its waves to hold her while he drank in the slightly dazed light in her gray eyes and the temptation of her soft lips. "Jess," he said.

"Hugh," she answered with a smile, tracing her finger over his eyebrow, along his cheekbone, and down to the corner of his mouth, her touch sending tiny flickers of pleasure over his skin. "I'm still not used to you."

He knew she meant how he looked, something he considered a genetic accident. He had long ago made peace with the fact that his appearance was a huge contributor to his success. When it came to Jess, though, he wanted her to love *him*, not his weirdly blue eyes. However, he made a joke of it. "Well, I intend to give you plenty of opportunity to become accustomed to me. All too soon, you'll take my good looks entirely for granted."

She cupped his cheek with her palm. "That will never happen." Her smile turned to a self-mocking grin before she pushed out of his embrace. "Like the good girlfriend of a movie star, I managed to lift my little finger and order us drinks and dinner from room service. Do you still like bourbon straight up?"

Eight years ago, he thought drinking bourbon neat was both sophisticated and manly, so he'd taught himself to like it. Now that he didn't have to worry about his image, he'd reverted to beer. But when Jess mentioned it, he had a sudden craving to taste the flavor of his aspirations. "It's exactly what I want right now."

"Hard day on the set?" she asked, taking his hand to lead him into the living room, where a decanter and several glasses were arranged on a tray on the coffee table. A half-empty glass of white wine stood near where she'd been reading.

She waved him to the sofa and poured the dark-amber liquid into a crystal tumbler. He simply watched her, taking in the curves of her backside under her jeans, the sure, efficient movements of her doctor's hands, the way her hair rippled and flowed over her shoulders as she leaned forward. He cherished every detail of her.

When she leaned back on the sofa to hand him the glass and snuggle up against his side, he wrapped his arm around her and sighed with contentment. "This is perfect."

"You haven't tasted the bourbon. It's a little better than the stuff you used to drink." Jess picked up her wineglass. "So's the wine, for that matter."

"The bourbon has nothing to do with it. It's having you beside me that makes for perfection. I could drink rotgut and still be happy."

"When you say things like that, I think . . ." She trailed off, and Hugh looked down, trying to read her expression. But she was staring into her wineglass.

"You think what?" His voice was sharper than he intended.

She lifted her head and smiled. "I think you are a mighty big flatterer."

"That's not what you were going to say."

"Okay, some things happened today that I need to talk to you about."

Alarm vibrated through him. "Good or bad?" he asked for the second time that evening.

"Both." She took a gulp of wine. "The good is that I hired that veterinarian you sent to me. She's terrific and starts tomorrow, so thank you for that."

For a moment he didn't catch the bombshell in her statements. He was about to say how glad he was when he realized she had somehow found out that he was responsible for Riya Agarwal's job application. "What makes you think I sent her?"

"She told me."

"That wasn't supposed to happen." He knew his voice was tight with annoyance.

"It was a misunderstanding. She thought I already knew." Jess turned toward him. "Why, Hugh? We weren't dating then, so I don't understand."

He shrugged. "A simple desire to help someone I'd treated badly. Maybe a little bit of atonement. You don't have to feel guilty, because I got my assistant to do all the legwork of finding someone qualified."

"You mean Trevor, who claims you're a dream to work for?" she said with a half smile. Putting her hand on his arm, she leaned in to give him a gentle kiss on the cheek. "Carla says never to look a gift horse in the mouth, so I'm just going to accept your vet with gratitude." Then her voice turned stern. "But don't do anything else like that behind my back."

He put up a hand in acknowledgment of his blunder. "I didn't think you'd interview her if you knew I was involved. But you're right. I overstepped a boundary."

"I like this new Hugh, who admits he made a mistake." Her smile was teasing, but the underlying truth was real.

"Eight years teaches you a lot of lessons." He grazed his lips against her temple. "I hope Dr. Agarwal works out, for reasons both altruistic and selfish. You need the rest, and I want more of you."

She melted into him, her head on his shoulder, her hand burning a brand on his thigh through the denim of his jeans. For a long moment, he allowed cowardice to get the better of him, stroking his palm up and down the soft wool covering her arm as her body heat soaked into him.

"All right, what's the bad?" he finally prompted.

She took a deep breath. "When I got to the clinic this morning, there were a bunch of photographers waiting. I might have yelled at them because they were upsetting one of my patients."

Hugh winced. He knew enough to imagine what those photos would look like. He didn't care for himself, but he feared it would upset Jessica. "Next time, call me. I have people who deal with that all the time."

"I have people, too, you know. Carla called the local K-9 unit. I patched up one of their dogs last year, so they brought a couple of combat-trained German shepherds to scare away the paparazzi."

Hugh threw back his head and laughed. "I wish I could have seen that."

"Unfortunately, they also figured out where I live."

His free hand closed into a fist as relief turned to anger. "How many?"

"About six or seven. There was kind of a swarm, so it was hard to count. Aidan had to bulldoze through them so I could get to the car tonight." She shifted against him. "I don't know how you bear it. They shouted horrible questions, asking if you'd cheated on me and that's why I'd dumped you." Her distress was clear.

"They're just trying to get a reaction on camera, but I'm sorry." He pulled her closer against him, as though he could protect her from the paps that way.

"You don't have to keep apologizing. You can't control them."

"But it's my fault that they're harassing you." He knew she wouldn't allow him to send a car and bodyguard to take her to and from work . . . yet. "We need to get in front of this story."

"What do you mean?"

"It's only news because it's new and we had a broken engagement. If we go on television as a couple and talk about it, there won't be any reason for the paps to bother you any longer."

"Go on television?" She pulled away and turned to stare at him.

"We could appear on *It's Showbiz* tomorrow night if I get Trevor on it right away. We'll do a quick interview and kill all the excitement about us."

She looked like a deer in headlights. "Do an interview on television? Like when you sit in one of those giant chairs and fend off scary questions from the host?"

"*It's Showbiz* isn't like that. They keep it friendly so people like me will agree to do the show. Even the chairs aren't that big." He made his tone light to ease her anxiety.

"What would I wear?" she asked unexpectedly.

"I know a stylist who can help you with that. So you want to do this?"

"Want to? No, but it makes sense." She squared her shoulders as though she were about to face a firing squad. "I don't want my patients and employees suffering because of me."

"Because of *me*," he said, the nagging sense of unease flaring up again. For the first time in years, he regretted the extent of his fame.

She reached up to brush her fingers through his hair, the gentleness of her touch sending tendrils of bliss curling through him. "I just have to get used to the side effects of being with you, that's all." She shoved off the couch. "Now let's eat. I'm starved."

He stood but stopped her from going to the table by taking her hands. "We need to talk with the security firm I use as soon as possible."

"A security firm? That seems extreme." Alarm clouded her eyes. "Won't the TV appearance solve our problems?"

"Up to a point." Since his rise to stardom had been gradual, he'd had time to layer on the barriers around him. Jessica was being rocketed straight to the pinnacle of celebrity without any preparation. "Let me give Trevor a call and then we'll enjoy our dinner." His voice dropped to a deep rumble as he thought of what he'd planned for dessert. "After that, we'll enjoy each other."

Chapter 19

Jessica clutched Hugh's hand as they followed their guide down the hallway to the set where Sherri Burns waited to interview them. Panic had wrapped a fist around her throat so she felt as though she couldn't swallow, much less speak. She drew in a deep breath and reminded herself that Sherri was friendly.

"You look like you're facing the guillotine," Hugh said, pulling them to a stop. He rubbed his palms up and down her arms and smiled at her, his eyes filled with encouragement. "Just be you, Jess. Say anything you want to. Talk about your work, the animals, the K-9 Angelz. Your passion will shine on camera. If there are any questions you don't want to answer, toss them to me. I'm used to this."

He'd told her the same thing in ten different ways, but she needed to hear it again. She nodded. "I'll be fine once I get started." She hoped to God that was true.

"Mr. Baker, we have to go," the assistant whatever-she-was said urgently. "This commercial break is short."

"It's all right," Hugh said, still smiling at Jessica. "We can always make an entrance."

His utter lack of concern about the timing or the content steadied her. She started walking again.

It had been a whirlwind of a day. Riya had started at the clinic. The new doctor found her footing very quickly, thank goodness, because that allowed them to get through more patients in less time.

Jessica had barely had a moment to feel gratitude for the success of the part-time vet before she had to race home to meet Quentin, the stylist. She was hugely relieved when Quentin said it was all right for her to wear trousers, because the thought of making sure her skirt didn't ride up on camera had fueled extra stress. He even permitted her to wear her own black dress pants, so she felt comfortable from the waist down, at least. Well, except for the sky-high black pumps he insisted on. He pointed out that she wouldn't be walking on camera, so it didn't matter if she wobbled on them.

"We want you to look hot sitting beside Mr. Baker," Quentin said as he held up a blouse on a hanger in front of her. "No, that color doesn't speak to me."

After testing three other blouses, he had her try on a periwinkle-blue silk blouse with a high scoop neckline. "That's the one," he said. "It gives your eyes interesting depths."

"It does?" Jessica peered over his shoulder into the mirror but didn't notice a difference.

"Trust me, the camera will see them."

He'd added small gold hoop earrings and a gold cuff bracelet. "You don't wear nail polish?"

"I'm a veterinarian. It would last about thirty seconds."

"Right, let's stay plain then. It goes with your backstory." He stood several feet away, his eyes narrowed in assessment. "What to do with your hair?"

Self-conscious, she touched her messy bun. "Is it that terrible?"

"Terrible? No, no! It's beautiful. That's why I'm having a hard time making a decision about the best style. So many options!"

She was pretty sure Quentin was sweet-talking her, but a glow of flattered pleasure flickered through her nonetheless.

In the end, he decided on a loose bun, but it looked entirely different from when she did it. Little waving tendrils drifted beside her cheeks while the rest of her hair was twisted into a soft, graceful shape at the nape of her neck.

"Okay, let's get you to the studio for makeup," he said, escorting her to the car waiting in front of her house. Evidently Hugh's people had done their thing, because no paparazzi skulked outside her door.

When he finished her makeup in the studio dressing room, Quentin had whipped off the protective cape and stepped back to evaluate his efforts. "You'll make everyone think that Mr. Baker is a lucky man," he said at last.

A few minutes later, she heard Hugh's voice in the hallway, and relief nearly swamped her. He walked into the dressing room and came to an abrupt halt, his gaze scanning over her and turning intense. "If Quentin wasn't here, I would say something improper," Hugh said, starting toward her again. "You look good enough to eat." He grinned wickedly before bending down.

Jessica laughed and put her hand on his chest to stop him. "Quentin has spent a long time dolling me up. Don't destroy his handiwork. And your intonation was quite improper."

The stylist snorted. "Nothing you say could shock me, and don't get me started on what I've *seen* go on in these dressing rooms."

Hugh dropped into the chair beside her and Quentin sprang into action, draping a clean cape over Hugh's silver-gray shirt. Of course, it took about one-tenth the time to make Hugh camera ready as it had her. He shrugged into the dark-gray blazer he'd carried in and was ready to go.

A technician came in to wire them for sound. Quentin took control of Jessica's tiny mic, pulling medical tape out of his kit and telling her to tape it in her cleavage so no bulge would show under her blouse.

"Let me know if you need help with that," Hugh said with a sideways smile while the technician clipped a mic under his jacket's lapel.

"Ha! You have it easy," Jessica said while Quentin ran the wire around her waist to the transmitter pack he had stuck in her waistband. "Next time I'm wearing a blazer, too."

Now as they walked down the hall, she focused on the strength of Hugh's hand around hers and the knowledge that he would step into any lull in the interview. But what really reassured her was that he genuinely didn't care what anyone else thought of her. He'd convinced her of that last night.

It was quite a change from the last public appearance she'd made with him.

The assistant led them past a forest of lights, cameras, and equipment whose purpose she had no idea of before they stepped into the brilliantly lit stage set.

Sherri stood up and air-kissed Hugh. "Thanks for giving me the first interview. I appreciate that." The talk show hostess was tiny, although her hot-pink sheath dress and heels that outdid Jessica's for height made her attention grabbing. Her hair was braided into fascinating patterns that swirled over her scalp.

"It's always a pleasure to be on your show," Hugh said, his smile so dazzling that Sherri actually blinked before she turned to Jessica.

"So nice to meet Hugh's new girlfriend," the hostess said with air-kisses in Jessica's direction. "I understand you have some interesting history."

"Not so interesting, really," Jessica said, answering Sherri's smile. "We just needed some time to figure ourselves out."

Someone called out, "Thirty seconds."

"Make yourselves comfortable," Sherri said, gesturing toward the plush gray sofa opposite her as she seated herself. "Sound check."

Hugh said, "Test, test," and nodded to Jessica to do the same as they settled onto the couch. She remembered to slant her legs to the side and cross her ankles, per Quentin's suggestion.

"All good," a disembodied voice said from the darkness beyond the set.

The countdown began, and Jessica felt her nerves tighten. She squeezed Hugh's hand to remind herself that she wasn't in this alone, but the thought of making a fool of herself—and by association, him—on national television made her heartbeat accelerate in an unpleasant way. When Hugh rubbed his thumb over the back of her hand, small curls of warmth eased her tension slightly.

Then Sherri greeted them all over again, which reminded Jessica to focus on their hostess and not worry about the gazillions of faces gazing at them on screens across the country. Sherri lobbed simple questions at Hugh, easing them into the interview.

Then she shifted to Jessica. "You're a veterinarian in South Harlem. I understand that your profession is what initially brought you into contact with Hugh. Will you share the story of your first meeting?"

Hugh had anticipated this question, so he and Jessica had rehearsed the story the night before, although it had quickly degenerated into a wildly embellished version as she and Hugh tried to one-up each other on the details. The memory of their laughter made Jessica relax a bit as she launched into the official version, ending with Hugh's proposal.

"So romantic," Sherri said. "But the engagement obviously ended. What happened?"

This was another question they'd known would come up, but Hugh spoke before she could. "I was an idiot." Which was not the response they'd rehearsed. Jessica stopped watching Sherri and turned to Hugh. "I thought my career was more important than hers just because it got more attention. But she was saving the lives of animals every day while I was just reciting lines." He angled his head toward Jessica so he spoke directly to her. "And it's still true. There's no comparison."

He'd gone off script, and she was lost in the depths of his blue eyes. He lifted her hand to brush his lips over the back of it, and Sherri sighed audibly. Then Hugh turned to the hostess. "Lucky for me, Jess believes in second chances, so I persuaded her to give me one. I don't intend to screw it up this time."

Even as his words sent joy zinging through her heart, she caught a flutter of movement from Sherri. "Oh my God, if Hugh Baker said that to me, I would be a puddle on the floor," the hostess said, her hands pressed dramatically to her chest.

Which made Jessica question how much of what Hugh said was meant for the cameras and how much was true. She hated herself for her sudden skepticism, but the ugly little doubt dampened her happiness enough to allow her to say with a naughty smile, "Sometimes it's hard to stay upright around Hugh."

"Ooh, a little double entendre," Sherri cooed. "I like this woman."

Hugh chuckled and gave Jessica a peck on the cheek before turning the conversation to her work. Sherri gave her all the right cues, and Jessica found herself waxing more passionate than she meant to about her clinic and the K-9 Angelz.

"My foundation has plans to replicate the K-9 Angelz in other locations," Hugh said. "It's an incredible program for the kids—and the dogs."

After that, Sherri finished up the interview before they went to a commercial break. Once again, she stood. "That was tremendous. The ratings will be through the roof."

Jessica let Hugh pull her up with him, using his grip to help her balance on the unaccustomed heels. Her knees felt a little shaky, too, as the anxiety-induced adrenaline began to drain away.

"You're a brilliant interviewer," Hugh said. "Always eliciting the best from your guests."

The hostess preened under Hugh's charm. "Come back soon."

And then they were being ushered off the set, passing the next guest in the hallway.

In the dressing room, Jessica threw herself into the makeup chair, her legs sprawled, her arms draped over the chair's sides. "That was utterly terrifying."

Hugh looked startled. "You handled it like a pro. Not a moment's hesitation or a wrong note. I thought you were fine with it."

"If you hadn't made us rehearse all that stuff last night, I would have just opened and closed my mouth like a fish out of water."

Quentin and the technician appeared at the same time. "You were fantastic," Quentin said, helping with the wire after Jessica peeled the tape gently off her skin. "A natural." He winked at her. "And Hugh was okay, too."

"Well, I know I looked all right, thanks to you." Jessica stood to hug Quentin. "I guess I need to give you the blouse and accessories back."

"No, the designer wants you to keep them. Just mention her name every now and then."

Jessica looked at Hugh, who'd been watching their banter with an indulgent eye. He shrugged. "Happens all the time. If you like them, take them home. Trust me, it's great publicity for the designer."

It felt odd to accept expensive clothing from a total stranger, especially when she was supposed to become a walking advertisement. Jessica flexed one foot out in front of her. "I can't imagine ever wearing these shoes again. They're just too high."

"Decide when you get home and let me know," Quentin said, closing up his makeup box. "I've got to dash."

He shut the door, leaving Hugh and Jessica alone.

"Was it that awful?" Hugh asked, worry putting a crease between his eyebrows.

"I was exaggerating for effect," she said, reaching up to smooth the furrow out. "What you said about why we broke up was really sweet. Did you mean it?"

Now anger made the blue of his eyes scorching. "Of course I meant it. I said it in front of millions of people."

"Well, that's why I wondered."

"Wait, you thought I said it *because* there were millions of viewers? That I was playing to the audience?" He raked his fingers through his hair as he looked away. "And here I thought that if I made such a public declaration you would believe me, and trust the truth of it."

The pain in his voice jabbed at Jessica. "I'm sorry, but this celebrity thing is new to me. I don't really know how it works."

She watched his chest expand as he took a deep breath. "I will never pretend anything with you, Jess, no matter how many or how few people are watching." He took her hands. "Every word out of my mouth was real. Do you believe that now?"

"Yes." She nodded as the joy bubbled up again, drowning all her creeping suspicions. "And I'm going to play the recording of that interview over and over again, just to hear you say it."

He smiled, but there was still hurt in his eyes.

Chapter 20

"That's a wrap!" Bryan shouted.

Relief surged through Hugh, but he fought the instinct to instantly roll away from Meryl and leap out of the bed. The actress had done her job in their love scene admirably, not to mention the fact that she was naked from the waist up. So he carefully extricated himself from their clinch and sat up, making sure to tuck the sheet around her to preserve any modesty she might have left after a dozen people had watched her strip and simulate sex with him. At least in Julian Best movies they kept the covers carefully draped over the more intimate parts of their bodies.

"Great work," he said with a smile.

"You inspired me, babe," she purred before tossing the sheet back and standing to take her robe from an assistant without any indication of embarrassment. She gave him a hot look. "It's not exactly painful to be pressed up against Hugh Baker."

He laughed, but he couldn't return the compliment. He didn't usually have a problem with love scenes, but the crush of her breasts against his chest had made him uncomfortable. He knew exactly why.

By a fluke of scheduling, he now had a four-hour break. After the intensity of this scene, he needed a completely different outlet, and Jess's living room walls sprang to mind. He hadn't lied to Gavin when he said he wanted to offer her something real, not something from his world of pretense. Fixing her wall made him feel grounded, in the same way Jess made him feel grounded. He belted on his robe and headed for the dressing room.

Forty-five minutes later, Aidan opened Jess's front door for him, the vinegary fumes of wallpaper solvent wafting out around him. "Good thing you texted. I was about to go out to grab lunch. By the way, why don't you get a key from my sister?" He grinned. "After all, the whole world knows you're together now." He stuck his head out the door and glanced around. "Notice the lack of lurking paparazzi."

Hugh stepped past Aidan into the front hall. "They weren't waiting for Jess this morning?"

"She didn't ask me to help her get through them, so I guess not." Aidan looked sheepish. "I slept late."

Hugh had asked her to text him if she had a problem and she hadn't, so he decided to let it go. "Let's get started. I've only got a couple of hours free."

Once he'd gotten set up, he fell into the rhythm of scoring, wetting, and carefully scraping the many layers of wallpaper from the plaster, letting the complications of his life fall away. The only thing better would have been Jess's company, but she was hard at work.

"I'm glad you came," Aidan said from his section of wall. He'd scarfed down a peanut-butter-and-jelly sandwich while Hugh started his task. "I've got a job interview tomorrow. I think I have a good chance at getting the position, so I may not have as much time to work on this."

Hugh could hire someone who would repair the walls faster and better than either of them, but he wasn't going to mention that. Jess might have something to say about the idea, anyway. "You promised your sister you'd finish the living room."

"I will." Aidan's tone was defensive. "It just might take longer."

Hugh had made his point. "What kind of company is it?"

"It's way cool. They deal with data exhaust."

Hugh laughed. "What the hell is that?"

Aidan went into a long, technical explanation that allowed Hugh to concentrate on peeling off the wallpaper as the jargon washed over him.

"I was afraid that Jessica getting together with you might be a problem, but Pete's cool."

Hugh's attention was jerked away from his task. "Why would Jessica's and my relationship cause problems for your interview?"

"I told you," Aidan said, letting a strip of wallpaper fall onto the drop cloth. "She was dating Pete Larson, who's kind of a big cheese in the company, until you came back into the picture. But he assured me it wouldn't affect my chances of getting the job."

Hugh didn't really care about Aidan's chances of landing the position right now. "Pete sounds like a stand-up guy." He yanked at the corner of wallpaper and cursed when a chunk of plaster came off with it. Stopping, he took a deep breath.

Aidan dipped his roller into the solvent and continued. "That's why I introduced them. He's from our hometown in Iowa and he's done real well for himself, just like Jess. I figured they'd have a lot in common."

Hugh didn't like the idea of a man who had grown up with the same people Jess had, who could probably reminisce about the same teachers in school, who knew the street names from her childhood. Even worse, who had followed a similar trajectory out of Iowa and into the big city. A man who would fit into Jess's life seamlessly, without any unwanted disruptions like Hugh would create.

Hugh forced himself to peel off another corner of wallpaper and tried to be subtle in his quest to find out more about his competitor. "You wouldn't find it awkward to work with a man who might be unhappy with your sister?"

Aidan shrugged. "They didn't date that long, so it's not like he's brokenhearted."

Hugh's tense neck muscles unclenched slightly at that piece of information.

"Besides, I would be working in a totally different area from Pete's. He's the CFO, and I'm tech."

A CFO. Pete was indeed a big cheese. Hugh rubbed at the back of his neck as it tightened again.

"I mean, she didn't even bother to tell you about Pete, right?" Aidan continued. "So it obviously wasn't a big deal. You know Jess. She's all about integrity and honesty and honor."

Hugh knew that, but he wished Aidan had kept his nose out of Jess's love life. And he didn't like Aidan's flippant tone when referring to his sister. "Those are rare qualities. They're part of what makes Jess such an extraordinary person."

The young man flushed. "Hey, I know. She's my sister. It's just that sometimes her standards are hard to live up to."

That was one of the many things Hugh loved about her. "You're fortunate to have a sister who cares about you so much that she offers you standards."

"Don't get me wrong, Jess is great," Aidan said. "She's always been really good to me, too. So I want to get this job to be worthy of her."

Aidan's lofty sentiments were conveniently in line with his own self-interest, but Hugh quashed his cynical response. The kid was a solid person. He just had some more growing up to do.

"She was pretty awesome in that TV interview with you." Aidan clearly wanted to change the focus of the conversation. "I told her how great she looked, but she said it was all because of the stylist. You know my sister—she'd rather wear scrubs than some designer gown any day." Aidan looked over again. "Is that piece of paper not coming off?"

Hugh looked at the dangling green-and-orange-swirled paper with the attached chunk of plaster that he wanted to bash Pete on the side of the head with, or maybe ram down his throat. "I need to put more solvent on, that's all."

"Here you go." Aidan handed him the roller. "You know, I'm glad Jess gave you a second chance. I mean, how many movie stars would strip their girlfriend's wallpaper?" Aidan stopped with a grimace. "Ugh, that sounds wrong."

Hugh ran the roller over the wall with more pressure than necessary and passed it back to Aidan, trying to banish the vision of a strapping Iowan farmer turned CFO with his muscular arms wrapped around Jess. "I'm glad to have your seal of approval."

"Jess needs someone like you, someone who can bring a little excitement into her life. She's gotten kind of, I dunno, too serious."

Hugh thought of the late-night trip to the clinic to resuture Zora's ripped-out stitches. "She's got more excitement than she really needs at work."

"Not all that blood and guts. The glamorous kind. Look how she did in the interview. It turns out she's a pretty great actress when she tries."

"She was spectacular, but it was because she relaxed and was herself." When Hugh had watched the show later in the hotel suite, just to see the effect, Jessica's genuineness and passion had radiated right through the camera lens.

"Ha! She fooled you, too," Aidan said as he eased a section of paper off the wall. "She was terrified about being on national television, but she didn't let it show at all."

"It's always hard the first time, but you get used to it." Hugh cringed inwardly at being the cause of such anxiety for Jess.

"Oh, I don't think she'll do it again. She kept saying it was just this once to keep the paps away from her patients." Aidan threw Hugh a look. "And for you. I think that's really why she was so afraid she'd screw it up. She didn't want to reflect badly on you."

Hugh knew enough to give up the painstaking task of separating the paper from the plaster. He stood with his hands shoved in his pockets, staring at the half-peeled strip. "I told her nothing she could do would bother me."

Aidan snorted. "She doesn't believe in failing. She gives everything she does everything she's got every single time." He glanced at Hugh. "You should know that."

He did. He just didn't want it to apply to something as inconsequential as a television talk show interview. To him, it was a mild irritation to be suffered and forgotten. To Jess, it was an alien, terrifying experience—and he'd forced her to go through it. Even worse, she'd twisted herself into knots just for him.

"She was perfect," Hugh said. And it ripped his guts out.

Jessica was stomping the salt and slush off her sneakers on her front stoop when the door opened and Hugh grabbed her wrist to pull her inside and spin her up against him. Delight rippled through her, turning to something much hotter when he kissed her long and deeply.

"Now that's what I like to come home to after a hard day's work," she said, grinning up at him when they finally leaned away from each other.

Her desire was reflected in the blaze of his turquoise eyes. "Something even *harder* than your work?"

"Get a room," Aidan called from the living room.

"What are you doing here?" Jessica asked Hugh as he helped her remove her coat. "Not that I'm complaining." She loved seeing him in her front hall, dressed in jeans and a T-shirt like a normal person.

"Finishing the job he started this morning," Aidan yelled.

"The running commentary is not necessary," Hugh responded. He wound his arm around Jessica's waist and escorted her into the living room, where Aidan stood on a step stool, peeling paper off a high section of wall. "I had a break in the shooting schedule this morning and came by to help Aidan for a couple of hours."

"Except he hit a troublesome patch and bailed on me," her brother said.

Hugh's arm twitched against her waist. "Ungrateful punk," he said. "I had to go back to work."

Jessica smiled, relishing the easy banter between her lover and her brother. "I'm so lucky to have two good-looking guys stripping off my wallpaper."

Aidan groaned. "Yup, it still sounds really wrong."

"Let me get out of my scrubs and I'll be right back," Jessica said.

"Let me help you get out of your scrubs," Hugh purred, running his hand up and down her back.

"Please do, and then get your ya-yas out while you're at it," Aidan said. "I can't take the overpowering reek of sexual tension."

Hugh laughed and squeezed Jessica's bottom, making her squeak. "I'll finish the last patch on the fireplace wall while you change."

"And then we can go out to some fancy restaurant?" Aidan asked hopefully.

"No," Jessica snapped out. Two heads swiveled toward her in surprise. "Let's stay home and cook dinner."

Aidan gaped at her. "Since when do you cook?"

"Just because I don't cook doesn't mean I can't." She could make three dishes with some confidence, so she'd pick one.

"Actually," Hugh said, "I'm a very good chef. *I'll* make dinner."

Now it was Jessica's turn to gape. "When did you learn to cook? Your specialty was pancakes out of a mix box."

"I played one of those self-destructive chefs—you know, alcohol, drugs, and women—in an indie movie a couple of years ago. I needed to learn knife skills, so they brought in a real chef to teach me the rudiments. We got along well, so he gave me a few other cooking lessons, too." Hugh shrugged. "I find it relaxing."

"You're on. Give me a list of ingredients, and I'll do the shopping while you finish the stripping."

"Do you know what jicama looks like in the raw?" Hugh asked.

"No, but my smartphone will." Jessica pecked him on the cheek and raced for the stairs.

By the time she returned with her purchases, Hugh had put on a clean T-shirt over his working jeans and was rummaging around in the kitchen for pots and pans. "This is going to require some improvisation," he said, holding up one of her ancient cast-iron frying pans to examine its dimensions.

"What are you making?" Jessica asked, setting the contents of her grocery bags out on the Formica countertop.

"It's a secret. You will just chop what I put in front of you." But he softened his command by lifting her hair away from her neck and kissing her just behind her earlobe.

"Mmm," Jessica said as sensation tingled over her skin. "Yes, master. I am your slave."

"Sex slave, I hope," Hugh said.

Aidan made gagging sounds from the other room.

Jessica laughed and turned on music from her cell phone, channeling it to a wireless speaker on the counter. "Now Aidan won't be able to hear us."

Hugh listened for a minute before shaking his head and pulling out his own phone. "I need hard rock for this job. And beer." He took two bottles of her craft brew out of the fridge. "At least you stock the truly important stuff." He flicked off the caps and handed her one. "Aidan doesn't get his until he's finished with the wallpaper. Drinking and stripping don't mix."

For the next forty-five minutes, Jessica alternated between chopping various vegetables and herbs and watching Hugh not only cook, but dance while he did it. When he came to collect the pieces from her cutting board, he would pull her into a little slow dance with him, his thigh thrust between hers, his hands on her butt, and his mouth against her neck, keeping her in a simmer of arousal. If her brother hadn't been a few feet away, she would have had sex with Hugh right there in the kitchen.

The three of them crowded around the small oak table to eat what turned out to be a dinner both delicious and healthy. The jicama had been transformed into low-fat french fries while the tilapia sported a crunchy pecan crust. Dessert was a featherlight angel-food cake with a strawberry puree. Aidan and Jessica's came drizzled with a warm chocolate sauce, but Hugh skipped the extra calories it added.

Jessica hadn't understood before how important the physical aspect of Hugh's profession was. His body had to be kept as finely tuned as his acting skills, at least when he was playing Julian Best. She was impressed by his dedication and discipline. Not to mention what a pleasure it was to run her hands over all those gorgeous, toned muscles.

They turned the music up again as they washed the dishes. This time Aidan joined them in boogying around the kitchen. Jessica got another glimpse of Hugh's talent when the two men played a duet on air guitar to an old Rolling Stones song. Hugh became Mick Jagger with every movement and facial expression. He even seemed to grow thinner.

As she ran a dish towel over the skillet Hugh had eyed so dubiously before, Jessica sighed. "I wish there were more dishes."

"You're weird, sis," Aidan said.

"Just the opposite. This is so wonderfully normal," Jessica said. She smiled at Hugh as she said it and caught an odd, stricken look in his eyes.

But her brother distracted her when he announced, "I'm going to bed. Want to be fresh for the big job interview tomorrow."

Jessica gave him a quick hug. "I'll wish you luck in the morning."

As soon as Aidan walked out of the kitchen, Hugh looped a dish towel around Jessica's waist and pulled her into him. "At last I have you alone," he growled.

"Could you pretend to be Mick Jagger again? I've always kind of had a thing for him," Jessica teased. "But seriously, how did you make yourself look skinny like him? That was amazing."

"Just actors' tricks," Hugh said. "Let's go upstairs, and I'll be anyone you want in bed."

"In bed, I only want you."

"Good answer." Hugh draped the towel around her neck and cupped her face in his hands. "Can I stay here tonight?"

"I'd love that." It would extend the illusion that Hugh was just a regular boyfriend.

He tossed the towel onto the counter and grabbed her hand, towing her to the staircase. Hugh kept stopping to kiss her as they made their way up the narrow, creaky steps, so it took a while to get to the bedroom, and Jessica was practically panting with the need to rip her and his clothes off.

"Where's Aidan sleeping?" Hugh asked as Jessica started to pull him through the door to her room. "I want to know how quiet we have to be."

"Don't worry, those Victorians were prudes," Jessica said, tugging him in with her. "They inserted a bathroom and two closets between the bedrooms, not to mention some thick plaster walls. Besides, Aidan sleeps like a dead person."

"Good, because I don't want you to hold back." The intensity of his gaze sent a prickle of heat through her.

However, he came to a halt just inside the door, his gaze skimming around the space. Jessica looked around, too, trying to figure out what he found so fascinating.

The only really standout feature was the star-pattern quilt she had hung on the wall between the two windows. Her grandmother had made it for her mother, and her mother had passed it down to Jessica. She found the bold green, yellow, and blue colors and the geometric pattern almost modern, even as it gave a nod to her Iowa heritage. She'd matched a simple matelassé bedspread to the royal blue of the quilt and added toss pillows that picked up the other colors in their prints. Other than that the furniture was solid but unremarkable Victorian oak.

"So this is your most private space." Hugh nodded. "It's you, Jess."

She frowned. "It's pretty basic."

"Not to my eyes," Hugh said. "I would know exactly how to play you in a movie just by seeing this room."

"Hmm, I'm not sure that would be as easy as making yourself look skinny like Jagger." She faced him and ran her palms over the hard, flat wall of his chest.

He laughed, but his gaze was scorching as he lifted his hands to the top button of her blouse. "I need to observe more closely the physical attributes of your character." He flicked open all the buttons in rapid succession, pushing the blouse off her shoulders. His eyes were locked on her breasts, so she threw her shoulders back to tempt him into touching.

"Being a method actor, I also need to know how they *feel*." He slipped her bra straps down to her elbows so the lace cups peeled away from her skin. He curved his hands underneath her breasts, lifting them as though gauging their weight, before dragging his thumbs across her already taut nipples. The friction sent an electric current arcing from the point of contact to the simmer of longing low in her belly, igniting it into a flare of arousal.

"Method acting is an excellent technique," Jessica managed to gasp as he drew circles with his thumbs.

"I need to know how they taste, as well." He bent, his hair brushing against her chest like frayed satin, making delight shimmer over her skin. When he fastened his mouth on one nipple, a streak of lightning lanced through her, making her arch into him and cry out. He sucked in, and she grabbed his shoulders to keep her knees from buckling under her.

When he switched to the other breast, her bones seemed to melt into molten desire. "Could you method-act us into bed right now?"

The warm, wet suction of his mouth disappeared from her breast, making her mew an objection, but then he stooped to hook an arm under her knees and scooped her off the floor. This time she didn't fight him while he carried her the few steps to the bed. She wound her arms around his neck and teased the side of it with her teeth and lips. "Being carried isn't so bad after all," she breathed into his ear, flicking her tongue against the lobe.

He held her poised above the bed as she combed her fingers through his hair and licked into the hollow at the base of his throat. His neck was one of his erotic trigger points. She could hear his panting and feel the uneven rise and fall of his chest against her breasts as she played there.

With a harsh groan, he put one knee on the bed and lowered her onto the bedspread. But he didn't follow her. Instead he leaned over and spread her hair out on the bed before running his palms down her shoulders, breasts, and bare torso. "So beautiful," he murmured.

"And so desperate for you inside me." Not that she didn't enjoy the compliment, but the ache between her legs was not going to be eased by words—unless maybe they were a lot dirtier.

His smile was wicked. "That's exactly how I like you. Eager and wanting more."

Jessica grabbed his belt and yanked the end out of the buckle. Unsnapping his jeans and pulling the zipper down, she thrust her hand in to find the hard length of his erection pushing against his black briefs. "Seems like you're pretty eager, too."

Another groan wrenched itself from his throat as she stroked her fingers along him. She tugged at the hem of his shirt. "That needs to go."

She kept her hand on his cock but savored the flex of his arm muscles as he crossed them to jerk the shirt over his head. His abdomen rippled with the movement, and she trailed her fingers over the sculpted muscles there.

He watched her hand move over his body, sometimes reacting with a contraction or an intake of breath. But when she got closer to her other hand, still wedged in his jeans, he suddenly grasped his pants and briefs and shoved them down to free her hand and his cock.

She circled her fingers around him and drew them down to the base and up again, loving the velvet solidity of him. His head fell back as he murmured, "Ahh, Jess." She did it again, and he grew harder.

She swung her legs around to kneel on the bed and leaned in to kiss the tip, licking the tiny white bead that had formed there. His groan sounded as though it came from his toes, and he clasped her head between his hands. "Once more and then you have to stop."

She swirled her tongue over him again, making his cock jump, but then he gently moved her head away from him. "I want this first time in your bed to last," he rasped.

She licked her lips with her gaze locked on his face. "We can always make the second time last."

His laugh was ragged, and she reveled in her power over this man who looked like a dark god come to earth. "We'll compromise."

"I don't know what that means, but I figure I can't lose either way." She lay back again.

"That's the spirit." He unbuttoned her jeans and worked them off, leaving her panties behind. She mentally congratulated herself on taking one lunch hour off to go lingerie shopping so she could wear pretty, sexy undergarments for Hugh.

"I like to see how wet your panties are," he said, trailing his finger down around one opening at the top of her thigh before he burrowed under the satin. When he found her clit and just feathered over it, the coil of longing wound tighter between her legs.

"You feel like silk and a warm Polynesian sea." He knelt over her on the bed, his hand still beneath her panties. Then he slipped one finger inside her and angled down to close his mouth over one breast.

The movement of his hand, the pull of his mouth, the brush of his thighs on either side of hers, made her undulate on the bed as delicious sensations hurtled through her from every direction. She closed her eyes and rode the wave of desire higher and higher.

When it was close to cresting, she grabbed his wrist. "You, not your hand."

"But I want to taste you," he growled against her skin.

"Then it won't last."

"Compromise, remember?"

"You've been warned." She released him, and he stripped her panties off with a few deft motions. Pushing her knees wide, he scooted down the bed to lie between her thighs. When his tongue touched her, she felt the first spark of her climax. He licked a long, slow stroke over her clit, and her hips came off the bed as her muscles clenched in a tidal wave of orgasm. "Hu-u-ugh!" she moaned as he licked her again and a second wave of pleasure rolled through her.

He coaxed another surge of release from her and then laid his cheek on her abdomen as she shuddered through the gentler echoes of climax while she came down from the peak. For a while she simply lay there, suffused with the glow of satisfaction, loving the scruff of Hugh's six o'clock shadow and the tickle of his hair against her belly.

Finally, he lifted his head and licked his lips in the same slow, sensual way she'd done, except she was certain that when he did it, it looked sexier. "That was my kind of dessert. Sinfully delicious and without calories." His voice was a low purr. He kissed her stomach and slid upward so they lay side by side.

Jessica snuggled up against him to bask in his body heat. "I'm pretty sure I burned calories. My internal muscles got quite a workout."

He huffed out a chuckle and nuzzled against her hair. His erection was hard against her hip, but he seemed to be in no hurry to satisfy himself. "My trainer would approve."

"Those muscles don't exactly show from the outside." She kissed his pec because it was there.

"Maybe not, but a satisfied woman has a visible glow."

She certainly felt as though she shimmered with the bliss of Hugh's touch. "I think it's time to give you a glow, too." She shifted her hip against his cock.

"No rush. I'll be here all night." His voice held a deep note of happiness, which she couldn't quite understand. They'd spent the night together before.

"Well, I might be in a rush." Pushing him over onto his back, she propped herself up on her elbow to watch his face as she feathered her fingertips over the length of him, trying different angles and strokes to see what pleased him the most. When she worked her way down to cup his balls, his eyelids fluttered closed over the blue blaze of his eyes, and the cords of his neck stood out as he pressed himself into her touch.

She draped her hair over one shoulder and slipped her mouth over him, tasting the salt of his arousal.

"Jes-s-s-s," he hissed, his hips bucking. He twisted his fingers into her hair and held on to it as she explored his cock at a leisurely pace. When she started to increase the rhythm, he gave her hair a gentle tug. "Inside you. I want to feel every inch of you against me."

His words seemed to run over her skin like liquid fire, stoking the still-radiant embers in her belly back into full flame. She scrabbled around for the condom he'd dropped on the bed when he stripped off his jeans, ripping the envelope open with her teeth and stroking the condom onto him with deliberately teasing touches.

"Vixen!" he said, somehow managing to roll her flat on her back and position himself between her thighs in one fluid movement. Not that she had any complaints when he braced himself on his forearms and began to push into her, slowly going deeper and deeper, while his chest brushed against the taut points of her nipples. "I want to watch you," he rumbled, flexing his hips slowly and deliberately.

But his breathing became ragged and his rhythm picked up speed until he drove into her hard and bowed back, his eyes closed, his arms straight, and his mouth stretched open in a howl, as her name echoed off the ceiling. The pump of his climax triggered the explosion of her own. She locked her legs around his hips and pushed him even farther inside her, so they could both feel the clamp and release of her muscles around his cock.

As her orgasm faded to an occasional twitch of sensation, Hugh lowered himself so he was on his forearms again, his weight pinning her to the bed from the waist down, his cock softening inside her. Dropping his head facedown beside hers, he heaved out a long sigh. "This is a great bed."

"You're giving the bed all the credit?" She cuffed his shoulder with a gentle smack.

"Setting is important." His voice was amused but turned serious. "You're in every molecule of the air in this room. I feel as though I'm breathing you in with each inhale."

"Wow, that's pretty poetic." For all her teasing, his words whispered inside her like a spring breeze, adding to her profound joy.

He lifted his head to stare down into her eyes, the angles of his face stark with solemnity. "This is your life, and I want to be part of it."

"You are part of it," she said, taking his head between her hands and locking her gaze on him. "You always will be."

"No one can promise that," he said, the set of his jaw going grim.

"If you walked out this door tomorrow and never returned, you would still be in my heart and in my mind. You would still have changed who I am in ways I won't understand for a while. You will be part of *me*."

He brought his face even closer to hers, and his voice held a note of vehemence. "When I walk out that door, I will always come back."

"You can't guarantee that, either." She smiled as she smoothed his hair away from his forehead. "But I know you will do everything you can to make it happen."

"Good." He lowered his mouth to hers for a long, tender kiss. When he ended it, he said, "I love you, Jess. Even more than before."

Happiness fizzed through her like champagne bubbles. "I love you right back. Even more than before."

"We owe that stray dog you were chasing a lot of kibble." He frowned. "Did you ever catch her?"

"No, but Diego, the kid who works as an intern at the clinic, did. She's going to have her puppies soon in a safe, new home."

He relaxed against her. "Maybe we could adopt one of the pups."

"That's the sweetest, most romantic thing I've ever heard."

"I just told you that I love you, but it's more romantic that I want to adopt a puppy? I should be insulted."

"Just think how irresistible you will be to me when you're holding a cute little puppy."

"That was my ulterior motive, of course."

Two hours later, Hugh lay beside Jessica, her delicious backside spooned against him. Instead of luxuriating in her declaration of love and his presence in her bed, he worried. When he'd brought up their television interview at dinner, she'd turned it aside with a joke about Aidan's upcoming job interview. He was afraid she'd been so upset by her brush with television that she didn't even want to discuss it. Which was very unlike Jess.

"I can feel you thinking." Her voice was drowsy but contented.

He hated to ruin the mood. "Usually people claim to smell wood burning."

"What's wrong?"

He forced himself to ask, "Was the interview as terrible for you as Aidan says?"

He felt her body stiffen. "I'm not going to lie . . . I was nervous. I've never appeared on national TV before. But I told you all that."

"He made it sound worse than nervous."

"You know Aidan. He loves drama." She blew out a breath. "Honestly, it was far stranger today having people give me curious looks and occasionally ask a question about you or what it's like dating a movie star."

"No paparazzi, though?" Hugh's PR people said they'd taken care of that, but you never knew how desperate one photographer might get.

"None, although Carla got a few phone calls from the press. She handled them in her own unique way." Her tone was amused.

"The excitement will die down, you know," he said, hoping to God it was true. "Once they see that you don't start wearing diamonds and furs to work, everyone will go back to thinking of you as just their beloved veterinarian."

"Well, Carla made me promise to show her any designer gowns I get to wear on the red carpet." But she sounded entertained, not upset.

"Jess, you have to tell me when you don't want to do something like that interview. I don't want to add more stress to your life."

She turned in his arms so they were face-to-face. Even though it was dark in the room, he could sense her gaze on him. "I deal with stress all the time. It goes with what I do and where I work. The interview was a kind of stress I haven't faced before. I just have to get used to this new element of being watched by a lot of people I don't know."

"I wish you didn't have to." He was afraid she would come to resent the lack of privacy.

"You're worth it." She found his lips with a heartfelt kiss. "Stop worrying about me and go to sleep. You have to get up earlier than I do."

He couldn't quell his uneasiness, though. He'd paid the price of fame knowingly. Jess still hadn't experienced how bad it could get.

Chapter 21

I got the job!!!! Aidan's jubilation came through the text message with its attached GIF of wildly dancing monkeys that pinged into Jessica's phone right after lunchtime.

"Yes!" Jessica pumped her fist. She propped her hip on the edge of the temporarily vacant examining table and texted back: Huge congrats! Champagne and steak to celebrate tonight! She'd pick up provisions on her way home and hope Hugh would cook them. The thought of Hugh dancing around her kitchen made her grin.

"You look like you won the lottery," Carla said, bustling in with a couple of patient files.

"Aidan got a job, a really good one."

"Thank the Lord! The boy is now gainfully employed and can stop sponging off you."

"Hey, he's doing a great job of fixing up my living room walls. I don't want him to leave too soon."

Carla snorted. "From what you say, that hunky boyfriend of yours could do a better job."

"Yes, but he has a full-time career of his own."

When Jessica got home at six with her load of festive food and drink, Aidan was lounging on the couch, which he'd cleared of drop cloths, drinking a beer and watching a video on his tablet. He must have done some work on the walls after the interview, because the acrid smell of stripping solution was strong. The old Aidan would have taken the afternoon off after he got the job offer. She was liking the new one.

He jumped up to take the bags, and she gave him a hug. "Congratulations, little bro! When do you start?"

"Friday I go in to fill out the HR forms so Monday I can hit the ground running. They've got a project they desperately need me on right away." He practically waltzed into the kitchen, his tousled curls bouncing along with his steps. She couldn't help wondering how much Pete had to do with his speedy hiring.

"The living room is really coming along," Jessica said, pulling the steak out of the butcher's bag. "You got a lot done today."

"Since I'm going to start work soon, I want to finish the project," he said, then gave her a rueful grin. "It was also a good way to keep myself from worrying about getting the job." He stowed the champagne in the fridge. "Is Hugh coming for dinner?"

Jessica glanced at the brass-rimmed wall clock. "He should be here any minute. Frankly, I'm counting on him to cook."

She'd been thrilled when Hugh had moved his things from Gavin Miller's to her bedroom. Seeing his T-shirts and jeans in her closet took her back to the early days of their relationship—before things got complicated. Of course, now things were ten times more complicated, but they could handle them better. She hoped.

She heard the front door open and called, "We're in the kitchen," walking out to meet him halfway. As he strode toward her through the ladders and buckets strewn around the living room, his long legs moved with the power of a big cat, his dark hair caught glints of golden lamplight, and the striking planes of his face were painted with light and shadow. But what made her breath catch was the look of joy that lit his intensely blue eyes when he saw her.

"Incoming!" she warned and hurled herself at him, wrapping her arms around his neck and her legs around his waist, knowing he would catch her. Laughing, he spun them both around before he lowered his mouth to take hers in a deep, possessive kiss.

"If that's the greeting I get every time I walk in, I'll keep working until I'm ninety," he said, lowering her feet to the floor and giving her bottom a squeeze.

"I won't be able to jump that high at ninety, but I'll give it my all," Jessica said. She hugged him again. "I just love seeing you in my house, even in this disaster of a living room."

She thought a shadow crossed his face, but when he slung his arm around her shoulders and steered them toward the kitchen, she forgot about it.

"Congratulations on the new job, Aidan," Hugh said, shaking her brother's hand.

"How did you know?" Jessica asked.

"I texted him, too," Aidan said, "since he knew about the interview."

Jessica hadn't thought she could be any happier, but seeing the growing friendship between the two most important men in her life lifted her joy to a whole new level. She was afraid she might explode into rainbows and sparkles at any moment.

"Jess is counting on you to cook the steaks she bought to celebrate," Aidan added.

"Hey, I was going to be more subtle than that," Jessica said. She turned to Hugh. "You'll do such a wonderful job of making those steaks taste perfect."

Hugh laughed. "Steak is my specialty." He turned to Jessica and put a hot note in his voice. "Not to mention that you will owe me for this, and I intend to collect later tonight."

"I'm willing to sacrifice my sister if it gets me a good steak," Aidan said. "But keep it down tonight, would you?"

A blush climbed Jessica's cheeks even as she said, "Your room is too far away to hear anything."

"If he has a problem with our activities, he can take his new salary and move out," Hugh shot back as he turned on the broiler. Then his face clouded over. "Actually, I have some bad news. It's supposed to snow in DC day after tomorrow, so Bryan is moving the shoot there to catch the weather. That way they don't have to make artificial snow and it saves a lot of money. I have to leave tomorrow night to be there in time for the first scene."

Jessica's fizz of happiness took a hit but rebounded. "Won't you have to return to New York after that to finish up whatever you didn't get done here?"

"Unfortunately, we can handle it all on a soundstage, so we'll move on to Miami after DC. But I'll get back here before we head to Florida."

"I could use a few days in Miami," Aidan said before he held up his hand to forestall any comments. "I know, I have a job, so I won't be going there until my first vacation days kick in."

Jessica was glad for Aidan's interruption, because it gave her a moment to absorb the prospect of Hugh's imminent absence. "Miami is only a three-hour flight away," she said. "How long will you be there?"

"Miami is a short stint, only three days, weather cooperating, but I'll work out a way to get back here when it ends."

"Because then you go where?"

Hugh grimaced. "Prague."

The fizz died. "Well, you'll have to finish filming sometime."

"It's going to be another couple of months," he said, running his palms up and down her arms as though she were chilled and he was warming her up. "I'll fly back as often as I can." His expression lightened. "There is one guaranteed trip home from Prague. Gavin's getting a major writing award, and I've been tapped to present it to him. The studio's PR people loved all the promo angles for that, so they insisted on a three-day hiatus in my shooting schedule, allowing me to fly back to New York for the ceremony. Will you come as my date?"

"Can I wear scrubs?" she ribbed him.

"And diamonds." He smiled down at her with such tenderness that her heart flipped.

It occurred to her that he hadn't suggested that she drop everything and join him on set. Some people might be upset by that, but she understood that he was being respectful of her own wall-to-wall commitments. "Maybe once Riya gets settled in, I can sneak away for a weekend or two myself. After all, I've never been to Prague."

Hugh's face lit up like a Broadway stage. "I'd like that very much." He leaned down to give her a kiss filled with gratitude. "And now, allow the creative genius room to work."

"Holy shit!" Aidan exclaimed, staring at his phone.

He was sitting at the kitchen table in plaster-dusted jeans and an Iowa State T-shirt, having just finished his wallpaper stripping for the day. Only one wall remained covered with old, awful paper. Aidan intended to finish it over the weekend, and he planned to help Jessica with refinishing the woodwork after that. In fact, her brother had reinspired her to work on her house.

At the moment, though, Jessica was putting together dinner for the two of them without enthusiasm. Hugh had been gone for less than twenty-four hours, but she felt hollowed out without his presence. Being in the kitchen made it worse, since she had such vivid memories of his sexy dance moves while he cooked.

"What is it?" she asked to be polite.

Aidan glanced up with an odd, dismayed expression on his face. "Sorry. Nothing important. Just a stupid video. I'm gonna go wash my face. I've got plaster dust in my eye or something." He nearly bolted out of the kitchen.

Jessica went back to slicing mushrooms for the gravy to go with the chicken breasts baking in the oven. She hadn't expected to miss

Hugh this much. After all, she'd had a very full life before he came into the picture and it hadn't eased up, despite the addition of Riya. Yet the hours plodded by, even when she was busy, because there was no hope of seeing Hugh at the end of the day. Texts and phone calls were no substitute for the intensity of his gaze, the heat and solidity of his body against hers, or the way the air seemed to scintillate with his unique charisma.

She drizzled olive oil in a pan and tossed the mushrooms in. As they began to soften and brown, Aidan walked slowly back into the kitchen, stopping right beside her with his phone held out. "Jess, you're not going to like this, but I think you need to see it. Just remember it's Meryl Langdon, not Hugh, saying this stuff."

"What are you talking about?" She gave the mushrooms a stir with the spatula before taking the phone. It was paused on a video clip of a typical talk show set with a host and a female guest seated on high stools. The banner across the bottom of the screen read *"Around DC with guest Meryl Langdon."*

She turned off the stove and hit the play button.

"So you're filming the next Julian Best blockbuster in DC for the next few days," the host said. "How does it feel to be the new love interest of the world's hottest spy?"

Meryl tilted her head back, showing the perfect line of her throat as she gave a sexy laugh. "Fabulous, of course. Who wouldn't want to do love scenes with Hugh Baker?"

"I hear the on-camera chemistry is scorching. How do you handle that off camera?"

"Hugh is the consummate professional," Meryl said with a demure smile as she tossed a long, shining lock of auburn hair over her shoulder. "But you don't get heat like that onscreen without a genuine spark. At the beginning of filming, there was definitely something . . . but . . ." She shrugged.

Smelling blood, the host leaned forward. "But an old love has come back into his life, hasn't she? How does that make you feel?"

"They share memories of a time when they were younger, less jaded, so it's hard to compete."

Jessica gasped. Meryl was trying to compete with her for Hugh? He'd never mentioned any romantic interest in or from his costar.

"But on-set romances are complicated," Meryl continued. "You don't know if it's the intensity of playing the role of lovers that draws you together or if there's something lasting between you. Although, with Hugh . . ." Her face took on a dreamy look.

"I can imagine," the host said when it became clear Meryl wasn't going to add to that. "I understand Mr. Baker's girlfriend is a veterinarian in New York City, so she has a career of her own. Will she be joining him on location?"

"I can't answer that question, but she is quite committed to her job." Meryl made it sound as though she were privy to Hugh's private life but couldn't share the information. She then looked at the camera and gave a smile that said the girlfriend's absence left an opportunity open for Meryl.

Jessica's blood began to boil, even as she admired the actress's ability to imply so much without uttering a word. "That b—witch!" She wasn't going to insult her canine patients by calling the actress a bitch.

"It's an interesting combination of careers," the host prompted. "A veterinarian and a movie star."

Meryl nodded, her expression pensive. "I think it's a difficult one. People with rigid, scientific brains have a hard time understanding those of us with fluid, creative talent. Right brain, left brain, you know."

"Rigid!" Jessica sputtered. "At least I *have* a brain."

"It's just a publicity stunt or something," Aidan said, reaching for the phone. "Don't let it get to you."

Jessica moved the phone away from his grasp, wanting to hear what other bombshells Meryl was going to drop.

"Two very different worlds colliding," Meryl continued. "She may find it hard to fit in."

Jessica's anger faltered in the face of that truth. Meryl might be annoying, but she wasn't wrong on at least one point. Now Jessica wasn't sure she wanted to hear any more.

Fortunately, the interview's time slot was at an end. She could tell the host was frustrated, believing he could get Meryl to stir the pot more, if he only had extra time. Instead he had to turn to the camera to do the obligatory touting of Meryl and the movie.

"How did you know about that?" Jessica said, handing the phone to her brother.

"I've got alerts set for Hugh and the movie title. When the paps started bothering you, I thought it might be a good idea. Just so you'd know if something blew up."

Touched by his concern, she squeezed his shoulder. "You're a good brother."

"Seriously, you can't get mad at Hugh about this," Aidan said. "He wasn't on the show."

"Don't worry. I'm not going to lose any sleep over what a publicity-hungry actress says to get attention." Jessica turned the burner back on and picked up the spatula. Aidan hovered for a moment and then went back to the table when his sister appeared unperturbed.

She knew in her heart of hearts that Hugh would have told her if there had ever been anything between him and Meryl. That she trusted him on. But she wondered if he was okay with the actress's innuendos. His fame had made him cynical about the stories the press published, but this seemed different to Jessica. Meryl worked with him, so her words carried the weight of real access. Would her staff and clients believe Meryl and feel sorry for Jessica now? Or even worse, think she was a gullible fool?

She cursed as she realized the mushrooms were turning black while she stewed about the unexpected drawbacks of loving a celebrity.

"You okay?" Aidan looked up from his phone.

"The mushrooms just got a bit burned." And so had she.

"What the hell does she think she's doing?" Hugh slammed the cell phone down on his hotel suite's coffee table, making his assistant, Trevor, wince, possibly because it was Trevor's phone being abused. "How long ago was this aired?" Hugh demanded.

Trevor picked up his phone and checked the screen's integrity. "About two hours."

"Shit!" Hugh vaulted off the sofa where he'd been reviewing tomorrow's script to stalk around the living room. "Where is my damn phone? I hope Jess hasn't seen this."

A ringtone issued from another room. "It's in your bedroom," Trevor said. "I'll keep letting it ring until you find it."

Hugh turned on one heel to veer toward the sound. Equal parts of anger and fear boiled in his chest. He knew Meryl had made the whole thing up, but Jess didn't. Would she believe him if he told her that? If it had been in a tabloid, she would, but Meryl was his costar and it had come from her own mouth on television. His anger escalated to fury. How dare Meryl drag the woman he loved into a sordid quest for media attention!

Instead of calling Jess, he scrolled to Meryl's cell number.

"Hugh, baby, I was just having some fun. No harm, no foul," she said without preamble, her voice amused.

"You're wrong about that. It was extremely foul. I'm pissed as all hell at you."

"Don't be that way." Meryl's tone shifted to cajoling.

Hugh came to a decision. "You're going to apologize to Jessica tonight. In person."

"Have you forgotten we're in DC and she's in New York? And it's snowing?" Now she sounded exasperated.

"That's what helicopters are for. It's not snowing hard enough to stop them from flying. Trevor will let you know when and where to meet me for the flight."

"Do you intend to make everyone who says something you don't like about your girlfriend apologize in person? Because if you do, you won't have much time to make movies. She'll need to toughen up if she's going to keep dating you. And by the way, I'm not being dragged to New York in the snow to grovel in front of her."

A red mist hazed over Hugh's vision, but his voice was arctic. "Don't forget that Irene Bartram thought she would play Samantha Dubois for the rest of the Julian Best series. Then Irene interfered with Gavin Miller's personal life. And now Samantha is dead."

Instead of being intimidated by his veiled threat, Meryl laughed. "Oh, Hugh, baby, you're far too honorable to do anything to damage my career. In fact, I sometimes wonder how you succeeded in this dirty business with all your gleaming integrity. Nice guys usually finish last in Hollywood."

That one was a right hook to his chest. He had not been at all nice to Jessica in those early scrambling days of his ascent to stardom. It was only because he'd made it to the top that he could afford to have principles now.

All the anger drained out of him. "Forget it. I don't need you there. But I'm going to give you some advice. Don't discount the power of integrity. Doing the right thing may appear inconvenient at times, but it breeds trust, which is a valuable commodity in this business." He didn't give Meryl a chance to respond before he disconnected.

For a long moment, he simply stared down at his cell phone before hitting Jessica's number on speed dial. A shudder of fear passed through him. What if she didn't believe that Meryl was lying?

Her greeting held nothing but pleasure at hearing his voice. There was no sign of anger or distress, so she must not have seen the interview. He dreaded the revulsion he might hear, but he had to tell her. "Jess, I'm calling because Meryl gave a television interview this evening and said things that were not only untrue but which could upset you."

"Oh, I saw it. Aidan has some sort of alert set up on his phone." Yet she sounded untroubled. "I kind of liked Meryl when I met her in your trailer, so it surprised me that she would do that. But I guess she wanted to stir up some publicity, right?"

Hugh winced at Jessica's matter-of-fact tone. He hated knowing his cynicism had rubbed off on her. Yet relief rolled through him that Meryl's insinuations hadn't sent her running for the exit. "Just to be clear, there has never been any kind of relationship between Meryl and me, other than a professional one." He didn't mention that Meryl had tried and failed.

"I never doubted that you would have told me if there was."

"I'm coming up there to prove it to you. Tonight."

"Oh, Hugh, you don't have to do that. I mean, I'd love to see you. I miss you all the time, but you have to work tomorrow." She sounded torn between happiness and distress.

"I'll text you my expected arrival time as soon as I know it. I won't keep you long because you have to work, too, but I need to talk with you face-to-face."

"It will be wonderful to see you." She sounded like she meant it. "I love you."

"I adore you." He disconnected and walked back into the living room to put Trevor to work on travel arrangements.

Two and a half hours later, the limousine pulled up at Jessica's house. The wrought iron lamp over her front door tinted the snowflakes drifting down with a golden glow, and the solid, brick Victorian town house projected an air of timeless serenity that he envied.

Unfortunately, the trip had given him far too much time to think about what Meryl had said. He had tried to dismiss her comments about Jessica needing to be tough as sour grapes, but she'd planted the seeds of misgivings in his mind, where they'd taken root. His righteous anger had diminished into an uneasy sense of guilt by the time he exited the limousine.

Jessica opened the door just as Hugh walked up the steps, so he could enter straight into the warmth of her home and her presence.

She wore jeans and a purple sweater, and her hair fell in a shining curtain over her shoulders. He wanted to stand and bask in the sight of her after just a day's absence. He hated to think how intensely he'd miss her after the weeks his foreign filming schedule would keep them apart. Meryl's words about exactly that echoed through his brain.

He bent to brush his lips against Jess's, tamping down his desire to pull her against him so he could feel every inch of her body. "Hello, my love. I'm so sorry to arrive late on a work night, but this is important."

He searched Jess's face, trying to read what she really felt about Meryl's stupid ploy. But her expression wasn't giving anything away. So he simply wrapped his arms around her, folding her into him as he inhaled the fragrance of her soft hair, and the warm, feminine scent that was just Jess. "I'm sorry, my love," he said again.

She melted into him, her arms tight around his waist. "Hey, it got you here when I was missing you like crazy, so I'm not complaining."

Hugh closed his eyes. Only Jess could have the generosity of heart to see this as a positive. He ran one hand over the silk of her hair.

She continued, her voice muffled again his chest. "I just have to get used to this sort of thing, and I might as well start now."

The guilt sliced at Hugh. "No, we should at least be able to trust my colleagues to behave like professionals."

"It wasn't that terrible, because I didn't believe her." Jess sighed, her breath a whisper. "I'm more worried about what my clients are going to think. They're not used to having a celebrity's, um, girlfriend in their midst, so they don't know that most of that crap is made up."

Remorse sank its talons deep into Hugh's chest. He hadn't considered the impact on her employees and clients. He lived in a bubble with his multimillion-dollar houses, chartered private helicopters, and staff to ward off unwanted intrusions. But Jess had to deal with the fallout from stunts like Meryl's. Expecting her to join him in his majestic isolation was out of the question. Her work was part of who she was. He couldn't cut her off from that. Yet Meryl had reminded him of the conflicts it would create.

"Can you enlist Carla's help with that? She tells it like it is." Hugh knew that was a cop-out, but he was grasping at straws.

Jess tilted her head to look up at him. "Carla would be happy to run interference, but I have to handle this myself. It won't be the last time gossip will circulate about us. I need to learn not to care."

"No!" Her words ripped into him like bullets, making him face the truth. "Caring makes you the person you are. It's why I love you." He somehow forced his arms to fall away from her. He took a long step back so that she had to release him, too. "You were right back then, Jess. You don't belong in my world." His world of isolation and pretense, of meaningless air-kisses and backbiting gossip. "It was wrong of me to try to draw you back into it."

She stood with her arms still slightly curved as though ready to wind them back around his waist. "What are you talking about?" she said. "You didn't draw me into it. I came willingly."

He curled his hands into fists so he wouldn't reach for her again. "You don't understand the price you would pay. Even I didn't understand it until now." He made himself tell her the unpleasant realities he had been withholding. "You know my limo driver? He's also a bodyguard, specifically trained to deal with the possibility of armed kidnapping. You'd need someone like him."

Her expression went from baffled to stunned, but he didn't stop.

"When I'm making a Julian Best movie—and I will make one every two years now that Gavin's overcome his writer's block—I spend a solid six months traveling with virtually no breaks. We would have a hard time seeing each other, given that you have an important job to do."

She started to speak, but he lifted his hand. "And no matter how many interviews we give, the paparazzi will never go away. Something like Meryl's stupidity will happen, and they'll stake out your clinic, interfere with your clients, and make themselves a pain in your ass until you'll give up and stop working there." He shook his head. "I can't do this to you, Jess."

She went silent, and he could see her absorbing the truth of what he'd said. But then anger flashed in her eyes. "Don't make decisions for me. I love you. That makes it worth dealing with all those other issues."

He wished that were true. "Eight years ago, you hated all the trappings that went with my job, and it's a thousand times worse now." He scraped his fingers through his hair, trying to explain his nightmare. She would hate it, and she would want out. Again. "I was tough already—I needed to be—so I didn't have to change. You would have to alter the most fundamental qualities about yourself. You would come to resent, if not me, then our life together." As pain joined the anger on her face and clawed at his gut, he realized why he'd welcomed the anger. He deserved it.

"Why do you think I can't be strong enough to ignore gossip and still care about what's important?" Jess waved her hands in frustration. "I'm not that same naive girl I was when we met, you know. I live in New York City, for God's sake. Doesn't that tell you something about my toughness?"

"That's exactly the issue. You live in the real world. I can't anymore." He would never be able to make her understand how artificial his life was, how few people he trusted. Hell, that was why he'd fallen in love with her again . . . or maybe had never stopped loving her. She counterbalanced all of that. "I can't do this, Jess. It would kill me to see you come to hate me." And walk away. Into the arms of someone like Pete Larson, a normal, hardworking fellow Iowan who would give her a happy life with two kids, four dogs, and a white picket fence. Hugh wanted to rip down that picket fence with his bare hands.

Jessica closed the distance between them and poked a finger at his chest, her hair rippling with every movement. "You can't predict what I will feel. You can't decide this is wrong without my agreement."

He couldn't stop himself. He curled his hands around her shoulders, savoring the feel of her vitality under his palms. "I love you too much to destroy you."

His desire to kiss her one more time nearly overwhelmed his certainty that he'd be lost if he did. He clenched his jaw and simply tried to memorize all the beloved features of her face to carry with him when the darkness started to close in.

Then he bolted out the door.

Jessica stood in the hallway, staring at the oak panels of her front door. Surely Hugh would stride back through it at any moment, saying he had temporarily lost his mind. He'd come all the way to New York just to apologize. How had that metamorphosed into breaking up with her? Her mind refused to accept it, even as her heart began to crack into fragments of loss and anguish.

Her knees started to tremble, so she tottered over to the stairway and sat down on the hard wooden step.

She'd been so careful not to make a big deal out of Meryl's interview. He was the one who'd decided the incident was so awful that he needed to fly up here in a helicopter. She braced her elbows on her knees and dropped her face into her hands. What had she said to drive him away? Only that she needed to learn not to care about stupid gossip. How had that set him off?

He had spoken as though he was listening to some strange voice in his head, reeling off a list of reasons she would come to hate him, when she had thought he was there to make sure she still loved him.

Baffled, she closed her eyes and let the tears leak down her cheeks. Maybe he'd decided Meryl really would make a better girlfriend. The actress already lived in his world, as he kept referring to it. She understood the rules. It would be easier for Hugh. Maybe he'd realized that on the trip up to New York.

No, Jessica didn't—couldn't—believe that. Hugh wouldn't lie to her about his relationship with his costar.

She thought back eight years and saw that the pattern was the same. He didn't love her enough to allow her to adjust to the pitfalls of his fame. He needed her to fit in right away or he became frustrated.

Maybe he was right. Maybe she wasn't cut out to love a movie star, except in a brief, bright flare of passion. Maybe the price of loving him was higher than she could afford.

Desolation flooded through her, wrenching a sob from her throat.

The price of losing him seemed even higher.

Chapter 22

A text pinged on Jessica's phone as she finished up the notes on her last patient. It was probably Aidan. After she had told him about Hugh, her brother had appointed himself her sympathetic guardian, checking up on her multiple times a day. He even informed her he'd sent a blistering text message to Hugh, telling him what a heartless jerk he was. That had actually made Jessica smile, albeit with a sad twist. It took all her willpower not to ask if Hugh had responded.

The thought of Hugh sent a dagger thrust lancing through her, and she had to lean against the counter for a moment to get through the pain of his absence. She hadn't expected to feel this level of anguish. Hugh had only been back in her life for a few weeks. How had he become so necessary to her?

She sucked in a couple of shallow breaths before she pulled out her phone. She might as well send Aidan a reassuring message.

But the text wasn't from her brother. It was from Pete. She opened it with trepidation.

> I know tomorrow is your day off, so I hoped I might be able to buy you a friendly drink, emphasis on "friendly." Aidan says you could use one.

Jessica groaned. Aidan had evidently decided that five days was all she needed to get over Hugh, and it was time for her to move on. Or move back to Pete. But the truth was that she had been dreading the long, empty hours of her day off. She could use a drink with a friend. Maybe she should go.

Just then, Tiana ushered in a golden retriever mix and his owner. "Looks like Casimir has a hematoma in his right ear," the vet tech said.

Jessica shoved her phone back in her pocket and forgot about the text. Until another ping sounded a couple of hours later.

I'm thinking Aidan might be wrong. Feel free to disregard my earlier text. No offense will be taken.

He sounded so Iowan somehow that a little wave of homesickness struck her. It might be a good distraction to talk about things so different from Hugh. Before she could change her mind, she typed back: A friendly drink would be nice. What time?

Pete texted back that he would pick her up at six. Now all the reasons she shouldn't do this flitted around in her brain like bats, the principal one being that Pete might read something into it that wasn't and would never be there.

She shrugged. He'd been the one to put the emphasis on "friendly," so he should have no illusions.

Jessica swallowed the last of her Manhattan and ordered another one, even though she knew she had drunk the first one too quickly. She and Pete were at the same bar where they'd met for their last date, but this time they sat in wooden chairs on opposite sides of a square, tile-topped table. No more banquette seating. Pete was sticking to the "just friends" script like a champ. He must have come straight from work, because he wore khakis and a deep blue, button-down shirt that made his hair seem more golden than usual.

She wore jeans and a lavender sweater, her hair in a loose ponytail, keeping it casual and low-key, the way she wanted their friendship to be.

They'd talked about her patients, Pete's business trip to Vancouver, and some old friends from Iowa. The only personal topic had touched on Aidan. Pete had volunteered that Aidan's boss raved about his coding skills, which made Jessica proud and glad for her brother.

"He's always been a tech whiz," she said, picking up the fresh Manhattan the waiter had just delivered. "What he does is way beyond my comprehension."

"Mine, too," Pete said, his eyes crinkling at the corners as he grimaced.

Jessica took a sip of her drink and fixed him with a skeptical stare. "I think you downplay your expertise. A lot."

"I have to understand what the guys like Aidan are doing in a conceptual way, but I'd flounder around like a mule in a mud hole if you asked me to actually do it."

Jessica laughed at his simile. The combination of his folksy speech and the alcohol made her bold. "Since we're just friends now, I have something to ask you."

"Okay." He put down his beer.

"We didn't part on cordial terms, so why did you invite me out tonight?"

He sat back in his chair, making the wood creak. "I regretted our leaving it like that. And by the way, I think Hugh Baker is a complete idiot."

"Oh God, I'm going to kill Aidan." She took an oversized gulp of Manhattan and coughed at the burn of alcohol.

"He's protective, like any good brother."

"And he overshares." But Jessica was touched by Aidan's vocal concern.

Pete snared her with his pale blue gaze. "I'd rather have you in my life on your terms than not have you here at all."

Pleasure and discomfort spun in her chest, combining with the drink to make her a little dizzy.

Pete took a swallow of beer. "Look, I know I came on strong right away in our relationship. Maybe I pushed too hard. But when you find someone you know is special, someone who makes everything in the world look better and brighter when you're with them, you go after that person with all you've got, because they don't come around so often."

The dizziness was vaporized by a blaze of regret. "That's much nicer than I deserve, but thank you for being so honest and so kind."

Pete shrugged with a crooked smile. "No point in pretending otherwise."

She remembered how focused Pete had been in his pursuit of her until Hugh had come back into the picture. But she hadn't done the same with Hugh, had she? She'd allowed him to walk away with barely a fight. He'd hit her in her most vulnerable spot, taking her back to that little girl who always had to get everything exactly right, reminding her that she had grown up in the cornfields of Iowa rather than in the sophistication of LA or New York.

But Hugh's upbringing was no more sophisticated than hers. He had grown up in foster homes. Maybe that made his outside shell thicker, but he still had the small, unloved boy curled up inside him.

"Oh my God, that's it! That's why he did it." Hugh couldn't forget that his mother had bailed on him when things got too overwhelming for her. He thought Jessica would do the same thing because she'd broken the engagement before.

"I think your train of thought has left me behind," Pete said, amused chagrin in his voice.

"I know what I have to do," Jessica said, pushing back her chair and standing up with a slight wobble. "Thank you. I need to go home now."

Pete rose as well, putting out a hand to steady her. "Let me pay the bill."

"Oh, right. We're friends, so I need to pay my half." She fumbled with her purse.

"This one's on me." He pulled out his credit card and handed it to the waiter, who'd appeared at Pete's signal. "I have a feeling I might not get to buy you another one."

She shook her head. "No matter what happens, you will always be my friend. You've been a good one."

"I'll hold you to that," he said.

Jessica tried to carry on a conversation with Pete on the drive home, but her mind was taken up with how to convince Hugh she wouldn't leave him when the going got tough. For one thing, he was in Prague and she was in New York. An elusive thought darted around her alcohol-soaked brain for a long moment before she pinned it down. She smiled. He was coming back to present an award to Gavin Miller. She just had to figure out exactly where and when. And she had to find a way to be there.

"Cut!"

There was a long silence as Hugh slowly rose from his crouch on the stone floor of the Gothic church in Prague. "Did you get the shot?" he asked, trying to figure out why no one was moving.

"Yeah, yeah, we got it," Bryan said.

"Do we need another take?" Hugh asked, rolling his shoulders under the straps of the shoulder holster.

"Definitely not."

"Okay." Hugh started toward his trailer.

"Hugh!" Bryan called.

Hugh stopped and looked over his shoulder.

"You ripped my guts out. Great job," Bryan said before turning to his crew. "All right, set up for the interior pan."

Gavin Miller stepped out of the controlled chaos of the film crew and fell into step beside Hugh. "Bryan's right. You had me reaching for a tissue, and I wrote the damn scene."

Hugh unbuckled the shoulder holster and shrugged out of it as he walked. "You gave me a lot to work with."

He'd been dreading that particular scene, because it was the moment when Julian Best finds out that Sara, the woman he loves, is dead, and it's his fault that she's been killed. He knew if he chose to do it right, he would tap into all the soul-destroying loneliness and loss he felt over Jessica—and he didn't want to go there. However, he owed it to Bryan, Gavin, and everyone else on the film crew to suck it up and be a professional. Actors mined their own emotions, so he'd allowed his feelings to wreak their agony on him as he did the scene.

"You took what I gave you and raised it to a whole new level," Gavin said. "That scene is going to turn the movie into an extraordinary experience for the audience. You might even get nominated for an Oscar."

"They don't give Oscars to spy blockbusters." Hugh tried not to think about the other scene he shrank from for an entirely different reason. In fact, Sara is not dead. When Julian sees her alive and well, there would be a highly charged scene of lovers reunited. Where he was going to find the resources to pull that off, he had no idea.

The two men climbed the few steps into Hugh's trailer, which was considerably smaller than the one he had used in New York City.

"Where's Allie?" Hugh asked, glancing around. "I thought she was waiting here." Allie and Gavin had flown over on the same plane as Hugh so Allie could visit the set and tour Prague. Watching them together reminded Hugh of what he had almost had and lost.

"She decided to go shopping. Want a drink?" Gavin rummaged in the small bar, pulling out a bottle of bourbon.

"I'm done working for the day, so why not?" Hugh tossed the holster on the kitchen counter. "It will help me sleep on the plane."

He, Gavin, and Allie were headed back to New York for the INK Literary Awards. Of course, the cynic in Hugh wondered how much the possibility of his presence at the ceremony had factored into the committee's decision to create a special achievement award for Gavin, but he quashed it. Whatever the committee's ulterior motives, the writer deserved the recognition.

Gavin handed him the tumbler of bourbon and settled down on the trailer's sofa. "I know how you reduced us all to tears in that scene."

"By being a great actor." Hugh lifted his glass in a mock toast to himself before he sat in the chair opposite Gavin.

"By using your real feelings about Jessica."

Hugh sent him a warning glare and took a sip of his drink. The alcohol slid down his throat with a smooth, welcome burn. Maybe he could drink enough to forget about Jessica for a few hours, since he didn't have to face the camera again for three days. No one would care if he had a hangover.

"You see," Gavin continued, impervious to Hugh's dagger stare, "I know what's really going on here. You're not saving Jessica from a life of shallow pretense and vicious gossip. You're saving yourself from the pain of losing her when she discovers what kind of life you think you lead. It's fear, pure and simple."

"Thank you for the amateur psychoanalysis." Hugh wasn't going to let Gavin get to him.

"I've been there, Hugh, with my mother. I was so terrified of how she might react to me that I refused to even try to find her. Until Allie convinced me that it was worse not taking the risk than it was to be rejected. Now my mother and I are establishing a real relationship. You have no idea how healing that is."

Hugh did his best to fend off Gavin's prodding. "My mother is dead."

"Don't be obtuse. You're taking the coward's way out." Gavin leaned forward with unaccustomed earnestness. "No matter what you think, you deserve happiness. Don't reject the gift of Jessica's love because you're afraid it might be taken away again. Grab it with both hands and hold on for the ride, because it's a magnificent one. If it ends, at least you will have the memory of real joy to help you through the dark days."

"Yes, I know the poem. I even read it at a charity gala once. ''Tis better to have loved and lost than never to have loved at all.' Thank you, Alfred, Lord Tennyson." He was doing everything he could not to let Gavin's words sink into his heart, but he was failing. Little feathered bursts of hope stirred faster than he could quell them.

"Now you're being an ass." Gavin continued to skewer him with his gaze. "You've loved this woman for years, admit it."

"My fixation doesn't mean we're the right people for each other." Hugh finally broke. "She left me once because of my career, and that career has only become more intrusive."

"No, she left you because you made your needs more important than her needs."

"I had one chance to succeed. I had to take it." Hugh tried for a mocking smile but suspected he didn't quite achieve it. "You should be glad I did, since I'm the personification of your fictional super spy."

Gavin just looked at him. "Consider the fact that you're going to be in New York and Jessica lives in New York. Start there and attempt to reach the correct conclusion about what you should do." Gavin put down his glass and stood up. "I'll see you at the airport."

As the door closed behind his friend, Hugh swallowed the rest of his drink in one gulp. But all the bourbon in the bottle wouldn't be enough to allow him to sleep on the plane tonight. Gavin had made sure of that.

Chapter 23

Jessica tugged at her royal-blue scrubs as she sat in the back of the car service sedan with Quentin, en route to the INK Literary Awards.

"Stop fiddling with your clothes," the stylist said. "You'll ruin my masterpiece."

"I'm not used to them being so tight," she said, twisting her hands together in her lap.

"Honey, I could have made them a lot tighter, but that wasn't the image we were going for."

When Jessica had tracked down the stylist and explained her scheme, Quentin had embraced the project with so much enthusiasm that Jessica felt like she had been whirled up in a tornado. He'd tailored her scrubs so they fit like a designer ensemble, found a jeweler who would loan her a real diamond necklace and earrings, and forced her feet into mile-high silver sandals with slender ankle straps. Her hair was spun onto the top of her head in a complex, sophisticated updo.

When he'd allowed her to look in the mirror, another woman had stared back at her in shock. The woman in the mirror had curves, but elegant ones that made her waist look tiny and tempting to a man's hands, and her exposed neck was as graceful as a swan's. Jessica had had no idea she could look like that, and she gaped at herself until Quentin handed her a jeweled clutch and told her to put her cell phone in it.

The well-connected stylist also knew someone who knew someone who could get tickets to the awards ceremony, and he'd offered to accompany her for moral support.

"Thank you for everything," she said, reaching over to squeeze his hand on the car seat. "You've gone above and beyond for me."

"Are you kidding? This is the most romantic thing ever," he said, the city streetlights flashing over his smile of excitement. "I can't wait to see Hugh's face. Can I be honest? That's half the reason I wanted to come with you."

Jessica laughed with a nervous edge. "That makes me feel a little less obligated." She drew in a breath. "I just wish I had more of a plan."

"Your heart will tell you what to do when the time comes," Quentin said.

Jessica's heart wasn't all that trustworthy on these matters, but she didn't share that with Quentin.

All too soon the car pulled up in front of the venerable midtown hotel where the ceremony was being held. The red carpet leading to the entrance blazed with lights, and photographers lined both sides. A few slightly dazed-looking couples were running the gamut.

Quentin snorted. "Those people must be writers. They don't know how to work a red carpet. But the photographers are only here for Hugh and Gavin and their movie friends, anyway. Let me get out first and prepare your path."

He swung open the door with a flourish before turning to help Jessica out of the car. He tucked her hand into the crook of his elbow and faced them toward the carpet. "Now the fun begins."

Most of the photographers were standing around, talking and waiting for more interesting prey.

Quentin scanned the cameramen and fixed on one particular pap. "David, how *are* you?" he asked loudly.

The photographer stepped up to the silken rope cordoning off the carpet. "Quent, what are you doing at a literary event? Not your usual."

"I'm escorting this lovely lady on Hugh Baker's behalf. Jessica, meet David Bristol, an old friend of mine." Quentin winked at Jessica.

"Nice to . . ." David took in Jessica's unusual outfit and Quentin's comment about Hugh before he came to the right conclusion and swung up his camera. "You're Jessica Quillen! Give me a smile, would you, gorgeous?"

That was all it took to get all the other cameras clicking and whirring. Quentin stood back to let Jessica pose as he'd instructed her, one hand on her hip, one foot in front of the other. At first all the huge, glaring lenses intimidated her, but then she remembered that she was there to show Hugh she could shine in his world, so she held her head high. Confidence coursed through her as she flashed her most brilliant smile in whatever direction a voice called her. She could do this, anywhere, anytime, no problem.

"Why the scrubs?" one pap asked as he snapped.

"Because I'm a veterinarian. That's what we wear."

He laughed. "Okay, but seriously."

"It's a little inside joke between Hugh and me." Jessica took another step toward the door.

"I thought you and Hugh Baker had split up," another said bluntly.

"You shouldn't believe everything you see on entertainment news," she said with a sly smile that evoked a few more chuckles.

When Quentin decided enough photos had been taken, he said to the paps at large, "Make sure to tell Hugh his date arrived before he did." Then he guided Jessica through the entrance. "You handled it like a pro out there," he said as they followed the trail of guests through the opulent lobby.

"That was the easy part." Surprisingly, it *had* been easy once she got into the right mind-set. But now she had to face Hugh, who might be less than thrilled by her unexpected presence. "You're sure Hugh's not here yet?" She wanted time to brace herself.

"Trust me, he'll make a grand entrance with Gavin, so the paps can do their thing and INK can get their publicity. Also, he doesn't want to have to schmooze for too long before the ceremony starts."

As soon as they'd checked in and been admitted, Quentin piloted Jessica over to one of the bars set up for the preceremony cocktail hour. "Liquid courage," he said, handing her a glass of white wine.

Peering over the rim of her wineglass, she watched the swirl of guests, many of whom looked slightly uncomfortable in their fancy gowns and tuxedos. She liked that about them.

"Too much black," Quentin said dismissively. "It's the amateurs' safety net. They think you can't go wrong with black, but, oh, you can." He pointed out a woman in a black dress that sported both ruffles and fringe.

"It has lots of movement," Jessica said, taking another swig of sauvignon blanc.

"Just like Jell-O."

Jessica nearly spit out her wine.

Quentin continued to entertain her with comments on their fellow guests' apparel, and after she drank a second glass of wine, Jessica could appreciate the lavish surroundings of glittering crystal chandeliers, cream wallpaper with glossy gold stripes, and deep-piled burgundy carpet. Music from a string quartet provided a counterpoint to the hum of conversation.

They'd meandered over to inspect a large oil painting of New York in the 1800s when the voices picked up a sudden note of urgency and heads began to swivel toward the entrance all the way across the crowded room.

"And he's here," Quentin said softly but with a certain tension.

Jessica spun around, her heart pounding like a racehorse's at the starting line. She swallowed to clear the knot of tension tightening around her throat.

"Let him come to you," Quentin reminded her. "I promise you he will."

Somehow she stood still as she caught short, flashing glimpses of Hugh, devastatingly handsome in the tuxedo that fit across his broad shoulders like a glove. She tried to read his expression, but he wore his movie-star-meeting-the-public mask, giving nothing away. He smiled, he nodded, he shook hands, and he never stopped moving. She wondered with a sudden breathlessness if he was searching for her in the crowd.

Her nerves coiled tighter and tighter as he got closer, and she worried that her stomach might reject the wine she'd just drunk. Quentin was talking, but it was pure static in her ears. Her entire focus was on the man now just three knots of people away. How would he feel about her surprise appearance at the party? Would he walk away or hear her out? She scanned the polite smile on his face, the attentive angle of his head, the squared set of his shoulders, and his every gesture, desperate for any clue that might help her prepare for their encounter.

The crowd shifted as Hugh approached, leaving a clear line of sight between them. He froze into absolute stillness, his smile evaporating, his blue gaze locked on her like a laser, and she lost her ability to breathe. She summoned up a smile and nodded, just as he had been doing.

Without a word to the people around him, he came straight toward her, ignoring greetings and proffered hands as he passed. His dark tux and long, fluid stride conjured up a large, predatory cat prowling toward his prey.

She gripped her jeweled purse so hard that the frame pressed against the bones of her fingers as a quiver of nerves rippled through her.

When he was within three feet of her, he came to a halt. "Jess. I can't believe you're here." Astonishment rang in his voice. His gaze skimmed down her body, and a strange, tortured smile twisted his lips. "Wearing scrubs."

For a moment, she couldn't breathe, couldn't move, couldn't speak. Seeing him again wrenched everything inside her with longing and loss. Then her heart told her exactly what to do.

Turning to the guests nearest her, she said, "You should get out your cell phones. You'll want to take a picture of this." More proof that she was prepared to fight for him.

Then she walked right up to Hugh, put one hand on the back of his head, and pulled his mouth down to hers for a kiss that poured out all of the feelings churning inside her: the wired coil of nerves, the hollow, gray ache of his absence, the sharp-clawed fear of losing him, but most of all, the heart-stretching love for everything he was.

When he didn't respond, despair began to roll through her in a cold, dark wave, but then his arms came around her and he crushed her against him, his mouth slanting over hers as though trying to inhale her.

A rush of relief welled up inside her, and she allowed herself to simply revel in the wonderful, familiar feel of him: the silky texture of his hair, the exotic scent of his soap, the steel of his muscles under the wool of his tuxedo, and his mouth—oh, that clever, deft, sexy mouth! She felt the wisps of heat drifting through her body, fanned by the press of his lips to glow hotter and hotter.

As she became aware of a ripple of applause, Hugh broke the kiss, lifting his head to look around with a dazed expression. "I forgot we were . . . let's go somewhere else," he said, his arm banded around her waist as he headed for a plain door set in the wall near one of the bars.

She glanced back at Quentin, who gave her two thumbs up and a dazzling smile.

As Hugh swept her forward, Jessica noticed one guest with her cell phone raised to take a photo or video. "Hey, if you post that on social media, will you tag me?" Jessica asked with a grin.

The woman looked a little taken aback by Jessica's directness, but she nodded.

"What is going on with you?" Hugh asked.

"Just enjoying myself." And she was, because having Hugh's arm around her felt so right.

As he drew them through the crowd, people moved out of their way, some whispering, some smiling. More cell phones were lifted in the classic picture-taking pose. There would be plenty of photos out in the world, so Jessica had accomplished one part of her plan.

When they dashed through the door, they found themselves in a hallway with scuffed white walls, a green linoleum tile floor, and bright fluorescent lighting. Bangs, clatters, and urgent voices indicated that there was food or beverage prep going on in one of the rooms off the hallway.

Hugh ignored it all, spinning her around to face him as he gripped her shoulders. "Jess, what are you doing here?" She saw confusion, uneasiness, and—maybe—hope in his face.

"I'm being myself in your world." She waved down at her scrubs. "And having a blast, if truth be told."

His gaze flicked over her outfit again, his expression bemused. "You look amazing. Those are not your average scrubs."

"Quentin tailored them for me," Jessica said. "And the jewels are on loan from Cazier. They're real." She touched the diamond necklace. "You see, I can do the red carpet and still be Jessica."

"Oh God, I never doubted that." Hugh's words came out on a groan. "You can do anything you put your mind to."

"I've put my mind to loving you, and I'm not going to change it." She laid her palm against his cheek. "You can't scare me away with a few photographers."

He pulled away from her touch, sending a spear of hurt through her chest, but she held on to the memory of how he'd just kissed her.

"The photographers are just the tip of the iceberg," he said, his voice tight with frustration. "You have an important job. Being with me will make it impossible for you to do it."

She put her hands on her hips. "You yourself said that once the novelty dies down, no one will bother me at the clinic anymore."

"I lied." The muscles of his jaw bulged as he clenched it. He swept his hands out in a gesture of futility. "You can only survive by retreating into an artificial cocoon of security and isolation. I won't ask that of you."

"Good, because I won't do it." She steeled herself for another rejection when she reached for his hand, wrapping both of hers around it. "I won't leave you, either."

He left his hand in hers but without any sign that he wanted her touch. He looked away down the hallway and said in a low voice, "My life drove you away once."

The pain radiated from him, old pain, all the way from his childhood. She held his hand tighter. "You'd already left me for the glitz and the adoration, so I felt like an obstacle," she said. "But I didn't expect you to cut me out of your life as though I'd never existed. It made me wonder how real our relationship had been right from the start."

He whipped his head around to face her, his expression harsh. "Realer than any relationship I'd ever had."

She saw the stark truth of that in his eyes, and another wound of her own began to heal. "You wouldn't share yourself with me fully, though. You kept secret the parts of your past I most needed to understand who you were."

Now he drew his hand out from between hers, taking away the warmth and physical connection she craved. "Some things you try to forget," he said.

"You have to deal with them first. I want to be the one who helps you do that." She curled her hands into fists of determination. "I am not like your mother."

"I know that," he snapped.

She pinned him with her gaze, refusing to allow his anger to intimidate her. "I will not let you drive me away this time. I came here in my designer scrubs to fight for you, in front of all the paparazzi, if necessary."

He dragged his hands over his face in a gesture of weariness. "I'm not worth the trouble, Jess."

There he was: the abandoned child lurking inside the man. She caught the loneliness of him in Hugh's eyes, and her heart felt like it would crack in two.

"Do you think I'm stupid enough to fall in love with a man who doesn't deserve it?" She stepped closer to jab her finger in his chest. "You were always worthy of love. Always. Don't let your past convince you otherwise."

"This isn't about my past." His voice became charged with vehemence. "I've tried to convince myself that we can make it work. But every time I look into the future, I see your love corroded into resentment, your openness and generosity hardened into cynicism." His eyes darkened with a wrenching agony, and his voice dropped to a near whisper. "I don't have the guts to face that."

She held out her work-roughened hands that even Quentin's ministrations couldn't make elegant. "You see these? They're damn strong. You should know that, because you've felt them on your body. So get rid of your image of me as a fragile innocent. My vet practice is in South Harlem. I treat police dogs shot by drug dealers. I spend time at the Carver Center, where some of the kids come from backgrounds that make you cry. Yet I haven't run away."

He stared down at her hands, suspended between them as she willed him to reach for her.

When he didn't move, she stretched up to brush back the lock of hair he'd mussed, startling him into meeting her gaze. "I love you, Hugh, with every ounce of my strength. You need to trust me enough to love me back."

Something flickered in his eyes, a glimmer of yearning. "I want . . ." He shook his head. "I can't survive you leaving again." His voice was raw with a fear that sliced into her heart.

He stood with his head bowed, his wild, dark beauty so potent that it lit up the dingy hallway. She wanted to wrap him in her arms and cradle his head against her, so he could feel the love vibrating through her. "Come home with me," she said. "Tonight."

His head jerked up, his eyes bright with a flare of hope, of desire, of longing.

She held her breath, waiting to see if he would give her the response she so desperately wanted. If he would finally believe in her. She nearly swore out loud when the door swung open and Quentin stuck his head though it.

"I regret the interruption, but Mr. Miller is currently fending off a worry-crazed committee of writers who want to know when they can start the awards ceremony. Evidently, you're the opening act," Quentin said to Hugh.

The light in Hugh's eyes faded. "Hell and damnation!" He raked his fingers through his hair before he said in a low voice, "I'll come home with you . . . to talk."

Jessica nearly pumped her fist. She'd heard that one before. However, she allowed herself only a nod.

Hugh crooked his arm and held it out from his side, his sharp-edged smile a challenge. "Will you accompany me into dinner?"

"It would be an honor." She returned his smile as she slipped her hand through the hollow at his elbow, loving the feel of his hard, muscled forearm under her palm.

Quentin held the door for them, raising his eyebrows in a question aimed at Jessica as she passed. She held her free hand down by her side so only the stylist could see it and made a "so-so" motion in response. Quentin muttered, "Keep the faith."

Chapter 24

As they crossed the expanse of burgundy carpet in the now-empty room, Jessica saw a group of people huddled around Gavin Miller near the main door. The writer glanced up before lifting a hand in greeting. "Mr. Baker is here," he said in a carrying voice.

All heads turned toward Jessica and Hugh before one tall, broad-shouldered woman dressed in a deep red pantsuit broke away from the huddle. "How wonderful to see you again, Hugh," she said, striding toward them. "I was afraid you might have forgotten that you are giving the opening speech."

"Never, Maggie," Hugh said smoothly as the woman fell into step beside him. "Not for an important event like the INK awards. May I introduce you to Jessica Quillen, an old friend of mine? Jessica, meet Maggie Stillwell, the chairperson of this splendid occasion."

Jessica peered around Hugh's shoulder to smile at Maggie, who gave her a curious look but made no comment other than a polite hello. As soon as they reached the crowd waiting for them, Maggie took charge, directing the other committee members to disperse to the ballroom while she escorted the celebrities herself.

Gavin Miller gave Jessica an odd, appraising smile before he introduced her to his red-haired wife, Allie. Jessica loved the other woman's slight twang of an accent, but they had no time to exchange more than a quick pleasantry before Maggie was marshaling them for their entrance.

Hugh kept Jessica's hand tucked firmly against his side as they followed the tall woman down the corridor, so she could feel the heat of his body radiating through his tux jacket against her bare arm. Just that little contact sent a thrill of excitement sizzling over her skin.

Gavin shot Hugh an amused, sidelong glance when they reached the ballroom's double doors. "Allie and I will go before you, so we don't dilute the crowd's first glimpse of Julian Best." And then he swept his wife along with him through the opening.

Hugh stopped in the doorway. "Let's give them a second to realize we're here," he said, his gaze sweeping over the vast room filled with round tables.

More and more guests swiveled on their chairs to stare in their direction, and the volume of the conversation dropped as people gawked and whispered. Jessica hadn't been prepared for quite so many pairs of eyes trained on her scrubs all at the same time, but she lifted her chin and gave them her best sparkling smile.

"And now we'll proceed," Hugh said, moving her forward with him. "Front table, dead center."

She slid a glance up at him to find that he was also smiling for the crowd and occasionally saying hello to someone at a table they passed. Although a few people eyed her unusual outfit askance, virtually all the attention was focused on the man at her side, a surprise benefit to Hugh being so famous—and gorgeous, of course. She could just lurk in his shadow.

The walk seemed drawn out, but they finally arrived at the table of honor, where Gavin, Allie, and Maggie were already seated, along with a few strangers and some prominent authors whom Jessica recognized from their book-jacket photos. There was a rustle of greetings as she and Hugh sat down in the last two chairs, making her wonder whom she had displaced. She also felt guilty about deserting Quentin, but he'd told her not to worry about him if things went well with Hugh.

Maggie allowed the greetings to finish before she stood and indicated that Hugh should come with her, leading him up a set of steps to the side of the stage. She ducked back into the wings while Hugh strode across the stage to the podium. Jessica drank in the lithe grace of his long legs, the tousle of his silky hair, the blaze of his turquoise eyes, and the sheer charisma that made the audience go quiet without a word or gesture from him.

He braced his hands on the podium and smiled out at the room. "Welcome to the eleventh annual INK awards," he said. "I'm Hugh Baker, your grateful servant, an actor who would have nothing to say without the words you all give me."

Of course he spoke from memory, as though he was just sharing his thoughts with the rapt audience. His speech was short but graceful, projecting a genuine gratitude toward the writers who filled the room. As he descended the steps, Jessica whispered to Gavin, "That was a terrific speech. Did Hugh write it?"

Gavin gave her a roguish look. "I might have assisted."

"I had a feeling," Jessica said. "Did you write his speech for your award as well?"

The author chuckled. "I offered, but he refused to allow me to sing my own praises. He knew I wouldn't hold back."

Hugh returned to the table, seating himself beside Jessica. "Wonderful speech!" she said. "Every writer in this room thinks you're brilliant."

"Because Gavin made sure I sucked up to them mercilessly," Hugh said, but amusement glinted in his eyes.

"Well, yes," Jessica said. "However, writers are pretty important to actors, after all."

"I like this woman," Gavin said.

"I told you that you would," Hugh said, sending a little wavelet of gratification rippling through Jessica. He'd discussed her with his closest friend in a positive way.

Then he swamped her with delight when he slid his hand onto her thigh beneath the tablecloth and gave it a gentle squeeze, his fingers strong and warm against the thin cotton of her scrubs. Her eyelids threatened to flutter closed while she savored the fact that he had returned to his old habit of touching her in public without seeming to do so. It was a good sign.

Allie leaned forward to catch Jessica's attention. "I love your outfit. It's got major pizzazz. You've inspired me to work harder on my PT scrubs."

"Yes, well, the diamonds might be a little over-the-top," Jessica said, her tone wry. She had been so focused on Hugh that she'd forgotten what she was wearing.

"Don't change a thing," Gavin said. "If you're going to prove a point—especially to someone as thick skulled as Hugh—prove it emphatically."

Jessica gave a little choke of laughter as Hugh tossed a dark look at his friend. "Of course, your thought process has always been a model of clarity," he said.

Allie leaned in again to say in a stage whisper, "I love it when these two get going on each other. It keeps their egos in check."

The banter was interrupted by a waiter serving appetizers of trout pâté. Jessica had just picked up her fork when a shrill, insistent alarm shrieked from her tiny clutch, sending her fork clattering onto the plate and her heart into a spasm of dread.

The sound was the clinic's emergency notification. That meant fire, flood, or burglary.

She fumbled open the jeweled purse and grabbed her phone to check the cause. Pure horror ripped the air out of her lungs on a gasp. "Oh dear God, it's *fire*!" She leaped up from her chair, somehow managing to keep her balance on the ridiculous heels she was wearing.

"Fire? Where?" Hugh stood up, too.

"The clinic. I have to go."

"Just a moment," Hugh said, seizing her wrist to hold her beside him. "Gavin, we need your limo. My apologies . . . I won't be able to present the award to you."

"Go!" Gavin said, his cell phone already in his hand.

"Wait, we?" Jessica said to Hugh.

"I'm coming with you," he said.

She didn't have time to argue with him, so when he released her wrist, she started toward the exit door, dodging between tables and chairs as fast as she could go, yet always aware of his presence behind her.

Just as she reached the door, her phone began pinging with text messages from Tiana and Caleb, the two vet techs who lived closest to the clinic and were on their way there. They would probably beat the fire trucks, even though the clinic's alarm was connected to the fire station, too. Of course, Jessica had expected to be within ten blocks herself. She hated for the techs to be the ones who got to the scene first.

Hugh rested his hand on the small of her back as they strode through the lobby, guiding and balancing her with his touch. She heaved a sigh of gratitude when she saw the limo waiting at the hotel entrance. Hugh snarled at the paps who scrambled to snap their pictures while he helped her in. The big car glided away from the curb, and Jessica began pulling up the clinic records on her phone, checking to see how many patients were boarding that night. Eight. She winced and sent the information to the two techs, praying the fire wasn't so bad they couldn't rescue the boarders.

Don't go in to get the animals unless the firemen say it's safe. Fill me in on the situation when you can, she texted.

Now all she could do was worry and wish the driver would go faster.

"You might want to remove the diamonds, since they're borrowed," Hugh said.

"Oh, right!" She unfastened the dangling earrings. "You didn't have to come. Now Gavin won't have your whiz-bang introduction."

"I couldn't let you face a fire alone." An undercurrent of anger ran through his voice.

"My techs will be there. We've prepped for this." She fumbled with the catch of the necklace.

"Let me help you," Hugh said, indicating she should turn on the seat. She swiveled and bent her neck to give him better access. The brush of his fingertips against the sensitive nape of her neck sent a tingle dancing over her skin. She closed her eyes against the thought that she wasn't sure if she would ever feel his touch again.

Then the heavy diamond necklace slipped off and fell into her waiting hands, adding to her burden of responsibility.

She cupped the glittering diamonds, staring down at the million-dollar pile in dismay. "What the hell do I do with these to keep them safe?"

"Put them in your purse, and we'll give it to Jaros, the driver, to take care of. He works for Gavin, so he's very trustworthy."

She opened the clutch and tipped the diamonds into the satin-lined interior before handing it to Hugh with a surge of relief. "I'm so glad you're here."

Hugh had always thought the sweetest words he'd ever hear from Jessica were *I love you*, but strangely, *I'm so glad you're here* sounded even better, especially after the sucker punch when she'd said he didn't need to come with her when her clinic was burning down. After what she'd told him earlier, he couldn't believe she would expect him to stand by and let her face it alone.

As he watched her tapping away at her phone with calm efficiency, awe bloomed in his chest and powerlessness twisted through his gut.

The only concrete help he could give her so far was handing over her jewels to the chauffeur.

"Have you ever had a fire before?" he asked.

"No, but we have an emergency plan, and the fire department gets the alarm at the same time I do. It's just that I expected to be there first, since I live the closest."

"Your staff members strike me as quite competent." Jess would hire only people she could trust in a crisis.

Her hands twisted together on her lap. "I don't want them putting themselves at risk. I've told them that, but I'm afraid they won't listen."

Because she cared about her people, and taking the risk was *her* job, of course. He caught a glimpse of the steel under her warm, compassionate persona, and her earlier words about her strength echoed through his mind.

He laid his hand over one of hers. When she instantly opened her fingers and wrapped them around his, pleasure washed through him. She had accepted his comfort.

Her phone pinged, and she released his hand to check it. She closed her eyes for a moment and he braced himself, but the news was good. "Thank God, it's not the clinic that's on fire," she said. "It's the bodega next door. The smoke is coming through a vent in the wall we share with them, and that's what set off our alarms. Tiana and Caleb got the animals out, and the fire department's there."

She slumped into Hugh, burying her face against his shoulder, saying in a muffled voice filled with relief, "The fire could still spread to the clinic, but the animals are safe."

He held her as the limo bounced over potholes and swayed around corners, her body cradled against his. He closed his eyes, soaking up the feel of her in his arms, while all the things she'd said to him earlier crashed around in his brain. He wanted to believe her about their future, but all he knew for certain at this moment was that he loved her almost beyond bearing, and he would do anything in his power to help her through this crisis.

After a few minutes, Jessica sat up and swiped at the moisture on her cheeks. She glanced out the window. "We're almost there."

As soon as she spoke, he saw the strobing flash of emergency lights and heard the rumbling of the big fire truck engines. Before the limo came to a full stop, Jessica had the door open and was climbing out, wobbling for a second on her high-heeled sandals as she got her balance on the water-slicked street.

When Hugh exited on his side, she was already talking with a man and woman behind the police barriers on the opposite sidewalk. A line of crates and animal carriers stood on the cement beside them. Despite the conflagration throwing angry flames high into the dark sky, the winter air sent needles of cold through the thin cotton of his shirt. As he strode across the street, he shrugged out of his tuxedo jacket. When he reached Jessica's side, he draped the jacket over her shoulders, hoping his body heat would provide some protection for her bare arms.

She looked at him with a startled expression. "Thanks, but I have to go into the clinic," she shouted over the cacophony of sound as she slipped the jacket off and held it out to him.

He ignored the clothing suspended between them. "What are you talking about? You're not going in there."

The street was churning with the controlled chaos of fire trucks, emergency vehicles, firefighters, and police, all washed in the scorching light of the furious flames pouring out of the building next to Jessica's clinic. The street and sidewalks reflected the blaze, making it appear as though even the ground burned.

She tossed the jacket at him and started toward the police barrier. "Geode's still in there. They couldn't find him before the firemen made them leave."

"Geode?" Hugh looked at the huge, angry flames and thick, black smoke pouring out right next to the clinic, and his heart twisted in fear.

"Our office cat. He has the run of the clinic, so he's hiding somewhere."

"You mean the streak of orange fur bolting out of your office when I walked in?"

"That's the one," she said before she ducked under the barrier and into the street.

Hugh dropped his jacket and vaulted over the barrier.

"Are you going to stop her?" one of the vet techs shouted.

"I sure as hell am," Hugh yelled over his shoulder.

He jogged after Jessica, catching up with her as a fireman roared, "Lady, you can't go in there. There are oxygen tanks that could explode."

His chest went hollow with terror. Dear God, he hadn't even thought of that.

"I know, but there's still an animal in there," she called back as she kept going. "And I'm the owner." When she noticed Hugh beside her, she shook her head and yelled over the din, "You heard what the man said."

The fireman stepped in front of them, his bulky suit creating an effective blockade. "It's too dangerous," he bellowed.

"The clinic is not on fire yet," Jessica yelled back. "I have to get my cat."

The fireman shook his head. "Try it, and I'll have the cops lock you in a police car," he threatened.

It would break Jess's heart if the cat died, but Hugh still felt a surge of relief. She would be safe, and he wouldn't be the one who prevented her from rescuing Geode.

Jessica whirled away from the fireman and headed down the street in the opposite direction from the bodega, skidding a little as her flimsy sandals hit a patch of icy slush.

Hugh grabbed her elbow to steady her. "We should go back to the sidewalk."

She shook her head and tugged her arm out of his grasp as she kept going. "I'm not abandoning Geode unless the building is in flames."

Hugh took a long stride and put himself in front of her, forcing her to stop. "You heard what the fireman said. The oxygen tanks could explode."

"It's only smoke right now, but it will kill Geode if I don't get him out," she said, steel in her voice. When she looked up at him, her jaw was set. "You're wasting precious time. Get out of my way."

He wanted to pick her up and carry her far away from the sky-licking flames and the suffocating, black smoke, but he knew she would never forgive him. And he would never forgive himself if something happened to her when he might have been there to help. "I'm coming with you," he said for the second time that evening.

She shook her head.

"Either I go in with you, or I haul you back to the sidewalk over my shoulder," he said, his tone as steely as hers.

"Hugh, it's too . . ." She swept out her arm in a gesture of refusal.

"Dangerous. That's why I'm not letting you go in alone."

She searched his face for a long moment, her gray eyes picking up reflected glints of orange and yellow from the fire. "Don't do anything stupidly heroic," she said before nodding.

"You should talk," he said, stepping aside even as his brain screamed at him that this was insane.

She started forward again, and his gut clenched when he saw where she was headed. Between the clinic and the pawnshop on the side away from the bodega, there was a narrow opening.

"Where does that lead?" he asked, hoping he was wrong.

"To the back entrance. Tiana said they unlocked it in case they had to exit that way." Without breaking her stride, she looked up at him again. "Stay here. I know the clinic like the back of my hand. You don't."

"Just tell me where to look first."

She hesitated for a long second but said, "My office. Check places you think are too small for a cat. He has a white tip on his tail, so look for that."

Hugh had to turn his shoulders sideways to fit through the dim, narrow walkway between the buildings. He didn't even want to think about what was crunching under their shoes, especially with Jessica's feet virtually unprotected by her barely there sandals.

When they reached the back entrance, she started to pull open the door, but Hugh slammed his hand against it to check the temperature. It was not hot, so he let it go. When it swung open, black smoke boiled out in a blinding haze. "On your hands and knees," he commanded.

They dropped down and crawled into the pitch darkness, Jessica leading the way without faltering. At least the lack of light meant there were no flames in the clinic yet, but the acrid smell of smoke made Hugh's eyes water and his throat burn. As they turned a corner, light from the front windows spilled down the hallway, illuminating the churning clouds of smoke just above their heads.

"I'm going to look in the other places Geode likes to hide," Jessica said when he came up beside her. "You go on to my office and yell if you find him there."

She turned off to crawl into another room, and he had to force himself to let her go, especially when he heard her begin to cough. His knees already felt bruised from pounding against the hard floor at high speed, but he slithered into Jessica's office. Thank God there weren't many nooks and crannies for a cat to cram himself into in the small space. Just as he was about to rise to kneeling height, he caught a tiny glimpse of white at the base of one of the tall oak filing cabinets. He scuttled over to find the tip of the cat's tail barely peeking out from the space behind the cabinet where he would have sworn no cat could fit. The creature must have been terrified to wedge himself in there.

He scrambled to the doorway. "Jessica! I found him! Jessica! In your office!"

When she didn't answer, every muscle in his body spasmed in terror, and he started out the door. "Jessica! Where are you?"

"Here!" Her voice sounded far away. "I'm coming!"

He didn't want to leave in case Geode decided to bolt, but it took all his willpower to stay. It seemed far too long before Jessica emerged from the smoky dimness, scooting along a cat carrier as she crawled.

Jessica shoved the case through her office door. "Where is he?" she asked between coughs.

"Filing cabinet," Hugh said, leading her around the desk while he fought down the urge to breathe deeply as his lungs begged for clean air. "I'm going to stand up and shift it. You grab Geode."

She looked up at the pall of smoke roiling above them. "Do it fast."

Hugh held his breath and leaped to his feet, thrusting up into the blinding, choking smoke. Squeezing his eyes shut against the corrosive haze, he shoved his shoulder against the cabinet. The shock of the impact radiated through his back, but the cabinet didn't budge. There was no time for finesse, so he took a step back before he hurled himself against the heavy tower, slamming his whole body into the solid oak. This time it skidded away from the wall with a loud squeal of wood on linoleum.

He dropped back to his knees as his eyes teared and burned while a fit of coughing tore at his chest. He'd probably bruised his side as well, but that was nothing compared to the craving for oxygen.

"Got him," Jessica said, slamming the gate of the cat carrier shut.

"Out the front!" Hugh shouted. "It's closer. Go! I'll bring the cat."

Mercifully, she didn't argue, leaving him the case and scurrying toward the door. He scuttled along behind her with the damned cat, wheezing, squinting, and feeling a tidal wave of gratitude that Jessica was safe.

The outside door was ajar when they got there. Jessica felt Hugh tug her upward into a crouch so they could run into the street, dodging around the emergency equipment. The dirty air of New York had never smelled so wonderful as when she drew it into her smoke-clogged lungs, while Hugh coughed as he jogged along beside her.

A fireman saw them and did a double take. "Where the hell—?" He glared at both of them before lifting his arm and shouting, "Get some oxygen over here. Two masks!"

Jessica pointed to Hugh as an EMT dashed up carrying two portable tanks with masks attached. "Give it to him first."

She turned as she spoke and saw that Hugh's face was streaked with black residue from the smoke, his eyes red rimmed and watery. But he pushed the mask toward her. "Take the oxygen, Jess," he shouted. "Your lungs are smaller than mine."

She took it to keep Hugh from arguing, but before she put it on, she asked the EMT, "Do you have a pet mask? The cat needs oxygen, too." The cat case was vibrating as Geode flung himself against the walls, no doubt freaked out by the din of shouts, engines, and roaring fire, as well as the wild pulsation of lights and flames.

"Come to the ambulance," the EMT yelled. "You can sit down where it's quieter, and we'll get the cat taken care of."

Jessica was worried about Hugh, so she put her mask on, picked up the tank, and hurried to the ambulance to make sure he and Geode got proper medical attention. Hugh slid the cat carrier onto the floor of the vehicle before he helped Jessica into the back, his grip on her hand reassuring in its firmness. Then he climbed in himself, settling on the bench that ran along one side, his tank by his feet, his eyes closed as his chest rose and fell, drawing in the oxygen he clearly needed.

Jessica clambered over to where the EMT was rummaging in a drawer. She took the cat-size mask and nodded toward Hugh, pulling away her mask to say in a low voice, "Will you make sure he's really okay? He inhaled a lot of smoke."

"I'll check him out," the medic promised, hooking her stethoscope around her neck.

Jessica knelt beside the cat carrier and swung open the door. Geode cowered in the back corner, his eyes wide, his fur smudged with black. "It's okay, sweetie. You're safe now." Jessica carefully pulled him forward enough to hold him while she positioned the mask over his nose and mouth. He surprised her by submitting without a struggle, which made her suspect that he appreciated the oxygen.

She glanced over to catch Hugh shaking his head as the EMT approached him with her stethoscope held out. Sighing in frustration, Jessica settled down beside the cat case cross-legged. At least Geode had the good sense to accept treatment.

Suddenly, a blanket descended over her shoulders. Hugh was leaning over to wrap the silver fabric around her. His tie was missing, his pleated shirt was splotched with black and ripped on one shoulder, and a clean streak down his smoke-smudged cheek showed that his eyes were still tearing.

Her body began to tremble, racked by deep, violent shudders as the fear she'd refused to feel—for all three of them—finally hit her. She should have refused to let him come into the clinic with her.

Hugh yanked off his mask. "Jess, what's the matter?" His voice held panic. He turned to the EMT. "You need to help her."

Jessica shook her head, keeping the mask on Geode with one hand while she pulled her own down. "It's only the adrenaline draining out of my system." The tremors made her teeth chatter slightly as she spoke. "I didn't have the luxury of being afraid before. I just need to sit here for a minute."

In one swift movement, Hugh was on the floor beside her, drawing her against him while his hand moved up and down her back in long, soothing strokes.

She leaned into his strength, profoundly grateful that he was alive and well when she might have gotten him killed. The solidity of his body and the gentle movement of his palm eased her tremors until she could relax against him.

"You scared the hell out of me when you didn't answer me in there," he said into her hair.

"There was too much smoke. I had to hold my breath until I got farther down the hallway." She pulled her face away from his chest to look up at him. "How did you know to crawl? I was going to pull my shirt up over my mouth until you said that."

"The fire scene in *Best Laid Plans*. Bryan decided that authenticity would make it grittier, so he brought in a fire chief to advise us on how you really should behave in a fire. Smoke kills more people than flames."

"I can't believe you went in there. You are crazy." She loved him so much that she thought her heart would burst out of her chest.

"No crazier than you are."

"I'm supposed to be insane about animals. I'm a vet."

His grip tightened, and he kissed the top of her head. Closing her eyes, she savored the living, breathing presence of him. She swallowed hard to fight back tears at the memory of Hugh's head and shoulders disappearing into the terrifying black smoke when he stood up to shift the cabinet.

"Jess! Oh my God, are you all right?" Aidan appeared at the open back of the ambulance, the lights and flames turning his face into a mask of worry.

"I'm fine," she said, pulling away from Hugh to sit up straight.

"You don't look fine," her brother said before turning to Hugh. "And neither do you. Tiana said you were supposed to stop Jess from going into the clinic."

Hugh's mouth twisted. "I tried. I even considered hauling her away bodily, but I knew she would hate me if Geode died." He kissed her temple. "I couldn't bear that thought."

Tiana came up beside Aidan, her gaze going to the cat case. "You got Geode! Is he okay? Here, let me take care of him." She climbed into the vehicle to take over Jessica's ministrations.

"The cat? Really?" Aidan shook his head before he reached out to take Jessica's hand in both of his. "Don't do that again," he said, his voice holding a distinct quaver. "You could have been killed, and then I'd be an only child."

Jessica answered him with a hard squeeze, her heart warmed by his concern. "Let's hope there's never another fire. How did you know about it anyway?"

Aidan rolled his eyes. "Text alert, remember?"

Jessica gave a laugh that turned into a cough. Aidan peered at her. "Maybe you should put the oxygen mask back on."

"Nope. Hugh's the one who got a lungful of smoke." She leaned away to inspect him once again. "You should let the EMT check out your chest," she said to Hugh.

He waved a grimy hand in dismissal. "My knees are killing me, but otherwise I'm good."

"Mine, too!" She massaged her battered kneecaps. "Crawling is a lot harder than it looks."

Aidan blew out an exasperated breath. "I don't understand why you guys broke up when you're so much alike."

Jessica gave Hugh a searching look. Even after what he'd just done, she didn't know where they stood. "Are we broken up?"

He gazed at her for a long moment without answering. "Let's step down from the ambulance," he said, pulling her up with him as he stood. He jumped down onto the street before he put his hands around her waist to lift her down, setting her feet on the pavement as carefully as though she were a porcelain statue.

Then in an abrupt movement, he dropped to one knee, his breath hissing out in a grunt of pain as he made contact with the pavement.

Her heart started to imitate Geode banging into the walls of his cat carrier.

Taking her dirt-smeared hand in his equally filthy one, Hugh turned his smudged face up to her, his eyes blazing in the madly dancing light of the fire. "Jess, you showed me—in a terrifying way—how to have the courage to love. You convinced me—with more drama than was comfortable—you would never abandon someone you care about." The lines of his face seemed to soften, and his voice became a caress. "I want you in my world. And I want to be part of your world. I think tonight proved that we can make that work. Will you marry me?"

Joy flared through her, brighter than the fire. "Yes! Yes, I will!"

He rose with only a slight wince, but he didn't pull her into him, even though she tugged at his pleated shirt. "I should have fought for you eight years ago," he said, sadness shadowing his face. "I feel like I've wasted so much time."

"Well, we're just going to have to make up for it, aren't we?" she said and yanked on his shirt harder.

This time he took the hint and enfolded her in his arms. "Starting right now." He lowered his mouth to hers and sealed his proposal with a scorching-hot kiss.

Epilogue

Jessica stood in front of the new entrance to the South Harlem Veterinary Clinic, the scissors she held glinting in the soft spring sunshine and not a single paparazzo in sight. A small crowd was assembled on the sidewalk in front of her, including the staff members of her clinic and the Carver Center, her brother, and her husband. She still couldn't wrap her mind around the fact that the man who looked like a god dressed in jeans and a white button-down shirt was now hers for the rest of their lives. She smiled straight into those intense turquoise eyes and got a slow, sexy smile in answer.

"I'd like to thank everyone on my staff for putting up with the incessant hammering, banging, and cursing, as well as the workmen's bad taste in music, for the last couple of months." That got a laugh. "Seriously, your suggestions for the new place have been invaluable. Who knew a burned-out bodega could be transformed into such a great addition to our vet clinic?"

She turned her gaze back to Hugh, who shook his head almost imperceptibly. He'd told her to keep him out of the limelight, but she couldn't bring herself not to acknowledge that he'd had a pivotal role in the project. In fact, he'd made it all possible by purchasing the bodega and then funding most of the construction costs. "I owe a debt of gratitude to my wonderful husband for the idea of using the building to expand the clinic. Of course, he then left for exotic locales, so he didn't have to suffer through the daily renovation disasters of hidden water leaks, surprise termite damage, or load-bearing walls that wouldn't bear a load. However, he heard about them—at length—every night."

Even Hugh laughed, despite her public mention of him. Happiness bubbled up in her chest at the thought of how much thought, effort, and love had gone into this building.

"We're all here because we care deeply about the creatures we hope to heal," she said. "I am awed daily by the commitment each and every one of you shows. That is what I thank you for the most."

She couldn't get any more words past the lump in her throat, so she was grateful for the loud applause. When she snipped through the purple ribbon strung across the facade, a cheer went up. She waved her hand in front of the electric door, which magically opened, a convenience for her clients with reluctant dogs or large critter carriers. "Come on in and eat!"

Hugh slipped his arm around her waist and gave her a peck on the cheek. Just that casual touch sent heat flooding through her veins. "Good use of humor in a ceremonial speech," he said. "That's why I'm not annoyed with you for dragging me into it."

"You didn't really think I would leave you out. We're married, after all. People expect it."

"I'm still not quite convinced we're married. It seems almost miraculous," the superstar who could have any woman he wanted actually said.

Their wedding had been a miracle in her eyes, one of romantic beauty. Hugh said they'd had an eight-year engagement already, so he wanted to marry her right away. Gavin had offered his Southampton beach house—actually, mansion was a better description—for the celebration. Gavin's wife, the amazingly down-to-earth Allie, had orchestrated most of the planning. By the time they'd decided on lavender and silver for the color scheme, the two women had bonded into fast friends.

The ceremony had taken place around the indoor pool, which Allie had filled with floating, lavender-scented candles. The huge, potted ficus trees were wound with twinkling white lights, turning the vast, glass-enclosed space into a fairyland. Jessica had walked to Hugh on a platform running down the middle of the pool, which had made her a little nervous. To reduce the danger of tripping and falling in the water, she'd requested flat shoes from Quentin when he was helping her choose her bridal ensemble. It turned out to be a smart move, because when she'd seen Hugh standing at the end of the walkway, his elegant, black tuxedo highlighting the stark beauty of his face, she'd forgotten where she was. When he smiled at her, she'd lost her breath.

Since then, she'd only fallen more and more in love with him.

Her reverie was interrupted when Gavin strolled up, holding hands with Allie. "You know that relationships begun during a traumatic event don't last."

Jessica laughed. Once she'd gotten to know him, she'd come to enjoy Gavin's needling, not to mention the occasional serious insights he offered into Hugh's character. "I might worry, except our relationship started nine years before the fire."

"I thought being married to a wonderful woman like Allie would mellow you," Hugh said.

"This *is* Gavin being mellow," Allie said.

Gavin raised his eyebrows. "I reserve my pleasant side for my wife and a few special friends like Jessica."

"Because your pleasantness is in such short supply, you're afraid it will run out?" Hugh asked with a snort.

"Enough!" Jessica said, holding up one hand. "I need to eat or I'll start to sound like Gavin."

"Have I been insulted?" the writer asked.

"Yes," Hugh said with a wicked grin before he swept his hand across in front of the door to open it for his friends.

Jessica elbowed him in the ribs as they walked into the spacious reception area, where the food was laid out on Carla's new kingdom, a huge, granite-topped half circle of workspace.

"Hey, Doc," Diego said, strolling up with a well-filled plate in his hand, "this is mad dope."

"There's something I want to show you," Jessica said. "Give your plate to Hugh and come with me."

Diego looked dubious about using a movie star as his plate holder, but Hugh solved the problem by taking it out of Diego's grasp. "Don't be too long or I may eat it myself," he said, inspecting the array of goodies the boy had chosen.

She led Diego down the wide, new hallway with its fresh, cream-colored paint and pristine, blue tile floor, to the farthest room at the back. Opening the door, she waved him into an antechamber that contained a scrub sink, a laundry hamper, and shelving stocked with rubber gloves, smocks, and cleaning supplies. From there a glass-fronted door opened into a small, empty space, floored in concrete that was painted a shiny gray with a drain set in the center.

"What is it?" Diego asked, peering through the door.

"A quarantine room. With its own ventilation and drainage system so there will be no danger of contamination to the rest of the clinic. I thought you'd appreciate it."

Diego's face glowed with delight. "So I can bring contagious dogs here and never get the Carver Center in trouble again."

"You didn't get the Carver Center in trouble in the first place. It was just bad luck to be visited by a grouchy health inspector," Jessica said. "I've always wanted to be able to treat highly infectious cases in-house. Your situation inspired me to install a facility for it, so thank you!"

She'd thought the boy couldn't look any happier, but somehow he did. "Now I can't wait for another case of giardia," he said.

She wrinkled her nose at the memory of the stench. "Let's not go that far."

When they returned to the reception area, Diego retrieved his plate from Hugh with a sideways look and brief thank-you before he fled.

"You still make him nervous," Emily said as she joined them along with her husband, Max, a genius chemist who also served on the board of the Carver Center.

"It's amazing how many people truly believe I can kill them with my bare hands," Hugh said.

"I can't imagine Diego's worried about that," Emily said, her expression a little sad. Since Jessica knew about Diego's father's penchant for violence, she understood. Then Emily brightened. "Hugh, I hear you're taking on a new role soon . . . on Broadway."

"*The Wrong Side of Truth*," Hugh said. "I haven't done live theater in years, so I'm not straying too far from what I know. I play a cop who's obsessed with finding his mother's murderer because her death put him in foster care."

Jessica couldn't believe he was nervous about it, but he was. He'd told her that she'd given him the courage to take such an artistic risk, which had made *her* nervous about it. But she'd been running lines with him at home, watching as he added layers to the character, so she knew he would be brilliant.

"We'll get you tickets for opening night," Jessica promised.

"Oh my goodness, that would be dope," Emily said, making everyone laugh.

A couple of hours later, Jessica locked the front door behind the last of the catering staff. Even though it was a Saturday, they'd decided to close the clinic for the day, giving everyone a weekend day off for once. Most of the staff had departed to enjoy their unusual holiday, but Carla and Diego remained behind, chatting with Hugh while lounging in the comfortable new reception chairs that all matched. Contentment and a sense of accomplishment floated through her.

317

As Jessica turned, Carla raised her hand to signal silence. Jessica followed her gaze toward the archway that now connected the old side of the clinic to the new one. Geode stood in the opening, his head lifted as he sniffed the air. Up until now, he had refused to abandon his favorite hiding places in the old building, despite the staff's attempts to lure him over. Jessica suspected it was the mouthwatering aromas from the catered food that had brought him to the threshold.

He sniffed a few more times before sauntering into the reception area and looking around. Then he turned to amble down the hallway, his tail ramrod straight up to the white tip that curled over. Jessica tiptoed along behind his fuzzy little rear end, feeling the presence of the other three observers at her back.

Geode stuck his head in each doorway he passed but continued until he reached the entry to Jessica's new office, which he padded into. Since the only furniture she'd moved from the old place was her treasured ergonomic chair, she wasn't sure how Geode knew it was her space, other than by scent.

All four of them crowded into the doorway to watch the cat sniff around each new piece of furniture before he leaped on top of the built-in credenza and curled up on the brand-new cat bed she'd placed there, in hopes he might someday deign to use it.

Carla lifted her hand for a high five. "That darned cat finally did something he was supposed to," the receptionist said, shaking her head.

"That darned cat convinced Hugh to propose to me," Jessica pointed out.

"Well, I might actually have gotten around to it without the cat's help." Hugh's tone was dry.

"Huh," Carla said, giving him a skeptical glance before she sauntered back toward the reception area, taking Diego with her.

Hugh nudged Jessica into her office and closed the door behind them. He ran his hands down her back and cupped her bottom to pull her into him. "You look happy," he said.

"I have Hugh Baker's hands on my butt. Any woman in her right mind would be happy," she teased.

He didn't smile. "This is going to work, isn't it?"

It amazed her that he still worried, although it happened less and less these days. "Never doubt it." She skimmed her hands up the warm, hard wall of his chest to curve around his neck, wanting him to feel the love suffusing her. "You give me the confidence to be myself."

"You give me the courage to take chances." The gratitude in his voice pierced her soul. "But the greatest gift you've given me is belief in your love. That it will be there for me always."

"Always," Jessica said, before rising on her toes to give him the kind of kiss that would convince him she meant it.

ACKNOWLEDGMENTS

Writing tends to be a solitary business, so I count myself very fortunate to have many people—and animals—to shore up my sanity, confer authenticity on my research, and turn my sweated-over manuscript into something that folks will want to buy and read. This is the fourteenth book that I have published, which means that I know a bit about the business. Let me tell you that I am blessed with the most fantastic team any author could ask for. I pinch myself on a daily basis. All my thanks go to:

Maria Gomez, my tireless, fabulous editor, who orchestrates every aspect of my work's publication. She does an amazing job of keeping all the balls in the air that are required to turn my manuscript into a real, live book. I bow down to her.

Gabby Trull, Colleen Lindsay, Adria Martin, Kyla Pigoni, and the whole incredible Montlake Romance author relations, PR, and marketing team, who make sure the world knows I have a book out there. Their hard work and creativity are second to none.

Jane Dystel and Miriam Goderich, my dream agents, who shepherd my career along in all the best ways. They are brilliant, tough, and always on my side. That's perfection.

Andrea Hurst, my treasured, insightful developmental editor, whom I've been fortunate enough to work with on every book published by

Montlake Romance. It's a pleasure and a privilege to have a long-term relationship with such a talented editor, giving my voice a quality and consistency that are invaluable. She is also a wonderfully sympathetic listener.

Sara Brady and Claire Caterer, my meticulous copyeditor and conscientious proofreader, who educate me on the niceties of grammar and usage, make sure my characters have the right names, check my math, and generally polish my prose to a high shine. They put the icing on the cake.

Letitia Hasser, my visionary cover designer, who brings my stories to visual life with such panache that readers will be desperate to find out what inspired that amazing artwork.

Rebecca Theodorou, fourth-year veterinary student and darling daughter, who—without complaint!—talked me through multiple scenes, filled in the veterinary details, sent me videos and tutorials on various surgical techniques, and did her best to edit out all the mistakes I made anyway. (All errors that remain are entirely my own fault.) She's the greatest research resource ever!

My critique group, Miriam Allenson, Lisa Verge Higgins, and Jennifer Wilck, who are the most extraordinary friends and writers. Their support carried me through a very tough time in my life. They were there for me in every sense of the word when I most needed them. I will never forget their generosity of spirit.

Noella Phillips, a fellow New Jersey romance writer, for her insight and perception at a time when those qualities were very necessary to me.

All the fur friends who have enriched my life, both past and present, but especially: Pie, my little gray cat; Papoose, my dapple gray pony; Max, the world's most perfect dog; Kelly, the canine companion of my childhood; and Brodie, my current big, goofy, golden pal.

Rebecca, Loukas, and Jeff, the precious family who have taught me about love: its depth, its heights, its profound effect on one's life.

Finally, a huge thank-you to all my readers, who buy my books and encourage me through social media, e-mails, and even the occasional snail-mail card. You close the circle for me, bringing my stories to life in your minds and hearts.

ABOUT THE AUTHOR

Nancy Herkness is the award-winning author of the Second Glances, Wager of Hearts, and Whisper Horse series, as well as several other contemporary-romance novels. With degrees in English literature and creative writing from Princeton University, she has earned the New England Readers' Choice award, the Book Buyers Best Top Pick honor, and the National Excellence in Romance Fiction Award. She is also a two-time nominee for the Romance Writers of America's RITA® Award.

Nancy is a native of West Virginia but now lives in suburban New Jersey with a goofy golden retriever. To learn more about Nancy and her books, please visit www.NancyHerkness.com, or find her on Facebook at www.facebook.com/nancyherkness and Pinterest at www.pinterest.com/nancyherkness.